THE
GENESIS
DECEPTION

Vatican Heresy

CRAIG STEVENS :: WAYNE SHEPARD

To the few that have lifted humanity from the darkness, and to Ram Dass and our beloved families and friends that believed.

THE GENESIS DECEPTION

VATICAN HERESY

INTRODUCTION

In May 1954, at the Bilderberg Hotel in Oosterbeek, The Netherlands, twelve select members from several disparate organisations including Freemasonry, Propaganda Due, Opus Dei, the Order of the Garter and the Knights of Malta demanded a highly classified meeting with the Special Assistant to the president of the United States. They sought total suppression of an antediluvian artefact captured from German forces in the last days of World War II.

Secured in a hermetically sealed vault seventy-seven feet below the Pentagon lies a stone block of indeterminate age. Cut with laser like precision the ancient block contains peculiar references to the genesis of man.

Today, the only clue of this ancient knowledge hangs on a wall at the House of the Temple, the sanctuary of the Scottish Rite of Freemasons in Washington, D.C. A photograph of astronaut Neil Armstrong standing on the moon in 1969, holding the apron of Freemasonry, commemorates the triumph and rebirth of a lost knowledge.

Like ripples upon a mountain lake, the global impact of this hidden knowledge has endured, veiled from humanity.

PROLOGUE

BERLIN, 1st MAY 1945

With the echoes of night bombing still reverberating in his head, the boy slivered under the cold metal scaffolding. The air was thick with the pungent smell of fire and death, the morning sun yet to creep above the horizon. Hidden from view, he spied on the small gathering only metres away.

A woman aged in her early thirties stood in front of a stone, candlelit altar with an immaculately attired SS officer. She had fashioned her singing career in the various clubs around Berlin and her enchantment greatly appealed to the SS officers who sought her company. Known only as Carla, she often spent time fraternizing with them. She despised their sleazy advances, but it was how she had learned to survive.

Carla also appealed to the German Esoteric Bureau. They solicited her other skill. It was in these moments before dawn that her talent was exploited. Still dressed in her finest show gown, Carla staggered forward and fell to her knees at the officer's feet. She appeared drugged, but the boy knew better.

The woman wailed in agony. She threw herself to the ground

and writhed in sudden convulsive movements, currents surging through her wracked body. Her flaxen coiffure collapsed and dangled in curled locks, obscuring her vision. Saliva flecked the corners of her mouth. Strange voices rumbled in her head like distant thunder. She was a ravaged, tortured soul on the edge of an abyss.

Abruptly, Carla stilled. She had migrated to calm, her eyes now clear and serene. Her trancelike state held the attention of a small audience, a strange rotund woman with a tangled mass of white hair and a thin, scrawny man adorned with a pectoral cross hanging from his Roman collar. A young male stenographer sat nearby controlling a state of the art Magnetophon recorder.

Uncontrollably, words babbled and then settled into a deep guttural monotone. Carla's voice was not her own. She was a puppet in a ventriloquist's hand.

The boy strained to comprehend the woman's words. He knew what was happening to her. He had witnessed the display before. This time however, a different Bureau officer had escorted Carla, and the boy had seen terror in her eyes. He had heard the angels speak through her many times, but he had never seen her chilled with fear. So he had followed.

There was nervousness in the stenographer as he taped the strange oratory. He shifted his posture and adjusted the controls. After several minutes, the monologue abruptly ceased. Carla slumped forward, exhausted. She breathed deep in an effort to regain her sense of self.

Helping her rise to her feet, the Bureau officer praised her by expressing the Fuhrer's gratitude. The accolade meant nothing. She didn't give a damn about the Fuhrer or his manic obsessions. He was finished.

In a swift and smooth, almost practised movement, the officer released the clip of his holster and raised his Luger. The blast splintered Carla's skull, a spray of crimson mist accentuating the growing morning light.

The boy jerked in fright. The collapse of Carla's body etched into his mind as though in slow motion. He remained deathly still, hidden in the shadows, as a previously unknown despair now possessed him. Tears welled and then drained from a young soul lost to a new destiny.

God had forsaken him.

"What the hell are you talking about? Hitler's bunker is just two miles from here. We'll be there by thirteen hundred."

The radio crackled, a burst of squelch piercing his ear. "Listen Hudson, this has higher priority. Get your arse over there now!"

The command was ludicrous. After the loss of millions of lives, the prize to capture Hitler and be the first to raise an American flag over a crumbling Reichstag was everything. It was the reason Central Command had chosen this elite force. In speech and appearance they were observed as Soviet soldiers and had gained valuable ground ahead of the Red Army advance. But instead of moving forward to glory, this insane order would back-track them through Soviet lines into streets offering little or no resistance. It was an open invitation for the Red Army to storm Hitler's refuge. Valuable documents and intelligence would be lost.

"Listen you bastard. We're almost there. What sort of shit is this?"

The scratchy metallic voice squawked back. "The shit comes from the very top. Central Command has been overridden, so move it. Now!"

Hudson's new orders almost made him puke. He had promised his men infamy, but this was just madness. Nights of bombing had opened the way for Berlin's capitulation. Fire and black smoke billowed from a city ravaged. For the past two days their mission had been aggravated by the misguided desperation of old men and Hitler youth. In every house, in every street, ordinary citizens had been asked to hold out for the Fuhrer. Unbeknown to Hudson the capture and interrogation of a key German scientist would change everything. U.S. military intelligence had uncovered a scientific and historic bombshell. It had now fallen upon Hudson's elite team to confirm the historic truth. The bunker would have to wait.

All around, the skeletal remains of buildings were filled with the stench of death. Women and children picked over the rubble, trying to salvage a moment of sanity out of the smoky gloom. Some wandered aimlessly laying blank stares on a wasted city, stupefied witnesses to the Fuhrer intent on ruin.

After eliminating a couple of teenage snipers, Hudson's men retraced their advance toward a non-descript, bomb-scarred building. Only hours before it had been secured by elite Waffen SS troops. Two machine gun nests were now strewn with the bloody corpses of those who were protecting something the Reich's inner circle had considered of incalculable value. And now, so did the U.S. military.

Hudson spat out his orders. It left a sour taste.

"Surround the building. Go!"

Within the vast edifice was an excavation site, the interior hidden from the outside world since 1937. Scaffolding held up the bomb damaged walls that shielded the excavation which lay eight metres below street level.

The German Esoteric Bureau had discovered the remnants of a third century temple built on the remains of a much older pagan site. The Bureau had dug below the temple exposing a sacred ring of stone slabs, the ritual centre of a long ago civilisation. A cuboid block of diorite lay in the centre of the ring bearing testimony to its ceremonial past. Carved into its sides were inscriptions and patterns outlining the movement of the celestial heavens. It revealed a precise knowledge of astronomy and advanced mathematics. The hieroglyphic style of runes disclosed events long hidden by the ages.

Hitler had long maintained an obsession with ancient religious artefacts, even possessing the Spear of Longinus, the spear believed to have pierced the side of Jesus at the crucifixion. But this treasure was deemed a mere trifle compared to the block of stone that held the ultimate of secrets – the truth of man's genesis and a new understanding of the universe.

Hudson moved toward the front entrance with his elite force. An explosive charge blew the bulky grill door from its hinge. Hudson was the first to enter. Four of America's finest worked their way through the deserted archaeological labyrinth, guns aimed, fingers tense and ready. They soon found their target.

Nestled against the ancient block of stone cowered a young boy. Quivering with shock he held a woman's head on his lap, her shattered temple caked in blood.

Hudson approached. Thin shafts of light broke through the damaged roof, casting a wraith like illumination on the stone. Particles wafted in the diffuse light. He sensed a strange, otherworldly eeriness closing over him. The diorite block was cloaked in a rich silken cloth with religious relics suitably arranged. Some arcane force had been at work here, a mystic ceremony laced with a malevolent intent.

Hudson spoke in fluent German, his accent clipped. "Come here boy. She's dead. There's nothing you can do for her now."

Innocence bled away in tears staining the boy's filthy cheeks. "She's my mother. The SS shot her."

"Come on. Come with me."

The boy peered up at Hudson through forlorn, rheumy eyes and uttered words of mystery. "She spoke to the angels. And to God. The SS officer recorded her messages."

Hudson reached over as the boy gently laid his lifeless mother to the ground. "What messages? What are you talking about?"

The boy was insistent. "The angels spoke to her. I want to speak to them too. I must. They were here."

Hudson knew the boy was distraught and bewildered, perhaps delirious. He decided to get him outside. The building had to be secured.

Under presidential Seal, Central Command had requested immediate removal of the inscribed stone block to be returned immediately to the United States for safekeeping. The Masonic Franklin D. Roosevelt and his inner circle had an abiding interest in such matters, but when he died from a cerebral haemorrhage on 12th April, his successor, the 33 degree Freemason and the 33rd president of the United States, Harry S. Truman issued the order.

Hudson's task seemed impossible. He was to smuggle the antiquity away from the Russians, and then to the North Sea where an American submarine was ready to ensure safe passage.

Like the Bible itself, the stone spoke of things most extraordinary. It referred to a time when the Elohim came to teach humanity. This was a golden time when the world lived in peace.

The boy was fearful of the Russian uniform and the men now surrounding him. Hudson reached out. "What's your name boy?"

"Antonio Valla sir, I just wanted to speak to the angels…"

1

THE REQUISITION

VATICAN CITY

Vatican Secretary of State, Cardinal Antonio Valla hurried up the curved marble staircase in long purposeful strides. Beads of sweat peppered his forehead and his flushed cheeks matched the colour of his authoritative rank.

How dare they take a contrary theological position, he seethed. Constant attack on the Word and the authority of the Catholic faith must stop. How dare we make concessions to modernity? We won't by God, we won't.

The tempestuous cardinal was a slim, classically handsome man. A slender face with formidable features, his dark brown eyes surveyed the world with a peculiar intensity. Now in his mid-seventies, his full head of hair was dusted with grey setting him apart from his contemporaries. He looked years younger. Yet there was something faintly disturbing about his presence, something only a few could detect.

Any softening of Church authority filled him with contempt for the fools who would allow it. Hope still echoed strong from the Second Vatican Council of 1978 and it needed to be silenced. The

Pope had gone too far back then and now the leash was straining. Battles for change were constantly being declared and occasional truces were made, but Valla was determined to win the war against those who would compromise the Word.

Now seated behind his Louis XIII desk of rare ebony and rich tortoise shell veneers, he instinctively knew what must be done. Rummaging through the desk drawer, he removed his medication. A capsule or two would do the trick. He needed to calm down. God had certainly favoured his rise, but the one demon he always struggled to exorcise was anger. The Cardinal poured a glass of spring water from a fine crystal jug and quickly swallowed the capsules. Slouching back in his thick leather chair, he relaxed, tension slowly morphing into firm decision.

The sumptuous office always had a calming effect on the Cardinal. It was his indulgent refuge. The elliptical antique desk was complimented with other quality furniture from the period. A large ebony cabinet on a carcase of oak and pine dominated one wall. Being the height of interior fashion in the mid-seventeenth century, its marquetry interior was adorned in ivory and select woods, together with mirrored glass and gilded balusters. The exterior was exquisitely carved with scenes of love between the goddess Diana and the youthful shepherd Endymion. Completing the room was a sofa and several chairs upholstered in gold brocade and fine needlework. Silk tapestries and renaissance paintings hung on the other wall, inert observers to the Cardinal's sombre moods.

Cardinal Valla allowed himself a moment of reflection. He had manoeuvred and coerced his way through the ecclesiastical ranks, and he intended to preserve the centuries of Holy tradition. It was his personal mission and any deviation would be decisively subdued.

Valla had always been uncomfortable with Pope John Paul II's approach to secular matters, fearing he had allowed too much leeway. It was true the time honoured dogma regarding the question of women in the Church had been preserved, as had the edicts on contraception, abortion and celibacy, but Valla had never approved the decision to fund the Jesuits in their research of the heavens. To grant the purchase of a huge telescope and allow a select band of scientific Jesuits in America to view the far recesses of space was sacrilegious. They were beginning to question the very nature of God.

There was much at stake. The long reign of John Paul II had finally ended and a more conservative Vicar of Christ now held the keys to the Holy See. Valla had backed and promoted the German, Manfred Cardinal Luft as successor; after all, he was a non-reformist and had promised the position of Segretaria di Stato, Secretary of State, for his unqualified support. It was a position Valla had coveted, assigning him added influence over the Curia.

The Cardinal had befriended Manfred Luft in the late-sixties when he returned to Germany after his formative years in the United States. Fate had again drawn them together, and based on the many discussions they had enjoyed over the years, Valla had been certain this man could be persuaded to stabilise the Church, thwarting those who sought even modest change. The papacy was about uniformity and consistency not popularity. Fortunately, the Holy Father had granted him the honour of retaining his previous position as Prefect of the Congregation of the Doctrine of the Faith in addition to his new duties as Secretary of State. In Valla's opinion, it was vital that he had done so. He would never resign as Prefect.

With his decision firmly made, he buzzed the intercom to his outer office. It was time the new administrative assistant retrieved some documents.

"Send in Angelo."

As the Cardinal placed his wire framed reading glasses on the bridge of his nose there was a subdued tap at the door. A young man immediately entered the room careful not to look directly at the vexatious Cardinal. The soft pile of luxurious carpet cushioned his stride as he timidly traversed the opulent office.

Angelo was twenty-two and had a bright future. He cut a robust figure, his six-foot frame chiselled from regular workouts at the gym. It was his only vice, a remnant of his late teenage years when he pumped the blood of subdued aggression through his veins. Weightlifting dispelled the frustration of powerlessness. At what age those feelings of inadequacy developed he couldn't fathom. His only physical flaw was fingernails gnawed to the quick.

His lucid black eyes diverted from scrutiny and appeared bruised with gloom whenever he was challenged. Once held in a gaze though, they burned with a fierce potency.

Angelo was intelligent and happily accommodated the orthodoxy of his beloved faith. Shy and retiring with a placid demeanour, he avoided drawing attention to himself particularly where authority was involved. The young man was still intimidated by the Cardinal's Vesuvian temper that could erupt at the most unexpected moments.

"Have you ever been to the Penitentiary Archives, Angelo?"

Angelo stared at the floor in front of him. His response was filled with respect and substance. "No Your Eminence."

Valla snapped with impatient displeasure. "Look at me when I speak to you."

"Yes Your Eminence."

"I need you to retrieve the Donation of Constantine and I also require the Bouyer file from the Penitentiary archive. Think you can handle that?"

"Yes Your Eminence."

"Something else," said the Cardinal, pointing an accusing finger. "The keeper of the Penitentiary archive is a deformed miscreant and an infernal troublemaker. Suffers from some sort of psychosis. I don't wish you to speak to him or you'll be doing penance for a year. Is that clear?"

"Of course Your Eminence."

The Cardinal dismissed Angelo with a nod knowing that the archivist's grotesque appearance would be enough to prevent too much conversation.

Angelo had been to the main Apostolic Library on several occasions and was still awed by the place. It contains over one million printed books and 75,000 manuscripts. Housed in rooms commissioned by Pope Sixtus V in 1587, the collection is one of the finest, containing original manuscripts from some of Europe's most influential thinkers, not to mention thousands of priceless religious texts. On this occasion however, he was required to enter the most protected archive in the Vatican, a place not usually visited by mere assistants.

The Secret Archives, L'Archivio Segreto, were removed from the main library under the orders of Pope Pius IV in the 17th century and are still housed separately. There are tens of thousands of documents and manuscripts – papyrus, vellum, paper. Browsing is strictly forbidden. Only selected scholars gain access, asking in advance for the precise document they wish to see. They must therefore know that the document exists in advance.

Even more secret, the archive of the Apostolic Penitentiary allows no access unless specifically requisitioned by Cardinal Orsini who held the position of the Major Penitentiary. Cardinal Valla was the only person with higher dominion.

Valla headed a panel of ultra-orthodox cardinals and bishops who dispensed canon law. When an accused sat before Valla, he crushed his opposition with a fist of iron. No case was ill prepared and the Bouyer file would help in his quest against a renegade Jesuit star-gazer who dared to challenge humankind's origins.

On the way, Angelo seized the opportunity to view one of his favourite rooms, the Stanza della Segnatura. The master painter Raphaello Sanzio had been deeply influenced by the works of Leonardo da Vinci and was summoned to Rome in 1508 by Pope Julius II. During this time, he completed the magnificent fresco entitled the School of Athens. This work of genius, framed in neo-classical style, glorifies the wise men and philosophers of antiquity such as Euclid, Pythagoras, Socrates, and the nobility and artists of Renaissance society – all gathered around the figures of Plato and Aristotle. Despite the beauty of the fresco, Angelo knew the Church had once regarded many of these philosophers as pagan heretics.

As he navigated the historic halls, Angelo wondered what a deformed miscreant looked like. *Why is he regarded as a trouble-maker?* More intriguing to Angelo was why this troublemaker was able to retain his job within the Church, especially given the Cardinal's penchant for firing staff for the slightest indiscretion. Cardinal Valla had once sacked a poor secretary for serving a cup of coffee he judged to be too cold. It seemed most odd for a psychotic to be holding tenure within the Holy City.

After a brisk five-minute stride, Angelo arrived at the entrance to L'Archivio Segreto. An archival monsignor, a burly middle-aged man with harsh, battle weary features and black eyes, spoke to him. His gruff tone suggested Angelo wasn't welcome.

"What are you after?" was his terse greeting.

"I'm looking for the Penitentiary archives, sir."

"Are you now? And on whose authority precisely?"

"Cardinal Valla," said Angelo, modestly handing him the requisition.

"Right. You'd better come this way," he commanded, surprised by the imprimatur of the Cardinal.

He handed the requisition back and led Angelo through the cavernous rooms. The young assistant drank in the antiquity as they ambled through a dimly lit, long narrow corridor straddled with some of the eighty-five kilometres of shelving. They were heavily laden with some of the most seminal documents for understanding the true history of the Western world – a history quite different to accepted dogma.

The librarian turned a wary eye to Angelo and ordered, "Avoid discussion with the keeper."

Curious about this second reference to the archivist, Angelo replied, "May I ask why?"

"He's a troublemaker. Be careful. Some question his commitment to the faith."

Angelo shrugged acceptance, now more intrigued than ever. The unlikely pair meandered past the floor-to-ceiling bookshelves containing the regular collection. *How many pages were housed in this place? Had to be tens of millions.* The walls dripped with history. Angelo was awed at the inestimable value and benefit that the collection could bestow on mankind. He felt privileged to be doing God's work.

Eventually, Angelo found himself standing before a pair of ornate bronze doors separating him from the man who was treated with trepidation and scorn.

The librarian's tone was brusque. "I'll wait here to escort you out; I can't stand to look at him. Remember, avoid conversation."

Angelo nodded as the epitome of intolerance sat in the stiff ladder backed chair furnishing the entry. *How ugly could this poor devil be?*

Angelo took a deep hungry breath to calm himself and knocked. It was time to meet this puzzling misfit.

2

THE EXCAVATION

NEAR BAALBEK, LEBANON

It's remarkable how a single event can shape a life. Sometimes consequences can ripple across the globe and echo back through the generations.

History was about to be rewritten.

Sonic geophysical research had indicated evidence of shallow caves located in the hills beyond the ancient ruins of Baalbek. Long before the end of the last ice age a series of caves had been obscured due to tectonic movement in the earth's strata. The quake had caused a major rock fall, forming a low escarpment and wall-like barrier to their entrance.

Over the course of four weeks, my team of graduate archaeologists and anthropologists had broken into three caves, and with great disappointment we had found no evidence of prehistoric habitation. Our official consents expired at midnight and our campsite had already wound up. During the cool of the morning, the team had finally disbursed eager to return to their everyday lives. Only my young assistant Jai Santini, a post graduate at Universitá di Firenze, had remained with me to finalise site remediation and complete our protocols. Jai had worked with me on three previous occasions and I valued his work ethic. He had the same manic passion that I recognised from my own youth.

I was packing the last of our gear when Jai started the hydraulic drill some fifty metres from our camp, well away from our closed work site. Jai had previously argued that the topography was worthy of further investigation, especially at the base of an expansive low mound about a metre higher than its surrounds. I was annoyed and chose to ignore him, but within ten minutes he was demanding my attention.

"Hey Aiden, check this out," he yelled, motioning me to join him. A trace of smoke wafted from the drill. I wandered over to take a closer look, navigating around the diamond tip. The rock at Jai's feet had been shattered, granules of dirt siphoning downward. Grabbing a pick, I hacked at the ragged edges to expose a larger gap, enough to peer into.

The mystery of human evolution was my holy grail. Modern man started to displace the primitive Neanderthal about fifty thousand years ago as the Cro-Magnon appeared via the Middle East. The origin of this new species, our own physical ancestry, obsessed me, particularly after preliminary tests on mitochondrial DNA had indicated they were not descended from the more primitive Neanderthal. The results had shocked the University of Munich and later the world. Preliminary tests demanded more research and interest had gathered in the anthropological community. If modern humans were not descended from the more primitive Neanderthal, as scientists had previously believed, then where did we come from?

I was in these hills for proof of Cro-Magnon's origin; unequivocal proof of interbreeding would have been a plus. If real evidence existed, I wanted to find it. Perhaps we were finally onto something.

On my hands and knees, I leaned forward and peered into the hole below. A thin cone of sunlight speared past my head and into the interior. Cool air, scented with loam caressed my face. This was no cave. "We need a flashlight here."

"Yeah, hang on a sec. I don't know how long it'll last, the battery needs recharging."

"Come on Jai, move it."

I waited impatiently as sweat prickled my scalp, peering through the distorted heat of the early afternoon.

Situated on a large hill in the fertile valley below, the ancient temple of Jupiter stood as a stark reminder to the power of Rome. Mainstream archaeology traces the history of Baalbek back to the Early Bronze Age, but some are not so sure. A few scholars have suggested the site had much earlier origins. I had no idea and right now, I didn't care. I had an investigation of my own to complete.

Jai handed me the torch. Excitement churned my gut at the possibility of a new find. It had always been the same. Discovery was my drug. I angled the torch into the small hole. A large chamber came into view. It appeared manmade, not what I had expected at all.

"Jesus! There's definitely something down here!"

I peered further into the cavity. It demanded closer examination, so I hacked at the edges with a pick. Slivers of rock tumbled into the blackness below. Under the relentless summer sun, rivulets of sweat streamed down my torso. Only the occasional breeze whipping across the barren landscape provided any respite.

Within moments, a large piece of rock gave way crashing with a thud below. Cool, tepid air seeped from the aperture, which was now large enough to allow access. Jai and I looked at each other, considering the possibilities.

What civilisation had built this place?

My torch exposed a floor extending well beyond the beam of

light. My addiction ached to be quenched. I had to find out what was down there.

"Get the harness Jai, I'm going down."

Twenty minutes later, with the triangular frame placed over the aperture and my harness firmly strapped, Jai lowered me into the darkness. The stifling summer heat was replaced by a rank, musty coolness. I was descending through the ceiling of an enormous crypt, the walls built from massive earthen blocks.

Moss and fungal spores spread in spidery tentacles across the structure. Clutching the torch, I saw the bones of two individuals, their bodies rendered to dust by the centuries.

"Hey Jai!" I yelled. "There's some good stuff down here. I'm taking a closer look."

Unhooking my harness, I carefully inspected the skeletal remains. There were two adult bodies, one of which had an ornate gold and silver pendant embossed with a faded red cross lying in the dust beneath its chest cavity. To the side was a gilded sword, again with a cross emblazoned into the hilt. *Who were these people?* I carefully removed the pendant without disturbing the bones and inspected it closely. The back was engraved in Latin, a few words that may help with the identification of its owner. I slipped it into my pocket. Both skeletons looked male, but would require a complete forensic inspection to determine age and possible cause of death. I left them undisturbed.

Within the structure was a four-point solar cross hewn into one of the large supporting blocks summoning entry into a wide passageway. The rest of the crypt was clear of any decorative markings.

Scanning my torch around the smooth floor, small black beetle-like insects scurried away from the light.

"You OK down there?" Jai yelled.

His voice was reassuring. "Yeah. Could be some kind of religious centre, don't really know." My expertise was being sorely tested, but curiosity drew me forward. "There's a wide passage down here. I'm going in."

Its route seemed to venture under our camp toward the escarpment.

The walls were made of cut limestone and beautifully decorated in reds, yellows, greens and deep bluish hues, the patina slowly faded by centuries of age. One side was a continuous mural, three panels in height. It depicted a magnificent chariot drawn by eight horses and controlled by a helmeted warrior reminiscent of Darius the Great, the Persian king who mastered these lands in the 6th century BC. But this character had an Egyptian quality, his coned helmet reminiscent of the pharaoh style headdress.

The other wall was unlike anything I had seen. This wall was possibly much older than the other. It may have been built at an earlier time. A large cone shaped tower dominated with large flame-like extrusions on all sides. Next to this was a colourfully decorated panel with twelve god-like beings completely encircled in rich golden discs filled with light. The rest of the wall was filled with intricate pictograms and unusual cuneiform markings.

The passageway led into an enormous pentagonal room. Here the walls were comprised of etched blocks with the largest ones towering high above. Somehow the builders of this place had hauled the largest blocks to a height of about fifteen metres, engineering them as load-bearing supports for the escarpment above. Each block must have weighed at least three hundred tonnes. *How could they possibly raise a block six stories high?* I reasoned that this place must have had some connection to the Roman temple of Jupiter in the valley below.

Twenty-four blocks, each weighing around four hundred and fifty tonnes, are visible at the site. Above six blocks on the western side, three larger blocks called the Trilithon were raised. Somehow these massive stones, each weighing up to twelve hundred tonnes, have been precision cut, quarried and stacked. How this ancient feat of engineering was built remains a mystery.

The Romans had conquered the site and built their temple on the foundations of an even earlier Phoenician temple dedicated to their god Baal. But the blocks of the Trilithon suggest the megalithic construction took place long before the Phoenicians.

How did the ancients build the Trilithon? I had heard some nonsense about a Phoenician legend suggesting 'Giants' had constructed it. I was to find out sometime later that an Old Testament reference in the Book of Numbers spoke of 'the Nephilim who came from the Giants'.

It all seemed plain rubbish as far as I was concerned, but those blocks did make me curious. The massive supports high above me did the same.

I suspected this chamber held some religious significance. The walls were adorned with dozens a colourful carvings and painted with Egyptian style hieroglyphics mixed with runic-like markings from perhaps a far later age. A rectangular stone altar took centre stage with a large, highly polished elliptical black stone lying at its centre. Carved deep into the altar were pictograms and symbols of the stars, planets and constellations. Some sort of sea craft levitated above the ground. People dressed in conical headwear looked down toward the ground below. As my spotlight struck the altar at different angles, shadows crept across the deep carvings in a movement of dance.

I was giving close inspection to the carved symbols when suddenly...CRACK!

The floor gave way. I fell hard and with a heavy thud tumbled onto a sandy floor. I was lost in a silent, velvet darkness.

3

THE KEEPER

APOSTOLIC PENITENTIARY, VATICAN CITY

The archives of the Apostolic Penitentiary are hidden at the rear of the more famous L'Archivio Segreto, the only clue to the inner sanctum being a pair of bronzed doors surrounded and almost totally obscured with a wall of centuries-old volumes.

A quiet voice beckoned from the other side. "Enter!"

Angelo edged into the inner archive's vestibule as he carefully swung one door ajar. Hunched over a computer screen, a lone and solitary figure sat at a large desk with his back to the door. Facing the desk was a thick double glazed wall protecting the most treasured manuscripts, maintained at the correct temperature, humidity and light intensity.

The cloistered man spoke. "Name?"

"Angelo DeMarco, sir. I have a requisition from Cardinal Valla."

"Valla?" he queried disapprovingly, "We haven't met before have we?"

"No sir."

The keeper cautioned, "They say I'm the disfigured villain, not Don Juan you know. Not that I've ever met him either." He amused himself with a seditious chuckle. "You won't be too alarmed when I turn around will you?"

Angelo swallowed hard. "OK."

"I hope you're not easily overcome by appearances."

"Not at all," said Angelo, bracing himself for what was to come.

The keeper swivelled in his chair and Angelo's fears turned to dread. A section of the man's face had been slashed to the bone. His skin was pleated with thick scar tissue that warped his appearance into a wretched caricature. He had a cavity instead of a nose, and his tight waxy skin contorted his left eye causing it to bulge lower than the right. There was a large bald patch on his head where a chunk of scalp had been sliced down to the cranium. Some crude medical work now covered the horrible wound.

"Most people just wait at the door with a librarian while I retrieve their requisition. You must be one of the brave ones," he said with a defiant snigger. "But then, not too many requests are made on this archive. In here I'm out of sight, out of mind."

Despite his appearance, Angelo was surprised by the eloquence of the man's voice and breezy disposition. There was something quite gentle and distinguished about him, educated even.

His grotesque features managed to contort a pucker of a smile. "Did they tell you not to talk to me?"

"Er, yes, I suppose," stumbled Angelo.

"Thought as much. So how's that pompous hothead Valla? Haven't seen him since his promotion, thank God. Flotsam always rises to the top you know."

Angelo reeled at the lack of respect for the Church's leading Eminence, a man who one day could be the Pontiff.

"Tell me Angelo, are you going to comply with their fear?"

The young man struggled to speak as a constriction affected his throat. "Er, no," he mumbled.

"Fear and greed," the keeper said bluntly. "It's what drives the world, especially empty intellectual palaces like this."

Angelo was concerned at the tone of the conversation.

"What do you mean?"

"You don't actually believe this religious fairytale do you?"

Fairytale? Disrespect was one thing, but this fellow was attacking the very authority of the Church?

"What do you mean?"

Ignoring the question another distorted smile registered on the disfigured face. He silently looked into Angelo's lucid black pearl eyes and liked what he saw. The keeper instinctively knew how to read people. He saw in Angelo a soul that shone from the depths of luminous innocence, and an honest desire to serve. *To serve what though? A pompous ass like Valla?* The keeper was mindful of an opportunity, a chance to overturn the incessant hum of archival monotony.

At least I've been warned about this misfit, Angelo thought to himself, uncomfortable with the keeper's unremitting gaze.

"How long have you been with Valla?" He could tell the young fellow was malleable, and hoped he would be able save him.

"I've been in the Cardinal's service for six weeks." Angelo was not prepared to divulge anything further.

"I see." The keeper's face furrowed into deep corrugation as he smiled. "My name is Comte. What text are you after down here?"

"His Eminence has requested the Donation of Constantine and the Bouyer excommunication."

Comte's face immediately lit up. He decided to challenge the young man again. "Now there're a couple of classics. Do you know what the *Donation* is about?"

"No sir," confessed Angelo uneasily. "It's not been in the curriculum yet."

"Well, I'll give you a head start. It's all part of the great lie," Comte pronounced boldly. "The document is the axis for most of the misery experienced in Christendom. It appeared in the eighth century with some clap-trap that it was written by Emperor Constantine four hundred years earlier."

"Are you saying it wasn't?"

A crooked grin said it all. "Of course."

Angelo averted his gaze, careful not to stare.

"It's a fake, a Church forgery. Everybody knows it. It's a clever subterfuge, and supposedly the very source of the Church's authority on Earth. It makes the proclamation that the Pope was Christ's elected representative on Earth, and because of his divine authority, he ranked above all the other monarchs. This, of course, gave the Pope the power to create future kings as his subordinates. He was even styled as Vicarius Filii Dei, 'Vicar of the Son of God'. All a clever trick designed to usurp the power of the European monarchs and take absolute control.

"The Roman Empire never died my friend; it was reborn as the Church. The Donation is complete nonsense." The keeper's defiant tone hardened. "The way I remember it, Christ didn't appoint anybody as God's representative."

An uneasy silence hovered between the two men as Angelo quickly tried to digest the unthinkable. *Surely it wasn't true. This Comte must be as crazy as people say.*

"But this is nothing," pronounced the keeper with a steely glare. "It's just the tip of an iceberg so vast it would swamp the whole world, not just the Church."

Angelo was uncomfortable about where the conversation was headed. "What are you talking about?"

"Look around this place; it's more deformed than I am. These archives hold the historical offal of Church persecution. The Bouyer file is just one of thousands. The whole place is riddled with cancer. Do you think any part of this is real?" He gestured with his deformed hand to accentuate the point.

Comte decided to challenge the young man's doctrinal brainwashing. "You believe in the Church, don't you Angelo?"

"Of course. It teaches the word of God."

"Does it my young friend? Did you know that the Bible speaks of other living beings? Nephilim, Ophanim, Elohim and Seraphim. Has any priest ever spoken to you about them?"

Angelo looked down. "Well, no."

"Has the seminary or anyone in the Church ever taught you about these other beings?"

Angelo stared blankly. "No."

"I didn't think so. It gives too much of the truth away. If you believe in the Bible, I mean really believe, you *must* believe in these beings. Yes?"

Angelo had been unprepared for Comte's savage denunciation, but something about this odd fellow struck a deep resonance within. This vault of religious historical knowledge prompted answers for questions unasked.

"Don't know," Angelo shrugged.

Comte decided to be conciliatory. "Thanks for your honesty. 'Don't know' is a far better answer than just blind acceptance. Know this though. Most things you believe are lies. What you don't think is possible is more real than my damaged face that offends so many in here. But you're not offended, are you?"

Angelo believed any criticism of the Church was a form of moral transgression, and was distressed at Comte's pronouncements. But intuition told him that Comte was a unique individual, harbouring a fierce intellect. If anything, he felt an abiding compassion for the man's physical disability. There was no question about his cynical irreverence, but it belied an astute single mindedness that Angelo found refreshing.

"No, I'm not offended. Look I'm sorry, but I have to get back. Perhaps you can get the documents now."

Comte was turgid, detecting Angelo's misgivings. "Sure, my pleasure, I can give you the Bouyer file. You'll need to get the Donation from the librarian waiting outside."

He raised himself from his chair and with pronounced effort hobbled toward the file's resting place. Angelo watched him disappear through the connecting door sealing it behind him. He was curious about the keeper and wondered what had turned him into such an irascible discontent.

After a few minutes, with Angelo sitting nervously in the anteroom, Comte returned with the requested document and gently said, "There are two choices in this world young man. One is to ask nothing and believe the things you've been told, the twisted and contrived. The other is to ask everything and seek for yourself.

"Didn't Jesus say, '*Ask and it shall be given you; seek, and ye shall find; knock, and it shall be opened unto you.*' If you really want to know about truth rather than the fantasies you believe then come back tomorrow night. I'll be here at 10:30. You'll have no access the way you've just come."

The keeper slipped an official after hours pass into the Bouyer file. "Show this to the Swiss Guard at the Porta Angelica. He will allow you entry. From inside the Cortile del Belvedere, take the steps to the basement. You'll find a narrow passageway that leads directly here. Knock and the door shall be opened."

4

THE DISCOVERY

NEAR BALBEEK, LEBANON

I had fallen into a large circular pit. Fortunately, nothing was broken. I was entombed in an oubliette, built by an unknown civilisation. My only escape was through the entry point some four metres above my head.

In the past, I had crawled through many underground chambers, cave dwellings and burial mounds, but this was different. There was an unsettling magnetism to this place that made the hairs on my neck bristle. Shining my fading torch in a wide arc, I spotted a low opening in the far corner. I clambered to my feet and approached. The edges of a tunnel had been cut through the rocky earth with almost mechanical precision. Stooping low, I entered.

My torch smeared the silent blackness. A deep cavity with unknown dimensions loomed at the yawning throat of the tunnel. I moved forward, a thick glistening web obscuring my vision.

I brushed it aside and entered another large chamber to discover a crude furnace complete with an ancient smokestack built up the wall and through the ceiling. A number of cavities were cut into the rock walls housing a range of decorated amphorae. Lying on the floor were the remains of broken clay bowls and saucers. A rudimentary stone bench near the far wall held a mortar, covered with a thin slab of stone. The pestle lay on the ground. *Was this an ancient laboratory?*

I carefully lifted the stone covering. A flaky dry paste basted the mortar's circular base. I rubbed my finger across the paste and it quickly disintegrated into a fine white powder. Curious about its composition, I placed a small sample on my tongue. *Definitely alkaline.* I wanted a sample. Retrieving two zip-loc plastic bags from my shirt pocket, I scooped in a few flakes for future testing.

My torch was fading. The anaemic beam wouldn't last much longer. I cast it above the entrance and noted a large stone relief of what appeared to be an Egyptian goddess. Through a veil of dusty incandescence, I noticed the carving was in remarkable condition, but it seemed oddly out of place. A solar disc was inscribed above her head. The Egyptian influence defied explanation.

And then something peculiar happened. My mind tumbled into itself. Perception of linear time became fused with the here and now. No past, no future, just now. A feeling of knowing engulfed me. There was a pristine clarity to my awareness as my mind transcended bodily awareness. But the fleeting splendour faded and I was suddenly drawn to painful ordeals. Events began to play out at super-luminal speed. I struggled to refocus. The white substance must have been either psychoactive or neurotoxic. Claustrophobia intruded. I took a deep breath, but the stale, rank air left me gasping. I dropped to the floor and switched off the torch to conserve energy.

I sat entombed within the unearthly darkness. I started to recall my past. The smashing of the front door, the sound of the shotgun blast, my uncle collapsing to the floor, my mother screaming as she grabbed to protect me.

Visions were replaced by terrible thoughts. If Jai did not come, this would be the end. I knew it would be a vile, painful ending. Dehydration would rack my body with delirium. My tongue would swell and harden in my mouth, eventually choking me from life-giving oxygen. It would be an agonising death, I'd be completely alone. My gut churned at the thought. But beyond the agony of dying, was there anything? As a man of science, I doubted the possibility, but I began to hope there might be something.

The darkness was stifling, like a thick smothering blanket. Sense of space was lost. I was alone with just my thoughts. Suddenly, there was a noise, like muffled breathing at the periphery of my senses. I calmed myself and listened. I could hear it clearly, the unmistakable sound of respiration and then, a hoarse rasp. There was someone in the crypt with me. I yelled for Jai, and the noise instantly vanished.

I sat cross-legged, stilling my thoughts, calming my panic. Slowly, imperceptibly, my mind drifted into a swoon.

Memories percolated.

The bombings, the sectarian hatred, the killings flashed before me. I saw loyalist thugs smashing into our Belfast home, and my uncle's face blown away in the shotgun blast. I was only six at the time, but the voice behind the gun now haunted me, *'Message delivered.'*

The scene was surreal, emotions crowding for expression. I inhaled deeply, focusing on the now. Try as I did, childhood images fluttered like anxious insects.

I was washed by scenes swimming into recognition, malignant with caustic memories long ago banished. My life history sped past like animated movie stills. I saw my wretched father. He wanted revenge, bloody murderous revenge. Then his violent drunken behaviour and pathetic brooding melancholy flashed past. It ended as always; my mother beaten to a bloody pulp as she protected me from him, then his pathetic remorse. I saw her lying on the floor with her lip split from a savage backhander.

He was a useless lowlife without her, so she finally got her way. Images of Australia came to me. Open spaces, blue skies, warmth and a chance to begin a new life. I felt my father's inane resentment toward me and for the country that had made us welcome.

I recalled the day I left home. I was sixteen and finally, I retaliated. Catholic guilt and a perverse loyalty had damned my mother to his torture for years. I put an end to it by almost killing the bastard. He was filled with grog and stupid aggression. He had staggered home and shamelessly smashed my mother's face against the wall for not having his dinner ready. Blood streaked the wall. I got lucky and knocked him to the ground, my boot then splitting his eye and breaking four of his ribs. He writhed in pain and I smiled at the fear in his eyes. At last, he knew I had the upper hand.

I screamed at my mother to get out. But the foolish woman just screamed back and went to patch up the bastard. I grabbed my jacket and left. He never touched her again, but he couldn't hold back from his daily rounds of emotional abuse.

She married for good or bad she had once said, but I knew it was guilt that made her stay – guilt for dragging him away from his vagrant retribution, but mostly by the wicked guilt laid on her by a religion that ruled her right to a worthy divorce. For his part, he had no ability to comprehend, let alone forgive, and I never spoke to him again.

The visions ceased as quickly as they had taken shape. I groped in the dark, my hand only touching the cool dirt floor. Steeling my thoughts I focused to keep myself calm. I reflected on why my father chose to be the person he became, his hatred for the English and his aggressive republican fervour. I understood and empathised with his sentiment, but not his wicked vitriol. The Irish famine of the 1840s had bred a resentment for the English that was well justified. The callous indifference toward the starvation of the Irish was nothing but wanton genocide. The English had unashamedly taken the food from their mouths and allowed my forefathers to die in their hundreds of thousands.

I was told he cursed me to hell when I completed university in Australia and went on to study at Oxford. As far as he was concerned, I was a traitor to the wretched English. Why didn't the bastard just let it go instead of giving my mother hell and drinking himself to death? Thank God she had a few years of peace. *Thank God?* I didn't believe in a Supreme Being. How could I? How could any man of science? A God of Love – it was a deceit, crap to feed the mushrooms.

Minutes passed like listless hours. The staccato beat of my pounding heart quickened in my ears, but curiously the sound came from outside my body. Passively inert, I listened for the sound of rescue. Gaining my composure, I breathed slowly and rhythmically.

I thought I heard a faint voice. *Rescue perhaps?* I called out. "Jai, is that you?"

Nothing. Just a wall of solid black.

The white substance must be hallucinogenic. My awareness intensified as I recalled the most obscure things in my life in minute detail. I even recalled a phenomenon discovered by Swedish artist Friedrich Jürgenson in 1959. He was taping the sounds of birdsong which revealed faint intelligible voices when replayed, even though no-one else was in the vicinity. He repeated the procedure and found that the recordings could be reliably replicated. A Latvian psychologist named Konstantin Raudive joined him in his work, and made over one hundred thousand recordings. Believing the clarity of voices could not come about through normal means, Raudive published a book in 1968 entitled, *'Breakthrough: An Amazing Experiment in Electronic Communication with the Dead'*. A satisfactory explanation to the electronic voice phenomena has never been found.

Slowly, my fatigued mind fell into a meandering, restless sleep…

5

THE HERETIC

———————

APOSTOLIC PENITENTIARY, VATICAN CITY

A ngelo's interest had been piqued, but so had his guilt. Pacing the lonely halls, he made his way to the archive for the 10:30 rendezvous. Angelo knew he would face a barrage of questions should he be spotted at this time of night. *What are you doing here after hours? Why are you near the Archive?* Worse, he could face disciplinary action.

Angelo feared questions from the Cardinal whose hypnotic stare would often reduce him to a dithering mess. After all, he was only an administrative assistant to one of the most powerful men in the Vatican. His duty was to serve God, but surely the search for truth was not a sin.

The Holy See took on a different atmosphere at night compared to its daytime visage. The intricate frescos and ornate architecture dedicated to man's concept of God appeared almost sinister, subtly transformed into a brooding mélange of shadows.

As Angelo hurried through the muted corridors, he knew he was treading in the footsteps of history. *If only these walls could speak,* he mused, *what number of saints and sinners have strolled these very passages?*

An eerie silence pervaded the hallowed passages. A Swiss guard secured the main entrance to the Secret Archive. The towering shelves cast long shadows from the faint security lights. Angelo was careful not to be noticed, making his way down the narrow hall-way leading closer to the secluded entrance which separated Comte from the rest of the world.

A heavy vault-like door came into view. Although Angelo hated the idea of consorting with a man who was regarded as a loathsome troublemaker, there was something alluring about the irreverent cynic, particularly in this bastion of pious conservatism. There was a captivating certainty about the man. Perhaps this was why he was considered dangerous.

Angelo knocked gently. No answer.

He knocked again, just a touch louder. Still no answer. *Comte must have forgotten.*

Just as he was about to start the long walk back, the electronic lock unlatched. The door glided open revealing Comte's grotesque features flashing a quixotic grin.

"Come in Angelo, come in my boy."

Angelo thought of a spider cleverly attracting its prey and tim-idly entered the Penitentiary's anteroom. Comte shuffled to his desk.

"Grappa?"

"No thank you."

"It's the only earthly pleasure they allow in here," smirked Comte, pointing to the uncapped bottle of liquor. "Hypocritical jack-asses!"

Angelo noted the label. The brand was expensive and would leave a powerful after-burn. He had only ever tasted the commun-ion wine, and even if he did partake, he wouldn't entertain drinking with someone with Comte's subversive profile. Angelo believed that only the Church had answers to the mysteries of life and death, but something about this man's nature had drawn him here.

He quietly watched as Comte deftly splashed a generous helping of the potent spirit. The poor man was horribly disfigured. Angelo admired his ability to handle the operation with half a thumb and only stubs for his fingers. His other hand was nearly as bad. He felt urged to help, but held back fearing he may offend.

"I know you're a good religious lad," said Comte, taking an audible sip. "I used to be a lot like you."

"Used to be?" Angelo threw a dubious glance. "What changed?"

"Pretty much everything really." Comte plonked his glass on the desk. "When I was younger, I was doing what I thought was God's work in Rwanda. Then the country went mad and I was attacked."

Inspecting the poor fellow's ravaged body, Angelo cautiously asked, "Did your injuries change your perception of things?"

"It was the catalyst. It helped me understand that I am not the flesh and blood you see."

Angelo's eyebrows creased. "What do you mean?"

"Oh, I think we'll leave that for another day. It's fair to say though, my concept of God and religion changed. You would have been a small child when Rwanda exploded into madness. Almost a million men, women and children were butchered in ten days of bloody carnage. In the process of saving a young child from the same fate, I was attacked by a crazed youth with a machete. I was lucky I wasn't killed. The world stood by and watched while the self-proclaimed policemen of the world, the U.N. and the U.S., did nothing.

"Worse still Angelo, this Church did nothing, *God did nothing*. Nothing. Most of those poor people were Christian for heaven's sake! It was as though humanity had lost its soul. Things I'd been certain of changed forever."

"What things? God works in mysterious ways, Monsignor."

"The name's Comte. Only my detractors call me Monsignor. Of course, that's pretty much everyone here."

Angelo measured the intent behind this comment and responded cautiously, "Fair enough."

"God might work in mysterious ways Angelo, but it's an explanation that's just a cheap, unintelligible cop-out. As for me, I work to further human understanding. Everything about religion is so different from what we've been told. Even everyday science and history have become a cover for a hidden truth."

Angelo was not prone to argumentative behaviour, but he felt his faith was being insidiously undermined. The sceptic in him played out.

"Can you back that up with an example?" he pressed, sensing a proof of either utter brilliance or borderline insanity.

"OK, let's start with the basics. You know of the Knights Templar."

"I've heard of them," Angelo' face registered caution, believing the Templars to be some sinister, quasi-occult religious sect. Worse, they had been in conflict with the Church.

"They changed the face of Europe," said Comte casually. "The world knew them as 'The Order of the Poor Knights of Christ and the Temple of Solomon', men dedicated to chastity, poverty and obedience, who vowed to protect the pilgrims travelling to Jerusalem. They became the wealthiest fraternity in Europe. Ironic, don't you think? Wealthier than all the monarchs in Europe combined."

"So what's that got to do with religion?"

Comte paused for a moment and dabbed at a dollop of saliva gathering in the corner of his twisted mouth. "Do you really want to hear this?"

Angelo shrugged. "Sure, why not?"

Comte's face lit up with mischief. "Because you may have to rethink everything you think you know. And it includes much of the theology you've been taught."

"Why do you say that? I'm not a complete fool."

"No, I don't think you are. For now, I'll just tell you about of the extraordinary Ark of the Covenant."

"What? The one mentioned in the Bible?"

"Yes that one." Comte slurped his liquor and wiped his mouth with the back of his hand. "Perhaps a little history lesson will help you. The origins of the Knights Templar come from the first crusade. In 1118, nine knights led by Hugues de Payens offered their services to the new King Baudouin II of Jerusalem. They were assigned a portion of his palace on Temple Mount above the ruins of the Temple of Solomon. These men believed they knew the precise location of the Ark, an artefact of immeasurable scientific and monetary value. Quite remarkable really."

Angelo was dismissive. "Yeah sure, I wonder what the Church has to say about it."

"Who cares," scoffed Comte. "Ignore what the Church says, just refer to the Bible. From the Book of Chronicles, we see that long after Solomon's reign Josiah decided the Ark should be returned to the Temple in Jerusalem."

"So the Ark was returned. So what?"

"The Knights had a great interest in it because it was a sophisticated electrical device."

Angelo looked sceptical. "How could a four thousand year old artefact be electrical?"

"Good question Angelo. It's a long story. Tests done by the Massachusetts Institute of Technology would suggest the Ark of the Covenant was a giant capacitor, storing millions of volts of electricity. That's why the Israelites only allowed the Levite priesthood to handle it. The Bible says the Ark was capable of turning people to dust and that it sometimes gave off sparks. More importantly, the Knights Templar retrieved it."

"Retrieved?" queried Angelo with scepticism. Despite his study at the Pontificia Università Urbaniana he had little knowledge of medieval history.

"Yes Angelo, retrieved. They knew from the Old Testament

texts that Jeremiah and Hilkiah's Temple Guard had hidden the Ark beneath the Temple 1,700 years before, below the very place where they now resided. Apart from the gold contained in the Ark, the Temple also held all the old Jerusalem bullion. Some think the Knights were motivated by greed, but that's nonsense."

"Perhaps they were just interested in the gold? Didn't you say they were richer than all the monarchs of Europe? Perhaps they were just common thieves."

Comte inwardly laughed at the superficiality of Angelo's knowledge, but admired the young man's challenge.

"Many would think so. But I can tell you these men fought and died for matters of principle. They resisted the demons of false authority and fought to the death for their beliefs. They gave their lives without fear."

"Just like other Christian martyrs by the sound of it. What made them any different?"

Comte shook his head. There was so much for the young man to learn.

"To truly understand Angelo, you must read and learn. At this stage, simply know the Templars retrieved the Ark and all the bullion. They succeeded where Nebuchadnezzar had failed fifteen hundred years earlier. This is confirmed by the inventory of plunder given in 2 Kings 25 and Jeremiah 52. Neither passage makes any mention of it.

"And when the Roman Senator Cornelius Tacitus entered the Temple in 63 BCE, he confirmed it as well by saying, *'the sanctuary was empty and the Holy of the Holies untenanted.'*"

Angelo was impressed with Comte's scriptural references and knowledge of biblical history. A life within the Church certainly helped in developing this ability.

Comte was becoming increasingly animated, his ugly features assuming a stoic look of conviction in the dim light. "The old

Hebrew text of Jeremiah 3 explains why the treasure couldn't be found. The Talmud records that Jeremiah hid the Ark in a vault deep below the Temple. After its discovery by the Templars, they formed the elite 'Order of the Temple' to protect it throughout history. They were eventually succeeded by the 'Order of Sion'. It came to be known as the Order of Elysius in the highest circles."

"So what happened to the treasure and the Ark?"

"That's a matter of history. The original Templar Knights had been assiduous scholars of the ancient texts. By 1127, they had retrieved priceless ancient treasure and of course, the Ark. It was all transported back to Europe and hidden by the Knights where it remains to this day."

Angelo was confounded by Comte's claim, wondering where the Ark might now reside. He decided he would do some research to see if Comte's outrageous claims could be verified.

"There was something else Angelo. The Templars discovered a parchment emboldened within the Key of Solomon. Understanding of the Key is now closely guarded by an elite faction of Freemasons that remain apart from the more common, business oriented guilds. Both the CIA and the Church have tried to decipher the Key, but I understand they've never cracked it."

Comte lifted from his chair and shuffled to a filing cabinet, pulling out a sheath folder. Inside was a set of symbols forming a cipher. "This is what it looks like. There are lots of theories as to what it means. I believe it's an astronomical map, a map of the stars."

Angelo looked baffled.

"I understand your scepticism, but my assumption is based on some powerful data. All fifty pyramids in Lower Egypt are configured to represent a string of constellations. The grand obelisk of Ra is placed dead centre, representing the blazing star in the Key. It's even symbolised in the United States with the Washington obelisk being placed in the very centre of the Mall."

"So what happened to the Templars?"

Comte wheezed a laugh as his disfigured face contorted with a perverse zeal.

"It was a great day for the Church and later, for modern versions of Christianity. When the last Grand Master of the Order, Jacques de Molay was captured in 1314, he was slowly roasted to death over an open fire. He challenged his betrayers King Philippe and Pope Clement to account for their actions at the Court of God before the year's end."

Pope? The word reverberated through Angelo's innocent mind.

"Within a month, the Pope died from a sudden onset of dysentery and the King died in the same year from unknown causes. God had finally dispensed justice. Just check your history books my friend. It's all there. Remember, seek and ye shall find."

Comte erupted with a bout of rebellious laughter and threw down the last of his grappa.

6

VISIONS

NEAR BALBEEK, LEBANON

My thoughts were replaced by a crystal serenity, accompanied by a sensation of falling. I was pulled through a kaleidoscope of feelings and conscious states. In a dreamlike sleep, my perception penetrated a series of membranes separating this reality from another. I was immersed in a vision of profound serenity. Darkness gave way to form.

With pristine clarity, I observed an enormous, decaying five-sided pyramid. It lay on a barren landscape littered with other tetrahedral and rectilinear structures. Far into the distance, I saw a mountain sculpted into artificial form. My vision was filled with an ecstasy so compelling I wanted to remain forever. Standing amid these decayed ruins, I knew I had been here before. It was more than déjà vu. The pyramid was very ancient, in some way connected with the primordial history of Earth. Years before, I had been told that in 1976 the NASA Viking Probe had discovered some artificial formations on Mars. Other artificial structures were confirmed by the Mars Global Surveyor decades later, results which were immediately suppressed as security classified.

My perception was perfect, clearer than anything I had ever experienced. Now I was skimming over the dusty landscape. I sped faster and faster. The topography was scarred with dry ocean beds and I saw deformations where polar ice caps had once been. Rather than a sequence of thoughts, knowledge unfolded as a single unified experience of pure consciousness.

The vision faded and a dream took hold. Something beckoned to deliver me an important message.

I observed a large illuminated wheel glowing in the darkness of night. It rotated slowly, iridescent lights fanning outward in a halo of colour. Oddly, the small sinuous hand of a child reached out to hold mine. I tried to turn to look at who was with me, but I was unable to move my head. My body failed to respond to my thoughts. Despite the strangeness of the event, I felt touched by the child's need. It yearned to tell me something

We strolled toward the huge glowing wheel. A noisy crowd blared just beyond a tall square-cut hedge separating us from the scene. Oddly, there were no stars in the clear night sky.

Rowdy activity enticed us. The corona of light from the wheel disappeared below the hedge as we walked along its perimeter. As we rounded the corner, I was dumbfounded. There was only a vast, barren plain of asphalt. Beyond, lay a pallid blackness, a void extending into the emptiness of space.

"Aiden, are you here? Aiden!"

I slumbered from my dream state, only half aware. I mumbled a few words.

"It's me – Jai."

White light punctured the dark. A shadowy form was sculptured out of the glare. With a stupid grin pasted on his face, Jai was kneeling in front of me holding an enormous spotlight. He offered a bottle of water.

"Thank God, man!"

I breathed deep and snapped back to the present. "God's got nothing to do with it. What took you so long?"

There was much to investigate. Pictographs and a form of hieroglyphics, with dozens of carved images and patterns, covered many of the walls within this room, all evidence of a significant civilisation. I was familiar with the Egyptian style of hieroglyphs and drawings, but most markings looked even more ancient, a throwback to an earlier civilisation maybe. *Was there a Babylonian connection?* Photographic evidence was the best we could hope for with our limited time.

We had official permission for our investigations, but our authority to be here was fast expiring. If we didn't move on, there would be hell to pay. We could do without questioning from the Hezbollah militia who often controlled this area and made occasional covert observations of our camp.

Until an official announcement of the find was made, it was important we covered our tracks. We made a special effort to camouflage the drill site so that the correct processes could be put in place, but more importantly so that plunderers would keep away. Finding a Neolithic cave always created administrative red tape, but evidence of a site occupied by a more advanced civilisation could be tied up for years, if not decades. Before anything was announced I needed some answers. This was way outside my vocation.

It was almost midnight before we drove southwest toward Beirut. The day had been a long one. After a couple of hours of weary driving, the lights of the city drew closer. Jai could barely contain his excitement. He wanted answers to questions not even thought of.

I was a little more subdued. We had stumbled on something extraordinary, but our mission had been to discover some evidence of modern man's origin. Real evidence of interbreeding between Neanderthal and Cro-Magnon, instead of the clap-trap previously published, would have given me some satisfaction, so I harboured a little disappointment.

Jai on the other hand wanted to shout to the world, but I made it very clear that for now, silence was the best policy. He knew this find would establish his credentials within academia, but he was sensible and loyal enough to be guided by my experience. It would give added weight to our announcement if we could identify and perhaps translate some of the strange writing from the crypt. We resolved to seek the opinion of an expert.

Upon reaching our hotel, I phoned Dr Keisha Petersen, Professor of Ancient Near Eastern Languages at the Australian National University in Canberra. Dr Petersen was a world authority in her field and I hoped she would examine our photographs. I had never met her, but her credentials were flawless, and she had a formidable, if not maverick reputation. There was an added advantage. It would give me a chance to visit the 'lucky country' again, the home of my youth. It had been far too long. I flew out of Lebanon late the next day and Jai returned to his native Florence to continue his postgraduate studies.

Jai left with the knowledge that his name would be linked to the discovery of an amazing crypt in the region near the ancient temple of Baalbek. We would publish our paper and I felt certain we could use some of the material in my next television series.

Unknown to us, forces were already at work to prevent us.

7

THE UNEXPECTED

FLORENCE, ITALY

Rosina Mastravino had coveted this moment for nearly three months. She yearned for her love. Casually dressed in T-shirt and denim, Rosina sat patiently, her long dark hair glistening in the warm Tuscan sun. She was the woman of all Jai's hopes and dreams. He too, was manic with excitement, having an urgent need to hold her. But that wasn't all. He couldn't wait to speak about his plans. She was the love of his life and there was much to tell her.

Jai Santini knew the discovery in Baalbek would open doors for his future and he was anxious to share his news with the world. If only he could tell her. He had wanted to ask for his girlfriend's hand in marriage for months, but he knew her father would find such a proposal unacceptable, at least until he had finished his studies and gained an acceptable position. The magnitude of his discovery with the well-respected Dr Keyes would now sway the scales in his favour.

The River Arno flowed sedately beneath the Ponte Vecchio as Jai paced the bridge to rendezvous with Rosina in the Piazza della Signoria. He swung past the entrance to the Uffizi Gallery, puffed with a sense of Florentine pride. He knew this was the most famous picture gallery in all of Italy and one of the most famous in the world. Yes, he was proud and exuberant, proud of the city of his birth, proud of his childhood sweetheart and proud of his new-found confidence.

Rosina had always waited for him on the steps of the Loggia dei Lanzi, a late Gothic structure standing to the right of the Palazzo Vecchio on the northern side of the square. She always enjoyed watching the tourists who delighted in the magnificence of the various sculptures sheltered within the loggia.

This morning was no different. Horse-drawn carriages were competing for patrons and a throng of tourists were gathered at Cellini's fine statue of Perseus, intently listening to their guide. The bronze masterpiece shows Andromeda's liberator, just after he has cut off Medusa's head. Resplendent in his winged helmet, the naked hero is personified by standing with his right foot on the lifeless corpse, holding the blood dripping severed head high in one hand and his curved-tipped sword in the other.

Jai caught Rosina's attention as he fought his way through the knot of people crowding Perseus. He smiled and waved, anxious to hold her in his arms. Rosina stood in anticipation of his embrace, teeth flashing through her smile.

Nobody saw it coming.

A man dressed casually in a grey polo shirt and blue denim jeans crashed out of the crowd just as Jai was about to clear it. In one swift action, a blade of steel sliced upward into Jai's chest, and an ice pick was slammed deep into his carotid artery. Both knife and pick were inserted with surgical precision. The instruments of death were left deep within the bloody flesh. Jai staggered in the crowd, blood pumping through his fingers, as he clutched the knife and held onto a fragment of precious life. The colour of deep red sprayed over the crowd from the pick imbedded in his neck.

Swaying wildly, Jai collapsed at the feet of Perseus, blood quickly flowing over the pavement. Rosina screamed, scattering the crowd as she elbowed through them and swept Jai into her arms. His body quivered, blood still spurting with every weakening beat. A promising life ebbed closer to the abyss. He sucked in a breath of air expelling it with a choked haemic cough that drooled thick over his chin.

The perpetrator had disappeared.

Panic, confusion and madness swept through the crowd as Rosina's tears mingled with the bloody mess in her arms. Jai's departure from this world left her knowing one thing. Lying under the raised arm of Perseus holding the severed head directly above, Jai spoke his last words.

In his dying breath, he whispered, "I love you…"

8

THE MEETING

_____

CANBERRA, AUSTRALIA

Dr Keisha Petersen was surprised when she received a phone call from the renowned paleoanthropologist and Professor of Evolutionary Biology at University College London, Dr Aiden Keyes. She knew a little of Keyes's reputation. He had recently hosted a six part series on the BBC about the origins of man and was being hailed as the Carl Sagan of anthropology. Keisha had caught the odd snippet from one or two episodes and had enjoyed them immensely. She likened the professor more to Sir David Attenborough, a presenter who enjoyed getting his hands dirty, fossicking around with an almost manic passion. It was obvious he liked the sun on his back.

Dr Petersen particularly remembered how Keyes had disagreed with his fellow researchers about what he called 'an inept grab for research funding'. He had publicly disputed their findings, saying future new evidence would reveal their folly.

His reasons for an appointment were obscure, some talk about photographs from his latest excursion. How she would be able to help was beyond her, but she was anxious to meet the man. She had admired his single-mindedness and his humorous cynicism. Any academic who was prepared to navigate stormy seas alone instead of the calm waters of his peers was to be admired.

Dr Petersen had observed from the television program that Aiden Keyes cut a tall, handsome figure. He had a cultivated Australian accent flavoured with a touch of Irish brogue. She had observed a strong personality, a man who knew his place in the world and a man who didn't suffer fools. He seemed brusque and opinionated, but she had also noticed a conspicuous boyish charm. A thin crease curled her lips. He was so ruggedly masculine. But she had also noticed how his eyes were frosted with sorrow.

It was a pristine sub-zero morning when I hailed a taxi for my eight o'clock meeting. A wispy fog blanketed the icy lake surrounding the city and the languid eucalypts exuded their unique fragrance in the crisp morning air. With refreshed and alert senses, I was anxious to meet the Professor.

Dr Keisha Petersen had a formidable reputation. She was renowned for her eccentricity and was considered something of a savant in her profession, uncompromising and unconventional. Nevertheless, she was widely regarded within academia as the best in her field and was regularly sought for her expertise. She was at the peak of her career and I was privileged that she had opened a space in her diary.

By the time my cab reached the University, the blazing winter sun had finally extinguished the remnant morning fog. The sky was now coloured a magnificent azure blue.

"The Linguistics faculty please."

The driver slowly rounded the narrow road stopping in front of a substantial concrete and glass building. Standing at the entrance in a long dark woollen coat was an extravagantly beautiful woman, her long blonde hair worked by the chilled breeze.

"Dr Petersen?"

"Yes. Dr Keyes I presume? Please call me Keisha."

The acknowledgement was accompanied by a pleasantly firm handshake. Her smile conveyed a warm, but discreet greeting and her pale blue eyes shone with a welcome openness. They held an infectious sparkle.

"Sure, call me Aiden. Everybody else does."

Keisha Petersen looked more like a stylish Nordic fashion model than a world authority on ancient languages. Not couture, but sophisticated. Aged in her mid-thirties, her feminine, well-balanced features and luxurious long blonde hair seemed out of place in the crusty academic world of unkempt beards and receding hairlines. She looked and smelled refined. Her polished manner captured the vitality of chic femininity with an intonation of demure and unde- manding sensuality. She was as fresh as morning rain.

As we walked to her study, I began to wonder about her aca- demic brilliance. She was exceedingly beautiful, quite sexy really, but was she as astutely erudite as so many had claimed? It had been an age since I had spent time with a woman as remotely appeal- ing as Dr Petersen and I found myself immediately drawn to her. However, my temptations would need to be subdued. After all, I was here to learn what she could tell me about my photographs.

Her study gave a hint to her personality. Spacious. Organised and clean. Modern and tasteful. Glass topped desk, work neatly stacked, slim Apple laptop and iPhone at hand. To the right, a wall of books, tidily housed. To the left, a large plasma screen hung on the wall above a modern white enamel credenza featuring two bronze- age artefacts. Classy understatement. I also noticed with interest, no personal snapshots.

After the usual preliminaries, I handed over my USB contain- ing the digital images. She inserted the drive into her laptop and allowed me to type my password. She quickly brought a plethora of images onto the screen. Shifting in her chair, she clicked on each, quickly scanning some, slowly pondering over others.

Her gaze remained on the screen. "Wow...these are very interesting Aiden. Where were they taken?"

"Confidential, I'm afraid."

"Just comment on the data, is that right?"

"Unfortunately, that needs to be the case." I hoped she would understand my need for secrecy.

The intensity of her perusal allowed my eyes to roam. In a long sweep from the open-necked blouse, I followed her curves from the subtly exposed shapely cleavage to her gracefully crossed legs visible beneath the glass-top desk. I took particular note that her long elegant fingers carried no wedding band, in fact, no rings whatsoever. Her nails were her own and neatly clipped. There was nothing acrylic about this woman.

Keisha sensed my detailed scrutiny, raising her eyebrows and glancing up at me. I'd been boldly caught out and as my eyes darted away from my captivation, she smiled with mischievous satisfaction.

I covered my chagrin with a comment, "Not married I see."

"No. And you?"

My handful of unresolved relationships over the years came to mind. "Never."

"Not interested or just too busy?"

Mmm...I had to play this carefully. Relationships were not my thing, but no eligible female wants to hear that, so I replied, "Still looking for the right woman."

"I see." Her tone was one of disinterest.

With my hand declared, Keisha went back to eyeing the digital images. I chanced a couple of discrete glances of her cleavage. Her coy smirk suggested she had again noticed my interest, so disappointingly I drew my attention elsewhere.

If I was going to succeed with her I would need to be subtle.

I knew that women this beautiful usually developed a 'princess complex' in their youth. Their families and friends doted on their beauty. In adolescence, she would have received the adoration of countless males, all practising their tacky pick-up lines. I would need to be different to shock her out of her self-satisfied complacency to become a contender. Long ago, I had developed the habit of examining the titles of books in the rooms of my peers. It was the surest way of gaining an insight into the essence of their personality. I wondered what they would tell me about her.

My eyes ranged across the bookshelf. The wall hugging collection was fascinating and disconcerting, a congregation of eclectic titles. Apart from the expected ancient language books there was a kaleidoscope of subjects – archaeology, anthropology, philosophy, comparative religion, quantum physics, ancient history, systems theory. There were books on biblical history, astronomy, Advaitism, computer science, and Jungian psychology. They were de rigueur for a first rate intellect.

My observation was abruptly interrupted.

Keisha stood and politely asked, "Espresso Aiden?"

"Oh, er…" As I began to shake my head, she interjected.

"It's very good here. My treat." Before I could answer she had bolted from the room.

My eyes drifted back to her library. This lady was obviously very different. In my experience, academics were usually dull, predictable people believing their particular discipline to be the epicentre of the intellectual universe. They rarely had much idea about a subject beyond their narrow field of expertise. Whilst I knew little outside my own field, at least I'd never been considered dull or predicable. As for Keisha Petersen, she was obviously prepared to push the boundaries of her knowledge. I liked that. The woman had style. And she had a beguiling, playful personality. *How* playful was the question.

One particular title caught my eye. Tucked to the right of the centre shelf was *'Religious Belief Systems of the Third Reich'*. I was intrigued. Not the type of book any serious academic would possess I thought, let alone one as esteemed as Dr Petersen. I was about to take a closer look when her quick return surprised me.

"How're you going?" she asked as she glided through the door. "Here's that coffee. Tell me if it's any good."

As she extended her hand, I noticed a white gold watch slip beyond the sleave of her blouse. It had a small moon phase regulator at the side of the dial.

"Nice time-piece," I remarked, probing for further clues to her personality. It looked expensive and I was curious as to how she could afford such an item on an academic stipend.

"It's a Vacheron," she grinned, offering me the cup.

"A gift?"

"No, just a special treat for myself."

I saw an opening to shake the princess complex. It usually worked. "Well, you have good taste, but I would have chosen the yellow-gold model. The white-gold doesn't suit your hair."

"Really?"

"Perhaps you can change your hair colour," I said, trying not to crack a smile.

"The men in this establishment wouldn't notice so thanks for the advice. I guess!"

Moments of subtle stress were a unique opportunity to get to know a lady. Keisha had handled the moment with aplomb. She was neither aggressive nor quarrelsome – good qualities in someone so damn alluring.

The aroma of the superb coffee wafted through her study, its rich flavour demanding comment. "You're right about the coffee, it's pretty good. You have an interesting book collection here. Quite a variety."

"You think so? I get bored easily so I spread my interests. Trained for four years as a physicist and then bagged it. I found I wasn't getting the answers to the really big questions."

"I thought physics answered 'all' the big questions."

"Only when you don't ask the hard ones." Her response was accompanied by a coquettish wink that suggested that she might be more playful than I had expected.

"You know Aiden, many years ago in Burma, an old monk told a mentor of mine about a doctrine from 'the Old Ones'. It explained hidden things about our existence. That's *the* big question I'm interested in."

"The meaning of life, eh. Now that *is* a big question."

"One worth pursuing don't you think?"

"I agree. Anything we don't know is definitely worth pursuing. Even about each other," I responded.

I had extracted a smile, but she remained the consummate professional. Before I could pass further comment her iPhone vibrated. She quickly glanced at its screen.

Her expression instantly darkened, her liquid eyes losing their sensual humour. Without any word, she deleted the message.

"Quick Aiden, there's a taxi waiting out front. A problem's developed and it's best we talk elsewhere."

"What sort of problem?"

"I'll explain later."

She slammed her laptop shut, slid it into a leather shoulder case and made for the door. I was unsettled by the change of events, but followed her to the entrance where the expected car was waiting, exhaust fumes condensing in the cold morning air.

Keisha and I scrambled into the back seat.

"The city please. Fast as you can."

Her attention turned to me, her expression rigid. "It's safer to talk away from the university. My walls have ears. Aiden, I've got bad news."

Bad news? How bad could it be, I hadn't even propositioned her yet. "What's going on?"

Keisha lowered her voice. "Your friend Jai Santini was murdered in Florence thirteen hours ago. These photographs may be the reason."

Blood drained from my face. *Was this a joke?* Keisha's expression suggested it wasn't. *Who the hell was this woman and how could she possibly know about Jai?* "What the hell are you talking about?"

She placed her hand on mine in reassurance, but my thoughts were elsewhere. How could anyone know about the photographs? Apart from me, the only people who knew they existed were Jai and Keisha. Surely Jai's death was coincidental.

I couldn't think. "Why would someone want to kill him? Nobody knows about those images."

"It seems you're wrong."

Keisha strained to look into the driver's rear view mirror. "Shit, I think we're being followed." She glanced through the back window. "Driver, the shopping plaza, up there on the left. Quick."

I was jolted into the moment. The driver flattened the accelerator and whipped through the traffic. As I turned to look behind, a black BMW careened out of hiding from behind another vehicle. Its windscreen was heavily tinted obscuring the occupants. We were thrown sideways as our car swerved into the open-air parking station, the car now close to our tail.

Before we came to a stop, Keisha threw fifty dollars at the driver, grabbed my hand, and together we dashed into the plaza. Another car backing out of its parking space impeded the BMW's progress. Two over-sized men wearing ill-fitting business suits immediately jumped out of the vehicle and took chase.

Adrenalin surged as we ran past several stores and through an exit into the opposite car park. Fortunately, a taxi rank had a waiting car, the driver standing outside the cab sucking on a cigarette.

"Driver! In the car now!" Outwardly unnerved, Keisha issued the order with cool composure as we clambered into the back seat. As our pursuers ran into the car park, our car sped off in a clean getaway.

Keisha panted as she caught her breath. "I think it's time we had a closer look at these." She patted the shoulder bag. "They seemed to have caught someone's interest."

My head cleared. "Keisha, who sent that text?"

Her reply was evasive. "I've always been looked after Aiden. It seems that you are too."

I was baffled and unnerved by the woman's ease. She was an enigma. Questions beckoned, but I decided to bide my time. I needed to be on guard. Even with Keisha Petersen.

9

THE BRIEFING

OVER THE ATLANTIC

Cardinal Valla was on his mission to the United States with a copy of the Donation in his possession. Compromise was out of the question and the recalcitrants in America would be brought to heel.

The Jesuits needed to understand that funding their astronomical fantasies would be cancelled once the keys to the Holy See changed hands. They had no right to question the nature of God.

And then there was the diabolical mess of the Boston diocese. Decades of endemic paedophilia had cost the Church millions. The problem had festered in Boston for years, and by God they could deal with the fallout themselves. For the press and certain clergy to sheet the blame on the edict of celibacy was sacrilegious. The authority of the Holy Office would be enforced.

The Holy Office received its current appellation in 1965 and was divided into four separate divisions. One such division, the Congregation of the Doctrine of the Faith was originally known as the Inquisition and has the mandate to safeguard Church Doctrine. Cardinal Valla received his appointment as Doctrinaire Head soon after his arrival in the Vatican in 1977. With his appointment to Vatican Secretary of State upon the death of the last Pontiff, he had no intention of passing this important position to lesser mortals.

Flying high above the Atlantic the droning silence was broken. The phone jarred him from his thoughts. It was rare for anyone to send a call during flight so it was likely to be of some importance.

"Valla," he snapped, stewing with impatience.

A contemptuous voice replied. "Good evening Your Eminence. It's Agostino here." The voice was laced with its customary sarcasm.

The Cardinal's blood ran cold, dread bleeding into his silent musings. Cardinal Giovanni Agostino was the maestro of elimination. As a senior Jesuit member of Opus Dei, Agostino had more than just influence within the Church. He had access to 'Secretum Omega', the highest security clearance in the Vatican. Agostino headed the highly secretive Servizio Informazioni del Vaticano, the Vatican Intelligence Service. A small faction of Jesuits who were aligned to the S.I.V. had become obsessed with the return to our solar system of a mysterious planet. Valla knew little of their objectives or operations and was intimidated by their secrecy.

Agostino relished the thought that Valla perceived him as a demon. He had built a reputation that fitted well and was Teflon-coated. Nothing would ever stick. Most importantly, Agostino knew the dark underbelly of the Vatican. He knew where the doctrinal and political skeletons were buried.

Agostino had cut his teeth in protecting the interests of the Vatican after the body of Roberto Calvi had been found hanging beneath London's Blackfriars Bridge in 1982. Chairman of the massive, privately owned Banco Ambrosiano, Calvi had been illegally siphoning money using the Instituto per de Religione, the Vatican Bank, to launder foreign currencies. Upon his death, a black hole of $1.3 billion opened to swallow his bank whole. It collapsed leaving the Vatican Bank vulnerable by holding a large proportion of the missing money.

Pope John Paul I had been on the verge of calling an investigation into the financial skulduggery and Agostino had brazenly limited the damage. The 'convenient' death thirty-three days into his Pontificate had made sure of it. Agostino caressed the innuendo surrounding the Pope's sudden death, giving him a reputation that had propelled his career. Enemies of Opus Dei within the Curia of Cardinals had been suitably shaken and the investigation was never called.

Agostino was also aware of Valla's rise in the Church. The Cardinal was a man seized by passion and ambition, and although his position as Secretary of State was secure while the German was Pontiff, the hold over his title of Doctrinaire Head was precarious.

Agostino had done his research and Valla knew it.

Decades before his tenure within the Holy City, Valla was forced through an accident of circumstance to witness his mother's execution in Berlin during World War II. An inner circle of the Third Reich had discovered something so astonishing it would undermine the very fabric of society. The young Antonio Valla had been confronted by a shattering truth, and in the madness that followed the War, he forged a pact with the Anglo-American military alliance that would promote his meteoric rise within the Church. The discovery could never be publicly revealed. The highest echelons of the intelligence community knew that if the world came to understand the truth, it would bring into question the very essence of civilisation. Many would become disenchanted with a life of ceaseless activity and competitive aspiration, making them difficult to control.

"What is it?" Valla was curt, his heart pounding.

"There's been a breach in the Baalbek region. We understand there's been an unauthorised excavation."

"By whom?"

"Dr Aiden Keyes, BBC television presenter and anthropologist renowned for his controversial views. He was looking for a cave apparently. P2 have dealt with his assistant. A Florentine by the name of Santini."

P2 – the infamous Propaganda Due. Secret and Elitist. Masonic. They had a reputation for maintaining shady allegiances and pulling the odd covert assassination. Back in 1978 they had orchestrated the murder of Italian Prime Minister Aldo Moro. Valla accepted the idea that the Church occasionally needed to exercise some muscle, but he worried about the organisation's allegiances.

The tentacles of P2 stretched deep inside the Vatican. Its membership was a virtual who's who – major industrialists, bankers, cabinet ministers, judges, high-ranking military and of course, members of Opus Dei, including Agostino.

For centuries, the Church had automatically excommunicated anyone who was exposed as a Freemason. Threats often fell on deaf ears and many members of the Curia were covert members of the Masonic P2. Curiously, when Pope John Paul II was at the helm, a new Canon Law was announced in 1983 allowing Freemasons to become members of the Church. This action cemented P2's membership within the Vatican. A new, more insidious order had been born. *Had the Holy Father been squeezed by Agostino?* No-one knew and neither did Valla. He didn't dwell on his suspicions, instead Valla did his duty, and obediently rallied behind the cause making sure the anti-communist regime was nurtured and supported. Privately, he had always harboured concerns.

With further Papal appointments, the Curia of Cardinals had been slowly stacked in a Machiavellian bid to perpetuate a right wing ideology. Valla understood and generally endorsed the ideology, but was disturbed by the extent of P2's penetration. They had operatives within the CIA, MI6 and Mossad, and through these agencies, clandestine connections with terrorist groups in the Middle East and beyond. However, there was something even more disturbing.

Valla had long ago been compromised. He had to answer to a more elite group with classification well above all of these agencies.

"What do you mean dealt with?"

Agostino did not speak. He allowed his silence to extend, conveying authority.

Valla's face tightened. "Damn you, who gave the order?"

Agostino knew the Cardinal would be livid. "I did Your Eminence." His words dripped with contempt.

"We should've talked about this."

Agostino made no attempt to hide his scorn. His response was designed to needle. "No need. You deal with theology Your Eminence and I'll deal with the real world. Can't have your masters taking all the credit, can we?"

Valla was cataleptic. He screeched down the line. "Fuck you. I want a full report, understand?"

Agostino replied with genuine amusement. "Certainly Your Eminence."

He enjoyed it when the Cardinal squirmed. The thought of Valla floundering with those who controlled him gave Agostino a smug sense of satisfaction.

Agostino decided to keep the Cardinal off-balance. "Just remember Valla, no-one is indispensible, including you."

A chill coursed through Valla's spine. He knew Agostino was issuing a threat. The bastard certainly had balls.

Another fucking problem, he thought as he slammed the phone into its cradle. *Another unauthorised excavation. And a fucking death.* The Cardinal fumbled for his pills and washed them down with a swallow of his cognac.

During his career there had been two previous incursions, with orthodox theology threatened on both occasions. Valla had been left to deal with the matter, suitably discrediting the insurgent archaeologists with his mastery of scriptural and historical spin. He had the wonderful black-art ability to make a discovery fit the dogma. Absorbed by the implications of this new incursion, he pondered a famous episode long before his time.

In the 1920s and '30s when archaeologist Sir Leonard Woolley unearthed thousands of inscribed clay tablets from some of the ancient Mesopotamian cities, the very genesis of the Bible was nearly exposed.

If the truth of Woolley's discoveries had captured popular imagination, the notion that the Bible is the Word of God would have been ridiculed. Fundamentalist Christianity would have been fatally compromised, because it was clear that the Bible had been copied from other much older sources. Some of Woolley's tablets described biblical stories. There was even an Assyrian record of the flood, and a disturbing account of the creation of man. The discovery had proved that stories within the Book of Genesis had been compiled from much earlier Babylonian texts.

Invaders from Syria and the Black Sea eventually ravaged Babylon and by the sixth century, all the great cities had been abandoned. Over the centuries, silt and sand from the desolate Plain of Shinar had covered an incredible truth that may have changed the world.

It will never cease until the masses end up rejecting the very Church itself, Valla agonised, throwing back the last of his cognac. He slouched back into his seat, a wave of tiredness flowing through him. Even though he had the appearance of a far younger man, the pressures of his position were beginning to bear down. He regretted that time was forever moving forward. He feared his life's work would eventually be to no avail, but whilst he still had breath he would fight to the very end.

The Cardinal had been well briefed over the years. Knowledge of unusual archaeological finds such as the stone celestial tracking stations in Guatemala, mechanical gears locked in Palaeolithic lava, perfectly engineered crystal skulls in meso-America and a sophisticated seismic machine from ancient China were conveyed to the Church from the highest U.S. and British intelligence circles.

There were literally hundreds of anomalies and artefacts from around the globe which made conventional history a complete nonsense. Compounding the problem were the Mayans who had developed the most sophisticated calendar in the world. A calendar so advanced, it actually tracked the terrestrial cycles of the earth against the 26,000-year 'precession' of the solar system through the galaxy.

Valla was the official Church voice on such matters. The thought that Agostino had instigated action without consultation made him shudder. One day, he mused, he would bring Agostino to heal.

The Cardinal reflected on what the sophisticated civilisations of the distant past would have thought of the today's world. An ego dominated death trap probably.

He knew that thousands of years before modern science had even discovered electricity, the ancients had mastered key aspects of the 'inner world'. They had understood that they were connected to a vast universe of multidimensional intelligence, something hidden by the royal-political elite since the time of the Pharaoh Amenhotep IV. If evidence of this was revealed and practised by the multitudes, the consequences to every modern religion would be devastating.

10

DISCOVERY

OLD STUDY ROOM, VATICAN CITY

Angelo couldn't sleep. He had been stirred by Comte's seditious claims. Difficult to comprehend – even more difficult to believe.

He vaguely knew that the Templars had been viciously repressed in the fourteenth century, but he figured they had been dangerous heretics, not heroes. The Church had always worked to further the Will of Christ, so there must have been a good reason for its action. God works in mysterious ways after all.

Angelo tossed and turned, thoughts crowding for attention. If Comte was telling the truth and the Donation of Constantine was a fraud, it meant the whole foundation of the Church's authority was a lie. The Church would have no more right to represent the authority of Christ than anybody or anything else. Worse still, they would have been responsible for a global fraud spanning centuries.

Angelo's innocent mind was being ravaged. His sleeplessness was pierced by the unthinkable. *What if everything about religion and God was wrong?* The claws of guilt pinched him for questioning the sanctity of the Universal Church. *Surely the Church taught the only authentic path to salvation? I need to get to the bottom of this just prove Comte wrong,* he reasoned.

It was 5:47 a.m. He would need to be at his desk by 9:00, but fortunately Cardinal Valla had left for an overseas trip. Access to the internet at his work desk was forbidden, but some quick searches should be able to confirm a few facts before he started work. Maybe he could resolve his deepening dilemma. His thoughts drew him to the Old Study Room adjacent to the Apostolic Library.

He quickly dressed and walked the short distance from his small bed-sit on Via di Porta Cavallegerri. Angelo's authority from Cardinal Valla to enter the Medieval Palace, the offices of the Secretariat of State, was enough for the Swiss Guard to allow him passage at this early hour. Heading toward the Old Study Room, he was disturbed by the muted shadows and perfect silences following his stealthy footfalls. He felt the beat of his chest, knowing the consequences of being questioned. As he approached a cross-corridor, a man dressed in a black cassock and purple facia silently glided past.

Angelo's muscles tightened. He recognised the man as a ranking bishop and luckily, he passed without notice. *Why was he out and about so early?*

There was a nervous lightness in his fingertips. He quickly typed >**Donation of Constantine**< into the search engine. Trawling the various hits, it took little time to confirm Comte's revelation. The man had indeed been telling the truth. The document was confirmed as a complete forgery. The authority it gave the Church was a sham. Angelo felt strangely violated. What disturbed him more was that the Church had even admitted it was a fake. This had never revealed at the pontifical university.

The sham of the Donation strengthened his resolve. The infallibility of the written scripture had been drilled into him since childhood and as a devout Christian he knew the Bible was the 'very'

Word of God. Being the Word of God, it followed that everything within the Bible must be true. *Absolutely everything.*

He continued to tap the keys with more searches, the cursor revealing an appalling discovery – stark contradictions within the Gospels.

The Gospel of Matthew said Mary was a virgin, but Mark made no such claim. According to Matthew 27:5, Judas Iscariot *'went and hanged himself'*, whereas in Acts 1:18 he died from an accidental fall.

Angelo was surprised to learn that Jesus was not born on 25th December. He knew other religious faiths celebrated on a different day, but he believed Christianity was the true faith. The date had originally honoured Saturn, the god of the Harvest, and had been chosen by Rome to merge Christianity into pagan culture, a culture supposedly reviled by the Church as heresy.

The strangest contradiction was the genealogy of Jesus. Both the Gospels of Matthew and Luke expand on this subject linking Jesus to Solomon in one account and to Adam in the other. But strangely, Joseph, the husband of the Holy Mother has a completely different father in each account, suggesting a totally different genealogy. If the Gospels are the Word of God how could this be? Even an idiot could discover these contradictions. *Why was the Church silent?*

He even found links to historical texts recording that Jesus had travelled to Persia, Egypt and even England between the ages of twelve and thirty. To his chagrin, he read that even today, there are Muslims, Buddhists and even Christians who venerate the Roza Bal shrine in Srinagar, Kashmir as the burial place of Jesus. The evidence seemed compelling.

But even worse than all this, Angelo discovered that the Church had spent centuries destroying controversial texts that recorded these events, punishing and discrediting anyone who spoke out about such heresies.

Angelo read about Origen, a Church Father who lived eighteen centuries ago. Origen is widely considered an intellectual giant and the most accomplished scholar of the early Church. He said that biblical scripture was nonsense if it was believed literally, being fit only for the instruction of simpletons. He claimed that many stories were obviously untrue or contradictory, and were designed to coax people into deeper inquiry. Origen observed that the Bible was written on three levels, corresponding to the body, mind and spirit, to be understood according to one's ability. He hinted at a hidden doctrine that would reveal the highest truths only to the most initiated.

Angelo went numb. His research had disclosed two disturbing conclusions. The Church had no authority and the Bible was probably not the 'very' Word of God. Maybe some of it was just the inspired word of God. His faith was being sorely tested.

A voice shrieked from behind.

"What in God's name are you doing here?"

Every muscle pulled tight as a sinew. The pit of Angelo's stomach leapt to his chest.

"Ah, some research," he choked, quickly turning around.

A Dominican cleric came close. Dressed in a black cassock, the man had a small, bald head with sober frog shaped eyes. His mien was ugly and vengeful.

"Exactly what kind of research?"

"Er, just random stuff," Angelo blundered. "I couldn't sleep."

"What random stuff?" An angry blue vein visibly pulsed at the man's temple. Intruding, he leaned over the screen and read the Google toolbar at the top of the screen. *Bible inconsistencies.* The words provided a case for the prosecution. "What's your name?"

"Angelo DeMarco, sir."

"I see! You work for His Eminence Cardinal Valla, is that right?"

"Yes sir."

The cleric backed away. "And you think questioning the Word of

God will somehow help the Cardinal and the Church?"

"No sir, I mean, it wasn't my intention to question the Word or the Church. I was just looking to verify…"

He was silenced with a damning interruption. Spittle hurtled toward Angelo as the cleric squealed. "Spare me you fool. You think you know more than the Church and its centuries of scholarship. Do you?"

Angelo held together and offered a mild protest. "Certainly not, but how does understanding history hurt the Church?"

The figure glared, pointing an accusing finger. "This is not the last you'll hear of the matter DeMarco, I can assure you. Your name will be mentioned. Be warned."

11

ODD CONVERSATION

_____

CANBERRA, AUSTRALIA

Had Jai really died? And for what goddamn reason? Maybe it was a case of mistaken identity. Somehow, I didn't think so. The whole event made me sick to the stomach. I still didn't really believe it.

I grabbed my cell phone from my pocket and dialled Jai's home and mobile numbers. No answer. _Was I being manipulated and if so, why?_

The waitress brought more coffee to Keisha and as we sat at our secluded table near the window at the Canberra Yacht Club, our view of Lake Burley Griffin was unencumbered. At this time of the morning we were the only patrons.

Her energy was alluring, but I needed answers to two questions. "Keisha, who the hell was that chasing us back there?"

"Don't worry Aiden. They're just the local spooks. Junior clerks cutting their teeth. The city's filled with them."

"What's their interest in you?"

"Not me, it's you who interests them. It seems you've upset someone and it probably has to do with these." She motioned to her laptop. "I'd say it's the reason Jai was taken out – to shut you up."

"About what for God's sake?"

"That's what we need to find out. Anything else?"

There was. "Who tipped you off about Jai?"

"A friend with ONA, the Office of National Assessments. He heard of Jai's death and knew I was meeting with you this morning. That's all."

What was so important to claim a young and promising life?

Keisha removed the laptop from her shoulder bag. As the computer booted into life, I inserted the USB and keyed my password. She quickly clicked on the file marked 'Last Excavation' and viewed the photo that had caught her attention at the University. It was the Goddess with the solar disc around her head.

"Do you know who this is?"

I shook my head.

"It's a relief of Hathor, an Egyptian Goddess. Beautifully preserved. Hathor mythology goes back to pre-dynastic times. This sun disc over her head symbolises the attainment of higher knowledge."

"I wondered about that; it looked almost Christian to me. You know, like a halo."

Keisha managed to live up to her eccentric reputation. She threw me a curve ball.

"Do you believe in God, Aiden?"

"What do you mean – God?"

She didn't cut me any slack. "It's a simple enough question."

"I don't believe in any form of religion, it's bullshit." My disdain for matters of faith had been formed in my youth. With parents like mine, I could do without it. There had never been a reason to change my mind.

Keisha was sympathetic. "Hey, it's OK. I didn't ask whether you believed in religion, I asked if you believed in God. There's a difference you know."

"Maybe, but the answer's still no. As far as I'm concerned 'you live and you die'. Look at Jai, what hope did he have? God's an illusion for those who need a crutch. You?"

"I do believe actually, but not in the way most religions teach. My beliefs are more like the early Christians who finished up being persecuted by the Church, many of them killed as heretics."

I let the statement go with a shrug.

Keisha just smiled, switched to a picture file within her own database and brought up another photograph.

"Ever seen this?"

I immediately remembered the image. It shocked me when I first saw it in my youth and it still did. It was the famous photograph of a Tibetan monk who had set himself alight in political protest. Sitting in the lotus position, the monk burned to death as his flesh melted from his bones.

"I've seen it. Weird he sat there so calmly."

"I don't have all the answers, but I know the Eastern adepts say the man experienced no pain."

"I don't believe that."

"That's what they say. His mind was purified, capable of transcending all physical phenomena, even the flames. At that very moment, he was in a state of ineffable Bliss and Absolute Existence."

Keisha was conscious of my enchantment and embarrassingly held me in her gaze. "Conventional science says there are many dimensions. Super-string theory suggests there's at least ten. What if our minds could access them? The ancient doctrines claim we can."

I thought she had lost the plot. "Not something I've ever thought about," I answered politely, trying not to offend her.

"That's what the solar disc symbolises. It's about access to the interior dimensions. There's something about these photos that had your friend killed so anything we learn about all this is important, don't you think?"

"Maybe, but my work has always dealt with physical evidence. I accept that the mind influences physical existence, but anything beyond that is just bullshit – surely?"

"Well, I'm not so quick to judge. There are other examples similar to this monk's experience. The Cathars of Europe faced the flames of their accusers just as calmly. You'll probably dismiss this, but both the Eastern adepts of today and the Cathars of the past claim that 'God' exists in a transcendental state beyond the physical. The adepts consider the entire Cosmos as a permanent state of suffering. Our very attachment to the physical universe is what we must overcome. It's our supreme duty in fact."

"That's a bit pessimistic, isn't it, to say the whole world is subject to suffering?"

"Is it?" she asked, taking a sip of her coffee. "Birth is suffering, old age is suffering, sickness is suffering, death is suffering and not getting what you want is suffering. Even getting what you want is suffering because in time it all passes away. Basically, if you're too young, too old, too sick, too ugly or too poor, then you'll suffer. If it's subject to 'time', it'll eventually pass away and you'll suffer. And everything in this world is subject to time. Aiden, I want to tell you what drives my research. Are you ready for some esoteric clap-trap?"

"I'm considered a heretic by my peers so go for it."

"There's evidence to suggest the Hebrew characters written in the original Old Testament books contain intricate mathematical relationships containing a hidden message."

Religion wasn't my thing, but Keisha's work did involve the study of ancient texts, so I was prepared to hear her out. "Sounds a bit deceitful – why not just say what you mean?"

"Persecution for having a different view from the Church was the main reason. So people veiled their knowledge. The hidden message is often subtle, but when it's fully understood it often leads to a higher truth. Also, people have different abilities to comprehend.

The hidden messages are recognised by those with insight and wisdom."

Maybe Keisha had a point. I knew my peers considered television as a biased opportunity for me to preach against their interbreeding hypotheses. The series was a menace to their hallowed profession.

"OK, but is there any real evidence for these esoteric messages?"

Keisha leaned back in her chair. "Definitely. It's what I'm currently working on. When Jesus said he spoke *the wisdom of God in a mystery* and that only one who is *born from above* is capable of receiving his message, I think there's something behind it. In fact, Buddhism says much the same thing by suggesting that humanity is divided into those who are capable of understanding the higher doctrine and those who aren't. The original Cabbalists who wrote the Old Testament had some provocative beliefs. The concept of 'you live, you die', as you put it was not part of their thinking. They believed in continuity."

"You mean all that reincarnation stuff?"

"Not exactly. The Western understanding of reincarnation is quite inaccurate according to Buddhist scholars. Yet, they believe time and space is linked therefore allowing existence to be renewed."

"If that's not reincarnation then what is it?"

"I must admit it's complex and I'm still struggling with it. The physical body ultimately decays and returns to dust – right? But we also know that energy can never be destroyed."

"Sure, every school kid gets taught that."

Keisha was adamant. "The Cabbalists believed that who we really are, the 'I', the 'experiencer' which dwells within each of us, moves through new states of existence after death, accumulating new experiences in its evolution." Keisha stretched back in her chair, taking an audible breath. "I love different perspectives. The Buddhists for example don't believe death is a tragedy."

"Of course it's not tragic. You live and you die. It's universal. At least you get a shot at life. No tragedy there."

Keisha stayed on track. "True, but they say that birth is the trag-edy because it brings with it the precondition of death."

"Hang on; I'm a bit confused here. Surely if we weren't born we wouldn't exist."

"Interestingly, the adepts would disagree with you on that one."

It was an absurd proposition, but I was beginning to understand Keisha Petersen's maverick reputation. She obviously didn't avoid controversy, but then neither did I. I liked that about her.

"Come on, how do we exist if we're not born?"

"Perhaps we've always existed and only take physical form to experience new realities."

Keisha reached across the table and placed her hand on mine. Her voice softened. "Aiden, I want to give you an example about the hidden message hypothesis. Is that OK?"

"Sure. Go for it."

She plunged into the pocket of her shoulder bag and withdrew a small dog-eared Bible. As she leafed through the pages, I began to wonder about her religious conviction. She carried a bible for Christ's sake. What was this woman all about?

"Yes, here it is. Genesis 6. Listen to this. *'And it came to pass, when men began to multiply on the face of the earth, and daughters were born unto them, that the sons of God saw the daughters of men that they were fair; and they took them wives of all which they chose. There were Nephilim on the earth in those days; and also after that, when the sons of God came in unto the daughters of men, and they bear children to them, the same became mighty men which were of old, men of renown.'"*

I tried to digest the passage. 'Sons of god' mating with 'daugh-ters of men'. What was it all about?

"Hidden messages you say?"

"It's a classic example. The Hebrew word 'Nephilim' is interpreted in most bibles by the word 'giants', but this is a spurious interpretation. 'Nephilim' means *those who came down*. And the original texts don't speak of 'sons of God' but the *'sons of the gods'*."

This was doing my head in.

"Mind if I have a look?"

She handed me the world's most popular text. I flicked the tissue thin pages to Genesis 6. The words were there in black and white. I was sure she knew more than she was letting on and wondered why our conversation had steered in this direction. *Were my photographs connected to this somehow?*

She continued, "The ancient Egyptian, Mesopotamian and Hebrew cultures described a race vastly more advanced than their own. They referred to this race as 'gods' who bred with the indigenous population. That's very different to the 'God Almighty' of modern religion. And it's a distinction that's been lost, if not deliberately concealed."

I looked at the text again. *Gods who bred with the indigenous population?* How far different was that to Cro-Magnon man interbreeding with the Neanderthal? Plenty – she was talking about a race far more advanced than the Cro-Magnon.

Keisha quickly stole a glance at her watch. "Aiden, I'm really sorry, but I have to catch a plane to Sydney in less than an hour. Can we reconvene tomorrow? Two thirty at the Hyatt? I'll buy you a drink."

"I think I need one now."

"Don't worry. I'll be back. I'm just sorry that I had to convey such sad news to you. Just be careful, OK? Until we have some answers to all this I suggest you don't go back to your hotel. You should take these."

Keisha passed a set of keys to me. "Go to the address on the tag. It's a friend's apartment. She's overseas at the moment, so you'll be safe."

"Isn't this a bit over the top?"

"Perhaps, but I want you around when I get back tomorrow. Your find is important to somebody and I want to see you again."

A coquettish smile and the playful stab of her finger to my shoulder accompanied her words. She turned and breezed out of the Club. Her delicate perfume lingered, enticing me to do her bidding.

It was still crisp and cloudless when I arrived at the 'safe house' overlooking Lake Burley Griffin and the grand parliamentary buildings of the nation's capital. Stretching behind were the eucalypt-studded mountains reflecting the grey, green and blue hues of the majestic Australian landscape.

After the news of Jai and our unexpected pursuit, I agreed it was best to play safe. However, amongst the morning's turmoil, one question reigned.

Exactly who was this intriguing woman?

12

CHALLENGE

APOSTOLIC PENITENTIARY, VATICAN CITY

Angelo was living in the eye of a storm. Many hours had passed and so far there had been no fallout from the Dominican's warning. Devoted to a life in the Church, Angelo believed he was performing God's work. But it was becoming increasingly clear not everything about theology or even accepted history was true.

The subversive Comte had shaken his faith, and Angelo remained fascinated by the man. Comparing the earnest and irreverent Comte with the insidious and threatening cleric, his course of action was clear.

He reached the vault-like door, took two deep breaths and knocked gently. The electronic bolt inside shunted as Comte stuck his deformed face outside the archive, the trace of a satisfied smile visible beneath his heavy disfigurement. He motioned Angelo to enter.

"How are you my friend?"

"I've been better. I was caught using the Internet in the Old Study Room. I wanted to check some of your facts and..."

Comte flashed a fiendish glance grabbing Angelo's arm. "Wait! Who caught you?"

"I've never seen him before, but he was a Dominican."

"The bald one with the weird eyes?"

"Yeah that's him."

Comte slumped in his chair putting his stumpy hands to his head. He scratched his patchy scalp. "Shit. Shit. He's a real twisted bastard that one."

"Is it that bad?"

"You don't know what a religious ogre he is."

"How can it be bad? I was just…"

"…thinking for yourself," Comte interrupted. "You don't know the consequences of thinking for yourself in a place like this. There's nothing they hate more than independent thought. You must maintain the facade of pliant subservience. Haven't you learnt that yet? How do you think Valla got to be Cardinal?"

Angelo hoped things weren't that serious.

Comte was silent for several moments. "The secrets of this place run much deeper than you know."

"What do you mean, I was just…."

"…thinking for yourself," he repeated. "Remember the lessons of history my friend. The Church has always extinguished contemporary thinkers."

Comte thought it necessary to labour the point. More to the point he wanted to disturb.

"Let me give you an example. In the year 415 A.D. a scholar of Plato was hacked to pieces. Hypatia was a renowned mathematician and student of philosophy. Led by a fanatical mob of Christian monks, she was pulled from her chariot, disrobed and dragged naked to the churchyard of Caesarium. She suffered the obscene cruelty of having her flesh scooped from her bones with sharp oyster shells before her remains were scattered in the streets of Alexandria as a public warning to heretics."

"Oh, come on, that was centuries ago," Angelo dismissed.

"Maybe they're not as violent these days, but if you're considered a heretic you'll certainly know about it. The Church is more insidious these days. You must understand the lessons of history Angelo. False edicts are continually promoted and sacred knowledge is suppressed. They can do what they like to me, but I don't want you getting into trouble because of me."

Angelo was confronted yet again. *Surely Comte was labouring under the delusion of some absurd conspiracy theory.*

"I accept you were right about the Donation, but the Church has admitted it's a fake. You make it sound as though the Church is a fake."

"Oh, it is my boy, more than you would believe."

"If you say it is, then come clean and prove it." Angelo retorted.

"That's a work in progress, so are you sure you want to hear me out?"

"Of course I'm sure."

Comte's distorted lower eye twinkled as he sat back in his worn leather chair, his face conveying a gentle satisfaction.

"Ask and ye shall find eh!" Comte sighed. He looked Angelo square in the eye. "During my periods of time off, I've had the privilege to work with a Professor in Ancient Near Eastern Languages. She currently works for the Australian National University, but spends a great deal of time in Europe. I've learned a great deal about the ancient texts. For example, in Genesis, the original word used for God was '*Elohim*' which comes from the root word El. The word's plural not singular. Therefore, the Bible refers to 'gods' not God."

Angelo was aghast. "Look, I've gone along with you up till now, but who are you kidding? That's impossible. It's damn pagan!"

Comte was emphatic. "That's where you're wrong, Angelo. No true biblical scholar would now dispute it. Of course, the plurality of gods presented an almost incomprehensible problem, so to get around it the early Church was forced to invent doctrines such as the Trinity. You know the idea – God the Father, Son and Holy Ghost. The plurality of the gods was buried under the contrived doctrine of the Trinity."

"That's conspiratorial nonsense. I don't believe it," Angelo ventured. "The Trinity is real!"

"It's a piece of intellectual nonsense that was fought over and voted upon at the Council of Nicaea back in 325 AD. Jesus Christ was proclaimed to be part of the Trinity, but it was by no means unanimous. Not all Christians believed it. Constantine the Great convened the Council and was seeking a comprehensive agreement on the matter, purely to galvanise Christianity and his authority over it. He was in no mood for conflicting doctrines. Constantine was no intellectual or theological heavyweight; he was more a vicious thug who knew how to get his own way. He was happy to murder anyone who obstructed him."

Unfortunately, classical history was not one of Angelo's strengths.

Comte poured himself his usual grappa. "You know about the conversion of Constantine?"

"Yes, I know about it." Angelo had been taught that it was a miraculous intervention by God, but he gathered that Comte was about to tell a different story.

"After the battle, Constantine decapitated his opponent Magentas and paraded his skewered head through the streets on his lance. Eleven years later, he murdered Licentious, the vanquished former Emperor of the East. He even killed his own son, and then his wife by having her boiled alive in her bath. His so-called Christian conversion certainly changed him, don't you think?"

Comte looked at Angelo solemnly. He enjoyed playing the cynic and could see the young man soften.

"More than a hundred million human beings have perished in the name of religion. What do you think Jesus would say about that?"

The core of Angelo's being was challenged and he resented it. It was unforgivable to air the dirty laundry of the Church like this. He retaliated. "What's your point then?"

"I just want you to understand that much of what you believe is based on palpable nonsense. Modern Christianity bears almost no resemblance to the poor Nazarene of the first century. You know Angelo, Clement of Alexandria, one of the early Church fathers, once said that the simple Christian faith was *suitable for people in a hurry*. I think he was right."

Disconcerted by Comte's devastating critique Angelo goaded, "So why in God's name do you work here? Surely you could request a transfer."

Comte shrugged, "Perhaps, but then I couldn't complete my work. Besides that bloated megalomaniac Valla prefers me locked away in here. I don't get to see anyone much and everyone likes it that way. Frankly so do I. It allows me to get on with my real work."

Once again, another of Comte's idiosyncratic outbursts had confronted Angelo, but he sensed Comte was holding something back.

"What work exactly? Challenging my beliefs?"

Comte hesitated, his eyes fixing on his glass of grappa. "You're free to believe what you want. I'm more interested in resurrecting the truth of the sacred doctrines, much of which is buried in the original Christian movement. Don't you find it strange that in the official Vatican version of these archives all the pre-8th century documents and manuscripts have disappeared? They're not to be found anywhere. They didn't all disappear by themselves. The documents only disappeared once *'they'* became involved." Comte's drooping eye rose as he jerked his head upward.

"They? Who're they?"

Comte ruminated visibly, tapping his desk with a pen. He was about to say something, but decided against it. Instead, he gave the Cardinal's young assistant some advice.

"Angelo, please understand me. I don't want you to get the wrong idea. The Church has multitudes of fine, devout and honourable servants paying a wonderful homage to their understanding of God and humanity, but unknown to them they serve a centuries old corruption. This perversion is not the Church or the Vatican as a whole, but an inner core of manipulators who've covertly controlled the masses long before Jesus showed The Way. These corruptors seek to hold the world in bondage. And believe me, they do. They've been behind the descent of humanity ever since the so-called Fall. I just request one thing of you. Never allow your own prejudice or disbelief to cloud the truth. If you search relentlessly, you'll come to understand how to triumph over this deception. On that day Angelo, you will truly see."

13

THE ORDER

HYATT HOTEL, CANBERRA, AUSTRALIA

A lonely evening at the apartment was laced with thoughts of lustful mystery. Ice-cubes clinked as I sipped my single malt. I had been magnetised. Keisha Petersen was exquisite, but also an enigma, just like my new living quarters.

Comprised of elegant kitchen with marble bench tops and stainless steel appliances, large open-plan living and master bedroom, it was furnished in the style of Keisha's office. Classy minimalist with the odd ornamental artefact. Strangely, there was little evidence of habitation. A close inspection revealed no personal trinkets other than a deluxe coffee maker with lavish accoutrements. The bedroom wardrobe was devoid of clothing and only revealed two fresh bathrobes. Even the bathroom cabinet was empty, save for new tubes of toothpaste and body lotion. It looked and felt like a serviced apartment made ready for the next paying guest, not the home of a friend travelling overseas.

My mind was cluttered with more important concerns. Jai was dead; the suggestion being that my photographs may have been the cause. Keisha had received the information from a friend in the

Office of National Assessments. Was she involved with them some-how? If not, why did her contact know about our meeting? Why leave the university in such a hurry? And why the car pursuit by people she claimed were the local spooks? Were they the colleagues of her so-called 'friend'?

I googled the online version of La Nazione, the Florence daily newspaper, and sure enough, there was a report on the murder of Jai Santini. Little was known; police were unable to get a description of the perpetrator. I was as angry as hell about Jai, but was determined to conceal it. I had a duty to find out what may have happened.

These unresolved questions about this beautiful woman created a conundrum.

I arranged a private table at the Hyatt, arrived early and waited. Keisha was fashionably late, but arrived in a flurry of unmistakable excitement. This lively blonde, her lips painted a glossy cinnamon pink, smiled as she offered her apologies. She was dressed smart for business, a tailored dark suit covering a light blue, turtle neck sweater, her silken blonde hair cascading the full length of her jacket lapels.

I politely ordered a superb bottle of Barossa Shiraz and asked what she knew about the local spooks. Whilst booting her laptop with my USB attached, her conversation turned toward the obscure.

"Intelligence agencies are a predictable bunch," she declared. "Their charter is to keep people safe, but that mostly means keeping us all in the dark. Some agencies have been employing psychics for years to study the subject of human consciousness. They know it exists independent of matter. But their research into the phenom-enon is rarely reported in the media, and never reported in main-stream science. I find that interesting."

"How the hell does a physicist come ancient language professor know this stuff?"

There was that mischievous grin again. "This is just my day job," she said, moving the cursor into position. "Now, your photographs."

"Why don't we give them a miss for now? Tell me, why are you always so serious?"

Keisha threw me a curious glance. "I thought you were in Canberra for my professional opinion."

I had to throw her a curve-ball otherwise I would look like another desperate with a hard-on. "Keisha – I don't think you're as boring as you try to appear."

She hesitated for just a second trying to digest the finely tuned insult. While she remained composed I knew she had taken the bait.

"Are you usually this obnoxious?" she retorted.

Now to close the trap. "Only when I'm around beautiful women."

Her annoyance fell away. She tried not to look pleased, but her blue eyes held an unmistakable glint of satisfaction.

She regained her composure. "Photographs remember."

I laughed inwardly. I would have to wait.

Keisha enhanced one of the images.

"How do they look?"

"Like I said yesterday, I think they're dynamite, particularly the murals on the walls. They're in excellent condition. The cuneiform writing is a form of proto-Akkadian and should be translatable, but there are added symbols which suggest a variant syntax. I think I can assemble a reasonable translation. It'll take time though. I'll need to run LITAN."

"LITAN?"

"It's an experimental program I helped develop. LITAN stands for 'Linguistics Integration Translation Algorithm Neural Net'. It's used to decode unknown languages. It scans the world's databases for similarities in languages relating to the unknown target language. It uses a new system of character and tonal pattern recognition which has the ability to self-modify."

"You mean the program can learn and adapt."

"Exactly."

She reached for her bag and rummaged around for a business card. "LITAN also has access to one of the world's largest privately owned linguistic, anthropological, archaeological and historical databases. You can access it at the following web address." She wrote down the address and password, and then handed me the card. "Do you carry an iPhone?"

"Yes. How long do you think the translation will take?"

"Maximum – two to three days, if we can access the Cray II. We'll definitely get something. That's assuming, of course, that I can copy these images."

I reluctantly agreed; there seemed no other option.

Keisha examined the photographs again. The image of the pendant I had retrieved from the body in the crypt filled the screen. The shot focused on the words engraved upon it. *'Ego Robertus de Bolbec, fecerunt Regi magno latebras. Consumpta templo suo Romam. Salva eius manet terreni Roma. Red City Circa Montes protege infideles ei'.*

She quickly translated from the Latin. *'I, Robert De Bolbec, have laid the Great King in hiding. His Temple destroyed by Rome. His Earthy remains saved from Rome. Near the Red City the Mountains of the Infidel now protect him.'*

"Who's Robert De Bolbec?"

"No idea. I removed the pendant from skeletal remains I found in the crypt. I presume it was him."

"Well, it's a clue worth following. The pendant is a Templar Cross, so maybe he was a Templar. Any other clues you remember?"

"There's a photo of a long sword with the same cross on the hilt."

"Mmm. A Templar knight maybe. *'His Temple destroyed by Rome.'* The Great King could be Solomon. If so, this suggests the remains of Solomon have been placed near the Red City. I wonder what it all means. I'll need to check it out. Let's move onto the other shots."

Keisha quickly flicked through several more photos before spotting something that again took her interest. She magnified the image and examined it in detail. Her eyes ate up the photograph.

"Look at this!" She inched closer and motioned toward the image. "See this symbol here? It's only ever been seen on two relics." Keisha was completely absorbed by the photograph. "It represents the Order of Melchizedek."

I stared at her blankly. "Meaning?"

"The Order is mentioned in numerous places in the Bible, but remains incredibly obscure. The Order is recorded in some of the most ancient writings known and it's said they have links back to the mysterious Neteru in pre-dynastical Egypt, some thirty-six thousand years ago."

I was well out of my depth and found it frustrating. "Neteru? Who the hell are they?"

"Well, they come out of nowhere anthropologically speaking. It seems they were so advanced they were considered divine by the ancient Egyptians."

I'd never heard of them and the suggestion was ridiculous. "Anthropologically speaking, they're an illusion. I mean come on Keisha; human beings were primitive cave dwellers just eight thousand years ago."

"A couple of ancient texts claim the antiquity of the Neteru is thirty-six thousand years. The Order of Melchizedek on the other hand made its appearance about six hundred years before Moses giving them a date of about 2,500 BCE. They seem to be the keepers of some great secret. Apparently the Church knows about some of this stuff. These days they've locked it away as the Secretum Omega – the ultimate, classified secret."

"Sounds unlikely?"

Keisha hesitated, gathering her thoughts. "The order is mentioned in the Pyramid Texts of Saqqara and they're utterly baffling."

"The pyramid texts of the Old Kingdom of Egypt?" I asked with genuine surprise. "Isn't that the oldest known writing in existence?"

"Supposedly. You know about them?"

"I read something about them once. All outside my field of expertise I'm afraid."

Looking up from the photograph Keisha explained, "I had the great privilege of having Professor Eli Rosen teach me how to translate cuneiform. He died recently, but as a legacy he left a series of books outlining the Creation stories of the Sumerians. Have you heard of him?"

"Can't say I have.'

"He's a genius, you should read his works. He also studied the Pyramid Texts and thinks that the content of these texts originally came from the Neteru via the Order of Melchizedek." She continued to scrutinise the images.

I shrugged. "I find that a bit hard to believe, especially when you say they date back thirty-six thousand years."

Keisha smiled at my uncertainty. "Of course Aiden, as an anthropologist you should be sceptical. Like the ancient Hebrew Cabbalists, the oldest Egyptian sources didn't believe their Creator was remote and external. Instead, they believed we are part of the Creator."

"Religion again?"

"It's difficult to fathom, I know. Our 'Higher Selves', or souls if you like, were symbolised by the Egyptians as the *Eye of Horus*, the 'All Seeing Eye of God'. As you would know, the Great Pyramid once had a massive capstone made from an exotic compound. Its purpose was to operate as a type of transducer to assist adepts in raising their consciousness – to experience what lies beyond death and the wisdom that connects us to the Divine."

It was a bold claim. "So you're suggesting the pyramid was used as some type of initiation chamber?"

"Yes, but I also reckon it was used to track mass human consciousness."

"You're kidding surely?"

Keisha's eyes flashed. "I'm afraid not. Scientists now know that the Great Pyramid precisely tracked the Earth's path across the cosmos as our solar system moves closer to and then further away from the centre of the galaxy. Somehow, the builders knew that the Earth's position in the galaxy affects human perception."

Her depth of knowledge about a range of subjects was remarkable. I wondered whether she was prepared to stand by her theories. "Are you sure about all this?"

Keisha flashed a luminous smile. "I guess we have a lot to talk about, don't we?"

14

TEMPLAR CODE

ROME, ITALY

Angelo retired to his tiny quarters, exhausted. It had been a long and stressful day. His desk had been piled with work. In addition, he had an assignment to complete for his university study.

He lay in bed between soft cotton sheets, allowing tension to drain from his tired mind. As he was drifting into meditative quiet, his attention was piqued by the buzz of his intercom. Opening his eyes, he was surprised to hear Comte requesting entrance.

"Come down. I want to show you something very important," he whispered. The archivist was trembling with excitement, an expression of mirthfulness pasted on his twisted face.

"Are you out of your mind? It's almost two o'clock."

Angelo regretted these words as soon as he had spoken them. There was no way Comte would have risked getting him into further trouble. He must have made some effort to find his rented room in a cluster of buildings near the spur of the Vatican railway track.

"Of course I'm out of my mind. Don't argue, just hurry."

Angelo quickly dressed and ran down the stairs from his fourth floor room. He moved into the street and found Comte on the footpath eager to go.

"What's up Comte?"

"Just follow me. You can't miss this."

The two men set off toward the Holy See with Angelo trailing behind. The Swiss Guard allowed automatic entry to the crippled Comte. They all knew the strange disfigured man and obliged him with small privileges. Angelo was surprised that at this late hour, he too, was provided access. Comte shuffled his way through a labyrinth of corridors, careful to use the cover of night to penetrate deep into the restricted parts of the Vatican. The injury of slashed tendons in his right knee and left Achilles were no impediment. Comte hobbled so quickly Angelo found it difficult to keep up.

Angelo was intrigued with the old, crumbling architecture, hidden grottos, dimly lit windows perched high on gabled roofs, and doors leading to God knows where. An eerie solitude pervaded the iconic recesses of Roman religious history.

As Comte led the way, he gave a hint to what was so important.

"Let me tell you something about the stained glass windows of the Templars. They're a mystery. No one knows how they're made. Even today's specialist glassmakers have no idea."

"What do you mean? We make stained glass windows today!"

"Not like the Templar artisans. Only theirs retain their exquisite brilliance in moonlight and convert harmful ultra-violet rays into beneficial light. Their secret comes from the Persian school of Omar Khayyam in the twelfth century."

Comte stole a glance at his watch and continued his pace.

"What's so important?"

"You'll see in a few minutes. The SS removed the windows from a small abbey in southern France during the war and gifted them to the Holy Father. A reward for our appalling silence over the Jews."

Shocked by more words of treason, Angelo remained silent. It was a stain that one day would need to be scrubbed clean.

"They were made by the master-craftsmen of the Order of the Rosy Cross, and were positioned specifically in France to denote the transition of the summer solstice."

Comte had thus far proven he was a man of integrity and surprise. Angelo was having second thoughts about this post midnight sojourn, but decided it was worth being patient to see what was so important to this controversial iconoclast.

Comte had led Angelo through a tunnel from the grottoes in the underbelly of Basilica San Pietro, and they had now emerged within the Santo Stefano degli Abissini, a church restored by Pope Leo I and assigned to the Coptic Friars in 1479. Incongruously nestled in gardens between the Basilica and the administration offices known as Palazzo del Governatorato, the church was meticulously decorated with symbols not normally associated with orthodox Christendom. Comte anxiously checked his time piece.

"What's with the watch?"

"You'll see in a couple of minutes."

"Yeah OK, I see the windows. So what?"

Fortunately, the night was cloudless and Comte and Angelo were bathed in pastel moonlight from the stained glass towering in front of them. The windows were decorated in the baroque style and contained the usual depictions of Moses, the Virgin Mary, Saint John the Baptist and the cherubic baby Jesus. The colours were spectacular, but so were hundreds of windows in a multitude of cathedrals throughout Europe. Angelo wondered what was so special.

"Any minute now," announced Comte.

"What am I looking at?"

Comte pointed his finger stubs to the opposite wall, toward a beautiful fresco of a naked Adam in the Garden of Eden.

"Spot on 2:33 a.m. Look. There!"

A melange of colour splashed the plastered panel below the

fresco with an archipelago of numerals slowly coalescing into form from the moonlight. The glass had filtered the moonlight, and the illuminated image clearly came into focus. They revealed themselves as Roman numerals below the fresco. Somehow, the numerals had been cleverly etched into the stained glass. It produced an interference pattern that had remained invisible until this very moment.

IIIVIII IIIVIV IIVVI IIVIIX IIVIIV IIIVII IVVV VIVI VVIVIII VIIIIIV

"I told you," chuckled Comte, his contorted face brimming with sublime satisfaction. "Clever bastards those Templars."

Angelo was dumbfounded. One by one, letters of the alphabet slowly peeled off onto the wall above the numerals as the moonlight traced its slow arc across the night sky. Angelo watched as the words *'PERMISSUM ILLIC EXSISTO LUX LUCIS'* projected themselves in a bright magical lustre.

"How in the name of God do those windows produce that?"

Comte grinned. "They're a crystographic masterpiece. You've forgotten that tonight is the night of the summer solstice. Every time the unclouded moon has filled that window since 1944, this sequence of letters and numbers has lit that wall.

"Permissum illic exsisto lux lucis – Let there be light. Remember the passage, Angelo. *'And God said, Let there be light: and there was light.'* These numbers shine in the light, the light of truth and understanding. I would love to know what they mean."

"You mean you brought me here and you don't know?"

"Not yet. I know that the Templars commissioned the making of these windows. It's a Templar code and for that reason alone I'll find out what it means."

"Maybe they don't mean anything."

"Then why go to the effort? The Templars always did things for a very specific reason and purpose, mostly unfathomable to those outside the Order."

Angelo inspected the luminous numbers on the wall again. Why did the Templars create the code, and why was this incredible event concealed in a Coptic church behind the Basilica? The SS had gifted these windows. Did they know the meaning, and if so, what was the Holy Church hiding?

Both men stared at the fleeting miracle of light optics. Comte decided the time had come to find out what it all meant. No matter the personal cost.

15

THE GODS

HYATT HOTEL, CANBERRA, AUSTRALIA

Keisha Petersen had won me. It was more than her sublime sensuality and breathtaking intellect. There was something deliciously enticing in the way she went about her business. I had deliberately arranged a table away from the spattering of other diners to ensure privacy and intimate conversation. The discussion was taking me away from my objective, but it was revealing a woman of uncommon conviction.

"The centre of our galaxy is about 26,000 light years away from the sun. In the coastal town of Hendaye on the French border with Spain, you'll see a mysterious cross in the town square. It was fashioned by a social outcast some three hundred and fifty years ago. The cross is a giant cosmological clock, marking the precession of the equinoxes over the Four Great Ages, a total of 25,920 years. It seems to predict a coming cataclysm."

"I'm getting lost here. The Great Ages? What are they?"

"As the earth moves closer to, or further away from the centre of the galaxy, human consciousness ebbs and flows. Each Age was divided into periods of six and a half thousand years, all represented by a specific metal symbolising the consciousness of the aeon.

"The four Ages began with the Golden Age, then Silver, Bronze and finally Iron. Spiritual perception gradually deteriorated over these vast periods. At first, humanity was aligned with higher principles and existed in harmony with the natural world and the greater universe, pristine and unsullied. Gradually, knowledge of the Great Primordial Wisdom fell away. It was progressively exterminated by more barbaric civilisations. As a consequence, human consciousness plummeted until we reach our own time, the Kali Yuga or Iron Age. In this Age, even religions that preach violence get taken seriously. Today we are at the bottom of the spiritual heap."

I decided to stick my neck out. "Is that why the alchemists claimed to transmute lead into gold? Trying to rediscover the knowledge of the so-called Golden age."

"I think so, Aiden. The Order of Melchizedek taught the 'hidden' things. In the middle ages, members of these sacred mystery schools were under constant threat of being tortured or executed by the Inquisition for their knowledge, so they used metaphors to transmit their wisdom. The alchemist's true goal was to transform ordinary human consciousness, designated as lead, into that of an adept, symbolised by gold."

Keisha's tone commanded authority. She obviously knew her stuff.

She glanced at the screen, "Finding this symbol isn't something I would have expected."

I paused for a moment, unsure whether to trust her with my strange experience of altered consciousness in the crypt. I took the gamble.

"There's something strange that happened to me. I haven't had time to show anybody this yet, but I discovered some white powder in a crypt."

"Really?" she replied, trading a puzzled glance. "Any idea what it could be?"

I shook my head and removed the zip-lock bag from my jacket.

"None. I dabbed a little on my tongue to test its acidity, but something happened that knocked the crap out of me. I experienced something I can't explain. Emotional feelings welled up, but then I had a strange vision. It was more of an experience than a vision."

"Hallucinogenic, perhaps?" Keisha held up the sample bag and inspected it against the sunlit window.

"I don't think so."

"Whilst we wait for LITAN, I can have it tested if you like. I know a forensic chemist who can run a spectral."

I decided to trust her. I had already split my sample in two.

Keisha gazed outside to a cluster of enormous poplar trees, their bare winter boughs glistening in the brilliant afternoon sun. A moment of silence passed between us.

"Aiden, I can't imagine this, but have you ever read the Bible in detail?"

"Like I said it's a complete fairytale as far as I'm concerned. Take out the dogma and maybe it's an average fairytale."

"Hey, I thought the same, but then I remembered its origins. The Bible's been heavily edited over the centuries, but its content is probably the greatest mixture of hidden fact and mythologised fiction ever assembled."

"What do you mean – fact and fiction?"

"The truth of the 'gods'," she answered bluntly.

"Gods? We're back to that subject again are we?"

"Yes, we are. If you don't want answers from me then we can call it a day."

"No need to get touchy. I'll hear you out."

"Sorry, Aiden, my trip to Sydney was more stressful than I thought. I've got a bit on my mind. In fact, I was looking forward to seeing you today. My study of ancient languages involves reading the ancient stories and the 'gods' are mentioned across different cultures and continents, and almost always with consistent time-lines. As much as you have an issue about religion, I can't get away from what the ancients wrote about."

"My issue with religion is the damage it's done, nothing more. I'm sorry; God talk doesn't do it for me."

"We have no disagreement there, Aiden. By 'gods' I don't mean anything supernatural. One person's 'gods' can be another person's race with superior technology, like when Cortez sailed to South America and was greeted as though he was their god Quetzalcoatl."

"Sure, but that only happened because of their mythical belief system."

"I disagree. The Sumerian and other pre-Egyptian civilisations were the legacy of these 'sons of the gods'. It's recorded in their own writings. The Sumerian texts of five thousand years ago called these gods the 'Annunaki'. And the Book of Enoch which actually pre-dates the Bible, called them 'the Watchers'. Have you heard of the Book of Enoch?"

"I've heard of it. That's all."

"Good. It's far more reliable than the Bible, because the Church didn't tamper with it. Unfortunately the King James Bible has had five different translations since the original texts, damaging their accuracy. The Ecumenical Councils continually altered scriptures to suit their political objectives."

Intriguing. Her knowledge was deep and deliciously heretical. "Tell me more."

"Much of the Bible was written from knowledge passed down from far older texts. The central 'god' of the Old Testament, Jehovah, was merely one god among many others. And the Bible even confirms it. In Psalm 82, Jehovah actually acknowledges the fact that he's one god among the pantheon of gods at the so-called Council of El."

"If that's the case, then I'm right. It IS mostly fiction."

"Well, for me it's all about interpretation. Like I said, there's a hidden message behind the outer story. Through dogma and fear, religion has been progressively politicised. In truth, Jehovah was a wrathful, vengeful god who sought to create his own dominion, and was later fraudulently appropriated as the One God. As part of this politicisation, the original Hebrew knowledge was lost and the truth behind the ancient texts was preserved only by the esoteric Judaic orders."

"Alright I believe you. There's obviously more to it than I was prepared to admit, but you've made some mighty claims."

"Nothing mighty, just the facts."

Keisha inspected another photograph. A long streak of hair fell across her vision and she fingered it behind her ear. She magnified and sharpened the image.

"Check this out. This is only the second time I've seen this marking. These characters here – see." Her finger hovered next to the screen, pulling my vision to the enhanced image. "They're a pre-Canaanite word for 'Elohim'. They're mentioned in the original texts as 'those who created the first humans' – Adam and Eve if you like. Aiden, this is very exciting. Your crypt might very well be a repository of knowledge about these beings."

I wanted to understand clearly what was at stake here. "You're saying this refers to those who created the first humans."

"That's what Elohim means in the Bible. This could explain who these 'gods' were and how they created the human race."

I had always considered religion to be smoke and mirrors, but I realised Keisha wasn't talking about magic. She was talking about a 'real' history gleaned from the walls of a crypt maybe thousands of years old. *How far did her theories go?* I decided to push on.

"So you reckon we've got something here."

"If this provides the information I think it does, it would add further confirmation to the story of Creation recorded on some of the early Sumerian clay tablets. It could well destroy the views of modern religion," she quipped. "The Church says God created man. But the actual word used in the original Hebrew texts is 'Elohim' and this here is pre-Canaanite. It derives from the root word 'Eloh' which means lofty ones. Eloh has a plural meaning."

"Yesterday you said Genesis referred to the 'sons of the gods' not the 'sons of god'. So this is the word that refers to them. Right?"

"That's right."

"What about Darwin then?" I wondered about Keisha's attitude toward the theory of evolution.

"Only the gullible and ungifted clutch to Darwin."

No room for debate there. "Yeah, well that's about one hundred percent of all academics, including myself? Don't tell me you're a creationist."

"Of course not. Darwin said we evolved by fortuitous mutation. If that were true, we would expect to see dozens, even hundreds of non-fortuitous human-like mutations fossilised in the rock strata for every beneficial one. They don't exist do they? Just look at the evolutionary gap between the Neanderthal and the Cro-Magnon, and they co-existed."

"OK, so the theory has holes, but what's the answer if you don't believe in Darwin or creationism."

"Maybe there isn't an answer acceptable to mainstream science? Maybe we're missing something."

"If what you are telling me is true, then I should reserve my judgement."

"I'll give you something extra to think about. What if the Sumerian story of Creation is correct? Eli Rosen recognised it as a story of genetic manipulation, where the DNA of a pre-humanoid species was altered to create modern man. His theory has been written off as a myth but imagine if it's true. Maybe there are those who want to keep this all secret."

I'd never heard of such a story. But Keisha was right, imagine if it was true. It might well explain the appearance of the Cro-Magnon, but the whole thing had to be pure fantasy.

Keisha dug around in her bag and removed her small dog-eared bible. Flipping over the first few pages she read, "'*Let us make man in our image, after **our** likeness*'. The Elohim, the ones mentioned here," she gestured toward the image on the laptop, "are quoted in the Bible as creating humans in their image."

Her lithe fingers flicked the page. "With regard to the Tree of Knowledge in the Garden of Eden it says, '*In the day ye eat thereof, then your eyes shall be opened, and **ye shall be as gods**'*. And further down, '*The Lord God said, Behold the man is become one of **us**'*.

"Note the words Aiden – 'gods' and 'us'. Plural. If we became one of them and we're physical, then these gods must have been physical as well. Your crypt may well give us some of the answers to the mystery."

I was struggling to keep up and needed a diversion. I wanted to lighten up. After all, nothing ventured, nothing gained.

"How about dinner tonight? I can stay an extra few days. Perhaps you can show me around."

"Show you around what Aiden." I spotted that mischievous smirk again. "The best I can do is to give you rain check, I've got another appointment."

I remained hopeful. "Tomorrow?"

"Busy, I'm afraid. I'll be out of action for three or four days."

I hoped my eagerness didn't show. "I'll want a comprehensive briefing on the LITAN search you know."

Keisha stood and planted a surreptitious kiss on my cheek. "You'll get your briefing as soon as I have something, don't worry. Must rush now. Bye."

She quickly turned swishing her perfumed hair over her shoulder and walked away. Her kiss lingered, and so did the stirrings of sensual vertigo.

She left me wanting more. At least I had a rain check.

16

DEMONS

BOSTON, MASSACHUSETTS

Cardinal Valla was torn by his predicament. For now at least he could quell the storm for change within the Boston Diocese, but it was the news from Agostino that really bothered him.

Without any preliminary briefing, Agostino had arranged for P2 to deal with the understudy of a prominent paleo-anthropologist. Worse still, his controller at Majestic had been informed. Majestic is an ultra-covert splinter group that directs the National Reconnaissance Office, with the highest level of security clearance. Their mission includes the tracking of unidentified aerial phenomena, material deemed too sensitive for the regular air force. Whenever action of this kind was taken by Agostino, Valla felt the pressure mount. The man's impertinent action was unfortunate, but the enmity between them needed to be kept in check.

He allowed his mind to wander back to those desperate final days of the War when he was spirited to the United States by Colonel Hudson. Orphaned and frightened, he had followed the Colonel who had taken pity on him. In truth, Hudson had been told to bring the boy to the U.S. He had been a witness to what had occurred in the excavation site. It was considered that the young boy may be useful. His indebtedness to those who had saved him from life under Soviet repression had eventually become his burden.

He had explained all that he had witnessed within the stone circle of the excavated building in Berlin; how the angels spoke through his mother and how on that morning, he had feared for her. It seemed a lifetime ago, a world away from the opulence of the Vatican. These days the Church would have had him exorcised for demonic possession if he revealed too much of his past.

Valla had never known his Italian father who had died soon after his birth. His German mother had been strictly religious and had returned with her young child to Berlin, the city of her birth. How she had got caught up in the madness that followed he didn't know, but he remembered how she had told him she was doing God's work. In those days he had witnessed things he still found difficult to explain.

The Cardinal remembered sneaking away from her dressing room that fateful night, to watch his mother and escort disappear down the steps of a closed bomb-shelter. At the bottom of the concrete structure, he followed her through a long dark passage that opened into a disused building. It was an excavation site, a ring of ancient ceremonial stones clearly visible.

Valla could see himself hiding under the scaffolding and watching as his mother convulsed. He remembered her glassy eyes and how she had spoken in a deep throaty voice, not her own. He recalled the SS officer and the stenographer recording her messages. He had learned much later from American intelligence that the other two observers were members of the Thule Gesselschaft. That information still bothered him. The Thule's had been influential in the early days of the Reich – a secret organisation with occult intent.

Tears formed in his tired eyes. The pink spray that ejected from his mother's shattered temple was not the reward she had deserved. The image still tormented him.

Knowledge that his mother had been a medium had changed him. He wondered how her messages might have influenced the Reich and the course of the War. Those ponderings were another torment.

But he continued to pray for her soul. Did his mother speak with angels or instead, demons? To converse with demons was a sin. He too, had wanted to speak to the angels. Thank God he hadn't.

Such was the reality of the evil war created by that madman, Adolf Hitler. He had fallen prey to dark forces that sought dominion within our world. But his desire to create a New World Order had been left unfulfilled.

Valla knew he should be grateful. He had received the best education, being one of the few accepted into the Society at Yale. He had been given a fast track to position and influence, culminating in his present position, but the Skull and Bones always extracted a price, even from the presidents of the United States who they had successfully nurtured.

Valla suspected his every move was monitored to ensue his debt was repaid. His peers made sure of it. Resentment festered deep within his psyche.

He played the ecclesiastical game, but was always cautious of those around him. He remembered the battle he had had with His Holiness John Paul II to remove that irascible gargoyle from his office all those years ago, but somehow he had a feeling this grisly individual still cast one of his grotesque eyes over his activities.

Thank God, I've hidden him away. He's just the type Majestic would use.

17

MYSTERY

CANBERRA, AUSTRALIA

Keisha Petersen had left an unexpected impression. Her blue eyes shone with a vivacity that lured me into pleasurable, but professionally forbidden thoughts. Although captivated by her sensuality and delicate beauty, it was her vitality and formidable mind I found most alluring. I tried to comprehend the sheer breadth of her interests. No idea was too extraordinary. Even the books she displayed demonstrated a voracious inquisitiveness. Why she had a copy of some Nazi ideology book confounded me. There must have been a reason.

I poured a neat Glenmorangie and silently mulled over our afternoon conversation. The spirit left the warm glow that only a superb single malt can deliver. There had been too many evenings alone over the past couple of years, but this night stretched more than most.

A thought pierced like a bullet. Maybe an understanding of Nazi beliefs would give me an added insight into Keisha's mindset. I had to know more about her.

I had three or four days to wait for LITAN and with Keisha

unavailable, I thought I would fill in my time. There was no urgency to return home to the U.K., so I registered as a reader and the Australian National Library. Forming one apex of the Parliamentary Triangle, the marble and glass monolith nestled against the man-made Lake Burley Griffin. Furnished with massive white marble supports, the building glistened against the enormous blue sky, its white angular silhouette contrasting with the hardy eucalypts in the foreground.

I decided to search the electronic catalogue and within minutes I submitted an e-call slip for *Religious Belief Systems of the Third Reich* by S. Van Der Platz. I waited for its retrieval and then proceeded to the main reading room.

Hitler had always been a complete enigma to me. I thought that a maniac's motivation needed understanding, if only to save ourselves from repeating their mistakes. How was it possible for one man to subvert and subjugate one of the most culturally and technically advanced countries of its era?

I found a comfortable chair and settled in. The book was compelling. It claimed the Third Reich had been seeded from a quasi-religious cult that believed in an advanced civilisation thousands of years before the rise of ancient Greece. Darwin's natural selection principles were used to validate Nazi ideology, propelling Germany to military conquest. I was discovering that the ideology behind Nazism was far more complex than I had imagined.

I was drawn in by the narrative and could scarcely digest the information fast enough. The motivational template for the Third Reich was laid out, complete with its twisted belief system. There were a number of so-called secret societies behind the formation of the National Socialists. One of the most prominent was the Thule Gesellschaft. The Order was formed in 1910 based on a combination of Sufism, Freemasonry and right wing political philosophy.

The influence of the Thule Gesselschaft and other esoteric societies on National Socialism was pervasive. But the truth lying behind their teachings was distorted to suit the Nazi brand of paranoia.

In a bizarre twist of fate, Hitler ended up banning the public practise of astrology, psychism and other such activities, and in 1937 he banned several groups including the Theosophists, the Order of the New Templars, the Hermetic Order of the Golden Dawn and the followers of Anthroposophy.

More beguiling was the Nazi expertise in psychological manipulation and social control. They pioneered mass manipulation at the Nuremberg rallies using symbolism, light and sound.

The book's author considered some of the greats of the past — Isaac Newton, Francis Bacon, Leonardo da Vinci and Johann von Goethe. They apparently all had connections with secret organisations, a practice followed by the Nazis. So too, did some presidents of the United States. Roosevelt, Washington, Jefferson and Woodrow Wilson were quoted as examples.

I wondered how these great men might have been influenced by their connections. And what about today? Are our minds closed to the influence from similar societies? Probably. I formed the view that they were. Mine was. I'd never even considered the subject.

In modern consumer culture, people rarely thought beyond the cost of their mortgage or the price of a hamburger. Such crass superficiality was frustrating. People's attitudes were so predictable, especially my peers whose agenda was measured by monetary grants.

Maybe that's why I found Keisha so enticing. She challenged the norm. But she was also challenging me. She was the wake-up call I needed. Apart from my disputes with the anthropological fraternity, I had started to fall into patterns of blind acceptance.

In some ways Keisha intimidated me. I enjoyed the challenge of excavating cave sites and burial mounds in the far-flung places of the world and liked action in my life, but I spent little time in deep reflection.

I knew Darwinism had holes, but I considered my work would eventually fill the ones I knew about. On the other hand, Keisha was challenging me with concepts that I had either long ignored or never considered.

During my reading, I sensed being scrutinised from across the reading room. I surveyed the scene and detected an odd-looking individual whose snake-like albino eyes quickly averted from their intense scrutiny. There was an unmistakable peculiarity about him. His complexion and his ill-fitting coat chilled me.

Surely he was one of the so-called spooks who had chased us through the mall? Or was he? I wouldn't stake my life on it, but when he looked up again and darted his serpentine eyes at me I was almost certain. The back of my neck bristled. Casually, and without drawing further attention, the man rose and walked toward the exit.

I reckoned it was time to go. I went to copy the remaining pages of the book when pale pink pupils glared in my direction.

The albino wanted me to notice. If he was trying to threaten, he was doing a lousy job. I would be happy to strangle the freak if he pushed his intimidation too far. I would not accept having Keisha and I pushed around by him and his cronies.

Once I had finished copying, I noticed he had disappeared. I could not fathom how he had vanished from his vantage point because the only way to exit was to walk past me. He never did. I checked the bookshelves behind me. Somehow he was definitely gone. Maybe I was just getting paranoid.

After savouring a magnificent steak and a couple of fine glasses of Coonawarra Cabernet at a crowded city restaurant, I retired to the balcony of my 'safe-house'. I watched the cars traverse the roads below like a convoy of fireflies, the distant violet hilltops dappled in glistening moonlight. This city reminded me of an oversized university campus rather than Australia's national capital. It was a paradise for chest thumping politicians and little else. *A cesspit for nothing more than mouth and trousers'* my mother used to say.

I mused over Keisha's explanation of the mysterious Elohim and the Order of Mechelzedek, and what my photographs might contain. If they could be translated and they confirmed Keisha's thoughts, then my whirlwind journey would be more than interesting. If I could get to present the findings in my upcoming series, Ivy League academics and the global media would go viral.

My reading at the library had reinforced Keisha's assertions. The section about secret societies claiming to have a lineage back to ancient Egypt had captured my attention. This lineage apparently conferred some sort of special knowledge that appears to have been strategically hidden from mainstream interests.

My research recorded that the Masonic president Franklin D. Roosevelt was a member of the Ancient Arabic Order of Nobles and Mystics with links to the Order of the Rosy Cross. Iconoclastic thinkers such as Goethe, Spinoza and Kant had also been members.

At the height of Nazi power in Germany, and after conferring with the U.S. Secretary of Agriculture Henry Wallace who was a practising esotericist, Roosevelt decided to have a Masonic emblem printed on the U.S. dollar bill. Wallace's idea came from Nicholas Roerich, a fascinating man who had travelled extensively throughout Nepal and Tibet, studying with the monastic lamas. Nominated for the Nobel Peace Prize in 1929, Roerich had made a notable contribution to the pact signed by twenty-two nations in a pledge to protect cultural property. Why these prominent and influential men were associated with arcane societies remained a mystery. *Why reside in the shadows?*

Thoughts of men with hidden agendas caused me to reflect on something Keisha had said. She was referring to one of my photos. *"If this provides the information I hope it does, it could well destroy the views of modern religion."*

What if the information was already known and it was deemed necessary to suppress it? Was that the cause of Jai's death? Perhaps the Baalbek excavation had exposed something considered too valuable to be declared. Perhaps those who resided in the shadows – the spooks as Keisha called them – had an agenda.

But Keisha had been more specific – *"It could well destroy the views of modern religion."* Could the Church have an agenda? Whatever the truth, Jai was dead, and I resolved to make sure his death wasn't in vain.

Suddenly the phone rang. Perhaps Keisha was available to enjoy the rest of the evening after all. She was the only one that knew I was here.

I picked up. "Hello, Dr Keyes here."

A deep baritone voice responded. "Yes, Dr Keyes. I know who you are sir."

"Who is this?"

"That's not important. What is very important is that you and your research are in serious danger."

The voice was cultured yet stern, with a touch of Oxford don about it. One of the spook field officers from yesterday maybe, but how did he know this number.

"Yeah, well it wouldn't be the first time. Declare yourself or I hang up."

"Don't be so hasty. More people know about your discovery in Baalbek than you think."

I had been ready to disconnect, but he knew about Baalbek. I hadn't breathed a word to anyone, not even Keisha Petersen. "What are you on about?"

"Your discovery may upset a delicate balance that has been maintained since the 1950s."

"Listen pal, I'm an anthropologist. I collect data, do research and publish results. That's my job. If you don't like it, then that's your problem."

"The world doesn't operate in a scientific fairytale Dr Keyes. Powerful interests rule what you think you know."

"Yeah, I know all about powerful interests. They're the paymasters behind research grants."

"You're forgetting something Dr Keyes. The history of the world is the history of the warfare between secret societies. Not my words, Doctor – Benjamin Disraeli's."

The anonymous contact was either trying to be helpful or throw me a false lead. The mention of secret societies was enough. I decided to play along.

"You've got ten seconds."

"You and I have common interests," he replied. "We both believe knowledge should be available to all."

"Five seconds."

A hearty laugh reverberated down the line. "Look, I know it's hard to trust a stranger who rings up out of nowhere, but I don't have time to explain. There's information which may give you a better understanding of your discovery and your colleague's death."

My blood ran cold. *How did he know about Jai?* "First, get out of that apartment. Take your colleague's death as a warning. Second, go to Dresden and meet Otto."

The mention of Jai honed my attention. "Listen, who are you? And who's Otto?"

"I'm your knight in shining armour. And Otto is just Otto. He's expecting your arrival. Schleissheimerstrasse 43. Get out now. Your work is important, my friend, so don't give up."

CLICK! The phone went dead.

18

HOODED MYSTERY

———

VATICAN CITY

Angelo was baffled by the Code.

His clandestine study of the Templars had made him aware of the numerous mysteries and countless speculations about the Order.

Angelo had been absorbed with their story. He accepted that the internecine battle between the Templars and the Church was not just over key spiritual principles, but also over control of precious artefacts excavated in Jerusalem. After the destruction of the Order in the fourteenth century, remnants of the fraternity went into hiding, vowing one day to re-emerge as a coherent force.

Comte had told him about his study of medieval intelligence documents hidden away in the archive. The records mainly drew on circumstantial evidence and had concluded that the Templars had managed, against overwhelming odds, to secure the most coveted of relics, including the Ark of the Covenant.

Incredibly, in 1867, Captain Wilson, Lieutenant Warren and a team of Royal Engineers re-excavated an area in Jerusalem and uncovered tunnels extending vertically from the Al Aqsa mosque, fanning out under the Dome of the Rock, the site of King Solomon's temple. Crusader artefacts were found in these tunnels. Further, the earliest written copies of masonic documents stated that Templars retrieved the Ark of the Covenant hidden in a cave under the site of King Solomon's temple.

It was a story ignored by Angelo's university. But it was a history that made the existence of the code more intriguing. *Why would such dedicated men hide a code in some stained glass windows at an obscure abbey in Southern France?*

Ever since meeting Comte, Angelo had been troubled in his sleep. His thoughts were constantly elsewhere. He was even distracted with his work in the Cardinal's office. Christian scripture had suddenly lost some of its lustre.

Like Comte before him, the Vatican was now a means of conducting personal research. What was real and what was theological propaganda? Those questions dominated his every thought and it was Comte who was his conduit to the answers he sought.

Angelo journeyed to the Old Study Room once more. He had finished work late, but his appetite for knowledge needed nourishment.

The walk to the library was now familiar, indelibly etched into his subconscious. The masterful frescos and ancient masonry continued to work their magic, his clandestine motives causing the shadowed hallways to seem more foreboding.

He contemplated what would be required to change the views of the Church hierarchy. Would dogma change if the message of the scriptures was overturned? History suggested otherwise.

His destination loomed. The Swiss Guard was not troubled with his entry, but he was concerned he would be spotted by the Dominican cleric. So far he had been lucky. Nothing had come of the cleric's threat. He determined to take extra care with this visit. Fortunately, the Old Study Room was vacant. It only had twelve desks, so Angelo arranged himself to take in the full view of the room. Nobody could approach without his knowledge.

He googled 'French abbeys' and surfed the wave of enquiry. His search entangled him, struggling to find anything relating to the Templar windows. Angelo was immersed, but came up for air as he decided to make a different search. Light taps on a keypad other than his own broke his concentration.

With a cataleptic stare at his screen, he listened, frozen to his seat.

He heard it again, breaking the hermetic silence.

Angelo slowly glanced past his screen. About five metres away and close to the entrance was a figure in a black hooded robe, half-turned in his direction. Such robes were uncommon in the Holy See, typically the preserve of some pious monastic order. No face was visible. It was recessed deep within the hood.

What now? He must have been seen.

Sweat soaked Angelo's forehead and shirt collar. His predicament was apparent. If he stayed, he felt sure action would be taken. Alternatively, if he approached, the consequences would be the same. This person could be the cause of his ruin. He collected his thoughts and steeled his nerves. The hooded figure continued to tap away, oblivious to his stare.

I won't be fearful. I'm doing nothing wrong.

Angelo quickly deleted the internet history from the control panel icon. No point taking chances, at least the computer was clean. He slowly rose to his feet and approached the intruder. It was best to leave quietly.

As he made his unscheduled exit, the mysterious figure looked up at him and threw back the deep hood. A bundle of luxurious, long blonde hair cascaded over the dark robe. It was a woman. A stunningly beautiful woman who greeted him with a warm smile and words that sounded like silk.

"Hello. You're Angelo aren't you?"

19

SINISTER FORCE

———

THE PENTAGON, WASHINGTON DC

"Majestic's really pissed off."

Ariel Goldstein recoiled. He didn't trust the ultra-covert agency. It had sinister motives with its black-ops programmes. But he enjoyed the challenges they presented. He was about to be involved again, whether he liked it or not.

"P2's intervened over an excavation near Baalbek," said Ernst Volker.

"Why do P2 give a damn? Excavations aren't part of their brief."

"You're right, that's why we've been called. If the discovery gets publicity, it might lead to discussion of the Elohim."

"What's the Elohim?"

"More like who, Ariel. You'll be briefed on all that later. For now, Majestic requires an intervention. P2's solved part of the problem. They want you to clean up the rest."

Ariel Goldstein was medium height, slim and wiry. Green eyes flecked with brown peered beneath a deeply creased forehead. Grey hair was cropped to crew cut. Small ears, no lobes. Thin mean lips. Street smart and feline quick.

Now in his mid-forties, he was a seasoned CIA agent who occasionally executed specific objectives for Majestic. There was none better than Goldstein. His enmity for the organisation was well documented, but his knowledge of CIA assassination techniques qualified him whenever the ultra-covert agency required.

Goldstein had a reputation for being both methodical and ruthless.

Ernst Volker was a desk jockey. Slightly younger than Goldstein, he was attached to Majestic as a researcher and adviser on archaeological history and 'extra-normal' events. Taller than Goldstein, his groomed locks of highlighted, sun streaked hair belied his studious demeanour. Fidgety and restless, he was in constant movement even when sitting. His mind worked overtime, always two steps ahead. Volker had an eidetic memory and knew of the historical existence of the Elohim. He understood their legacy which was recorded by many races, in many lands, many thousands of years ago.

He had studied countless Biblical texts on behalf of Majestic and knew of the numerous references to the Elohim and other beings, including the Nephilim, Ophanim and Seraphim. He also knew how these beings were never discussed at the Seminaries and bible colleges, how orthodox Christendom had strategically manipulated the original texts to ensure that modern interpretations ignored the real truth of such beings. At least the Koran acknowledged these things. Thankfully, the published works of the renowned Eli Rosen had not captured the public's imagination.

P2 had a common objective with Majestic, but this time their action had been hastily executed. There was a need to tighten the reigns.

Majestic's mandate was to explore phenomena that challenged

ordinary cultural norms. As an elite group of supra-national intelligence agents, they exist with a security classification higher than both the CIA and the president. The group was commissioned during President Truman's term to gather artefacts and to compile data on a variety of controversial subjects. If deemed necessary, they suppressed its dissemination through the media. Their responsibility was to ensure that the social, political and economic order remained stable. The power elites refused to have their carefully contrived paradigm compromised.

It was after the American War of Independence that various fraternities in Europe took an interest in creating the New Atlantis. These underground associations had long known of the biblical Elohim, beings who had taught the ancient Egyptian priesthood.

The skill on how to manufacture a special substance used to attain advanced states of consciousness was passed down through the Priesthood. This enabled the adherents to access the so-called 'super-sensible realms'. Commonly known as the Sacred Path in the Far East, the knowledge still remains hidden in the most ancient traditions, and subsequently became the precursor of today's orthodox religions.

The most remarkable revelation of the twentieth century, subsequently classified by the military and now protected by Majestic, was linked to this ancient knowledge. The few governments around the world that had the resources to track what was happening were frightened by what was witnessed.

Majestic's objective has remained constant: to condition nation states as passive players in the New World Order. This includes maintaining the current interpretation of biblical events. Regardless of cost, the core dogmatic theological position must be preserved to ensure global control.

20

UNCODED

THE PENTAGON, WASHINGTON DC

Angelo recoiled in surprise. He stared intently as her scent enticed him. *What was a woman doing here?* Crystal blue eyes and picture perfect Nordic features greeted him; a warm and undemanding smile curled the woman's lips.

Angelo flushed even more as he recognised his arousal. His vocal chords constricted as his eyes darted away from her scrutiny. He could only nod in reply.

"I was told you might be here tonight." She had a curious mixed accent that the young man couldn't place.

How could she know he was in the Old Study Room? Angelo was dumbstruck by the beautiful woman who had sought him out. *How in God's name did she get in here?*

Angelo stuttered. "M...me? Why have you come to see me?"

Keisha Petersen ran her elegant fingers through her dishevelled hair. "Your friend Comte is attending to some personal business with my colleagues and he'll be away for a few days. He intends to return, but I need to warn that neither of you may be safe here for much longer."

Angelo's heart sank. Why hadn't Comte told him he was leaving, and what was this nonsense about their safety? Could he trust this woman? *Maybe she's trying to incriminate me in a scandal. Maybe Comte's resolve to break the code has attracted unwanted attention.*

Angelo played it cautiously and gazed into the deliquescent shimmer of her ice-blue eyes. He could feel himself being drawn to her. Be careful with beautiful women, his father had always counselled. He was right. Be careful.

"Where's Comte gone?"

"I can only say that he wants to be back soon."

"Who are you? How did you get in here?"

Keisha thought to ease the young man's distress. "Let's just say I'm a friend of a friend," she said with playful charm.

"Comte you mean."

"No, not even Comte could arrange that. But he wanted you to know that he's broken the code. If he doesn't return by week's end, you'll need to get away from here. Don't ever come back."

It seemed there was no middle ground. He heard his father's voice again. *Be careful.* He played dumb.

"What code?"

Keisha smiled. "You know – the Templar code from the windows."

He ignored the response. "Where did Comte go?"

The woman leaned forward gently touching Angelo's arm. He felt a shiver course through his body. Her touch triggered a response he hadn't expected.

"All I'll say is that I belong to a group who have an interest in uncovering and preserving the ancient knowledge. We became aware of Comte's activities some years ago and decided to make contact with him."

Angelo was suspicious. "You've been spying on him? Why?"

The woman crossed her long graceful legs, shifting her weight in the chair. Angelo noticed her natural elegance, but remained on edge.

She replied, "No Angelo, not spying. Anybody who's able to decipher that code deserves the opportunity to further his research, wouldn't you say. I can't deny we've been monitoring him, but purely for his safety."

"What about me? Why are you concerned about my safety?"

"It's Comte who's concerned. I'm here at his request. You're more than welcome to join him in his activities if you wish."

Angelo's continuing work with the Cardinal without Comte would be unbearable, but he hedged. "I'll think about it."

Keisha stood up. "I must go now. Be careful, Angelo."

Angelo decided to take his chance. "This code, what did it say?" If Comte never returned he needed to know the meaning.

Keisha had wondered how long it would take for him to ask. She flashed a cheeky glance at Angelo's muscular frame, his face flushing with embarrassment. "He thought you'd want to know. You'd know of course that the Bible has undergone a number of linguistic translations."

"Yes, I do. I study at the Pontificia Università Urbaniana."

"I know you do, but it's a little more than misinterpretation. The texts have been deliberately obscured to prevent the uninitiated from penetrating their true meaning."

Angelo frowned. She was sounding like Comte.

Keisha removed a folded paper from her robe's pocket and opened it flat on the computer desk. The code was printed at the top of the paper with rows of numbers beneath.

IIIVIII IIIVIV IIVVI IIVIIX IIVIIV IIIVII IVVV VIVI VVIVIII VIIIIIV

Her eyes hinted at something astounding. "The code is one of the most elegant medieval examples I've seen. The key to its decoding is the very structure of the Bible itself. I'll give Comte credit – he's tenacious."

"I agree with you there," replied Angelo.

Written under the code were the numbers,

243 244 256 269 275 242 455 516 568 814

Under these was another set,

2-13-21 2-13-22 2-14-24 2-33-9 2-34-5 2-40-38
4-14-14 5-1-33 23-60-8 26-1-4

"This first row of numbers comes from the Roman system. See, IIIVIII is II IV III, or 2 4 3. Numerologically, the numbers expand out to those here in the last row. So 2 4 3, becomes 2 13 21. The numbers are simply references to passages in the Bible. 2-13-21 is Book 2, Chapter 13, verse 21. 2-13-22 is Book 2, Chapter 13, verse 22 and so on."

"OK," marvelled Angelo, surprised by the code's ingenuity.

"The Old Testament is taken from far more ancient texts and sometimes, the words lose some of their meaning."

From the deep pocket of her robe, Keisha drew out her tattered hand-sized bible. She fingered the pages and read in slow deliberate tones. "Book 2 is Exodus, 13:21 says, **'And the Lord went before them by day in a *pillar of cloud*, to lead them the way; and by night in a *pillar of fire*, to give them light; to go by day and night.'**

"This describes how Moses was helped in leading the Israelites out of Egypt. Now the next verse, 13:22, **'He took not away the pillar of the cloud by day, or the pillar of fire by night, from before the people'.**"

Angelo frowned. *Pillar of cloud, pillar of fire? What did it mean?*

Keisha nodded at Angelo's puzzlement. "There's no such thing as

a *'pillar of cloud by day and a pillar of fire by night'*. When the translations took place, it was difficult to be precise. The ancient Hebrew
word for 'pillar' is more correctly translated as 'stone'. So the witness
to this event was observing *'a stone of cloud by day and a stone of fire
by night'*. The Bible's full of such gems."

Keisha quoted again, this time the next passage of the code.
"Next coded number says, **'and it came to pass, that in the morning watch, the Lord looked unto the host of the Egyptians through**
the pillar of fire and of the cloud.'."

Angelo straightened as he focused on the passage. Why was the
Lord associated with this pillar, stone of cloud and fire thing? How
was the Lord actually 'looking through' this thing to the Egyptian
people?

Keisha paused to allow Angelo to consider the passages. "Next
number, Exodus 33:9, **'And it came to pass, as Moses entered the**
tabernacle, *the cloudy pillar descended, and stood at the door of the*
tabernacle, and the Lord talked with Moses.'"

"So the 'cloud pillar' actually descended," remarked Angelo,
perplexed.

"That's what it says." She continued, "Exodus 34:5, '**the *Lord***
descended in the cloud, **and stood with him there, and proclaimed**
the name of the Lord.'"

"So now the Lord is 'descending' in this cloud thing. What's
going on? How come I've never heard about any of this?" An uncomfortable resentment toward his pontifical study stirred within him.

Keisha allowed the gravity of the passages to sink in. Finally, she
quoted the last coded passage from Exodus. "'**for *the cloud of the***
Lord was upon the tabernacle by day, and fire was on it by night, **in**
the sight of all the house of Israel, throughout all their journeys.'"

"So the full code mentions similar quotes, does it?"

The woman nodded. "It seems it's only an entree to encourage further study. Many of the Old Testament books give similar

descriptions, as do some in the New Testament. There are a number of similar verses."

"So the Bible has other references to these cloud things?"

"Yes Angelo. Check the code for yourself. The truth is there for you to discover. Here, take the numbers. Remember the phrase that appeared in the windows – 'Permissum illic exsisto lux lucis'. Before I go, I'll give you something else to investigate. It seems all this may have been known to some initiates who portrayed the knowledge by the only means available to them. There's a painting in the National Gallery in London from 1486 by Carlo Crivelli. It's called 'The Annunciation with Saint Emidius' and has a disk formation in the clouds shining a beam of light onto the crown of the Madonna. It seems to show the 'cloud of the Lord'.

"I must leave you now. Be careful and know that Comte is safe. Maybe we'll meet again."

With those words, Keisha touched Angelo lightly on the shoulder and made her leave. Angelo was numbed by the interlude. He was urged to follow, but remained anchored to the floor. She had stirred feelings he had never before experienced. He didn't even know her name.

Within the private confines of his bed-sit, he decided to check the code. He recognised 4,14,14 as Numbers 14:14,

'**And they will tell it to the inhabitants of this land: for they have heard that the Lord is among this people, that the Lord art seen face to face, and that** *thy cloud standeth over them, and that thou goes before them, by day time in a pillar of cloud, and in a pillar of fire by night,*'

and then the next set as Deuteronomy 1:33,

'**Who went in the way before you, to search you out a place to pitch your tents in,** *in fire by night,* **to show you by what way ye should go, and** *in a cloud by day.*'

Angelo was in a state of abject disbelief. In Isaiah 60:8 he read,

'Who are these that *fly as a cloud, and as the doves to their windows?*'

He chuckled aloud. *Now these cloud things fly and have windows.* This is monumental. He flicked the pages over to Ezekiel 1:4,

'And I looked, and behold, a whirlwind came out of the north, a great cloud, and a fire infolding itself, and a brightness was about it, and out of the midst thereof as the colour of amber, out of the midst of the fire.'

Angelo believed the Bible was describing some type of flying vehicle from a period of history over three thousand years ago. The strange woman had also told him of another painting called 'The Madonna with Saint Giovannino' painted by Giovanni Bellini in the 15th century. On display in the Palazzo Vecchio in Florence it depicts a glowing disk hovering in the sky behind the Madonna. Even more revealing, she mentioned a mid-fourteen century fresco painted above the altar at the Visoki Dicani Monestary in Kosovo entitled 'The crucifixion'. She said it depicted two fiery, comet-like craft with men inside.

It was hard to accept. Angelo's main difficulty was how the Church had never revealed the truth of these passages.

He made another conclusion, one he found obscene – *We've been lied to for centuries.*

This changed everything. He suddenly felt very close to his friend, Comte.

21

CONTACT

DRESDEN, GERMANY

Get out I did. The mystery man knew about Baalbek and had offered a clue about Jai. *Take your colleague's death as a warning,* he had said. That was good enough for me. I left a message for Keisha on her iPhone asking her to contact me when LITAN had produced a result, but thought better of telling her my plans. The faceless man had somehow known to contact me at Keisha's 'safe house' and that created a further mystery. *Could I really trust her?*

Rubber squealed on tarmac. A dark slate-grey smeared the city, as thick, bold clouds swelled, ready to crack open. It was an unusual sky for a summer afternoon.

The carousel ejected my baggage and after passing Customs, I taxied to the Kempinski Hotel Taschenbergpalais for a much-needed shower.

Set in the heart of the old city, the elegant hotel was nestled among the Opera House, the splendid late-baroque Zwinger and the 15th century Royal Palace. The regal spires of the elegantly restored Palace clawed upward, teasing the brooding metallic sky.

It was hard to believe these magnificent buildings were virtually destroyed during two wanton nights of carpet-bombing toward the end of the War.

It was time to solve the mystery of Otto. Did he actually exist or was this some kind of elaborate exercise to extract information about my find in Baalbek? God knows what I was walking into. I had to get to the bottom of it, despite the risk, especially if it would help me translate the photographs.

I wasted no time. My taxi dropped me at Schleissheimerstrasse 43. An overgrown hedge with a daunting century-old, wrought iron gate fronted the street. It opened to a narrow, broken pathway overgrown by thickets of weeds bursting through age-old cracks. Branches from a clutch of trees grazed the shingled slate roof. Leaves rustled in the breeze as the sun now speared through wispy clouds high in the sky.

The house must have been 300 years old. The dark stone facade was covered with decades of grime, the slate entrance steps ground down by the tread of unknown feet. Narrow leadlight windows sagged drunkenly with age on each side of the heavy oak door. I knocked and waited.

The door eventually groaned open to reveal a tiny old man with a thatch of thin white hair, pale complexion and heavily lined face. He was fragile and stooped, just over five feet in stature.

"Hello, my name is Keyes. I was told that...."

I was cut off by the abrupt German accent. "Yes, yes. I know who you are Dr. Keyes, your reputation precedes you. Please come in. My name is Otto."

His hazel eyes glistened with alertness, but revealed a weary tiredness. He offered a bony hand and shook mine with a grip defying his age. Without reply, I entered the hallway and followed the old man into the house.

"You must be very tired after your long flight?"

I explained that I had rested well, but the old man's attention was elsewhere. "I'll fetch refreshments, please make yourself comfortable."

I scanned the large room. It was a step back in time. Nothing within it hinted of the 21st century. Wrought stone and large heavy furniture dominated the room. There was a huge oak table with matching antique chairs and an enormous blackened fireplace cut deep within the thick stone outer wall. A richly woven tapestry hung on a side wall depicting a medieval knight ready for battle, and at the back of the room was a heavy ornate bookcase crammed with an untidy array of dusty old books. I was about to investigate when Otto returned pushing a chromed tea trolley. I was quietly amused by the old man's quaint domesticity.

"I do hope you like strong coffee, Dr. Keyes."

I nodded appreciatively. "Very much. Call me Aiden if you like."

"Very well Dr. Keyes, Aiden it is. Have some cake as well; the recipe is a bit of a Saxony tradition. It's my grandmother's."

I spotted a hint of exuberant pride. The little man sank into the chair opposite me and beamed with undisguised admiration. Without any preliminaries, he confessed his subterfuge. "I know about your discovery in Baalbek. Forget how. What matters is its importance, but there are some things you need to be aware of."

His eyes squinted beneath his deeply lined forehead as they moved over me, studying me intently.

His confession and his perspicacious appraisal unsettled me. I had been compromised, so I brushed off his comment. "Not much of a discovery when everybody seems to know about it, so it can't be that important.

The old man looked forlornly into his lap. "Oh, it's important alright. That's why they're trying to stop you. It could well be a link to things not well understood anymore."

I was becoming impatient and wanted to get beyond the bullshit.

Otto sensed my annoyance and his scrutiny softened. "So you're wondering why you're here, eh?"

"After spending twenty-six hours to get here, that had crossed my mind."

"I understand your frustration Aiden. I had you summoned because of a nasty visit I had from a pimple-faced officer from the Federal Intelligence Service – the Bundesnachrichtendienst."

I raised my eyebrows. What was I getting involved in now? The Canberra spooks came to mind. Maybe they had tipped off their international counterparts.

"Oh don't worry; I've had plenty of visits by those idiots before."

"Why are they interested in you?"

"They're a bit concerned about our knowledge upsetting the status quo. It seems your discovery has brought them out from under their rock again. Damned hypocrites."

"Whose knowledge are you talking about here? Care to enlighten me?"

Otto squinted mischievously. "I'm associated with a centuries-old group that works to preserve the ancient knowledge."

The old man somehow knew about my discovery and had links to a possible subversive organisation. Was it they who were responsible for Jai? "What group are you talking about, Otto?"

The little man hesitated, carefully weighing his answer. "All in good time Aiden. I can assure you, you're in no danger here. I'll give you some background to make things a bit clearer. Is that OK?"

"Getting to the point would be a good idea."

"After the War, the U.S. government illegally brought important German scientists into the country under a secret operation called Paper Clip. The objective was to give the U.S. a lead in a number of fields, including weaponry, rocketry, over-unity energy, mind control and biological engineering."

"Yes, I'm aware of the rush to smuggle out German expertise."

"It wasn't just the Americans though. The connection between Hitler, his highest ranking SS officers and some of these scientists – and what the Reich had discovered as part of their esoteric explorations, particularly in the Far East, was eagerly sought. The U.S. military gave it their highest security classification. But our group has always believed that certain knowledge needs protection from those who would seek to use it for their own gain."

"That's all very interesting, but what's this got to do with me?"

"You're here to learn. Secret societies guard their knowledge well, but knowledge in the wrong hands can be catastrophic. Hitler's regime was living proof of that."

My tone was aloof. "So I'm here to learn secret knowledge, am I?"

Otto countered, "When you're ready, and that time is fast approaching for all of mankind. The true history and consequent destiny of human evolution has only ever been known to the very few. My connections believe in its gradual release. Our aim is to help the raising of human consciousness. But the masses today seek visible proof of any hypothesis. Only tangible proof can shatter the power structure of those in control."

"So the Intelligence Services are worried about the release of true history and this release would threaten them, is that it?"

"It threatens them all to the point of paranoia."

"Is this a joke? I have no idea what you're on about old man. How about getting to the point?"

"Aiden, the truth can only be disclosed when one is completely ready. One can't be half ready; the consequences would be devastating. So the time has come to move humanity forward. Truth needs to be gradual, but it does need to be released. Those who control the global information system will try their very best to stop it. I'm sure you realise you were in danger in Australia. Your understudy has already been dealt with, and your home in London is being watched as we speak. They knew where you were and will stop at nothing to silence your discovery."

There were obviously hidden forces at work, but I was wary of the old man's motives. "Yes, and it seems you knew where I was as well. Care to explain that?"

"It's true we've watched your back. Your credentials will give credibility to any future announcement about what Baalbek may disclose. Your safety is important to us. That's why we made it obvious you were watched. Do you remember our albino friend?"

What the hell? "You had him watch me?"

"To keep you on your toes, otherwise you may not have taken heed."

"So you think that scared me do you."

"Never. I know your reputation. You can look after yourself, but you may not have travelled here. As I said, your credentials are important to us."

"My credentials have nothing to do with you and so far there's nothing to announce."

The old man spoke in a hushed tone. "If your discovery leads to what we think it might, there will be plenty to announce and they'll stop at nothing to destroy its release. They'll destroy you too, make no mistake."

Anger welled up and pressed hard against my chest. "I'm in danger because I discovered something that might reveal a bit of history. Is that it? It's completely illogical."

"So you may think, but these people control history. They control the mythology behind religion. Always remember that history is written by the winners, and the winners are the masters of the political puppets. Control the money system and you control the governments that depend on it."

My brow curled. "So you think religion's a myth as well? That's at least one point I can agree with."

Otto remained calm. "That's not what I said, but the Baalbek discovery could blow the lid off their best-laid plans. If you look objectively at the biblical texts, it's clear that much of it is very different to what we've been told."

"So I'm beginning to learn."

Otto stroked his thin grey hair. "Yes, Dr Petersen is a marvel isn't she?"

The comment hit me like a hammer. It seemed all of my movements during and since Baalbek had been being monitored. *Had Keisha betrayed me?*

I went for the jugular, "Listen, I'm just about fed up with this crap. How do you know about Keisha Petersen?"

Otto remained implacable. "Dr Petersen has translated many manuscripts for our organisation. With her international expertise in ancient near eastern languages, it's not surprising you sought her advice. After all you were staying in an apartment she provided, were you not? She's the best in her field, and she's no fool. You would do well to take note of her views, especially with her expertise in ancient symbols."

"I'll take note then. How did you know where I was staying?" That question had bothered me since the call from Mr. Anonymous.

"All will be revealed in good time. I'm not your adversary, Aiden. I presume Dr. Petersen is helping you, correct?"

My response was deliberately terse. "I'm not sure yet."

"She will help you with the deciphering of symbols that are the keys to the hidden truth. I'll give you a very simple example. That OK with you?"

"Go on then," I nodded.

"A classic symbol of Christianity is the fish. Right?"

I was getting bored. "Yeah, I've seen the bumper stickers."

"The fish has important significance, veiled by those who control the Church. As you know, Jesus and his disciples were called the 'fishers of men'. Members of the community were called *pisciculi*, 'little fishes'. Even their baptismal fonts were called *piscina* or 'little fish ponds'. The first letter of each Greek word in the phrase 'Jesus Christ, Son of God, Saviour' spells the title ICHTHYS. It means fish and is no coincidence. All these references point to an epochal event opening the way for a change in mass human consciousness."

"So the fish represents what?"

"The Age of Pisces – the Age of the Christ principle. Those who wrote the original texts dated key events using star configurations. Important epochal events were recorded against the alignments of the stars. Remember the Magi travelling to Bethlehem to herald the birth of Jesus?"

"Yeah, the Christmas story made for children."

"You're not far wrong. It's a story based on superficial readings of the ancient scrolls. The Magi were Persian priest-astrologers who'd been waiting for the precession of the equinoxes with a rare triple conjunction of Jupiter and Saturn in Pisces. It coincided with the birth of 'Kyrios', the 'Bearer of Light' for the dawn of a New Age. Hence, the Age of Pisces, the age of the fish, represents the birth of Christ."

I was beginning to understand how the ancient texts differed from the conventional view. The Baalbek crypt obviously held a secret considered worthy of Jai's death, so I decided to hear Otto out.

"I presume the Magi's gifts were symbolic too?"

"Of course, gold is the symbol for royalty, frankincense for the authentic priesthood and myrrh for the sacrificial role of Jesus. Even at his birth, they knew He would be a 'sacrifice' to the Eternal Truth."

Otto leaned forward and poured more coffee, filling my cup almost to the brim. "May I tell you a story?"

"You're lucky. I'm still listening," I said, annoyed that I had traversed the globe for this type of discussion.

"When I was six or seven, my father bought me a pup and like all kids, I loved that dog more than anything. A year later she died unexpectedly. I remember my father burying her behind an old shed in the garden. Through my youthful tears, I wondered what had become of her."

Otto shifted in his seat. "I was raised as a Lutheran, and I asked the pastor whether the dog's soul would go to heaven. He told me animals didn't have a soul. I just couldn't accept it and as it turned out Albert Einstein had already answered my question."

"Einstein?"

"Yes, he proved the interchangeability of mass and energy. Of course, the Indian Vedas explained it all thousands of years ago, but that's another story. Remember the equation $E=MC^2$?"

I struggled to see the connection. "What does this have to do with your dog's death?"

"When she died I knew her consciousness or soul was missing, some kind of energy if you like, the difference between life and death." The old man paused. "The entire universe consists of either matter or energy, and both are interchangeable. If we accept that consciousness or soul, or whatever you want to call it, is not physical, then it must be some kind of energy."

"Maybe, but maybe there's just plain nothing."

"Energy is not nothing. It can't be destroyed, it exists forever. It's a universal law, and it means that if my dog's consciousness is some form of energy, then it must still exist somewhere in the universe, in some form."

I followed the old man's logic, but remained silent.

Otto eyed me enthusiastically and eased out of his chair. "I want to show you something."

I followed him to a room the size of a large closet. He reached down and folded a tattered carpet square to one side. He then punched a keypad positioned on the wall. 1314. Otto made no effort to conceal the password. Part of the floor electronically dropped and slid to one side. Metal steps descended to the basement below.

"Come Aiden."

22

MANNA

PONTIFICIA UNIVERSITÀ URBANIANA, ROME

Angelo was now reading the Bible in a different context. *Why haven't I noticed this before!* His mind reverberated with the implication of the coded verses.

'*Who are these that fly as a cloud, and as the doves to their windows?*'

Someone was flying like a cloud in a vehicle with windows. *This was from the Bible!* He had never heard of such a thing. Angelo's familiar world was rapidly falling apart.

The indignant rage of the frog-eyed cleric burned hot. *"You think you know more than the Church and its centuries of scholarship. Do you?"* Angelo didn't, but right now he was full of questions. The dangerous course had been set by Comte, and now he felt vulnerable.

The Dominican's final pronouncement stabbed his thoughts. *"Your name will be mentioned. Be warned."* Perhaps the beautiful woman in the Old Study Room was right. Maybe he wasn't safe.

"Angelo!" screamed Vincenzo Lamech. "Have you been listening to anything I've been saying?"

Silent looks fell upon him. His fellow students were taken by surprise at the sharp outburst. It was the first time Angelo had ever been named during class.

"Ah, yes sir. I heard most of it," he replied evasively.

Lamech peered down his pointed nose and over the rim of his dangling glasses.

"Really? Then perhaps you can explain why Satan embodies original sin in this defiled world."

Angelo had switched off during Lamech's monologue. It was the usual fire and brimstone rant. The lecturer's face was now contorted with anger, his eyes blazing with black fury.

First the cleric and now Lamech, thought Angelo. *What's wrong with these people?*

The young assistant had always believed that the Church's teachings offered the only authentic path to salvation. But now, with thoughts of visitations by flying vehicles three thousand years ago, with these events actually mentioned in the Bible, he was less certain. Besides, there was something wrong with the idea that only those who followed the sanctioned scriptures could be 'saved' from purgatory or hell. What about those who had never heard about scripture?

Angelo decided he would challenge Lamech's self-righteous indignation, if for no other reason than to stay true to Comte. He vacillated no longer.

"Sir, I don't believe Satan embodies original sin."

Lamech's face bloated, his ears turning bright red. "Really?" he snapped.

To prevent any further dissent, Lamech prepared to humiliate. He had always ruled with an Orwellian zeal.

"So, DeMarco what do you believe then? Please tell me, I'm quite intrigued. In fact, we're all intrigued." With artistic flair he gestured with his hand in a wide arc at the other students.

Twenty four eyes focussed in curious anticipation. Glances and veiled smirks were exchanged. Fellow students looked toward the normally meek assistant as though he was the bravest man in the Rome. Angelo's demeanour was charged with new found confidence. The class knew Lamech would not let such impertinence pass without a fight. The unshakeable truth of scripture was being challenged.

Angelo stared his interrogator down, buoyed by his friendship with the irascible keeper. "You only have to think about it," he pronounced. "Let me read the Gospel of John, Chapter 1 verse 1-3."

Lamech grimaced at the impertinence, but he allowed him to continue, intent on humiliating the young upstart with his superior knowledge of scripture.

Angelo flipped the pages of his bible and read aloud,

'In the beginning was the Word, and the Word was with God, and the Word was God. The same was in the beginning with God. All things were made by him; and without him was not any thing made that was made.'

"Sir, do you believe that?"

Lamech was annoyed by such an obvious and stupid question. "Of course. It's the Word of God!"

Angelo glared with arrow-like precision at Lamech. "In the beginning, if there was *only* God, then there was nothing outside of God. Correct?"

"Yes, of course!" seethed Lamech impatiently, wondering where this idiot was leading.

"So when God made everything that ever was, what did God make it from?"

"What are you talking about DeMarco? Get to the point."

"Well, if there was only God, then everything ever made must have been made *from* God. After all, you agreed there was nothing outside of God."

Lamech paused. "So?"

"Do you believe God makes mistakes?"

"Of course not you fool."

Angelo knew Lamech had fallen for the trap. *Perfect.* "If, in the beginning there was only God and he created all that there is, then all that was, is, and ever will be, must have been made **from** God. True?"

"Of course, so what?"

"So it follows that Satan was not only created by God, but…" Angelo paused for effect. "…Satan must have been created from God. If Satan came from God, then he must be a part of God, like everything else in existence."

The class was hushed as Angelo's gaze swept over his fellow students.

His dialogue continued. "God's creation is Him, creation comes from Him, is part of Him. So God must 'let' Satan do his work at each and every moment. After all, you agreed God doesn't make mistakes. Therefore, your so-called interpretation of scripture doesn't make sense."

Lamech was infuriated. He stumbled for an argument. "God does this because God wishes to give people a choice."

Angelo had anticipated this piece of theological nonsense. "OK, let's assume that's true. If God is infinite and all knowing, creating every being in the universe, why go through the charade? God must already know the outcome. After all, everything came from Him. Everything is a part of God, even the existence of thought, the existence of sin. How can Satan, who was created by and from God, embody original sin? If Satan does, then sin must have existed within God in the beginning."

Angelo pushed further. He was ready to incite. "To lecture me about such a stupid notion is ridiculous. I don't buy it and anybody that does is a fool!"

Lamech propelled himself to his feet, his chair crashing back-ward to the floor. The stench of malice reeked from his pores. He trembled with rage.

"The devil be with you DeMarco! How dare you. Where did you get such sacrilegious lies?"

The whole class felt the heat of the maelstrom.

The temperature of Angelo's response was steady. He quietly and passionately answered, "God gave me an intellect to use reason and logic, and that's exactly what I intend to do."

Lamech scanned the classroom. Students were either smiling or trying not to laugh. *I may have lost the battle, but not the bloody war.* The gloating triumph of this intolerable agitator would be dealt with. He marched for the door and before steaming out of the room, he screamed, "You'll regret this, smart-arse."

Three hours later, still buzzing from his victory, Angelo found a scrawled note under his bed-sit door heralding an invitation. *Come and see me you crazy bastard!*

He smiled. There was only one person who could have written it.

23

REALITY BITES

APOSTOLIC PENITENTIARY, VATICAN CITY

Comte's invitation was fortuitous. Angelo knocked and heard the usual muffled reply.

"Enter!"

The automatic lock shunted open. Comte quickly placed a manuscript into his desk drawer; Angelo's sensing it was not for his casual gaze. More animated than usual, his mischievous grin contorted into form. "I know what you're going to ask, so don't, it's a long story."

The day's events had worked upon Angelo like an aphrodisiac and he was still oozing self-confidence. "Don't tell me that Comte. Where the hell have you been?"

Comte savoured Angelo's curiosity. "I've been filling the gaps of my research. So you got my message."

Angelo flushed at the thought. "Yeah, I did. She said you were leaving."

Comte wouldn't be drawn. "Keisha said she spoke to you. I need to finish up my research here, so sometime in the future I will be getting out of here."

Angelo's heart dropped.

Comte noticed the disappointment. "I'll be here for a while longer and you can leave with me if you wish. The time is coming to reveal the Truth. Would you like to be involved?"

"I don't know, Comte. The Church has been my life."

Comte changed tack. He scratched his blotchy scalp and solemnly shook his head. "I know, but right now I'd say you're in some trouble."

Angelo felt his gut churn. "So you heard about what happened with Lamech."

"Of course. He's an officious weasel, a toady pushing the same worn out dogma at the University. The news of your dissension is all over the place."

The young man's response was cautious. "Should I be worried?"

"I think you should be."

"What for? I've never said anything that I didn't think was true."

"I know, but it's like this Angelo. I want you to listen and listen well. Nobody gives a shit about me because they think I'm crazy. I get away with things, but you're different. You're the perfect, unblemished new assistant for one of the biggest bastards in this place. You've never put a foot wrong until now. Your indiscretion with Lamech will be reported to Valla. Don't underestimate him. Valla and I go back a long way and he's only made it to the top because he's the arsehole I know he is."

"Perhaps, but…"

"But nothing. The raw truth is often dangerous." Angelo looked anxious, struggling with the gravity of his predicament. "I'm just saying, be careful. You're treading on dangerous ground. Just remember, today's Holy See is the same institution that was once the Inquisition. They mercilessly tortured anyone who questioned their dogma. Don't get too brash because they'll knock you down so fast you won't even see it coming."

Angelo resented the reminder. "So what's kept you here so long?"

Comte indicated the sealed storage room behind. "I have full access to the archives. It helps me understand."

"But why do you bother? You don't believe in any of this, so I don't get it."

Comte's disfigured face warped into a bemused smile, "It's about those who keep knowledge for themselves. I resent that attitude, so I'm their bête noire, their black beast, ready to annoy the hell out of them."

Comte decided to satisfy Angelo's thirst by furthering his education with a confirmation.

"Don't get me wrong, I like what you told Lamech. You're more on the mark than you might think. Using your intellect is good progress."

Angelo felt his ego puff. Comte continued, "The first Christians never sought an organised religion. There was no retinue of priests, bishops, cardinals and Popes to act as intercessors between God and themselves. They believed in the ancient tradition which is now denounced as 'pagan'. They believed God could be accessed directly through inner experience. That's why what you said causes the Church trouble. Imagine telling the congregation that they don't need a priest because God can be found *within*."

Angelo's brow furrowed. He wanted assurance. "The original Christians thought that, did they?"

"You don't have to believe me. Believe Jesus in Luke 17, *The kingdom of God does not come visibly, nor will people say, here it is, or, there it is, for behold, the kingdom of God is within you.*"

"I know the passage. So what're you getting at?"

"Angelo, it means exactly what it says. What is 'within' is wisdom, feelings, emotions, perceptions, consciousness. Consciousness alone is the bridge to God. It's the whole point of religion. God is the end game to all inquiry. Of course, just knowing this doesn't help you cross the bridge. Only the individual can walk across. I'm proud of you my boy, you've started on the Path."

Angelo was still unsure. Understanding theology was how to reach God, surely. *But today, I spoke out against dogma. Maybe I am on the Path.*

Comte elaborated, "The Bible mentions a substance called 'manna' which sustained the Israelites during their escape from Egypt. It's a white powder." Angelo instantly recognised the biblical name. "There's evidence that it heightens perception by raising consciousness into higher realms. The Mesopotamians called it *she-manna* and the Egyptians called it *mfktz*. Perhaps this is how Moses 'spoke' with the Lord, and how the ancients had direct access to God."

Comte had fired the coals of Angelo's imagination. "Did you learn about this while you were away? From that woman you sent here?"

"Keisha has always been helpful. She's helped me connect a lot of dots. I've learned about a race of beings that existed thousands of years ago who achieved things which today we barely understand. It gives some credence to the code embedded in the stained glass windows.

"Keisha's been actively involved with translators who are studying the Pyramid Texts of Saqqara. It's a massive exercise. Hieroglyphs cover forty rectangular walls and twenty triangular gables, over four thousand columns of writing in all.

"Much of the text is considered pure mythology, but Keisha's connections are getting a different picture. One of the texts describes the King's journey after death to a place called the Field of Mfkzt, to the realm of existence beyond the physical world. It's also called the Dimension of the Blessed, or as Jesus might say – The Kingdom of Heaven."

"Are you referring to the use of manna?"

"They seem certain of it. Coincidentally, the substance was reported in *Scientific American* back in 1989. They described it as a monatomic superconductor. It's able to alter gravity, and therefore space-time. When ingested, consciousness is 'raised' to higher states beyond our current understanding. Amazingly, there's a slight weight reduction in the brain as part of our mind is transported to a different space-time reference. Consciousness is intensified, penetrating realms beyond our normal sensory perception.

"I told you about the Knights Templar and their retrieval of the Ark of the Covenant. The Ark contained a massive amount of the substance, making it a giant superconductor. A portal in effect."

Portal? Supersensible realms? Angelo was dismayed. It seemed Comte was being influenced by people with some exotic motives. This was just all too weird. But if Scientific American had reported this phenomenon, then maybe there was some truth to it.

"It seems like science fiction to me. I thought a life in the Church would give me peace, but since I've met you that's all changed."

"You started on the path all by yourself, my boy. The choice will always be yours. Only you can decide."

24

SHADOWS

THE PENTAGON, WASHINGTON DC

"Fuck!" Volker cut the cellphone connection with the stab of his thumb.

"They want to move now. They reckon our P2 friends have overstepped the mark. They're edgy and want to kill off the Baalbek incursion. Apparently our friends were clumsy with an elimination. Too public and messy. Good news is there's no apparent motive. At least that's the way we made it appear."

Goldstein was nonchalant. "They want us to put a lid on it do they?"

Majestic feared the inscriptions from the Baalbek crypt would be translated and leaked to the press, leading to a full-scale excavation. The truth of human genesis had to be suppressed. The world was not ready. The inevitable loss of political and economic control would undermine the New World Order objectives. Collapse of orthodox religion was unthinkable.

Truth had always been traded for comfort and in a world of power and privilege the elites would fight to the very end. Just as oil was used to galvanise the fiat currencies used in global exchange, so it was with ideas. Truth was always the first casualty. Simplistic religious dogma was the oil of the mind, manipulated by the few to control the many.

"Luckily they're all idiots out there," scoffed Goldstein. "If academics represent the pinnacle of societal thinking, it's little wonder your job is so much easier."

Ernst Volker wasn't so sure. "In this case, Aiden Keyes is a real maverick. He used his television series as tool to tell his peers where to get off and brazenly told his viewers that he would prove them wrong. If he figures out what he's uncovered, he's the type to yell from the rooftops."

"Didn't you tell me once that the Vatican dispenses with embarrassing disclosures by using the media to ridicule?"

"Not so sure this time. The Vatican's not as powerful as it used to be. Not like the old days when you could just torch the heretics in the town square. The public are more interested in image these days and Keyes has it all – good looks, popular public profile and rock solid support from his University, let alone the BBC. This latest excursion of his was even funded by them. They see him as the Carl Sagan of paleo-anthropology."

"Nothing a little accident couldn't solve."

"That's a no-go zone, I'm afraid. That's why P2 took out his assistant. Hopefully, he'll get the message."

"And if he doesn't."

"We do what's necessary, but you have to wonder how long we can hold them all off. Just think about it. In the nineteenth century, the world's best archaeologists said that Homer's City of Troy was pure myth, even though Homer said he had received the information from an ancient Egyptian priesthood. Only a few intellectual heretics insisted the story was real. Academics claimed Troy couldn't possibly exist, then Heinrich Schliemann discovered it in 1871, exactly where Homer had described. The same was said about the Minoan civilisation, until it too, was discovered by Schliemann. It's the Schliemanns of the world, and now the new breed like Keyes who make it difficult."

"I suppose. Look what they've come up with to attack the discovery of the so-called hobbit in Indonesia. The idea that they're not a new species of human and actually suffered a degenerative disease will keep the half-wit academics arguing for years."

"Probably. Majestic just want to keep the cattle from straying too far, that's all," said Volker sternly. "It's a pity P2 got involved. They should have stuck to what they do best."

Volker reflected on Majestic's major objective. "Majestic doesn't want a repeat of the Petrie incident. If people had understood the significance of that discovery, modern religion would have been wiped out. To think that Petrie discovered an ancient foundry in the Egyptian Temple of Mount Serabit, three thousand years after Moses, is explosive enough. Imagine the consequences if people understood what the Brotherhood produced there. Fortunately, people are still motivated by fear and greed. Anyway, it's all academic. The decision's been taken. We've been summoned, so let's just get it over with."

25

SACRED LIBRARY

———

DRESDEN, GERMANY

Light splashed into the dimly lit passage beneath Otto's house. The old man was nowhere in sight.

His voice crackled. "In here."

I stepped into a tiny square room where an old wooden table and one rustic chair stood beneath a single dusty globe. The table was heavy with tattered old books and manuscripts, their thick brown pages in various states of disrepair, some falling apart at the spine. Otto was in the shadows silently inspecting a bookshelf.

He turned with a puzzled expression. "Ever feel you don't fit into society?"

I knew the frail old man was eccentric, but I answered honestly. "The thought has crossed my mind."

"Well don't be too worried about it," he replied. "Those who seek the highest state are never worried."

Worried about what? I wondered. Worry was not a word I had in my vocabulary. "What's the point of worry? You live, you die, you do your best," I retorted.

"Is that right? Maybe that's why you're here then; to learn about your choices."

I had always hated psychoanalysis, especially when I was the subject. It was such a bore, so I changed the subject. "Where did you get all these works?"

"Many are copies from the Library of Alexandria."

I knew the old German was serious. "The one that was burned down nearly two thousand years ago?"

"Yes, that one. As you probably know, on the orders of a fanatical Christian Emperor, the place was obliterated in 391 AD. The curator knew the attack was coming and was able to save few things. Over the centuries they were copied, but all the originals are now lost."

"Thousands of texts were burned, weren't they?"

"Hundreds of thousands, Aiden. The greatest storehouse of historical and scientific knowledge – completely gone."

Otto explained how priceless works of art, and papyrus and parchment texts from ancient Egyptian, Arabian, Indian and Hebrew history were smashed and burned. The local Bishop had considered the place satanic because the texts contravened Church doctrine, so Emperor Theodosius employed the edicts of the Council of Nicaea, and organised an angry mob to destroy every relic and text that could be found. The event allowed a convenient rewriting of history.

Otto spoke with caution. "Since Babylonian times a small elite have spun an elaborate web of lies that have resulted in the dominant religions. A patriarchal priesthood has promulgated only the most literal concepts of doctrine."

"Patriarchal? Didn't the ancient world venerate the Goddess?"

"You're right, but the Divine Feminine, once held to be of equal standing with the masculine was strategically isolated. Jesus knew the folly of this isolation. His disciples Peter and Andrew however, clung to literal views and were confounded by the role

Mary Magdalene played in Jesus's life. They preferred the narrow scriptural interpretations that reflected chauvinism and ignorance, ideas that Jesus specifically warned against.

"There's a new force gathering Aiden, and the restoration of the Feminine principle is part of it."

Otto extracted a dilapidated book from his collection. "There are many other things...."

He stopped mid-sentence. A touch of sadness overcame the old man for the slightest moment as his silent contemplation wandered. My thoughts switched to Keisha, a modern day woman genuinely seeking esoteric understanding through her work.

I prompted, "You were saying."

"The numbers in my Order are small, but we are powerful and well connected." The old man examined me closely. I held my thoughts close. "The Order is a repository of arcane knowledge. Many are now ready to understand more."

Otto's scrutiny of my demeanour was annoying the hell out of me. He threw another curve-ball, a question I had never contemplated. He asked, "Do you think your birth, life and eventual death are a random accident of the universe?"

I was being challenged again and resented it. This old man was beginning to sound like Keisha and I much preferred her company to his. "I'm not sure I have an answer to that."

"Aiden, science says everything in the universe has a cause. In a sense, who we truly are has already chosen its path. The purpose of life is to understand the choices we've made, and more importantly, why we made them."

I thought for several moments. "If you're telling me life has a cause even before we're born, then I'd say you're wacko. You sound like one of those new age loonies."

"Understanding comes slowly," Otto sympathised. "Select monks have always practised a path of self-knowledge through contemplation, and in their meditations some have pushed memory back to when they first recalled the concept of 'I': the first experience of being separate to the physical world. This occurs around the age of three, but centuries ago, some took it much further than that. They attempted the recollection of events before childhood, a practise confirmed in this parchment. It's an old copy of the Egyptian Book of the Dead. Have you heard of it?"

"I have, but I don't know much about it."

"It's a baffling document, but it's also important. It describes the liberation of the 'Ka', sometimes referred to as the 'light body'."

The conversation was still bonkers – the light body for Christ's sake. What was next? *Crystals?* The old boy's marbles were clearly intact, but I was finding this diatribe tedious. It was late afternoon and I felt like a strong drink. I decided to humour him. "Care to elaborate?"

"There's an aspect of ourselves that survives death."

"I'm sure you mean well Otto, but it's all just fantasy. You're beginning to sound like Keisha Petersen."

"Really, I'm glad she took up my suggestions."

Otto approached the bookshelf and pulled out a very old looking, leather folio. Opening the tattered yellow pages he quietly quoted a passage. *"I stand before the masters who witnessed the genesis, who were the authors of their own forms, who walked the dark, circuitous passages of their own becoming."* He carefully rolled the page. *"I stand before the masters who witnessed the transformation of the body of a man into the body in spirit, who were witnesses to the resurrection when the corpse of Osiris entered the mountain and the soul of Osiris walked out shining – when he came forth from death."*

"That makes a little more sense than the resurrection of Jesus. At least Osiris rises in a spiritual body and not a physical body, but I still say it's a convenient cop-out."

"Thought so. Even the Church considers the concept a heresy.

So you have good company."

"The Church has nothing to do with my view. It's just that reincarnation has no scientific basis."

"So you may think, but you'd be wrong. Pharmaceutical drugs were used in the MK-Ultra programme undertaken by the Americans during the 1950s. They wanted to understand the nature of mind, and to probe pre-existence using hypnotic regression techniques."

"I've heard something about those experiments. It was pretty fiendish stuff apparently."

"Evil I'd say. But my interest stems from the misunderstanding by scientists about the separate nature of the physical and conscious realms. True initiates of the practise study with rigorous mental inquiry. Jesus even confirmed that Truth was hidden. I think he said something like, 'To you, the mystery of the kingdom of God has been given. But to those who are on the outside, all things are done in parables; so that they may indeed see but not perceive, and they may indeed hear but not understand.'"

I couldn't for the life of me figure out what this was all about. "Otto, perhaps you can explain something here. I get an obscure phone call and I'm told my life is in danger and to seek you out. I fly halfway round the world and you tell me you belong to some obscure organisation having a heritage that pre-dates the Egyptians. I find that comment hard to believe. Then you say I'm here to learn. And now you're telling me about parables. I mean, cut the crap. What's the real reason you called me here. I didn't come for a history lesson, and I'm just about to call it a day."

Otto's eyes softened. He knew it was time for a straight answer.

"Knowledge in the wrong hands is a dangerous thing. You're here because I needed to assess your intentions."

"Intentions about what?"

"Your discovery. The truth of what you may have found needs to be revealed, but the truth threatens the status quo like never before."

I had lost patience. "What truth? Give me an answer for fuck sake, or I walk right now."

"We think your discovery confirms the truth behind mankind's creation. And if it does, there are forces that will try to stop you. Your profile will add valuable credibility to the discovery, but you must first understand it."

I was aghast. "You know the meaning of my discovery?"

"The answer to that is 'maybe'. You've sought out Dr Keisha Petersen. Work with her, she is the best mind in her field. We're relying on her to help you unravel this thing. As for you, be true to your goal. I'm convinced your cause is honourable."

"If you know what the secret of the crypt is, I'd like you to tell me."

"If I knew, I would. All I can say is that you need to become more conscious. Once in the sacred flow things just happen. It's the same for everybody everywhere."

"What do you mean?"

"Let's leave it at that for today Aiden. You must be tired after your long flight. Come tomorrow at ten. I'll gather some documents that will give you a background to what I hope Dr Petersen will find."

The afternoon sun struggled to rid the air of a light misty rain. The wispy moisture refreshed me from the gloomy confines of Otto's basement library. Thoughts of conspiracy and Otto's unknown Order had me intrigued. Naturally I would continue my search. The only problem was I didn't know what I was looking for.

26

DARKNESS OF EVIL

APOSTOLIC PENITENTIARY, VATICAN CITY

Comte remained steadfast. "Monastic orders in the Far East have accessed states of mind we can barely conceive. Even the Essenes referred to it in their Manual of Discipline. Something along the lines of '…*the Revelation of the Mysteries, which has been kept in silence through all time eternal, are now manifested.'*"

Angelo almost wanted it not to be true. "I don't know Comte, it's hard to accept."

Comte's jaw tightened. "So is Higgs-boson theory, but that doesn't make it wrong. Just because enlightenment can't be physically proven it doesn't mean it doesn't exist. Do you believe in good and evil Angelo?"

"I'm not sure anymore. I told Lamech I didn't believe Satan embodied original sin."

Comte nodded with satisfaction, "…*and by their deeds you shall know them*, Angelo. Do they preach truth? Do they reject mindless fundamentalism? Are they opposed to violence? Do they foster wisdom? Most religions emphasise blind faith, demanding we give up intellect. It's intellect that separates man from the animal kingdom.

That's how you challenged Lamech today. You used your intellect. God gave you a brain to use, something ignored by the Lamech's of the world. The Enlightened Ones of the past and present reject blind faith. They believe in direct access to the creative principle without the need for an ecclesiastical intercessor. They evolve to know the higher realm directly."

"So where does Jesus Christ fit in with all this?"

Comte knew an explanation was necessary. It was time to reveal a hidden message. "Do you understand the difference between Jesus and Christ?"

"What difference. Jesus is Christ?"

"Not exactly," Comte replied emphatically. "There's a distinct difference between 'Jesus' and 'Christ'. In the beginning of his story he was known simply as Jesus, or Jesus of Nazareth, but during his baptism something remarkable happened. Matthew 3:16 says: *And Jesus, when he was baptised, went up straight away out of the water: and lo, the heavens were open to him, and he saw the spirit of God descending like a dove, and lighting upon him.*'

"Jesus saw the spirit of God descend and light upon him, Angelo. He saw it. The next verse says, *And lo a voice from heaven, saying, this is my beloved Son, in whom I am well pleased.*'

"Only when the spirit of God descended did the voice say 'this is my beloved son'. The spirit that descended is the beloved son. Jesus heard the voice say it. That spirit is Christ. Christ is the beloved son and Christ descended, alighting upon Jesus the man. Take particular notice Angelo that only after this event was Jesus known as *Christ*."

"I've never actually thought about it like that before."

"Jesus was human and born of woman, but Christ is spirit and born of God. During the baptism, Jesus the man was infused with the 'Christ Being'. The Christ is the Logos of Consciousness that assists humanity's evolution. For the few who understood his message, and there is doubt as to whether all twelve disciples truly did, he unlocked the hidden doctrines of the distant past, re-establishing the Law of the Ancients. Something the Holy Church still rejects."

The two men sensed the conversation had run its course. Angelo wanted some space and bid Comte goodnight. The implications of Comte's message required contemplation.

Angelo decided to take a solitary walk into the heart of Rome, clearing his thoughts in the warm night air. It was only a matter of time before Comte left the Vatican and he didn't know how he would cope in a world he no longer understood.

Angelo passed St Peter's Square and entered the Borgo Santo Spirito. He headed for the Tiber, happy to stroll along the tree-lined walk-way skirting the river. The warm night air invigorated him as he tried to make some sense of his life. Deep in thought and oblivious to the footfalls coming up behind, he was cravenly struck down.

…Thump! Crack!

Three masked assailants attacked. Wooden batons came down hard battering his athletic frame. Angelo faced the savage blows. He kicked and flayed in defence, but the powerful blows continued to rain down, felling him like a tree. He tried to cover his face in protection, but kicks to his head and body pierced his defence. An ugly cut opened above his eye and through the blood soaked dark he watched the cowards run.

It ended as quickly as it had begun. He was pulverised, unable to move. Blood had splashed the pavement and pooled against his face. His mind faded into unconsciousness.

It was a dream, a flashback maybe? No, that nightmare ended years ago. This beating was different. I always did as I was told. Why did I wet the bed? I remember my father. Why that evil school? I only ever saw him at Christmas. Why can't I remember my mother? I never remembered her. Why did she leave?

"Never trust beautiful women," father would say. "Never trust them." I loved him, so why did he forsake me? I can feel the beatings. I complied and the agony stopped. Yes, the agony stopped. I survived. I remember now. It's simple. Comply and the agony stops.

Angelo curled into a bloody ball like a damaged foetus, steeling himself from the pain.

27

OMINOUS FOREBODING

DRESDEN, GERMANY

I strolled the Outer Neustadt, an area populated by the more chic examples of Dresden culture. The assortment of students reminded me of my undergraduate days when alternative was the way to dress and be seen. I'm sure the punk teenagers and hip-hop kids thought I was out of my league, but I didn't care, I just needed the air and some space away from my hotel. Otto's warning about my safety was reason enough.

I entered a retro café and checked my iPhone for email. Sure enough I had a message from Keisha.

> Aiden,
>
> Extremely interesting breakthrough. LITAN has made a defini-tive match on quite a few characters. The program managed an interpolation between ancient Akkadian and a proto-Sumerian dialect. The anthropological origin of the language is unknown, but I have already translated some tracts of wording.
>
> Remember what I said about the *Elohim*. This new language has a word that corresponds with the word *Annunaki*, which in

Sumerian cuneiform translates as 'Heaven came to Earth'. The *Annunaki* have no known orthodox anthropological or sociological genesis, but I feel these Annunaki are linked with a number of groups such as the *Nephilim*. Remember reading Genesis 6:1-4 with me? And remember me mentioning Eli Rosen's works?

The connection with the Annunaki is extremely interesting. I think we are onto something. Will keep you posted.

I received your message about leaving Canberra at short notice. Looking forward to seeing you soon. My turn for drinks remember.

Regards, Keisha.

END OF MESSAGE.

Interesting. The discovery appeared to confirm the existence of the mysterious Annunaki. An elixir of prejudice and personal bias had clouded my views on the Bible and no doubt my understanding. Perhaps the passage in the Book of Genesis was a threshold test about human genesis. If I could understand the passage, maybe I could penetrate the meaning of the Bible even further.

I googled the more alternative sites relating to the Bible. I discovered that the earliest known Bible is dated from the fifth century with the King James Version being five linguistic translations removed.

Apparently, the word 'Nephilim' became to be regarded as the angels who had morally fallen and been 'cast down' by the Almighty. The Church imparted a sinister, immoral character to these 'fallen angels', possibly for their own strategic reasons.

In fact, I discovered 'Nephilim' comes from the root word NFL, which simply means *'to come down'* or *'to descend'*. They were portrayed as non-physical beings or spirits, but if they bred with the daughters of men then this was nonsense.

I discovered a reference in the book 'Antiquity of the Jews' by the famous first century Jewish historian, Flavius Josephus. He wrote: *'Many angels of God accompanied with women, and begat sons that became unjust...on account of the confidence they had in their own strength'.*

Surfing cyberspace resulted in some controversial material. I wondered what LITAN had to say. After typing the web address, an interface appeared prompting me for the password Keisha had provided. Entering the configuration, I was acknowledged.

> User: 501214.
>
> Welcome Aiden.
>
> Message from <Keisha Petersen>
>
> Been expecting you. Will talk soon.
>
> Take special care,
>
> Keisha.

I keyed >**Bible History**< and an extensive list of sub-topics was presented. It was becoming clear that orthodox Christianity had been contrived for political motives.

I learnt that in 1415, one of the Avignon popes, Benedict XIII, known as an anti-pope by Rome, ordered the destruction of all copies of the Latin treatise Mar Yesu and later ordered the destruction of the Book of Elxai. The Rabbinic fraternity had great reverence for these manuscripts as they were the original records reporting the life of Rabbi Jesus. It appears Benedict did not approve of the references to Him.

Later in the 15th century, Pope Alexander VI ordered all copies of the Talmud destroyed, while the Council of the Inquisition required the burning and destruction of as many Jewish writings as possible. Over 6,000 volumes were destroyed at Salamanca alone.

And again in 1550, Cardinal Caraffa procured a Papal Bull from the Pope disallowing priests to read the Talmud because it contained, '*...hostile stories about Jesus Christ*'.

Why had the Church been so touchy? After all, Jesus was a Jew and nobody had been more meticulous at recording the ancient writings than the Jews. Had the Church tried to obscure the true story of this man?

There were even more shocking examples. According to LITAN, in 1554, a converted Jew, Solomon Romano burned thousands of Hebrew scrolls, and in 1559 every Hebrew book in Prague was confiscated. Ancient copies of the Old Testament and the original hand-written texts were consigned to the flames.

No different from the book burnings carried out by the Nazis in 1933, I thought. *What were they trying to conceal?* The crimes and the attempts to rewrite history went deeper than I had ever suspected.

Rewriting Christian history was easy. The populous struggled for a living and were mostly unable to read or write, while the ecclesiastical classes of priests, bishops and cardinals were educated and spoke Latin. They held the impoverished in their hands.

"Schließende Zeit!" the young attendant shouted, slowly scraping a greasy curtain of pitch black hair away from his eyes and tucking it behind his heavily studded ear. The café was deserted. I'd been too engrossed in research to notice it was closing time.

───── ✺ ─────

Peaceful sleep was elusive. As I drifted out of waking consciousness, the vision of the glowing Wheel returned.

I stepped forward as the huge apparatus slowly rotated, coloured neon lights illuminating the darkness of night. A corona of colour captivated my attention. Although alone, I sensed I was being observed. For some reason beyond my comprehension, I was being drawn to this place. *What was I meant to see?*

The scene changed. The veil of darkness receded and twilight broke in an orange glare over the horizon revealing a vast barren plain. The Wheel had vanished. In its place was a large, very ancient stone gate. I walked closer...

Sunlight lanced the gap in the heavy window drapes. I woke with a start. I was going to be very late.

I arrived at Otto's at 10:40am, ready to apologise for my delay. I darted up the short overgrown path and knocked.

Silence.

I knocked again and waited. Nothing.

Finally, I tried the handle and the door groaned open.

A foul smell of smoke hung in the hazy air. I noticed smoke swirling from the hallway. I raced to the tiny room that concealed the basement entrance. Thin veils of yellow-grey wafted through the floor hatch. Something was very wrong. I punched the password into the keypad. The floor hummed open.

Disguised behind the mustard smoke, hungry tendrils of orange flame suddenly howled in the updraught. The choking fire gasped for life-giving oxygen. In a flash of heat and flame, my face was almost scorched as I lurched backward. If Otto was down there, he was surely incinerated. Nothing could have survived the inferno.

I quickly stabbed the keypad to quell the flames. The sliding floor spliced the outburst as it buzzed back into its locked position. Then I noticed something disturbing. Wet splotches of red. Small drips became dribbles, and then a sordid broken stream. The bloody trail led toward the kitchen and then outside into a large overgrown courtyard. My stomach clenched. I followed the trail with morbid curiosity.

And then I saw it, the hideous and sickening sight of a heavily mutilated body. It was hanging by its feet like a fresh slaughterhouse carcass. The head had been bludgeoned and the torso had been slit from the lower abdomen to the chest. Intestines and entrails hung from the open cavity. The heart had been hacked out and lay beneath the corpse, stabbed into the ground with a utility knife. The death had been executed by a butcher, a depraved amateur. Flies were already feeding on the carcass.

The sadistic mutilation was all that remained of an old man, decades of life desecrated by some vile, sub-human lowlife.

The slaughter was fresh, very fresh, blood still dripping from the entrails into a congealing pool below. Panic surged through me. *What if the killer was still here?* I was unable to hold back. Remnants of my meagre breakfast splashed at my feet. Primal instinct suddenly took hold. I rushed to the front door and with measured self-control calmly walked into the street.

My mind was infused with the monstrous image of the sickening depravity. *What kind of psychopath was capable of this?* My nervous gait turned into a run.

A kilometre or two later, I slumped onto a park bench to catch my breath. *Who? Why? Why Otto?* Then a wicked thought. *Had I been set up?* Cold dread coursed through my veins. I would be the number one suspect surely. My fingerprints were everywhere; even my DNA announced itself from my spewed breakfast. Over and over, a squall of questions screamed. *Who would commit such savagery?*

Otto said he was visited by the intelligence service. *Was he a threat to them?* Surely not. Perhaps it was his knowledge of my discovery at Baalbek. First Jai, now Otto. Then the old man's words screamed at me. *"If your photographs contain what we think they do, they'll stop at nothing to destroy the knowledge. They'll destroy you too, make no mistake."*

Just like Canberra, another threat. First Jai, now Otto. I had to get out and get out quick. I needed a safe haven to think and make sense of what was happening. Within the hour, I had checked out from the Kempinski and was in the airport lounge. There was a flight to Zurich in seventy minutes. I hungrily drained a double scotch and then another.

Zurich would give me the chance to rendezvous with an old friend. Mac and I had formed a special bond during our university days when we shared the experience of undergraduate youth. There was no person I trusted more.

These days Mac lived in the solitude of the Swiss Alps detached from the maddening banality of common life. He was a remarkable man and, although I hadn't seen him for about three years, I knew he would provide sanctuary.

Mac completed his secondary schooling at fifteen, and proceeded to Cambridge to study pure mathematics with a major in particle physics. After gaining his PhD, he developed his own research company and patented some sort of data-compression technique. The U.S. military bought the patent in 2002 for an undisclosed sum and Mac dropped out to live as a recluse. He spent the first two years with Buddhist monks in Nepal and subsequently retired to his mountain hideaway doing whatever he does these days. I knew the prodigious intellect of my friend would help me sort out the madness of the last few days.

Mac was probably the most complex person I knew. He defied any sort of psychological categorisation. Some would say he was borderline pathological. But that's said of many geniuses, especially those who search for their personal truth, no matter what the cost. Mac regarded society with a good degree of ambivalence and cynicism. In the past, he had referred to society as *'animals squabbling over finite resources'.* This opinion typified his relationship with people in general and society in particular. His attitude to academics was even more scathing, believing them to be *'tenured prostitutes reinforcing the status quo'.* This view developed when he briefly held an Associate Professorship at Stanford. He believed his research was being compromised by buffoons, so he left and formed his own company. The friction he suffered with the rest of the world manifested into a drinking problem. Perhaps the solitude of the mountains was helping him control this excess.

I wondered whether he had mellowed since I last saw him, whether he had lost his cynicism and contempt for mere mortals. Had he lost his dark and irreverent sense of humour, and his complete disdain for all forms of authority? Never.

Amid all the unfolding mayhem of the past few days, I looked forward to seeing the crazy bastard again.

28

MAJESTIC

WEST VIRGINIA, UNITED STATES

Ernst Volker gave a warning. "I know you hate the prick, so do I, but just toe the line OK. Majestic treats the CIA like shit these days, but hey, I have to take my orders from them so take my lead."

"I should release some dirt on the fuckers and get their funding cut," grumbled Goldstein. "Why I have to clean up after them I'll never know."

'Majestic funds itself, so if you want to end up dead, go right ahead. Just relax will you?"

"Fuck 'em."

Ariel Goldstein hated the methods employed by Majestic. He was CIA born and bred, used to the more subtle methods employed by his agency. He was a trained killer and considered his profession an art-form where he executed his orders in a way that attracted minimal attention.

Majestic is the most elite covert operation in the world with a security classification thirteen levels above the president. Enforcing the geo-political and socio-economic game plan devised since the formation of the infamous Club of Rome was paramount. Presidents come and go according to the prevailing electoral winds and it is never wise to divulge the entire global strategic plan to a mere politician. The ordinary citizen required protection and control.

Majestic was formed to execute these specific objectives, and they acted wherever and whenever they decided, directing the subordinate National Reconnaissance Office. Veles Kane was the Intelligence Director of Global Studies, a deliberately loose title designed to thwart any opposition to his real purpose. He was responsible for containing those discoveries that might undermine the status quo. Populist religion regardless of its persuasion is a key pillar to this objective. Majestic had carefully nurtured overt fundamentalism into a strong, subversive force within world affairs. It served their cause perfectly. Problem-Reaction-Solution was the modus operandi used to template global hegemony.

Majestic also nurtured and protected their inside men, funding them and smoothing their path. Various evangelical Christians, a spattering of radical Muslim clerics and right-wing Jewish rabbis served Majestic well, but the jewel in the crown was their man within the Holy See. They were all regarded as 'mindless, but infinitely useful'.

Volker knew the game. He had honed his skills to advance his career within Majestic, working with Kane closely over recent years. He didn't like the man, but had learned to respect him. Kane never took prisoners. You either performed or disappeared. Volker had learned to keep his thoughts to himself.

Examining and researching unexplained artefacts still thrilled Volker, but in recent times the bar had been raised. He was often sickened by Kane's methods. Thankfully, he was never involved in the killing; he wasn't cut out for it. As he drove the black SUV toward the guarded checkpoint, he glanced across at Goldstein.

"Just take it easy Ariel. You've never met the man so be open-minded."

"Open-minded for fuck sake, that bastard ordered the old boy disembowelled. I've never worked with such a mess. They reckon P2 was clumsy. The only thing decent about the whole thing was the timing. Keyes arrived at the house late, but he couldn't get out of there quick enough. White as a sheet, dumb son-of-a-bitch. Never knew what hit him."

"Let's hope he disappears for a while. If his breach in Baalbek doesn't get out, then you've solved the problem."

Goldstein was smart enough not to ask what the breach was all about. What he didn't know couldn't be used against him. He drew deep on his cigarette, blowing the smoke though his nostrils.

"So why does he want to see us. I'm happy dealing with you and you alone. I can do without meeting the bastard. Why're we meeting him?"

Volker had only received sketchy details. "Don't know. Something to do with an artefact."

"Another one? Haven't they collected heaps of them since '47, what makes this one so special? Christ, how much of that crap have they got stored at Edward Airforce Base and the Smithsonian?"

"All I know is they've found some type of device in Western Tibet. They've also captured the device's guardian, a monk of some kind. They're trying to get him to show how it's used. Apparently the device emits some sort of Tesla field effect."

Volker knew something was up. Goldstein had never actually met any Majestic personnel, so Volker suspected they were being assigned to something big.

Their drive through the Appalachian Mountains in McDowell County, West Virginia was depressing, despite the rugged beauty of the place. Twenty years or more of coal mine closures and large job losses had turned the area into an economic wasteland. With the highest poverty rates, lowest education levels and biggest drug problems anywhere outside the largest cities, a disused mine of a now defunct mining operation offered the perfect cover for Veles Kane's clandestine operations from within the United States. The centre housed a Cray II supercomputer that was linked to CIA, NSA, FBI, MI6, Mossad, Interpol and many others. Majestic's hardware is equivalent to the Pentagon.

A security compound protected the mine site. It appeared like all the others, rusted dilapidated out-buildings surrounded by a high fence and signed with 'Keep Out' and 'Dangerous Mine Site' warnings. A security camera attached to one of the buildings zoomed in on the occupants of the SUV. Facial recognition and infra-red signatures confirmed their clearance.

The security gate slid open. Volker drove to a dilapidated brick edifice not visible from the road where two armed militia approached. They checked the men's security papers and searched the vehicle. Volker was given approval to drive further, down a secluded valley road that eventually led to an ominous non-descript building built into the face of the mountain.

Volker eased the SUV into the new checkpoint for the next security procedure. A large roller door raised in front of them, exposing an interior space the size of a large aircraft hangar. Several guards surrounded the perimeter as a red security light flashed. Volker was motioned forward into the huge expanse and parked near a cluster of offices.

Veles Kane approached. He was not as Goldstein had imagined. The man was of medium stature, but held himself tall with shoulders back and head high. His gait was as a light as a dancer. His Italian shoes were fashioned from expensive leather and shone like a mirror. Dressed in an Armani suit with white business shirt and classically designed grey tie, he looked more like a successful movie producer ready to sign off a new contract. His hair was dyed black and neatly groomed. Goldstein wondered about the man's sexuality.

"Morning Ernst. Ariel Goldstein, pleased to meet you at last." Kane held out his hand and Ariel Goldstein took it with an iron grip. Kane was the first to unclench confirming to Goldstein that the man had seen no action. Kane exchanged a few pleasantries with Volker and led them to a briefing room.

Kane announced the reason for the men's summons. He slid an envelope slowly across the table. "It's official now Ariel; you're attached to Majestic. These papers will give you your new history. There's now no record of your career with the CIA. Every time I have required your services, they've tried to stick their nose into our operations. I can't trust those slow-witted flatfoots anymore, so now you're with us."

Goldstein heart sank. He felt like strangling the little shirt tosser. He shot a glance at Volker. He read his partner's equal surprise and chose to take his advice. He remained silent.

"It's become necessary gentlemen for a new cell to be created directly under my control. Ernst, I want you to head it up. Ariel will be at your disposal. I've been prompted into action because of the stupidity of P2, so we're taking full control of operations. We made a deal with the Vatican back in 1954 and they haven't strictly adhered to it. Their intelligence service has overstepped the mark for the last time. We can do without foreign agencies getting involved. Both of you will need to have a full understanding of what we are dealing with. You will be at my disposal for intensive briefing over the next day or two. Any questions?"

There were none. Goldstein wanted to instantly reject the proposal, but that was not an option. It was obvious his superiors at the CIA had no choice and were required to sanction his transfer. It was more than an order. The bitter taste in his mouth was sweetened by the knowledge that he would be working with Volker.

Volker was quietly pleased. It would give him an authority

he welcomed and it would allow him to work more closely with Goldstein. As much as Goldstein was a cold-blooded killer, he respected the professionalism of the man.

Kane proceeded to give Goldstein a standard briefing of Majestic objectives, explaining how research commenced by the Third Reich had continued in the U.S. after the war with the formation of the OSS, the Office of Special Services. The detail of the information blew Goldstein away. It was heady stuff.

Kane explained how NASA had been chartered to progress rocketry; the CIA charter was to progress intelligence gathering and to exercise covert political influence, and Majestic were commissioned to investigate, categorise and cover-up anything that might challenge the 'orthodox view' of the world. Majestic's involvement in close encounters of unidentified aerial craft was well documented in the strategic ruse code named Project Blue Book. By virtue of Majestic's statutory powers, the organisation had become involved in every aspect of unexplained phenomenon. They also had a mandate to recover 'anomalous artefacts' that were discovered anywhere in the world. Majestic, in conjunction with the subordinate National Reconnaissance Office, were in and out of a region before a host government had even identified an issue. Majestic's satellite technology was two generations ahead of any sovereign nation, including Russia and China.

Prior to their official formation, a handful of celebrated discoveries had leaked into the public domain. Among them were the giant stone balls found in Costa Rica in 1940. The perfectly spherical manmade objects that weighed up to 16 tonnes were cut with industrial laser accuracy. How such precision was achieved by the pre-Columbian cultures that made them without sophisticated cutting technology still needed explanation. In 1898, a small Egyptian wooden artefact was found at Saqqara that looked similar to a model aeroplane. It was aerodynamically designed and could actually glide. And some years later, in Central America, a thousand year old object had been found that could be considered a replica of a modern delta-wing aircraft.

Majestic had catalogued hundreds of these artefacts, but perhaps one of the most problematic was the Great Pyramid of Giza. Majestic ensured that the incredible mathematical and astronomical knowledge imbued in the structure never received any credibility in academic circles. Rogue researchers were subject to funding cuts, character assassination or even physical harm if they published their research. But of course, in recent years a plethora of theories had been espoused, with a multitude of television specials, but nothing truly captured the public's imagination. Majestic had been successful in manipulating how the information was delivered. On the U.S. networks, truth was successfully cloaked by a 24-7 compliant media, designed to bind the masses to their basic instinctual and social urges. Stupefaction through corporate controlled news and mind-numbing reality TV entertainment was a stated policy. Combined with the ceaseless activity of modern society to maintain perpetual debt, ideas and discoveries that could release humankind from suffering and ignorance was successfully kept under wraps.

Kane was quite candid with his dialogue. His now ex-CIA pupil was listening with interest. It signified to Volker that something decisive was about to be divulged.

Kane explained how the elite of the Third Reich understood the significance of these 'anomalies'. As a poor Viennese artist, Adolf Hitler had spent a great deal of time in the city's libraries. The grinding poverty of his vocation and the freezing Austrian winters provided a compelling invitation to indulge in reading some of the most obscure books in Europe. Interest in great ancient civilisations was once commonplace among the educated classes of Europe and as Hitler became aware of such things, he was determined to seize absolute power and regain the ancient knowledge.

After the rise of National Socialism, Hitler formed a faction within the SS to survey the lands of the races he believed were descended from an advanced civilisation destroyed long ago in a cataclysm, with the Great Pyramids an enduring legacy of this past civilisation. During this time, the Third Reich attempted to decipher the ancient texts, recovering significant artefacts wherever possible. Untold millions of reichsmarks were spent in trying to decipher the complex knowledge of the Tibetan llamas. After the war, the true motivation for this research was then deliberately suppressed during the Nuremberg trials. The Office of Special Services along with its later instrumentality, the CIA, classified much of it as 'Above Top Secret'.

Majestic recovered nearly all of the knowledge gained by the German Esoteric Bureau during the war and with the latest technology, and decades of additional research, they now held an unrivalled repository of esoteric historical and future-science knowledge.

Majestic was well aware of the hidden events during and after the war. The German army had amassed the necessary hardware in Antarctica in preparation for their survival. The Parisian newspaper Le Monde had even carried articles on the Antarctic hideaway, information that is now security classified.

Secret unconfirmed reports indicated that in the late afternoon of the 30th April 1945, a Messerschmitt 332 departed for Norway with Hitler on board. A fleet of U-boats sailed from Bergen with gold and supplies, together with Martin Boermann and sisters, Gretel and Eva Braun. Recent forensic efforts gave weight to these reports. It was suggested that for propaganda reasons, the Russians had deliberately faked the burned bodies at Hitler's bunker. Recent research on the charred remains indicates a deviation from the bonafide dental records.

Not generally known to the public, the might of the U.S.

Navy subsequently attempted to destroy the German presence in Antarctica. Unfortunately for the Allies, even more formidable forces had long taken an interest in the region.

29

REVIVAL

VATICAN CITY

Angelo had survived with split eyebrow and lip. Gashed cheek, bruised neck and shoulder. Cracked ribs. Overall, he'd been lucky, his kidneys were swollen, but the prognosis was good. He was young and fit, and would mend.

His flashback into the world of nightmare was once again erased from his memory. The flashback was intended, it was part of the process. He was a valuable asset who had now been manipulated into action.

Angelo thought of Keisha's warning and then Comte's. *Who were his attackers? Why?* He wondered whether it was a random mugging or something far more insidious. Angelo recalled Lamech storming out of the auditorium, but surely even he wasn't capable of organising such despicable cowardice. Another contender was the frog-eyed cleric. Comte had told him to be careful and claimed the Church had methods to veneer such acts, but Angelo had his doubts. It made no sense.

Angelo slept with fitful dreams, wrenching hidden, sordid memories from an obscured past. Dreams of beatings, abuse, deprivation and bed-wetting. During the night, his subconscious was dragged through hell, only coming out to shine in the light of day. When awake, he remembered a previous life of mental inquiry and reverence for the wonder of God. He had sought his spiritual home within the Church, and had received his wish, but since his savage beating he struggled with a dreamlike past that veiled a tragic secret. Somewhere beyond his waking consciousness was a horror seeking expression. *Surely, he thought, it was all just a dream.*

He yearned for Comte, the only person he could trust. He had developed a heroic appreciation for him. Comte's resolve to overcome his afflictions despite the rejection by his peers was to be admired.

More and more, he realised that Comte was a lone beacon of strength in the stormy waters of resistance against pious religious deceit. Only now with his injuries, Angelo understood the unremitting agony of a profound disability. He needed Comte's wise council.

Angelo returned to work immediately. His body was damaged, but he was determined to show his contemporaries that he suffered no fear. He wanted to know whether the investigation into his beating had revealed the perpetrators. There had been little progress.

Everything Angelo had believed was steadily eroding. First it was Comte and now it was a cowardly attack. Angelo thought His Eminence Cardinal Valla might show some sympathy, but it was just business as usual. Perhaps Comte's enmity toward the Cardinal was duly justified. He certainly seemed heartless.

Valla maintained his eternal aloofness and his ability to tap anger at will. Angelo did, however, detect a subtle change in his manner. He carried an air of automation and remoteness, an implacable strangeness. Perplexed, Angelo silently wondered whether his perception had been warped by his recent trauma, impairing his youthful judgement.

Late that afternoon the Cardinal summoned him. Angelo was

issued the usual instructions. His speech to the Curia needed to be copied and distributed. Angelo was handed a bundle of papers for processing and the Cardinal droned in his usual fashion.

Angelo took the opportunity to speak. "Your Eminence, may I have a word?"

"Make it quick."

"Your Eminence, I feel that much of what I hold dear is being challenged. I didn't deserve what happened."

"You may think that is true, but God has ways of testing us. You would do well to remember it. Now do as I ask."

The reply rang hollow and Angelo prepared to speak again. He was cut short. It was the usual outburst of ill-temper, but this time flavoured with manic ranting. Something about Jesuits and their damned telescope. Something about heresy. Something about bringing the mongrels to heal.

Angelo's thoughts strayed to Comte's claim about Valla. Did this man who always held an inner fury, this pillar of Church authority dressed in fine ecclesiastical splendour know anything about Comte's revelations? And if he did, did he care? The mere thought of Comte's subversive activities from the bowels of the Vatican, right under the nose of Valla, gave Angelo a thrill that coursed the length of his spine.

Valla paused, preparing for his next outburst. This time the Vesuvian tirade was about questioning authority. Angelo seized the innuendo. Perhaps it was a warning toward him. His averted gaze drifted upward to take a cursory hold of the Cardinal's glare. He detected something quite disturbing. Reptilian eyes burned back at him. Valla's familiar guise had all but disappeared, replaced by a gaunt caricature of his former self. Something grey like a dark auric shroud. Angelo blinked, and instantly the vision disappeared.

The inferno of abuse slowly dampened. Angelo quickly gave his leave. He needed to talk to Comte.

30

OLD FRIENDS

———————

ZURICH, SWITZERLAND

"Aiden, you old bastard!" It was the familiar voice, the trademark smirk, the usual form of greeting – a hug and slap on the back.

"How you doing Mac?" He looked great. Slick bastard.

"Better than you that's for sure. You look like shit. Come on there's three years to catch up on, so let's get a drink. I haven't had one since breakfast."

With Mac there was never a clear line between reality and fiction, and I was never sure when he was joking. This time he wasn't. Without any thought of leaving the airport, we headed straight to the bar.

Mac hated small talk, so I gave him a quick synopsis of the last few days, ending with Otto's murder. Nothing fazed him. Mac was always a good listener, a prerequisite for a prodigious intellect. After downing a couple of Löwenbräus, he broke off my story.

"Time for a drive. Tell me more later."

Mac led the way to the car park. The day was set with a deep blue sky, punctuated by the occasional wave of strato-cumulus. I recognised his vehicle immediately. It was the representation of his personality.

"It's a Ford GT40 replica, better than the real thing. Supercharged 351 cubic inch boss engine made in the good ol' USA – will trounce a 430 Modena no problem."

I had no idea what he was talking about and as usual, he was visibly enjoying my trepidation.

The four-point harness into which I was now strapped suggested power, function and ruthless efficiency. Mac depressed the ignition and the engine fired with a voluminous rumble. The car shuddered, as the cabin was swallowed by the growl of its ludicrous supercharged V8.

Once away from heavy traffic, he punched the accelerator with a brutal shove, the engine bellowing with metallic thunder. I uttered a few complementary expletives as Mac grunted the vehicle through its gears.

Along the narrow mountainous roads, the towering conifers whipped past my door, the branches hanging low over the road. The further we went the faster Mac drove. His speed was not designed to impress, it helped him breathe and to stay alive. Living on the edge had always sustained him.

Mac informed me that the GT40 was designed to win races against Ferrari. Minor issues such as speed around corners had only nominal significance. Steep crests were treated with contempt. The engine blasted us along the winding roads like a homing missile. My head pressed into my headrest whenever Mac accelerated, the exhaust's deep aural bass heralding our approach.

For me, it was thirty minutes of gut wrenching, adrenalin fuelled horror, but for Mac it was a pleasant Sunday outing. It might have been exhilarating, but I was happy to arrive at Mac's residence in one piece. I always hated the thrill of carnival rides and this was no different.

Mac's home was a classic architectural statement. It reflected his complex persona, a combination of functional modern and classical renaissance. It was a mixture of unforgettable Bauhaus design wrapped in old world Bavarian charm, infused with traces of modernity. Touches of brushed aluminium, dark hardwood and stone were nestled against the shade of a thick, gently swaying alpine forest. The house was the perfect metaphor for Mac's incongruous personality.

If the outside looked pastiche, the opposite was true of the interior. Simplicity, technology and elegant function dominated. As expected, there were the usual gadgets. Dominating the large living area were five enormous glass windows overlooking a panoramic view of the mountains, still dusted with remnants of late winter snow. The room proudly displayed a magnificent pair of Acapella Excalibur speakers with a state of the art music system aimed to blow the mind. I threw down my bag and sunk into the soft white leather lounge. Mac was quick to pour some drinks.

I needed his prodigious intellect to start delivering some answers. "I could really do with some advice about what's been happening over the last few days. My questions will seem a bit stupid though."

"There are no stupid questions," he said with his usual smirk, "only stupid answers. Just hit me with the detail."

I rambled for over an hour. Mac drank and listened, only interrupting for the occasional point of clarification and to top up his glass. I told him about the location of my find, how I had told no-one, yet the old man Otto knew it was Baalbek. I divulged as much as I could remember about his rantings and of Keisha's theories. He nodded every now and then, and after I had exhausted the conversation, he sat in quiet contemplation.

Finally, he blurted a comment. "You seem surprised by all this."

"Of course I'm bloody surprised! Jai and Otto murdered. For what? Some bullshit about Elohim in the Bible, secret societies, even Hitler for Christ's sake. What am I supposed to think? It's lunacy!"

"It all makes sense to me. You've touched a nerve, that's all."

"How the hell does it make sense? And whose nerve for fuck's sake?"

"The controllers – those who have lied to us about Pearl Harbor, Kennedy, 911, weapons of mass destruction, the GFC, and anything else of major importance. Do you really think the so-called free world has a free press? It's only free to report idiotic trivia to misinform us. Since living here I've taken quite an interest in some of what you've spoken about and the way of the world is not as it appears."

I knew Mac had taken an interest in Eastern philosophy, but his disclosure was more than I expected. His previous attitude had never given any clue of his interest in the subject.

"So fill me in here. Most people would never have heard of any of this."

"Apathy Aiden. Simple as that. People don't give a shit. They think I'm a lunatic, especially that time when I blew my wad at Cambridge. But I'll take lunacy over apathy anytime. You know how it is. Society has always been split in two. The first group survives through fear. So what do they do? They escape into apathy, mundane activity and working themselves into an early grave to make the banks rich. Then there's the second, much smaller group who let go of fear. These are the people who invent and discover basically everything the first group takes for granted. You know them, the non-conformists."

"Well, you fit the second group like a glove."

"Forget it, I'm in neither."

It was good to have this mad bastard back in my life. I was feeling better already. "You've never liked society very much have you?"

"Hey, I like people. It's just that I feel better when they're not around." His lips spread into a wicked smirk. "Seriously, what pisses me off is that we're still dealing with suppressed information, limited thinking, wars and starvation because a few at the top refuse to share."

"C'mon, life's not that bad?"

The alcohol had started to kick in. "In thirty years or so, everybody we know will be dead. How fucked is that?"

"You'll be dead, that's for sure," I grinned.

"Damn well hope so. Tell me, what do you reckon would change all that?"

"I don't know, maybe proof that God exists."

Mac surprised me again. "Ah, the question of God! It's important, but it's just a sordid distraction. A more important question is 'what happens to us when we die?'"

Wow! Mac was touching on something I never thought he would. He knew my history and how I had dealt with it. He had always thought like I had – when you're dead, you're dead. Mac had never been the reflective type. *What the hell happened to him up here?*

"Have you been hitting the weed again?" I stirred.

"I've been hitting something, but it's not that," Mac grinned.

He touched where Otto seemed to be leading. He explained the hypnotic regression work conducted by one of his former colleagues at Stanford. Under hypnosis, the subject's memories were taken back further and further in their life experience. A number of subjects reported existence within the womb, and some even reported pre-uterine existence. If some people could accurately remember their existence in the uterus, then perhaps their recollections before being in the womb were also accurate. The theory had emerged with Carl Jung, but many scientists continue to ignore the data.

"It doesn't fit their little models of the universe," pronounced Mac scornfully. "The usual drivel is sprouted. I mean, listen to this. An eminent physicist – eminent they call him – has claimed consciousness is something that comes from physical phenomena. What a load of bollocks. Mind and body certainly interact, but to presume the physical somehow 'creates' the mind is idiotic. Surely it's obvious. The clown should stick to blowing balloons up his arse."

"I don't mean to be thick Mac, but it's not obvious to me."

"You've been digging in caves for too long, that's your trouble. If everything can be reduced to electromagnetic waves, why is the physical required for consciousness? Quantum physics destroyed linear cause and effect decades ago. Listen, this woman Keisha you mentioned is right. The ancient doctrines never spruiked God as some all powerful, singular entity directing the laws of the universe. Instead, God was seen as an integral state of being, underpinning and interweaving all manifestation.

Mac's tone was circumspect. "When I was twenty-one I'd already bagged my PhD, and was earning a tonne of money. I had the Ducati, remember, and my girlfriend, Tina."

"How could I forget?"

"One night I went camping with her and after a raunchy session a thought suddenly hit me like a brick. Lying naked under the billions of stars blew me away. The Earth and the Life on it is just a speck in the Cosmos. Most academics I worked with were more concerned about their little egos and their next trite paper. How you still put up with that shit is beyond me."

"I know all about the egos and trite papers, Mac."

"Yeah, I know. I've followed your tantrums. Just keep it up, don't let the bastards get to you.

"OK, but since when did you take up an interest in all this stuff?"

"When Tina and I split."

"You've never spoken about it before."

"Well, you were on your own trip. It's only since I've been living up here that I've really contemplated the question. I reckon it's the clean air. The more you discover, the more you realise what you don't know."

Changing his reflective mood, Mac cast a more excited glance.

"I'm bloody interested in your findings at Baalbek though, especially from what this Keisha said about them. What's she like? It's about time you hooked up with a hot woman with some brains."

I smiled inwardly. If Mac knew of my interest he was bound to wind me up, so I let the matter drop. Instead, I offered to refill our glasses. Mac often faded into binge drinking whenever given the chance and my presence was an excuse that he had often used. For the first time, I noticed the pained sense of tragedy in this solitary man seeking truth in a disinterested world. The unremitting banality of modern society was never sympathetic to his kind.

I opened up a new line of discussion. "What do you know about secret societies?"

"Not much really, but I know their impact on history is pretty significant."

"What makes you say that?"

"You're familiar with the symbolism on the U.S. dollar bill, aren't you?"

"Sure. Apparently, there's something Masonic about it."

Mac stood and approached a double-sided Japanese dresser that acted as a stylish room divider. He produced a wad of U.S. notes and removed a dollar bill. "Here we go. See the date on the bottom of the Great Seal." I spotted the numerals – MDCCLXXVI. "1776 right? Most people think the date relates to the American Revolution, but they'd be wrong. It actually signifies the founding of the Illuminati."

"Well there you go. I was wrong."

Mac explained how the true and authentic traditions had been subverted on two fronts. The first was by imperial Rome, an obvious, overt assault ultimately leading to the rise of the Inquisition, the crushing of free thought and spiritual practice. This led to people being driven underground where they formed societies to continue their practices in secret. The second assault was more covert, designed to suppress these groups and convert them into political agencies, beginning with Adam Weishaupt, the founder of the Illuminati.

Mac pointed at the dollar bill. "Look here, above the pyramid. It's the symbolic Eye of God surrounded by rays of light signifying Illuminism. Illuminism was a force in the French Revolution with this symbol appearing during that time. The flat pyramid represents the loss of Ancient Wisdom due to the merciless onset of Roman religious dogma."

I gave a slight nod, trying to recall what I had once read about the symbol.

"George Washington believed the creation of the United States was a divine mission. Whether we believe in divine mandates or not is of little consequence, because it profoundly influenced Washington. He thought he was an instrument of higher powers, and with the participation of the Rosicrucians and the Freemasons, they changed American history. They helped plan the American Revolution, write the Declaration of Independence and draft the Constitution."

"Washington was an active Freemason wasn't he?"

"Yep. See this here." Mac pointed to the all-seeing eye.

"This motto *Annuit Coeptis* translates to 'He favours our under-taking'. These societies believed they were performing the divine will."

I could tell Mac was enjoying the discourse. He threw back another dose of scotch to fuel his enthusiasm.

"The reverse side of the Great Seal contains the words, 'Novus Ordo Seclorum' or 'New Order of the Ages'. No doubt you've heard the term, New World Order."

"Of course. George Bush Senior used the term when he attacked Iraq back in the nineties."

"Yeah, the Bush clan is another story altogether. We can discuss them another time. The original idea of the 'New Order of the Ages' was considered the best way to replace the repressive and autocratic monarchies of the time. The ideal was democracy, where workers could keep most of the gains from their labour, rather than being crippled by feudal taxes and unbridled usury. Societies were pivotal in breaking down the feudal system."

He threw back another gulp of his whisky. 'Novus Ordo Seclorum' has an even deeper significance though. You know about the Earth's 26,000 year cycle through the heavens?"

I gave a vague shrug. "Yeah sure. This is weird because Keisha touched on this."

"Now she sounds like my kind of lady. You must introduce me to her. Come on, what's she like? Don't bullshit me. I bet she's as hot as hell." Mac almost made me laugh. "Made a move yet Aiden?"

"Shut up you silly bastard and get back to the point."

"Mmm, touched a nerve. She said no, did she? If she did, you've got no excuse not to introduce me."

"You'll get nothing from me, so get back to the subject."

"OK. A couple of questions. How did primitive people without the use of computers and satellites know about the Earth's movements through the heavens? Second, how could the Egyptians build the Great Pyramid with 2.3 million blocks of stone, cut so accurately that a razor blade can't fit between them, and more to the point, construct it in a way that actually tracks this movement via the stellar constellations. The corporate media have conditioned us to believe that thousands of workers coordinated their efforts to build it. Yet, the miracle is not the manpower; it's a matter of technology."

"Makes you wonder I know."

Mac's eyes glistened against the gentle fire that spilled its subtle warmth across the room. Was it his curiosity or the effects of the single malt? A few scotches always fired him up.

"The scientific community has a general hostility to hard questions. If the data doesn't fit their expectations they reject it. To be frank, I can't stand them. They're a pack of sexually repressed toss-bags. That's why I was fired from Cambridge." Mac cracked a smile.

"Well that, and for having it off with the Chancellor's personal assistant. Messed up his desk a bit."

I grinned. "Are you serious?"

"Yeah, well, all in the name of research. Of course, the research needed repeating several times to confirm the data, but the Chancellor wasn't happy."

We both laughed, evoking memories of our university days together. The mood had shifted from heavy conversation. We needed a break. I felt thick and lazy with alcohol. We had talked into the early hours. So much had happened, and yet with the mercurial Keisha Petersen keeping in touch and now with the raw genius of Mac, I sensed I would finally make some progress.

Mac fixed a couple of strong ristrettos and headed out into the chill of the terraced courtyard. The night had been a heavy one, heavy on conversation and heavy on the scotch. He casually lit one of his Gauloises Kreteks, a tobacco and clove concoction that I loathed. An occasional joint was a vice that still held him, but his damn Kreteks always capped off one of his drinking sessions.

The cold air and spicy smoke revived the senses as the platinum sky splayed the distant mountains with a purple hue. Daylight was nearing. The whole valley was animating to a cacophony of morning birdsong. The scene conjured the beauty and charm of a world I had lost touch with. I thought of Keisha, also beautiful and charming, and so cool in a crisis. I wondered about her safety and the progress of the LITAN analysis.

And then Otto came to mind. Who would want him dead and why? Bile flooded my stomach. With my fingerprints all over Otto's house, it would be easy for the authorities to build a case against me. After all, how could I ever explain my presence there? And what about Mac? Was I endangering him by being here? Probably. But I knew he would back me to the very end.

31

IRON THRONE

APOSTOLIC PENITENTIARY, VATICAN CITY

Comte stuck out his twisted face from behind the door. Angelo felt a sense of relief. The familiarity of the keeper soothed his concern over the Cardinal's latest outburst.

Comte was shaken at the sight of his friend's bruised face and the heavy stitching over his swollen eye and across his cheekbone. His other eye was heavily bloodshot, his left ear puffy and engorged.

Comte tried to make light of an ugly situation. "Perhaps it's time you considered a career change."

"Go on say it."

"Say what?"

"I told you so."

"I've never received any pleasure in that practice, so I won't start now. My God Angelo, I didn't realise you were so bad. Here have some grappa. It'll get the blood flowing!"

This time Angelo didn't decline the offer. He threw the velvet liquid down in one gulp. The burn stung, but happily soothed his nerves. The alcohol perversely allowed a greater appreciation of Comte's controversial remarks.

"Lamech's a fool Angelo, but I don't think he'd be involved in this. And that Dominican cleric has always been a sanctimonious jackass, but it isn't his style either. I reckon that bloated arsehole Valla is somehow involved. Your behaviour would have tested him, and Valla's network runs deep. I've tried to fathom his paranoia for years. There's definitely something weird going on."

Angelo suspected Comte was right. After recharging their glasses, Angelo mentioned the Cardinal's outburst, the spluttering about Jesuits, telescopes and the celestial heavens. He was about to discuss his perception of Valla's change in appearance, the gaunt reptilian shroud that fell over him, but decided against it. Comte might think he had a problem with his mental health. After all, it was Comte that was meant to be the crazy one.

Comte continued to provide further insight. "Valla's enmity toward the Jesuit astronomers verges on the paranoid. I've never understood it, but when I heard what happened to you I started digging. I had trouble getting access, but Valla has had an interesting past. Some would say peculiar. He was an orphan at the end of the war and finished up being educated at Harvard. I don't know the full story, but it wasn't the Church that helped him. It seems he received a privileged upbringing. Someone at very senior levels helped him, and I'm not talking about the Almighty. His U.S. immigration papers show that his foster father was one, Gerald Rankine, the Deputy Director of the Office of Strategic Services. This was the forerunner to the CIA. Rankine was a high ranking Freemason and was intimately involved in the formation of NASA. The man had many influential friends in Washington."

"Interesting Comte, but it doesn't mean Cardinal Valla was somehow involved with my bashing."

"True, but it may explain why he's paranoid about the Jesuits."

"I don't follow."

"Haven't you noticed his tattoo? When he left the U.S. he had it placed on the nape of his neck. It's a reverse red tick, almost like an arrowhead. It's the main feature of the NASA logo."

"So what?"

"NASA specifically chose this insignia which also features an ellipse and the constellation of Sirius. It must hold some significance to Valla."

"So he's got a tattoo. Maybe he just liked the logo," reasoned Angelo.

Comte was matter-of-fact. "No. That bastard would have had a reason. He always does. I know it's circumstantial, but he has links to the Freemasons and has remained intimately attached to his connections in the States. Whenever he goes there on Church business, he always has a meeting with his cronies there, always on the quiet. I know; I've been able to hack his itinerary from here."

Angelo smiled causing a sharp pain under his swollen eyelid. "You follow him around do you?"

Comte was direct. "My friends have kept a dossier on him over the years. Valla is of immense interest to them."

"Why in the name of God do they care?"

"It seems he has some unsavoury friends. They didn't tell me who, but somehow, I think it has more to do with history than anything else."

Angelo had come to enjoy Comte's ranting on his historical perspectives and encouraged him to continue. "Go on, I want to hear it."

"Since independence, various high ranking Freemasons have been sponsored to become presidents of the United States. The founding fathers had links with Freemasonry and the Rosicrucians, so they knew something of importance about the ancient Egyptians."

"This is going to be controversial is it?" queried Angelo sceptically.

Comte sculled the last of the grappa. "Perhaps, but symbolism is important. Why is an Egyptian obelisk so proudly displayed in

Central Park in New York, in the Place de la Concorde in Paris and right here, out front in the Piazza? They went to a lot of effort and you have to wonder why."

Angelo failed to see the significance. "OK, so there's an obsession with Egypt. So what? What does that have to do with the NASA logo?"

Comte yanked the cork from another bottle of grappa. He recalled the words of Christ when he said, *'Don't cast pearls before the swine'.* But Angelo was no swine. He was a young man without compromise, greed or ambition. Comte knew he was special. He was also a young man who was battered and bruised. He decided to confide in him.

"I've told you very little about my recent absence, but after I understood the meaning of the Bible code I needed answers to further questions. Like the founding fathers of the U.S. my contacts are also protecting an ancient knowledge. They want to bring this knowledge to the world in a more contemporary manner and are looking for ways to achieve it. This is very difficult today, with the narrow commercial interests that control global media. My contacts pushed me in a direction with conclusions that are, to be honest, astonishing. And Egypt holds an important key. What I'm about to read to you is the reason why NASA designed the logo the way they did and why I reckon Valla has his obsession. Egyptian pharaohs were obsessed with the dog-star, Sirius."

Comte opened his drawer and removed the file Angelo recognised as the one 'not for his eyes'.

"These are quotes from the Pyramid Texts of Egypt. They're the oldest known human writings. In Utterance 221, the text reads,

'**The King is a flame, moving before the wind to the end of the sky and to the end of the earth...***the King travels the air and traverses the earth...there is brought to him a way of ascent to the sky.'*

and Utterance 332, 'I am this one who has escaped...*I have ascended in a blast of fire* having turned myself about. The two skies go to me.'

and Utterance 483, 'May you remove yourself to *the sky upon your iron throne.*'

Then there's Utterance 673, 'O my father the King, such is your going when you have gone as a god, *you're travelling as a celestial being...*and *sit on this throne of iron at which the gods marvel.*'"

The words were a confirmation. Angelo's thoughts percolated to the mysterious blonde woman, Comte's friend Keisha who had revealed the Bible code to him. The utterances seemed similar to the verses thrown up from the stained glass windows.

Angelo was ready to articulate a bold statement. "You know what this means?"

Comte replied excitedly as he grabbed a new page, "Wait, just wait, listen to this. From another place, another culture, another race. Listen."

"The flames of the *Brahmastra-charged missiles* mingled with each other and surrounded by fiery arrows they covered the earth, heaven and space between and increased the conflagration like the fire and the Sun at the end of the world.... All beings who were scorched by the Brahmastras, and saw the terrible *fire of their missiles,* felt that it was the fire of the cataclysm that burns down the world."

Angelo saw the significance. Missiles, fiery arrows. This description went beyond the Bible code.

Slowly and meticulously, Comte continued,

"Oh you, Uparicara Vasu, the spacious *aerial flying machine* will come to you – and you alone, of all the mortals, seated on that vehicle will look like a deity",

Flying machines. These ancient words were even more descriptive than the verse from Ezekiel. Angelo understood.

"The gods came in their *respective flying vehicles* to witness the battle between Kripacarya and Arjuna. Even Indra, the Lord of Heaven, came with a *special type of flying machine* which could accommodate thirty three divine beings."

Comte beamed with unreserved delight. "These words were written in antiquity and are quotes belonging to the *Bhagavata Purana* and *Mahabaratha*, texts that are thousands of years old. Our world was very different then, but they are talking about flight, Angelo. Flight! No wonder Valla's obsessed. And no wonder the Church is so obstinate about their deception!"

32

THE ARTEFACT

WEST VIRGINIA, UNITED STATES

Volker was anxious to discuss operational matters. "So why did you bring us here, Veles?"

Kane's tone lowered. "We've discovered a genuine artefact."

Goldstein shrugged. "There are plenty of artefacts. Hell, I saw a FOX program just last week on crystal skulls."

"Yes, we approved the episode. In fact, we approve of the network, but this artefact has its origins in Atlantis."

Goldstein shook his head in disbelief. *Maybe Majestic weren't that hot after all.* "Atlantis? You don't fall for that shit do you?"

Kane dismissed the gibe with icy finality. "You're not CIA anymore, so listen and observe. You're not here for your intellect."

Goldstein sarcastically recanted. "I think I get the message loud and clear Sir, but come on, Atlantis is a bit out there."

"You need to get used to something right now, Goldstein. The difference been Majestic and the CIA is that we do our research more thoroughly and limit what we share with those fools. We have access to virtually all Western databases and unprecedented amounts of historical and scientific data. We make the rest of you look like pre-school amateurs. We study what nobody else wants to think about and we take decisive action. Your job here is to do what I tell you. That's why I sent you to Dresden. Decisive action. Understand?"

Goldstein understood without equivocation. The orders he received for the elimination in Dresden could only have come from the mind of a psychopath.

Volker headed off the impasse. He pushed for more information. "OK, so what've you got?"

"You'll see it soon enough, but first, a little background. The Nazi inner circle rediscovered something in Tibet during their excursions in the thirties."

Creases spread across Volker's forehead. "You said rediscovered?"

"Yes, meditation techniques that enabled them to make channelled contact. Typically, the knowledge gained was callously abused."

There was an uneasy silence between the three men. Goldstein was on guard to avoid another confrontation. *Maybe these guys are mostly demented,* he thought. "Contact with what?"

Kane held the two men solidly in his gaze. "Contact with an off world intelligence. Back in 1955, General McArthur publicly stated that the next World War would be interplanetary. The reason for his conclusion had its origins within Hitler's manic obsession."

Goldstein looked at Volker like a teenager who had just been told the 'facts of life'. His smirk was comical. Volker stared back blankly hoping Goldstein would get the message to shut up.

Veles Kane continued, "The Reich used these meditative techniques to make contact with extraterrestrial powers. Hitler believed they had contacted 'Supermen', but in reality they had contacted those who have been interfering in human affairs since the beginning of civilisation – regressive intelligences. Primitive civilisations mythologised them as 'gods'."

The word 'fascinating' rolled off Goldstein's tongue involuntarily. It was spiked with sarcasm. He regretted his response immediately.

Kane eyes burned at him, and he sensed a lack of conviction. "You're CIA through and through, aren't you?"

Goldstein nodded imperceptibly.

"Then you'd be aware of Operation Paperclip where the most valuable Nazis were recruited to the U.S."

Goldstein's nod was more prominent.

"What you wouldn't know is that the Nazis tried to take control of the planet with knowledge obtained from the most ancient sources."

Volker chipped in. "So their search for doctrines in Tibet, Egypt and the Far East helped them in their quest?"

"Only to some extent. They thought detailed records about the genesis of man were hidden millennia ago in both Egypt and Tibet. If they could find those records, they believed they would find documentary proof of the existence of their Supermen, the extraterrestrials who the Nazis had been surreptitiously contacting, all in an endeavour to create new technologies. The Nazis had put their knowledge into practice. The allied pilots who witnessed the so-called 'Foo-Fighters' during their bombing raids over Germany toward the end of the war were dumbfounded. The sightings were a widespread phenomenon at the time, but the Allies covered it up. Observers to those events, and subsequently the media, were either coerced into believing it was a hoax or they were discredited with talk of post-traumatic stress. Of course, all this was followed by the famous mass sighting of hovering craft over the Capitol in 1947. Even the OSS had trouble denying that one."

Goldstein was captivated. Volker had once told him of the controversy surrounding the unidentified craft over the Capitol and now his imagination was captured. "So how did the Nazis make the breakthrough with these beings?"

"It all began with Karl Haushofer, a professor at the University of Munich. He was a man with enormous intellect, spoke eight languages including Sanskrit, Chinese and Tibetan. He was aware of the regressive forces influencing world affairs, and was the first person to use the term 'geopolitics'. Haushofer studied with the Lama's in their monasteries and spent considerable time with the Bon Priesthood in Tibet. He had a distinguished military career and served as a General in World War I. While commanding troops at the front, he had the uncanny ability to anticipate future events.

"The man who eventually became the Deputy Fuhrer, Rudolf Hess, served under Haushofer and was enthralled by him. Haushofer went on to form the *Vril Society*. This group and Rudolf von Settendorf's *Thule Gesselschaft* had a profound influence on the young Hitler. The Thules wanted to re-establish a society based on a civilisation apparently mentioned in some of the ancient texts of Tibet. During this time, two members of the Vril Society with a highly developed psychic function made contact with what was believed to be advanced intelligences.

"During later explorations in the East, a scientific investigation unit decoded a few fragments of the Secret Doctrine and discovered the fourth dimensional nature of this knowledge."

Goldstein was perplexed. "Fourth dimensional – meaning what?"

Kane appraised Goldstein, measuring the level of disclosure necessary. "The Secret Doctrine deals with the manifestation of hyper-dimensional physics, the very basics of which are known as sacred geometry. Of course, there's nothing actually sacred about it. It's just highly advanced.

"Both the Thule and Vril Societies had tried to improve humanity, but they lost control of their protégé, Hitler. The Thules had two branches, one dealing with esoteric matters and the other dealing with the more mundane exoteric issues. Publicly, they presented themselves as honourable establishment figures, like major industrialists and bankers. But the very institutions that had helped Hitler into power were eventually subverted by him. He was out to destroy them. The round-up of Freemasons into the concentration camps is a classic example. This show of power had the effect of intimidating the Vatican. If the Catholics within Germany were to speak out, he was quite prepared to make life extremely difficult."

Kane paused to deliver his instruction. "Right now we're preparing for an interrogation off American soil. Be ready at a moment's notice to leave."

33

NIGHT MENACE

ZURICH, SWITZERLAND

Although exhausted, repulsive images kept me awake. I was having difficulty locking away the sight of Otto's gutted torso. Whoever committed that atrocity would clearly stop at nothing. I didn't want Mac in danger and decided my stay would be brief.

Memory can be vague. It can play tricks. I saw an emerald light and recall a strange odour. There was a sensation of falling, accompanied by a faint buzzing, much like the sound of a foraging bee. I was completely paralysed, unable to even move my mouth. This was no dream. I could still hear the clock ticking in the hallway. Something unspeakable was happening.

Sensation passed away as two dark figures stood motionless at the foot of my bed. My body was inert. Only the hazy silhouettes were visible. My mouth was dry as sandpaper and my tongue rasped against the roof of my mouth. I was trapped in a twilight state between wakefulness and sleep.

I screamed out, but my voice trailed off as a cold silver light enveloped me. I drifted into unconsciousness…

…The Wheel was missing. I stood at the foot of an enormous stone gate. Pitch black asphalt extended to the horizon. No stars were visible in the night sky, only the pall of obsidian blackness. I turned to look at the child and was repulsed.

Small and deathly grey with spindly arms, the child looked up. Its eyes bulged, like an enormous blowfly. He reached for my hand, but I recoiled in horror. I struggled to let go and ran.

I turned to see if it had chased after me, but the child just stood there, bewildered. Ailing and listless, it slowly sank to its knees. It was desperately sick and needed help. This understanding was conveyed without words. Whilst I knew the strange child meant no harm, I was unable contain my fear.

It was silently pleading for my help…

34

SIRIUS

APOSTOLIC PENITENTIARY, VATICAN CITY

The keeper dabbed a film of saliva from the corner of his mouth. "The Old Kingdom of Egypt was the legacy of a much earlier and more advanced civilisation. They venerated the divine intelligences, Osiris and Isis. Isis was the female spirit who gave birth to humanity. She was symbolised by the star system Sirius."

Angelo listened intently. "So you're right. It is connected to history."

"Yes and I'm sure Valla is trying to continue what the Church has done for centuries. Hide the truth."

"I wonder what's so important about Sirius."

"Before I was attacked in Rwanda, I spent some time travelling through Mali. I met some members of the Dogon tribe, a scattered people of around three thousand persons whose origins go back to ancient Egypt. Anthropologists in the 1930s documented the beliefs of their shamans and found they possessed a detailed understanding of astronomy that wasn't confirmed until the development of radio telescopes."

"You're kidding?"

"Not at all. It was very clear that the shamans were speaking of Sirius and its two celestial companions. What they called 'Po Tolo' is now known as Sirius B. It's invisible to the naked eye and was discovered in the '60s by radio telescope. It was finally photographed in 1970. Anthropologists had assumed the Dogon story was a primitive myth, but they not only knew of its existence, they also told how it orbited Sirius every fifty one years. Technology eventually proved they were spot on. Even their knowledge of a second celestial companion was confirmed when Sirius C was discovered in 1995."

Angelo frowned, "How could a primitive nomadic tribe know all that? How?"

"Makes you wonder doesn't it. But the most interesting thing is their talk of the '*Nommo*' who arrived on Earth amidst fire and thunder. Same old story, Angelo. Fire and thunder. It's like the code in the Templar windows. Clouds of fire. Incidentally, the Dogon also knew about Saturn's rings and Jupiter's four major moons. They followed four separate calendars for the Sun, Moon, Sirius and Venus. They knew the planets orbited the sun thousands of years ago and knew the orbital sequence of the Sirius celestial bodies."

Angelo breathed deep and reached for the grappa. "Do you believe their story about the *Nommo*?"

Comte shrugged his shoulders. "I believed in the Church, the Pope and the Curia of Cardinals. I believed in Life and then I witnessed the results of almost a million deaths in Rwanda. So now I just believe in data. I'm not one for elaborate religious dogma or speculative science. And I don't reject anything just because it doesn't fit my narrow belief system. If a primitive tribe has knowledge of astro-physical data thousands of years before Western science has confirmed it, then I find that compelling. Drawings on a cave wall showing precise representations of our solar system can't be dismissed. If this tribe say the 'Nommo' landed on Earth 40,000 years ago, then I can't automatically reject it. When you look at the numbers, the law of probability overwhelmingly suggests there should be an abundance of life across the universe. I mean marine biologists are still discovering new forms of life in the hidden volcanic depths of the oceans for heaven's sake!"

Faith was certainly being challenged. Angelo agonised, "But how could the Dogon know this?"

Comte shrugged. "If proof was provided that the Nommo came down to Earth and they coexisted with an indigenous tribe in Africa, the likes of Valla would be quick to theologically disprove it with his ecclesiastical clap-trap. You know he's the master of spin. You've prepared his briefs. He would consider it demonic."

Angelo believed in the scriptural interpretation of the creation of mankind. The Book of Genesis said the 'Elohim' had created man. He had believed this to be God himself, while others in the Church believed the Elohim were the Angels of God. Maybe these Angels were some form of extraterrestrial being, perhaps the Nommo even.

Comte decided to push the young man further. "I'll tell you something else from another race, another culture on another continent. In Coricancha, near Cuzco in Peru, there once stood the Inca Sun Temple with a wall covered in solid gold. Before it was plundered and destroyed by the Spanish, the golden wall depicted the story of creation. The god Viracocha was said to have taught the Incas everything from writing to agriculture, astronomy to stone engineering. According to the inscriptions of the Sun Temple, Viracocha was depicted as coming from a special place in the sky. And that place was Sirius."

35

INSIGHT

NEAR LUGANO, SWITZERLAND

"He's coming around."

The voice was soft, feminine. There was a flicker of light, then a flash. A white haloed vision hovered over me. The haze cleared and adorable features leaned forward shining a penlight across my pupils.

"Don't be afraid. You'll be alright now. When you're ready, follow these two men down the hallway. Do you think you can do that?"

I wriggled my toes. At least I was conscious.

The woman flashed pearly teeth and disappeared from view. I blinked, gathered my focus and slowly sat up. A light medical garment covered my body.

I was in a white sterile circular room. There were no overhead lights; instead, the illumination emanated from the opaque walls. Two men clad in white medical coats silently helped me to my feet and handed me my clothes. I felt like I was coming out of deep anaesthesia.

Without comment, I was guided down a stark corridor, our

journey ending at double white doors. My minders tapped the key-pad and we entered a large formally decorated room. It was a stark contrast to the previous austere clinical spaces. Timber panelling. Maroon leather armchairs. Renaissance art. I was reminded of an exclusive London gentleman's club.

I was ushered toward a stately door, the entrance to an inner sanctum. A small red light illuminated and the door unlocked with a click. I stood at the threshold of a sumptuously appointed office. A man of indeterminate age with delicate elfin features sat behind an enormous desk. White shoulder length hair covered a set of elongated earlobes.

"Come in Dr Keyes." The man stood and extended a sinewy hand. "Please take a seat."

My minders silently retreated. I stepped forward and tentatively sat in comfortable leather.

"Dr Aiden James Keyes. Born 4th October 1965. Professor of Evolutionary Biology and BBC television presenter. You specialised in paleo-anthropology after completing a bachelor degree in archaeological science. Why on earth did you choose archaeological?"

The voice was educated and formal. Erudite and in control.

My experience had been dreamlike. I had taken some time to gather my thoughts, but now I was boiling with rage.

"How about I ask a question? Who the fuck are you?"

The man's voice was cultured, but flat and stripped of emotion. "You have my apologies for our unorthodox introduction. They sometimes use a magnetic resonance hemi-synch to make an introduction. Fortunately for you, your mind is strong and hard to subdue."

"Cut the crap. Where the hell am I?"

The man made a concession to my vitriol. "You're still in Switzerland, but perhaps you'd like to know why you're here."

"That'd be a start."

"We've been watching out for your friend Alex or Mac as you like to call him."

I suspected the worst. "What do you mean? Is he OK?"

"Don't worry Dr Keyes, you'll see Alex shortly. There are many people we look out for, but so do the others."

Others? "What are you on about?"

"Belial." He remained impassive and spoke calmly. "They're a group of controllers who master an organisation known as Majestic, a powerful network who have co-opted most of the world's governments and the intelligence apparatus. They've corrupted religion, the financial system, withheld beneficial science and confined our knowledge of the wider cosmos. They have undue influence over the media, academia and the global agenda."

Nothing made sense. I felt like Alice in Wonderland talking to the Mad Hatter. I ignored his babbling and fired another question, "Why would you want to spy on Mac?"

The man shifted in his chair and spoke with proud authority. "I didn't say we were spying on him. We try to care for the special ones, and Alex is certainly special, wouldn't you agree Dr. Keyes."

"Like I said cut the crap."

The man's tone hardened. "I never speak crap as you call it. But you do deserve an explanation. It all came to a head with your discovery in Baalbek. We've been able to make a translation with the help of LITAN and we need to keep Belial away from your discovery. In addition, the pendant has opened a line of enquiry we would like to pursue."

Baalbek? LITAN? The Templar pendant? I was outraged at the disclosure and theft of my property. "How do you know about Baalbek and the pendant? And what the hell is Belial?"

"Aiden, please remain calm. All your questions will be answered. And please call me Philip."

"We're on a first name basis now are we? Listen pal, just get on with it. Start talking!"

There was a cautious edge to the man's refined tone. "As you please. Firstly, Belial was originally a faction of the Watchers mentioned in the Book of Enoch. The Sumerians called them the Annunaki."

Watchers! Annunaki! Keisha had mentioned them. *Where's all this nonsense leading?* "I've heard of them recently, but that's it."

"The Book of Enoch is an important document. Its translation is virtually uncorrupted, purely because it was left out of the Bible. The Ecumenical Councils that butchered the translations and precepts of the Bible didn't tamper with the Book of Enoch; hence it contains a more unadulterated truth." He released a cautious smile and continued, "Enoch actually means 'initiated'. He was unique because like Adam he actually 'walked with God'. Enoch claims that the Watchers were destined to, *'afflict, oppress, destroy, attack, do battle and work destruction on Earth'.*"

"Fascinating, but you didn't answer my question about Baalbek."

Philip's tone hardened. "Then I'll make myself clear. You're well known for your BBC series. You have the same passion as Attenborough."

"Cut the celebrity crap."

"Crap maybe, but that series has given you the forum to communicate your views as you ponder the genesis of man. It was common knowledge that you were searching the hills near Baalbek to prove your theories. And anything discovered there would be in your next series. Correct?"

I hedged, "Maybe. I haven't decided yet."

"As I said, Belial is the unseen force behind a highly secretive organisation called Majestic. They exist to keep the truth of man's genesis a secret and to keep us all in bondage. If you find the truth and splash it on television screens around the world, then you're a real threat to them."

"I don't really give a shit about that at the moment. Mind explaining why I'm here?"

"You're here for your own protection."

"Give me a break. Protecting me from some unheard of group with connections to some old book. I mean, who the hell are you guys?"

"All will be revealed, but first let's get you clean."

"What?"

Philip ignored my question, stood up and gestured toward the door. "Please follow me."

I didn't comprehend the request, but I needed answers about Mac and what this man knew about Baalbek. Philip opened the door, my minders ready to receive his instruction. They led me back down the corridor to another circular room. A sleek reclining dental chair with arm and leg restraints, overhead lights and a workbench with stainless steel surgical tools arranged in neat rows told me I was in trouble.

I swallowed hard. "What's all this?"

"We won't hurt you Aiden, but we believe you're infected."

"Infected with what?" I bristled. "You'd better start explaining what's happening or I'm out of here."

"Sit down Aiden. Please. We had hoped to attend to this before you came round. I'll show you everything before any procedure is performed. Let me just say that Alex is clean and it's important that you are too."

I glanced at the two men. They were heavy duty muscle ready to do what was necessary. I didn't have a chance to fight my way out, so I sat in the chair, my stomach turning with anxiety. One of the men fetched a small cylindrical object that resembled a tranquiliser gun.

"Just hold still," Philip reassured. "This device transmits a low intensity electromagnetic signature to detect minute foreign objects. There's absolutely no pain."

Just as I was about to decline any further involvement, they pressed the device against my temple and it immediately beeped. Philip was right. I felt nothing.

"He's tagged."

"What the… hey stop that! Get off me!"

The two gorillas quickly snapped the arm and leg restraints into position. They pushed my head back and locked it into the sculpted headrest, strapping my forehead tight.

"Let me out you motherfuckers!"

I tasted bile as I struggled against the restraints.

Philip spoke quietly, "Please, if you hold still it'll only take a second."

I knew the pain was coming. The bastards could get it over and done with.

With clinical precision, one of the men swung a small laser-like device above my temple. A harmonic frequency was pulsed through my head, creating a small puncture. In less than a second, a needle-like extractor plunged into the wound creating an excruciating jab of pain that permeated every corpuscle. My mouth went dry.

"Got it!" A miniscule implant dropped into a Petri dish as my muscles relaxed. "You're OK now."

Philip held up the bloodied device between a pair of tweezers. "You were carrying this. Belial uses them to track and control individuals they regard as subversive. You, my friend, are now free."

36

THE TRIP

ROME, ITALY

Life was challenging Angelo. His robust physique had helped his prognosis. He was mending quickly.

Cardinal Valla had shown the young man no sympathy and thankfully, he was once again away on Vatican business giving Angelo time to think. Disenchantment had taken hold. His work had lost all purpose.

Angelo thought of Comte often, but since his beating, something deep within his psyche had prevented him from seeking out his friend's company. Although loathed to admit it, his savage beating had shaken him. It triggered a hideous fear.

But it was more than that. There was something abhorrent that festered within his subconscious. He was waking early every morning, startled and drenched in sweat. *Are they just nightmares or memories of the forgotten past?* One thing was certain, he recalled childhood episodes of bed wetting and cold fear, but the answer as to why was beyond him. Angelo had no idea that demons were gathering to prey.

He felt awkward serving the Cardinal, but the thought of leaving the Church provoked trepidation.

Comte buzzed the intercom for Angelo's apartment. "Wake up you lazy bastard!"

Angelo was tired and his body ached. It was past 9.00 a.m. The last time Comte had woken him the encounter ended with the mystery of the Templar Code. *What could it possibly be this time?*

"What's up?"

As usual, Comte refused to say much, but he was like a child with a new toy. "We have the day off, remember. Get yourself ready, we're going for a stroll. There's something you need to see."

Angelo rarely had the opportunity to saviour the beauty of the city in which he lived. He mostly used his free time to catch up on study. To spend a day in the heart of the metropolis would be a release, a therapeutic respite. The colour and vibrancy of Rome would be a welcome diversion. Besides, Comte's eccentricity would add to the occasion.

Within the hour, the two men were relaxing at an alfresco café on the skirt of the Piazza di Spagna. One man was blemished and disfigured; the other handsome and statuesque, with facial cuts and bruising that were rapidly fading. They were the objects of idle amusement as glances and stares from passersby penetrated the warm Roman air.

The usual glut of tourists loitered on the Spanish steps. The attraction of this city icon had always amused Comte because in his opinion, Rome had so much more to offer. No matter, the tourists and locals loved the steps and the happy snapping of their cameras was always a curiosity. It was a dazzling morning with the sun, cutting swathes of brilliant light down the fashionable and elegant Via Condotti. Angelo soaked in the ambiance of his surroundings. He watched as designer-dressed locals participated in the play of life.

Comte was sipping a ristretto. "Remember when you met Keisha in the library?"

The mysterious blonde. The very mention of her gave Angelo goose bumps. "I'll never forget her."

"What she told you is right you know. We're in danger. I reckon they're planning to come after me."

"What makes you think that?"

"Don't know, but I can sense it," he replied bluntly.

Angelo suspected his beating was payment for questioning theology, so the possibility of Comte being harmed for exposing fraudulent scriptural interpretations was possible, especially given recent events. "Why now all of a sudden?"

"Keisha thinks my computer's been hacked. I bet that bastard Valla is behind all this."

"You've spoken with her? What did she say about me?" he babbled.

Comte eyed a curvaceous brunette in a classic red miniskirt as she ambled by. She cut a glance at the two men and visibly recoiled at the sight of the hideous keeper. "Keisha also warned you, didn't she?"

An uneasy quiet descended on Angelo as he inquisitively stared at Comte. It was just a matter of time before he would need to make a life-changing decision. But how and to where? Despite this, the ceaseless tide of beautiful people and excited tourists subdued his dark melancholy. It snapped Comte into action.

"Come on, I didn't drag you here to look at skirt. We've got something to see. Keisha has arranged a meeting and it's time to go."

"Where are we going?"

"We've got a flight to catch in a couple of hours, so finish your coffee."

37

TORTURE

NEAR POSITANO, TYRRHENIAN SEA, ITALY

According to legend, the sea surrounding the islands of Li Galli was where the sirens tempted Ulysses on his voyage back to Greece. The islands had been held in private hands for almost a century and on the largest, Il Gallo Lungo, a villa was built on the ancient Roman ruins by an American choreographer back in 1924. The islands changed hands over the years, one owner being a world famous ballet dancer who held the property until 1994. Through a series of blind trusts, they now belonged to Majestic, having been purchased for €200 million.

Kane led his guests to a basement room within the expansive villa. It contained two curious items. The first was a large metallic contraption, a strange tetrahedron suspended from the ceiling with a number of protruding wires providing an earth polarity. The second was an A-frame with a small Asian man, naked to the waist and strapped to it with wire. He had already been tortured.

Volker's eyes flickered with restless movement, his gaze not focusing on the Asian man. He found the scene distressing, so he looked through the captive as though he was invisible. He focussed on the tetrahedron.

Goldstein was more interested in the primitive extraction technique that was being implemented. He remembered the images of Abu Ghraib prison in Iraq and the wicked attempt to extract information. It was rarely useful. He wondered how Kane could be so vulgar. The CIA had long used various methods of 'stress inducement' to interrogate prisoners, but this disgusting effort repulsed him. Kane was a twisted bastard.

The prisoner's wrists were strapped together above his head and wired to the frame, as were his legs that were spread wide, only his toes being able to touch the ground. His head was held in place with wire pulled tight around his neck. Callipers forced his eyelids apart. Congealed blood oozed from gaping wounds around his wrists and ankles where the wire had cut deep. The captive sucked in a wheeze of air as his eyelids twitched.

Kane puffed with pride. "He's a Tibetan monk, a senior member of the Bon Priesthood."

Volker pointed to the pyramidal device attached to the ceiling. "So what's this thing meant to be?"

"That's what we'd like to know. It seems it's used to access a fourth dimensional field. Buddhists call it penetrating the jhana."

Goldstein shook his head in professional disgust. "That dimensional stuff you mentioned before?"

"Yes. It seems this technology was used in pre-Egyptian times to gain spiritual knowledge."

Volker was Majestic's adviser on archaeological and biblical history and this disclosure surprised him. "Are you sure about this Veles? The Great Pyramid was certainly used as an initiation centre and the Pythagorean Mystery School was involved with transmitting this knowledge to other monastic orders, but I'm not familiar with any reference to this type of contraption. I'm aware of the dimensional effects of shemanna, but I've never heard of anything like this."

Kane replied. "With its capstone the Great Pyramid was a powerful columnar wave resonator used to tune the resonant frequency
of the adept, stimulating advanced states of consciousness. Am I
correct?"

"Generally speaking, yes, and I presume this contraption does
likewise."

"We believe so. And this bastard knows how to use it."

Goldstein was trying to make sense of the discussion. "Are you
saying we have a soul or something?"

Volker hedged. "Well, that's difficult to say. It's been suggested
that during sleep some aspect of our self travels through various
vibrational densities. Fragments of these vibrations are reported
back as pictures during REM sleep."

Kane joined in. "Most people dismiss anything beyond the
ordinary waking state. However, the few who have attained the
highest levels of consciousness claim to experience their true self.
It seems the Tibetans and the pre-dynastical Egyptians understood
the nature of consciousness, not only beyond the waking state, but
also beyond death. Majestic has been researching the characteristics
of consciousness ever since the first MK-Ultra experiments."

Goldstein pointed to the device on the ceiling and sniggered.
"So you think this came from the Atlanteans."

Volker noticed the scepticism in Goldstein's remark and decided
to diffuse any heat. "I'd agree that most of what is written about
Atlantis is bullshit, but don't dismiss the idea completely. Recent
sonar-resonance tests have discovered the likely remains of Atlantis
on the seabed between Cyprus and Syria. Walls of what was no
doubt a city extend for almost three kilometres. Incredibly, the features and layout of the underwater acropolis are corroborated in
over seventy references made in the Plato dialogues, Timaeous and
Critias."

Kane took the lead. "We want the public to think that Atlantis is bullshit Ariel, so you can be forgiven for your cynicism. If people come to understand Atlantis, they'll ultimately understand its science and then by implication, the inter-dimensional nature of the universe. That's why I sought your help with the Baalbek problem."

Goldstein pointed to the monk. "So how does this poor bastard fit into the picture?"

Kane shot a scowl at the tortured man. Bloodied, dry eyes blazed back. "He knows how to use this thing. We've tried everything to get him to talk. So far – nothing. He says he doesn't fear death because he understands it. It's time we tested his claims."

Kane circled the Tibetan. He reached for his cell phone and punched a key. "Send in the translator."

Goldstein noticed the prisoner was in bad shape. Burn marks from high voltage electrodes were visible at his temples. Controlled beatings had left yellow-brown welts all over his back, neck and shoulders.

The translator entered. A short, fragile man with fine Indian features blinked through thick round spectacles. He walked nervously down the steps and faced the sardonic Director. An indignant disrespect simmered behind the soft-featured face.

Kane spelled out instructions as he pointed to Goldstein. "Tell the monk that this man is an expert interrogator and I'll have him burn out his eyes if he doesn't start talking."

Goldstein inwardly flinched at the suggestion, but the translation was odiously issued as instructed. The monk spluttered a meek response through bloodied teeth.

The translator repeated the words. "He says this world means nothing and he will never yield to the unworthy. You may do as you wish."

Kane spat back. "Is that right! Perhaps I'll just do this myself."

He removed his tailored jacket, folded and brushed it smooth, handing it carefully to Goldstein. He then reached for the cabinet behind him and removed a small blowtorch canister. An intense blue flame crackled into life.

"Tell him this is his last chance. No more evasion! He tells me how this thing works or he'll burn."

The translator spoke ruefully, holding an innate compassion for the resolute gentleness of the Tibetan. The monk remained silent. With blowtorch in hand, the menacing Kane inched forward.

Goldstein was perversely amused. Matching the size of the tiny blue flame, he figured the Intelligence Director didn't have the right sized balls to inflict the pain.

How wrong he was. Kane stood close and dispensed his wanton cruelty.

In a shadowed recess, a figure silently observed the proceedings. Dressed in an immaculate silk cassock with lashings of scarlet, Antonio Cardinal Valla nervously removed the ecclesiastical ring that wrapped his first finger.

Today, he was not proud of his rank.

38

SION

NEAR LUGANO, SWITZERLAND

My mind rebooted with cold rage. "What the fuck is that?"
Philip leaned forward, "You're OK."

I had no time for subtleties. "I'm not fucking OK. I want answers you twisted maggot."

Philip remained composed. "In one form or another they've been used since the '60s, although these days their insertion and removal leaves no more than a pin prick. They're mostly used to modify behaviour, but they also act as accurate tracking devices. More so than a cell phone."

Behavioural implants? Tracking devices? The implications were unthinkable. "Yeah, but why? Who? What the hell is going on here?"

"This is a Belial device, so it confirms our thinking. They obviously have an abiding interest in your Baalbek discovery. I suspect you were tagged once the Lebanese Government approved your application to work there. That area has been under the control of the Syrian backed Hezbollah for years and they've been heavily infiltrated by Majestic. They were obviously concerned with what you might find."

"So they know I'm here then."

"We placed a jamming device on you when we picked you up. This facility is also shielded, so nobody knows your whereabouts. That I can assure you."

"So where exactly are we?"

"You're still in Switzerland, not far from Lugano. You're very safe."

Actions had occurred beyond my control, but I was starting to feel that Philip was no threat. If they wanted me dead, it would already have happened.

We returned to his inner sanctum and I slumped back into the same leather chair, exhausted by the theatrics.

I had watched Philip closely and noticed his distinctive features. He had the palest skin with eyes of aqua, not unlike the green-blue hues of the deep ocean. His demeanour was aristocratic and his enthusiasm defied his age.

I figured conciliation was a better approach to get the answers to my questions, so I tempered my aggression. "I'd like to know who or what you represent."

"Let's just say our existence is one of subterfuge. There's no possible way we can overcome the forces of Belial and their control of Majestic. They oppose us at our every move, so we covertly work with them."

I tried to make sense of Philip's response.

He clarified. "More correctly, we work *within* them. A group within a group. It gives us the advantage of using their resources and knowing their agenda. Those who harbour our objectives naturally filter our way, but they are few. Our objective is to bring Truth to the world and allow humanity to be free. It's been our purpose since the beginning."

"If you surreptitiously use Majestic, then why should I trust you? You said you used LITAN to translate my photographs. I want to know how you got hold of them."

"Your contact with Professor Petersen made life a little easier for us. Keisha has been operational for a few years now and she's been active in decoding your photographs. The results are very, very valuable. We had to intercept you before Belial got to you."

I was paralysed with surprise. *Keisha Petersen was a covert operative?* Everything about her was a lie. *How could she possibly be caught up with these people?* No wonder my photographs were common knowledge.

"So Keisha betrayed my discovery? What gave her the right? Money?" The woman's duplicity made me want to strangle the bitch.

"Keisha never betrayed you Aiden. In fact, she delivered you from evil as it were. She was concerned for your safety and asked me to help you. Love and compassion for your wellbeing shouldn't be misunderstood as betrayal. Even Otto sacrificed himself for you."

"You know about Otto?"

"Of course, Otto was one of the few I referred to. Our contact within Majestic informed us of the murder of your friend Jai, so we knew they were onto you. The call you received in Canberra came from us. We wanted you to get some background to the implications of your discovery. We're just sorry to have lost Otto in the process."

"Couldn't you have stopped it?"

"We didn't know until after the event. And even if we did, there was no way to intervene. It would have exposed our source."

"So you allowed the poor man to be disembowelled?"

"Otto knew the danger in meeting you. He knew we were closer now than ever before."

"Closer ?"

"Closer to actual evidence of the creation of man. How Cro-Magnon came to be."

Now that was unexpected. That was my life's work and there was no way anybody was taking this from me. I could feel the drug kick in.

"And Baalbek gives a clue."

"It gives more than a clue."

"So why do you give a damn about all this?"

"Our organisation has existed in various forms since 1152. Back then, we were known as the Underground Stream. Majestic know us as Elysius. But there's a crucial difference between us and every other movement, regardless of whether they're religious, political or otherwise. Our peerage goes back thirty-nine thousand years."

I almost choked. The claim was preposterous.

"Thirty-nine thousand," I repeated. "Your lineage goes back to prehistoric cave man, eh? Now that's utter drivel!"

Philip placed his thumb and forefinger on the bridge of his nose, indicating his weariness at my animosity.

He persevered. "As a hypothesis Aiden, let's imagine a world in the long distant past, a civilisation where the inhabitants had reached the pinnacle of their abilities. Now imagine a privileged class who sought a closed technological system and opposing them were those who struggled to attain an open system that was freely available to everyone. Imagine that war became inevitable between the opposing factions.

"Now imagine this war was on an interplanetary scale. During cataclysmic battle, all was destroyed; civilisation driven to its demise by a bitter battle for supremacy. In the end, the players of this war know that all their power and knowledge is lost. So what's left?

"A desire by the survivors from each faction to salvage what they can, to salvage what they once knew and what the other side didn't. A power play is born. And here on planet Earth, Majestic and Elysius represent this power play. Elysius seeks an open system for all. Open energy systems. Open wealth accumulation without debt. Open science and spirituality. We continue to fight against the repressive forces that would hold it for themselves.

"We can discuss all this later, but for now, I suggest you see your friend Alex? He's a rather bright fellow you know."

39

CATACOMBS

———

VIENNA, AUSTRIA

Angelo felt the butterflies fluttering within. "We're going where?"
"Vienna. We're going to Vienna!"

"Will we be back by tonight?"

Comte was delighted at the thought of Valla's explosive rage and consternation. "No, let's play truant."

"What about work tomorrow?"

"Forget it. Valla's not around at the moment, so he can get stuffed. You don't owe him anything."

Angelo shrugged. With all that had happened he still held a loyalty.

"Vienna's important. It's been arranged."

Why am I afraid to go? pondered Angelo. "Why can't you just tell me what's there?"

"Because I want you to see it for yourself. Don't worry, I've organised everything." Comte waved the flight tickets with child-like delight.

The flight was punctuated with the now familiar glances and stares, people screwing their faces in disgust at the unsightly keeper, or averting their eyes in feigned ignorance. Only the few paid no attention.

The two men checked in at the Astoria Hotel within three hours. Located in the heart of Vienna on the fashionable Kartnerstrasse, the hotel is decorated in traditional style, exuding a subtle elegant charm.

Vienna is structurally adorned with architecture from the Ottoman Empire and proudly boasts some of the best Byzantine, Baroque and Gothic buildings in all of Europe. It was home to cultural icons such as Mozart and Goethe, a place of learning and art. Mercifully, the city was mostly untouched by the wars that ravaged Europe during the last century.

The Gothic magnificence of St. Stephen's Cathedral has dominated the city since 1147. It had been the tallest building in all of medieval Europe. Today, it stands as an inspirational beacon, framed in a backdrop of classic architecture. During the 18th century, the cathedral was decorated with baroque altarpieces, the panel of the main altar showing the stoning of St. Stephen, the first martyr of Christendom.

Angelo was keen to explore his romanticised vision of the city, but Comte had other plans. It was 3:42 p.m. and he was anxious to move. They needed to be at their destination by 4:00. Eighteen minutes would normally have been plenty of time, but the hobbling keeper and the recovering Angelo needed to hurry.

"Where're we going?" asked Angelo, noticing Comte's unbridled exuberance. He imagined the headline, *'Vatican understudy arrested for breaking and entering'.*

The brooding splendour of the cathedral loomed into view against a bright azure sky. Angelo followed Comte to the entrance of the catacombs next to the North Tower elevator. A queue was waiting for the four o'clock tour. At exactly four, the trail began to move. Comte stood his ground.

As the line of tourists disappeared beneath the cathedral, Comte's contact walked into view. He motioned the two men toward the interior of the cathedral where they descended a stairwell into the catacombs. The bones of more than fifteen thousand Viennese were stacked and racked like kindling, ceiling high in different cavern-like recesses tunnelled into the earth.

Comte's contact led them away from the tourist areas and fumbled with a bunch of keys to unlock a metal security door. He found the light switch and bolted the door behind them. Only then did he loosen up to speak.

"How are you my friend?"

"Well, very well." Comte's face was pasted with his warped lyrical smile. "Angelo, meet Childeric."

"Pleased to meet you."

Childeric nodded in acknowledgement and irritably wrestled with a bolt attached to yet another grille door.

Comte found it hard to contain himself. "Come on Childeric, let's have a look."

"It's over here."

At the base of some makeshift steps, the men from Rome followed the man from Vienna into a small recess. They were three metres below the floor of the catacombs at the very base of the cathedral's foundation. The area was bathed in incandescent yellow, filling Angelo with apprehension and yet, a nervous exhilaration.

Childeric explained, "Like many cathedrals in Europe, this one is no different. Many pagan temples were destroyed with the advent of Christianity, but often the site's importance was preserved with these massive monuments dedicated to the Christian God. We've found remnants of an earlier Christian church here dating back to the 6th century, but even that was built over an earlier pagan centre."

The musty air choked Angelo's lungs. For reasons unknown, a tenuous anxiety took hold. Comte on the other hand was ecstatic.

"So this is where you found the manuscript?"

Childeric gestured to a shelf cavity deep within the recess. "It was found right here seven months ago. We're sure it's late twelfth century and was placed here during the construction of the Cathedral. There are eighty-seven pages in all, pinned tight with iron clamps between two wooden covers and finally, thickly wrapped in linen. They're in exceptional condition."

"Where are they now?" queried Comte.

"The original is safe and is being carefully preserved. I can show you a copy this evening."

"What does it tell us?"

"Early days Comte, but it mentions the Egyptian mystery schools and Melchizedek. We think a Templar knight hid his journal here on the way back from the Holy Land. It doesn't reveal his name, but the story is dynamite."

Angelo pricked his ears. The Templars again! Childeric explained further. "The journal is in three parts. It briefly tells of the Templars recognition at the Council of Troyes in 1129, before describing the author's travels and exploits leading up to Saladin's victory at Acre when the city surrendered in 1187. Page after page is filled with a detailed history of the campaign. It's a first-hand historical document. After Acre, the knight resides in Constantinople and becomes a scholar to a *philosopher of the East*.

"Much of his study centres on what he calls *raising the spirit within*, by the use of an intricate form of meditation and psycho-mental training. He says this was practised by the *scholars of Melchelzidek* and *in the schools of ancient Egypt*.

"The third part of his journal is a short commentary passed to him from another source. It tells of the removal of an ossuary from a site near the Jerusalem Temple. The burial chest is taken to Damascus where it resides until the city's fall in 1154. It's subsequently removed again by three knights who vowed to ferry it to safety. Dressed as the infidel, these three knights travel across North Africa to the mountains in the far west. Here, a site had been prepared for its final burial, safe for all eternity. This is where the story ends.

"The Templar legends seem to have given rise to the medieval Grail stories, but it seems the chalice of the Melchizedek was the original 'Cup of Immortality', which conferred Eternal Life. It seems the Melchizedek came into existence through the rather strange King of Salem, king and priest of the 'most-high god'."

Comte was thrilled by the revelation. He shook with excitement. "Yes, yes. The god was called El Shaddai in the original texts, meaning Mountain Lord. Melchizedek comes from 'Melek' meaning King, and 'tsedeq' meaning 'Righteousness'. The King of Salem was the King of Righteousness."

Chideric grinned at the keeper's animated display. "Indeed! The Templars rejected the Church's view on the Resurrection of Jesus. After all, Adonis in Mesopotamia, Osiris in Egypt and Dionysus in Greece were all reborn into Eternal Life after their death, so the story was nothing new. Of course, the Church conveniently discarded all the other stories of resurrection as nothing but pagan myth. As far as the Church is concerned only the Jesus story is true, all the others are nothing but heathen lies."

Although this was another wound for Angelo to deal with, each new laceration became shallower. "Are you saying the story of Jesus is a lie as well?"

Comte provided the answer. "He's saying that resurrection was known in other cultures and other civilisations long before Jesus. Even the Norse deity of wisdom, Odin was hung on the Yggdrasil, the World Tree, to gain special knowledge. He suffered a form of crucifixion."

Comte's memory kicked in, quoting an Old Norse sage, "'*Wounded I hung on the wind-swept gallows, For nine long nights,*

Pierced by a spear, pledged to Odin.'

"Of course, Jesus too, was crucified, pierced with a spear and gained Eternal Life, but Odin preceded Jesus by centuries. Remember your studies Angelo? Mark 16:12 where, after the crucifixion, Jesus manifested 'in a different form'. Despite his disciples following him for years, they didn't recognise him. None of them. Doesn't that strike you as a little odd?"

Angelo shrugged. "I haven't really thought about it. I suppose it does."

Comte pushed harder. "What do you think this different form might be?"

Angelo shrugged again.

"Jesus appeared in his 'Resurrection' body Angelo, not his physical body. He appeared in the body of spirit and couldn't be seen through physical eyes."

Childeric caught Angelo's attention. "The Templars never believed the Resurrection was a physical event. These men eventually settled within a society that became known as the Cathars and they believed immortality was only achieved in the realm of pure spirit. It's the reason they were exterminated from the face of Europe."

Comte was on a roll with his quotations. "We are so much more than just physical Angelo. Read Revelation 2:17 when you get the chance. It says: *'To him that overcomes will I give to eat of the hidden manna, and will give him a white stone, and in the stone a new name is written, which no man knows save he that receives it.'*

"We've talked about manna before. Once ingested, it raises consciousness much the same as intense meditation. The 'new name' is the recognition and finally, the illumination of your identity in the form of spirit. Jesus received his instruction from the Order of Melchizedek. Hebrews 5:6 and 6:20 confirm it. The Israelites used manna to unlock the transcendental universe. In the original text of 1st Corinthians 10:3, manna is confirmed as spiritual food. But when this sacred knowledge was suppressed by the early Church, the science of achieving these states of consciousness was lost. The medieval alchemists tried to rediscover the secret and maybe some of them did, but there are stories that the knowledge was preserved by the neo-Templar, The Order of the Rosy Cross."

40

MISSION

NEAR POSITANO, TYRRHENIAN SEA, ITALY

Albrecht concentrated on the monk's upper torso, the stench of burning flesh causing Volker to dry-reach. The Tibetan didn't flinch. He refused to yield. His expression remained steadfast.

Goldstein had inflicted much pain during his career, but he was disgusted by the determined fervour of Veles Kane. He may be the Intelligence Director, but he was an amateur when it came to extraction techniques. The man had no originality. The monk was clearly in control although Goldstein couldn't understand how it was possible. It was as though the house was burning and nobody was at home.

Kane stepped back and irritably wiped the back of his hand across his sweaty forehead. "This bastard understands how to use that contraption and he WILL tell me."

Volker was still nauseous. It was soul destroying to watch the religious man burn. Somehow it only seemed justified with a murdering terrorist.

"What now?" questioned Goldstein.

"It's time for Hawass. That's what now. He's an expert in the pain management business and as skilled with a knife as a surgeon. A real Gulf War pro. We rendered Afghani POWs to his Egyptian lair after 9/11. He's the man who got results."

"Yeah, the torture got plenty of useful info. They only told you what you wanted to hear," Goldstein mocked.

Kane threw daggers from his steely glare. "I told you before to cut the commentary. I won't tell you again."

Kane punched his handset. The vile spectacle that Volker and Goldstein had just witnessed was about to be upstaged with the entrance of one of the most reviled pain-managers in the business. He was known by his peers as The Beast.

Hawass was a bear of a man. His slimy grin was plastered with a cluster of nicotine yellowed teeth. Jaundiced and pock faced with long greasy hair platted to his waist, two words oozed torment. "This one?"

He moved close to the Tibetan. Hot, fetid breath fed into the captive's nostrils. A thick hairy hand with filthy pointed nails lifted the monk's chin. His dark evil eyes bore into the face of human compassion.

"Leave him to me. His brain will function so he can speak, but the rest of him will be food for worms."

Kane spat a command. "Don't kill him, you hear? Gentlemen this way. Now!"

As they left the room, long amnestied memories stabbed a tortured conscience. A howl from the shadowed recesses cut the air like a scalpel. The Cardinal could take no more. He slumped to his knees and prayed for forgiveness.

The three men retired to Kane's private office overlooking the mirrored waters of the Amalfi coast. The islands were surrounded by a protected marine reserve. On this occasion, a tourist boat was anchored nearby with several snorkelers frolicking amongst the rich marine life. It was the ideal location for Kane's sanctum. Whilst they were private islands, they attracted no special attention from the day-trippers who were a constant decoy to Majestic's evil machinations. Kane figured too much secrecy would attract unwanted attention, activity nearby acted as the perfect cover. Hidden in plain sight, in a beautiful location, suited him perfectly.

Volker and Goldstein were still unsettled by what they had just witnessed. They had spotted the Cardinal seated in the darkened recess of the interrogation room.

Goldstein was curious and showed his disrespect for any form of authority that was not military. "What's with the Catholic?"

Kane was prickly. "You noticed he was Catholic did you? How astute. When I want to discuss the Cardinal with you I will. And I didn't bring you here to witness the handiwork of Hawass. These islands are my domain, so they're totally secure, regardless of what you see out there with the sightseers. We operate a tourist centre in Positano and run the boats out here on a daily basis. It means we control the area.

"The reason for this discussion is that I want you to eliminate another recalcitrant. What I'm about to tell you is classified Security 12. Any leak of this conversation will be dealt with in the harshest manner. Understood?"

Goldstein was convinced the Director suffered from some form of lunacy. The man was insufferable. He realigned his posture. He knew what the term 'harshest manner' meant.

Kane didn't wait for a response. "At the beginning of World War II, a special bureau was commissioned by the German High Command to investigate all religious artefacts, and to assess the veracity of all religions preceding Constantine the Great. Special attention was given to Egypt and Tibet. After the war the OSS ensured that the most important Nazi discoveries were suppressed. To ensure global stability, the U.S. and U.K. governments, together with the Vatican, agreed to support the mythology of Constantine Christianity to ensure certain facts remained concealed. The German Esoteric Bureau had discovered an ancient science recorded by an advanced civilisation that had been decimated by tectonic disturbance and sunk beneath the oceans."

Goldstein opined, "You talking about Atlantis again, right?"

"Actually it preceded Atlantis, a continent referred to as Lemuria."

Goldstein considered the statement fanciful, but knew there was no room for debate. His concentration hid his incredulity.

"Apart from the physical evidence uncovered, they managed to decipher a number of old legends that spoke of past cataclysms. These myths and legends have been critical to the preservation of arcane knowledge. The legend of Phaethon is a classic example. The truth of this story lies in the cyclical movement of the stars and planets which periodically destroys a great deal of terrestrial life with fire and flood."

Goldstein failed to see the importance. "Everyone knows the world's had cataclysms. There's nothing special about that."

"Of course, but what is special is the origin of man. The original race came from a group of extraterrestrials who have continued to visit the planet since their genetic breeding of Cro-Magnon Man."

Goldstein was gobsmacked. "Hang on. Everybody in intelligence has ideas about incursions into our air space by so-called UFOs. But you're saying that really happens and that we were genetically created by these ETs."

Kane had captured his attention. "Perhaps now you'll appreciate the importance of our work. It's thought our human forefathers, the Cro-Magnons, evolved around 50,000 years ago from the more primitive Neanderthal. Analysis has shown that the mitochondrial DNA was so different to the Neanderthal, it's impossible for the Cro-Magnon to have been descended from them.

"Archaeologists know the Cro-Magnons were far more

sophisticated in clothing, art and lifestyle. Even their brain cavities were different. So the question remains. Where did the Cro-Magnon come from? They were so radically different from their supposed ancestors, the ordinary theory of selective evolution doesn't account for their origin. Anthropologists have debated the issue ever since Darwin. Even Darwin himself expected the 'missing link' would be found in his lifetime. The idiots are still looking.

"Our friend Dr Keyes has been stirring up trouble for years. He was part of a European team that released a scientific paper claiming both species interbred. Keyes subsequently recanted, saying there's nothing in the fossil record to confirm the theory. He made a big point of it on his last television series. He's now intent on gathering hard evidence to prove them wrong. Baalbek holds a key to discovering that evidence, a key with the lock still missing. That's why Keyes is potentially dangerous to our cause."

"To suggest we were genetically engineered by ETs is quite a claim," ventured Goldstein.

Volker was twitchy, eager to tell it his way. "He didn't invent the idea, Ariel. It's actually written in the records. The Book of Jubilees and the even more remarkable Book of Enoch were never included as books of the Bible because of the secret history they clearly exposed."

Goldstein found the assertion far-fetched. "What? The secret history of ETs."

"Enoch spoke of the 'Watchers'. They were the sons of gods who mated with earthly women. The Watchers had learned the 'eternal secrets' of the gods. In the Book of Jubilees, the sons of the gods slaughtered the primitive indigenous hominids. The offspring of these sons of the gods became Cro-Magnon – Afro-Asian Homo Sapiens."

Goldstein kept his mouth shut. He remembered this information was Security 12 classified.

Kane followed up. "The reality of the off-worlders became public when Major Gordon Cooper testified before the United Nations. He piloted the 1963 Mercury capsule and saw a metallic, glowing green object during his final orbit. The solid object was confirmed by the Muchea tracking radar in Western Australia. Consequently, all astronaut sightings have been classified since this time. We've ensured media silence across the board."

This particular sighting was news to Volker, but it was Goldstein who was audacious. "Maybe Cooper just lost it when he was floating around up there."

Kane didn't rise to the bait, but mentioned other sightings that backed-up the Cooper story. He claimed that James McDivitt and Ed White photographed a strange craft from their Gemini capsule as they passed over Hawaii in 1965. And in the same year, James Lovell of the Gemini 7 mission spoke to Mission Control about several sightings of 'bogeys'. Even Buzz Aldrin and Neil Armstrong said UFOs monitored their presence on the moon in 1969.

"So what does all this have to do with me and your need for an elimination?" Goldstein asked.

Kane had anticipated the question. "We can't let understanding of human origin gain widespread acceptance. Every time the mainstream media gets near the question of human origin we make sure the researcher is suitably discredited and publicly humiliated. That's where the Cardinal comes in. Unwitting fool. He's the Secretary of State for the Vatican and he uses the power of Church doctrine, and that wonderful word 'faith'. It's been used to great effect over the years. They can't burn heretics at the stake anymore, but the Church's modern methods are still getting results. Whilst Keyes is a potential problem, we've now got a more urgent one."

Goldstein mouthed a smart remark. "I thought you would have it all under control."

"Too many agencies have been involved in the past, so I've

decided on a small operative cell under my command. You two are its primary recruits. Your first job Ariel is to rid me of a recalcitrant who has found a connection to the 'Watchers' mentioned in the ancient books, and is likely to divulge their connection to mankind. Even the Cardinal wouldn't be able to discredit this man. If he tried, it would be a total embarrassment to him and the Church. So it's up to us to stop him."

41

TEMPLAR STRONGHOLD

NEAR LUGANO, SWITZERLAND

Philip stabbed the intercom. "Please ask Mr MacIntosh to join us."

I was still fuming. Yet I held a tinge of excitement. The pugnacious irreverence of Mac would be welcome. Maybe he could make sense of all the nonsense.

The door opened and Mac strolled in looking as though he had just taken a Caribbean holiday.

"You haven't got any more handsome," he smirked.

"I was better before I had half my head removed."

"Yeah, I heard about that. You OK?"

"How can I be, I can't make any sense of all this."

Philip broke the banter. "Now that you're reacquainted, I'm sure you both want to know how Aiden's photographs fit into all of this."

Mac nodded. "Go for it. What're we dealing with?"

"We obtained information that Majestic was tracking you Aiden. They obviously knew about your excavation. If Keisha hadn't made the connection we're certain you would have faced an unfortunate accident."

"Why does this Majestic or Belial as you call them, give a damn about some photographs?" I enquired.

"Because the illusion would be shattered, society would finally break out of its perpetual servitude. Political and financial structures would be threatened. People would come to know who they truly are."

Philip's spoke as though he were a teacher at Junior Primary. He was trying to wake a sleeping infant. "Aiden, don't let the illusions of the world fool you. Belial has been controlling the masses since Babylonian times. Their method of manipulation has varied little. To control the flock you only need to control the dominant leaders. Stragglers can always be dealt with later. A firm hand over the dominants gives total control. To achieve this goal, historical and literal truth has been replaced with a litany of lies. Control of the media has been crucial to their goals."

Philip explained how the exiled Israelites compiled their written texts around the 6th century BCE, but much of it was taken from earlier Babylonian records. Scribes made numerous translational and interpretational errors and by the 2nd century BCE, Belial had infiltrated the religious orders injecting their own spurious mythological element into the texts. Destruction of the authentic records was part of the process of their control, the loss of the great Library of Alexandria being one such example. I remembered the collection of Otto's tattered copies that were equally destroyed.

"Is this your reasoning around Otto's death and the burning of his books?"

"We don't think so. They know what those manuscripts contained. It was more a warning to you and to us, but I'm sure they saw the fire as an added bonus. However, hard evidence of the Annunaki will reveal the true history of Earth and they will try everything to bury it. Your implant and young Santini's death makes that clear. The manuscripts of Alexandria contained knowledge of the all the known sciences, especially the great spiritual works passed down since pre-dynastical Egypt, a time known as Zep Tepi, some forty thousand years ago."

I glanced at Mac and repeated my previous declaration, "Can you believe it Mac? Forty thousand years. Man had just developed the skills to spit a paste on the walls of caves thirty two thousand years ago to create the first paintings, but eight thousand years before that, man was supposedly passing down great spiritual works. Somehow, I don't think so!"

Mac's reply was authoritative. "Hear Philip out, Aiden. I've learned to do so." His tone left little room for dissention.

"Go on then, I'm listening."

"The Cathars were the last society in Europe to be blessed with this knowledge. It radically undermined all faith based religions and threatened the political and monetary elite."

Philip explained the Cathar demise in detail. Word of their religious persecution had spread and around the year 1210, Raymond de Péreille built a protective fortress at Montsegur. It was rumoured that the citadel held the legendary Grail treasure. A papal decree known as Ad Abolendum had already been prescribed in 1184, specifically condemning the Cathars for heresy. Known as the Albigensian Crusade, the Church crusaders set out to destroy. They extracted a death toll in excess of one million souls over a fifty year period. Not only were the Cathars murdered, but so too were those who refused to condemn them. Much of population of southern France was decimated.

The fortress at Montsegur was the final bastion of hope for those who refused to bow to official theological doctrine. Precariously perched on a peak above the surrounding countryside, the whitened ruins of today are from a later period because the fortress was pulled down by royal French forces after it was besieged in March 1244. The original castle had held for nine months, but finally through an act of treachery, the invaders scaled the cliffs. As the castle succumbed, the defeated occupants marched down the mountainside singing. They were offered lenient terms if they renounced their heretical beliefs, but not one of them recanted. They chose death rather than renounce the sacred doctrine. Over two hundred Cathars were burned en-masse below the fortress at the behest of the Church. Men, women and children were marched into the bonfires that had been prepared for them. Their faith was more powerful than the agony of the searing fires or the earthly attachment to life. Today, a solar cross stands as a silent sentinel to this unspeakable crime.

The Church believed the Cathars also had possession of the Ark of the Covenant, and other priceless treasures which they assumed were hidden somewhere in the Languedoc area. These artefacts threatened ecclesiastical power. Hence, at the siege of Beziers in 1209, when asked how to distinguish the Catholic faithful from the Cathar enemy, an edict was declared by the Cistercian papal inquisitor, Arnaud Almalric. He announced, *'Kill them all! For the Lord knows them that are His'.*

The Cathars and other Gnostic groups were linked to the Templars, and had a spiritual knowledge that far surpassed the contrived theology of the Church. They were the guardians of the sacred gnosis. The Albigensian crusade rooted them out and attention was then focused on the Templars. By the beginning of the 14th century, they had consolidated into the wealthiest fraternity in Europe. But King Philippe IV of France was determined to bring them to heel in a bold attempt to absolve his indebtedness to them. With the French Pope, Clement V, under his influence, the Knights eventually faced the blind savagery of the Inquisition. Clement conspired with King Philippe in an effort to eradicate the Knight's knowledge of human genesis, the truth about Jesus, the Resurrection and most importantly, their understanding of the authentic doctrines.

I quizzed Philip with this historical exposé. "Otto told me that history is written by the winners. How do you know this version is true when they were the obvious losers?"

Philip was steadfast, "It's our job to know. You're in the latest stronghold of the Order of Elysius, the sole successors to the Knights Templar."

42

HERESY

VIENNA, AUSTRIA

Although Angelo had always been deeply religious, he found talk of the spirit realm disturbing. In the Church, such notions were left to interpretation and pronouncement by the religious hierarchy. Nevertheless, the mysterious Order of Melchizedek was clearly linked to Jesus, although nothing was known about the association. Angelo was puzzled.

Comte tried to placate him. "What we now call theology was once a combined science of the physical and the mind. The Order regarded physical science as important, but nowhere near as important as the science of human existence. Like the Egyptians, it was the knowledge of what lay beyond death that consumed them."

"Only God knows what happens after death. How can anyone possibly know?"

Childeric turned and stared. In the subdued light, his eyes were shadowed by his heavy eyebrows, his glare not penetrating Angelo's vision. "They did, and they didn't think they knew, they *did* know."

Angelo sheepishly acknowledged with a nod. He wasn't convinced by the confident matter-of-factness.

Childeric pushed. "Have you heard of the chakras and Kundalini?"

Angelo thought this type of discussion was the sharp edge of heresy. "Not really."

"Traditional concepts are slowly being unravelled. Even psychics look toward these ancient truths. Super-string theory claims there are at least ten dimensions of space and time. Everything we observe manifests because of its vibration. If the rate of vibration changes, so does the nature of reality, most often to something we can't see or perceive. Do you understand what I'm saying Angelo? *Everything changes but we don't necessarily see it.*"

Angelo had followed carefully and nodded acceptance.

"In these spatial dimensions the old monks of the Far East and also some of the original Christians experienced oneness."

Angelo thought through the proposition. "Tell me if I understand what you're saying. If you're watching a reel of film and could only see one in every six frames, then theoretically there are six separate movies on the reel. Those watching the first frame of every six would see a different film from those who watch the second frame of every six. Am I right?"

"Excellent analogy, Angelo; couldn't do better myself. The Order of Melchizedek knew how to access transcendental realms. In the past 'yoga' was focused on manipulating consciousness. It wasn't associated with the physical ritual practised by the West. 'Yoga' means 'union' with the spiritual world. In Eastern yoga, they understand that electromagnetic points on the body interact with different dimensional realities. These points are the chakras, each one manifesting at different vibrational rates. Make sense?"

"I think so. These chakras somehow interact with different realities."

"Yes. Chakras act like tuned antennae. The first chakra rules our survival consciousness and the second stimulates sexual arousal. The third stimulates intuition and when a person feels 'in love', their fourth chakra is active. For most people, the fifth, sixth and seventh are rarely activated. These are gateways to higher realities."

Comte interjected. "Activating the higher chakras allows the rise of 'Kundalini' energy up the spinal column to the pineal gland where Enlightenment is achieved. It was practised by the Egyptian Therapeutate whose symbol of two snakes coiled around a winged pole is still used by medical associations around the world. It represents our link to the spiritual."

Angelo was once again intrigued by Comte's obscure knowledge. He was being opened to further counsel that Comte was now willing to divulge.

Comte took a deep breath in the musty air. "At the moment of sexual orgasm Kundalini travels from the base chakra and escapes to the second chakra. You know that feeling?"

Angelo gave an embarrassed shrug.

"The sexual impulse has been completely misunderstood by the Church. It has nothing to do with 'sin'. Rather than releasing Kundalini it in its lower state, the true adept allows it to rise up through all the chakras to the seventh. In this way, consciousness is refined and raised to the point of ultimate transcendence. The objective is nothing less than union with the Creator. In Old Egyptian, Kundalini was called Sekhem, meaning Serpent Energy – the energy that sustains the entire universe, the creative principle itself that manifests as the Cosmos. Its origin is simply known as God by the common religions."

Angelo's efficacious mind thought of the serpent that tempted Eve with the knowledge of Good and Evil. "Is this why the serpent is both revered and denigrated in various civilizations and societies?"

"Now you're thinking, Angelo. The Old Kingdom was obsessed with attaining 'Second Sight', the Eye of Heru, known today as the Eye of Horus, more valuable than all the material wealth in existence. After all, we can't take our possessions with us when we die, but we do take our spiritual evolution with us."

43

ORME

___

NEAR LUGANO, SWITZERLAND

Mac grinned in silent admiration. Elysius – successors to the Order of the Knights Templar! It obviously struck a chord within him. I saw it in his expression. I could imagine his thoughts. *'Poor bastard's still trying to get his head around it all.'* He was right.

Mac knew the history of the Templar downfall well. He was keen to expand my understanding. I discovered that in the beginning of the 14th century, the Papacy had become an instrument of French policy with the Papal Court based in Avignon. The focal point of Christendom had collapsed, the popes being nothing more than absentee landlords of the Italian Papal States. Civil war raged among the prominent families and Rome had been left to the mercy of thieves and killers. By the time of Christendom's jubilee year in 1350, as fifty thousand pilgrims a day arrived to pray at the tomb of St. Peter, cows actually grazed on grass within the dilapidated apse. Rome was in abject decay.

In June 1305, in an act of selfish advantage, King Philippe IV of France arranged the election of Bertrand de Got as archbishop of Bordeaux who was eventually crowned as Pope Clement V. In fear of his life, Clement never went to Rome and he settled in Avignon where the papacy owned two vast estates. The papacy remained there for another seventy two years with seven popes in succession being French.

Philippe was hugely indebted to the Templars and he deceitfully leaned on Clement. He drew up a list of accusations and with the Knights disregard for a great deal of Church theology they became easy targets for charges of heresy. Individuals were interrogated, tortured, imprisoned and burned to death. Paid witnesses gave false testimony accusing them of all manner of evil, including sorcery, homosexuality, necromancy and blasphemy. Philipe's other objective was to capture the Templar hoard excavated from the Holy Land. It was never found.

Philip interposed, "So true Alex. It was Jacques de Morlay; the 23rd Grand Master who ensured the treasure was removed. It was spirited away on a fleet of galleys from La Rochelle on the Bay of Biscay."

"The fleet went to Scotland, right?"

"Some of the galleys did, but a few harboured in Portugal."

"Which ones were the decoys?"

"The final resting place Alex is still a secret, even within our Order."

Mac smiled and pushed further. "OK I'll let that go, but can you tell me what was so special about the Ark?"

Philip paused for a few moments, as though considering the best way to answer. "It's apparent from the Old Testament that the Ark was the most blessed of all the Israelite artefacts. It's recorded that the Ark killed people if not handled correctly. Its description suggests that it was a dielectric capacitor."

"You reckon they had the skill to create a capacitor?"

"Unlikely. It was probably a remnant from a more technically advanced civilisation. The Bible indicates the 'fire' that sometimes emerged from the Ark was preceded by a glow. This electrical ionising effect was described as the 'glory of the Lord'.

"The surviving Templars eventually gathered together, but to protect what they knew they had to remain clandestine. This helped to retain the Ark's other secret. It was also a receptacle for what the Israelites called Manna. Early last century, Sir Flinders Petrie found the substance after he and his team scaled Serabit el Khadin on the Sinai plateau. They discovered the ruins of a Temple of Hathor dating back 4,600 years to Pharaoh Sneferu. Modern research indicates the substance is an ORME."

Mac casually muttered, "Orbitally Rearranged Monatomic Element."

Clever bastard. "A what?"

"It's the latest thing in physics," Mac declared. "They're a rare group of super-conductive metals where the electrons don't cancel each other out as would be expected. It results in a unique magnetic field with no polarity, repelling other magnetic fields."

"Give me a break. Talk plain English."

Philip explained. "Our scientists have discovered that when this substance enters its super-conductive state, it loses 44% of its weight. It reduces gravity fields and consequently bends space-time."

Mac noticed my dumb frown. "Any substance that loses weight must lose it to somewhere. The matter must be transported to somewhere else. True?"

I reasoned the statement was correct. I nodded in agreement.

"If substance is lost to our dimension and it still exists, then it must pass to another dimension."

Philip's eyes sparkled. "I'll let you in on the secret, Aiden. The Egyptians called it Mfktz and it was used as an inter-dimensional gateway of the mind. Through the process of induction, it caused a portion of the human brain to lose weight. A small amount of matter was temporarily translocated into another realm. The Hierophants, the pre-dynastical Pharaohs, and those who came before them, used to ingest the substance so that their consciousness could penetrate the realm beyond death. The Egyptian Book of the Dead describes how the minds of the hierophants were transported to the blessed Dimension of the Orbit of Light.

"Now's as good a time as any to tell you about that white powder you ingested at Baalbek. Keisha had us test it for you. Your sample displayed all the characteristics of an ORME. It would explain your strange experience. No wonder Belial is threatened."

44

GODS & DEMONS

APOSTOLIC PENITENTIARY, VATICAN CITY

Cardinal Valla sensed something wrong. It wasn't like Angelo to be absent. He weighed the unpalatable possibilities and one cause became likely. *Comte!*

The mere thought of Comte provoked suspicion and vexation. Valla had wanted him removed from the Vatican on a number of occasions. The man possessed a powerful and contemptuous intellect with the ability to tear holes in centuries old theology. He was a loose cannon. Fortunately, his tenure as the keeper of an obscure archive had kept him quiet. *'In the past a man like Comte would have been treated as a heretic. And that alone would have been his end.'* He prepared for a confrontation with the hideous keeper and commenced the walk to Comte's den. If Angelo was there, he would have hell to pay.

He traversed the cavernous *L'Archivio Segreto* and entered the secluded anteroom. He knew it! The disgusting keeper was nowhere to be seen. Anticipating this, he dug deep in his pocket for the physical key that provided access to Comte's inner lair. It acted as an override to the electronics. His entry would not be recorded.

Valla scanned the keeper's ordered desk. Files were neatly stacked, various manuscripts ready for permanent scanning onto the Vatican mainframe, with others waiting for file reassessment. His eye curiously honed in on various post-it notes sticking out from a printout sandwiched between folders in Comte's desk tray. Valla reached for the files. He quickly rummaged through them to access the printout. What he found pummelled him like a boxer's right-hand jab. It was titled *The Book of Enoch* and was secured with a fold-back clip.

Valla was incensed. His cheeks flushed with anger. The book was a dangerous enigma, revealing far too much about the history of humankind. The keeper was now an insidious threat. Enoch had referred to the 'Watchers' saying their ancestral spirit was destined to, '...*afflict, oppress, destroy, attack, do battle and work destruction on Earth*'.

The Cardinal knew all about Enoch. His name in Hebrew meant 'initiated' and his status was unique; he had 'walked with God'. Valla believed attacks on Church authority came from faithless and misin-formed fools who would never accept the role of the Church. Comte was hardly misinformed and certainly not a fool. The Cardinal knew he would also be aware of other texts like the Book of Jubilees and the Book of Noah.

Flicking through the pages of the computer printout, Valla was deeply shaken. His dark brown eyes burned into a passage Comte had deliberately highlighted. Enoch 108:4: '*And I saw there something like an invisible cloud; for by reason of its depth I could not look over it, and I saw a flame of fire blazing brightly, and things like shining mountains circling and sweeping to and fro.*'

The Book of Enoch had been describing the flying vehicle of the gods. Valla considered the phenomena demonic, but like Enoch, Valla's controllers did not. The Cardinal noticed Comte's thoroughness. Highlighted text near the beginning of the printout outlined Enoch's summons to the mothership. Enoch 14:8 read: '*And the vision was shown to me thus: Behold, in the vision, clouds invited me and a mist summoned me, and the course of the stars and the lightenings sped and hastened me, and the winds in the vision caused me to fly and lifted me upward, and bore me into heaven.'*

There was further damaging material in the folder. The Apocalypse of Lamech, one of the original Dead Sea Scrolls, describes the son of Lamech as more like 'the children of the angels in heaven' than a human being. *'More like the sons of the gods.'* Lamech had questioned his wife about the paternity of the child, *'Behold, I thought then within my heart that conception was due to the Watchers and the Holy Ones ...and to the Nephilim ...and my heart was troubled within me because of this child.'*

The chill of inevitability swept over the Cardinal. *Comte had to be contained.* Valla's soul had been bought long ago and now, another progress payment was due.

From the deep folds of his soutane, he reached for his cell phone and dialled the encrypted number.

45

AGENDA

VATICAN CITY

If the fractious mutant dared to set about destroying social norms, then some collateral damage would be necessary. It carried the added bonus of a stark warning to the Vatican Secretary of State. *Perhaps a crucifixion of the disfigured traitor in the Piazza San Pietro would send the right message.*

Kane screamed into the encrypted phone link. "Maybe it's time to cut you loose, Your Holy Fucking Eminence! For Christ's sake, how could you let that monstrosity threaten everything we've worked for?" The words were sharp and gravelled, laced with threat and intent rather than accusation.

"Look, I didn't realise things were so bad. I shoved him away in that archive years ago. I thought he was under your control, he's your man after all?"

Kane's face hardened with fury. "You fucking thought! You're getting old and sloppy Valla. Why would you think I need a socio-pathic freak like Comte? You listen and listen well. You made an oath – remember. The society at Yale groomed you to have position within the Church and groomed me to have control over you, not

Comte. Understand!" His words dripped with malice.

Valla tensed, "I can do without the reprimand, so keep you're shit together. I've given you information about a potential problem and I've passed the mantel. If you want control, you've got it. What more do you want?"

"You've given information. What a fucking joke. I own your position Valla. Just remember that. I already know about this Comte, we've hacked his computer. Thankfully, our intelligence in your little paradise runs a lot deeper than just you. I dispensed my elimination order on the freak when you lost your nerve with the Tibetan. God, if we relied on you, who knows what mess we'd be in. Just when I need you to tell me where this Comte is, you've suddenly got no fucking idea."

Valla was tired, so tired of the shackles that chained him. The rebuke was salt to the wound. *I've always known I've been watched. If not by Comte, then who?* Valla had always thought Comte was his nemesis. He had struggled hard for the Pope's approval to have him removed from his staff and into the obscure archive. Now, Kane had told him about intelligence running much deeper. If not Comte, who? *Agostino?*

He played the matter down. "Look, it's not that bad. How much could he have worked out anyway?"

Kane snapped back. "Are you a complete fool? You gave him unrestricted access to manuscripts going back thirteen centuries for Christ sake. The man has a pathological tenacity and a major axe to grind, mainly against you for putting him there. That's a volatile combination."

"I know he's had access to those documents, but how deep can his knowledge go. There's hundreds of thousands of manuscripts in there, the vast majority having absolutely no significance. You've just told me you've had him watched, so how dangerous can he really be?"

Kane's intelligence was fresh. His contact had just become active after a long incubation and he wasn't about to expose him. Valla had remained reasonably composed, so Kane went for the jugular. "He's aware of the Church's dispatches with the Nazis during the war. He knows about the meetings between the Pope's envoy and the German Esoteric Bureau. He's copied the minutes. Shall I go on? Jesus Christ, man, if their activities are exposed, the pact Eisenhower made with the off-worlders will be finished. If this gets out, I hope you've written your epitaph. We've been able to deny their existence for more than half a century, but a breach would be fatal."

It was the same old garbage about off-worlders. Why couldn't the man just call them demons? Valla reacted, "Don't threaten me with my epitaph. The Nazis abused and killed my mother, and I'll meet my maker soon enough."

"Listen, don't lose your zucchetto. Just keep your end of the bargain and you'll keep your scarlet silk. Comte needs the ultimate restraint. Otherwise you're obsolete, do I make myself clear?"

Valla drew a deep breath. "Of course, you're right, but maintenance of faith is becoming increasingly difficult. I don't need you reminding me of the agenda."

"Good. The concept of religious faith has certainly been helpful to our cause. But we need to be more vigilant. Having a madman like Hitler backing one faction, while Roosevelt backed another, has only made our job more difficult. Look, this Comte is either very lucky or is one of the most extraordinary analysts I've come across. Our real concern is that he's dug deeper than we suspect. We discovered complete dossiers on his deleted files. He's recorded the pivotal role of Hess and Haushofer, and the impact of the Aldebaran's on the Nazi military-industrial complex. Fortunately, nothing from his computer has been emailed anywhere. But he's printed reams of material and I need to know what he's done with it all."

Valla had made it his business to understand those critical end days of the War. His mother had been his last living relative and he didn't want her death to be in vain. At the age of ten, he had little choice and journeyed to the States with Colonel Hudson. Authorities wanted his eyewitness account of his mother's activities. As an adult, he studied the significance of Haushofer and Hess, and concluded they had been possessed by the devil.

During his youth and his years at Yale, he discovered little about his mother's activities. They were considered highly classified. Only when he had risen to power within the Vatican and had the necessary security clearances did he learn the secret. It was Veles Kane who had filled in the blanks. The man was tedious. His oration about the 'off-worlders' was never backed with physical proof, just severe warnings of the meaning of classification security-12.

Kane had told him of the events surrounding a woman known as Maria Oršić, a member of the Vril Society. In December 1919, she presented telepathically channelled messages to a small group of Vril and Thule Gesselschaft members. She claimed that the messages had originated from a being that dwelt in the solar system called Aldebaran, 68 light years away from Earth in the constellation of Taurus. Revulsion for the economic disparity suffered by the majority on Earth, aberrations that fuelled conflict and war was claimed as the motivation for the channelled transmissions. Blueprints for free energy and affordable mass transportation devices had been clairvoyantly received in an effort to create prosperity and peaceful interaction. The messages also contained instructions for the building of a circular flying machine.

Dr W.O. Schumman from the University of Munich studied the details and realised that viable physics for the construction of a flying machine had been bestowed. By 1922, preliminary work on a prototype was underway.

Subsequently in 1924, together with Rudolf von Sebottendorf, the founder of the Thule Gesellschaft, Maria Oršić visited Rudolf

Hess at his apartment in Munich. Hess was unnerved by her trance state during her performance. Her slumped sitting position, her gaping mouth and her rolled back, capillary filled eyeballs disconcerted him. During the session a thick guttural voice came through, the proponent claiming to be from the planet Sumi in the Alderbaran system. It was claimed that the Sumi's were a humanoid race that had briefly colonised the Earth and were the ancestors of the Aryan race.

Sebottendorf was sceptical and asked for proof. Oršić, still in trance, scratched a scribble of markings. They turned out to be ancient Sumerian characters, something the medium had no knowledge about.

Hess had always been beguiled with Hitler's oratory ability. He mistakenly believed he could lead the world to a golden age. Haushofer was also intrigued with what he thought was Hitler's grasp of esoteric concepts. If his ability was used wisely, the result would surely be a better world. In 1933, when the National Socialists came to power, Hitler was astute enough to use some of his limited knowledge. In an act of thorough brilliance, he took his cue from Abraham Lincoln and with like-minded inspiration, he transformed an economy. He decided to thwart the international banking cartel by taking control of the issuance of money. This act reformed Germany from a basket case into an economic powerhouse and was clearly the basis for Time Magazine bestowing upon him the coveted title of '1939 – Man of the Year'.

Hitler was complex and had the cunning ability to decimate opposing political arguments. Back in 1923, after the failed Munich Beer Hall Putsch, a coup d'état that sent Hitler and Hess to jail, Haushofer witnessed Hitler's speech at his sentencing hearing. It made a powerful impact upon him and he misguidedly decided Hitler could be used for good purpose. Haushofer visited them in jail. He even contributed a full chapter to Hitler's Mien Kamph. After their release, it was Haushofer who established the blueprint for Germano-Japanese domination of the globe, the so-called Axis Alliance.

According to Maria Oršić and her fellow medium Sigrun, the humanoids from the Aldebaran system colonised Mars before arriving on Earth where they genetically seeded the Sumerian civilisation. This became the catalyst to the insanity of Hitler's pure race.

In due course, the Reich commissioned an esoteric research bureau to discover and incorporate knowledge from the ancient doctrines. They conducted extensive explorations into Tibet, Egypt and the Far East. They had a measure of success discovering a few ancient relics and codices. Before the end of the war, the Reich had decoded a few fragments of the doctrines and had discovered the extraordinary fourth dimensional nature of science. Sadly, the Reich's inability to understand the doctrines resulted in the many horrors of the War. A number of senior members of the Reich had unwittingly locked themselves into a regressive consciousness.

During his speeches, Hitler was transfigured by malevolent energy. Somehow he captivated a nation. Hitler's aide, Hermann Rauschning, believed that Hitler was a form of 'channel'.

Despite the search by the Nazis for the ultimate doctrine, they could never do more than breach its outer walls. Valla's mother, Carla, met Maria Oršić in Munich when the young Antonio was a toddler. She was dazzled by Maria and her fun-loving bohemian friends. They were passionate women filled with hope for a better world. Carla soon discovered she had the gift as well and, she too, would channel. In March 1945, Oršić disappeared. The war was already lost, but the SS elite who had always taken a particular interest in Carla used her until the very end. It saddened the Cardinal deeply that she had channelled for those who had brought the world to the edge of total destruction.

Valla was conflicted. He believed most of Kane's disclosures were the manipulations of the devil. But at the same time, he acknowledged that in 1954, the father of rocketry, Professor Hermann Oberth, a man of prodigious intellect and science stated, *'It is my thesis that flying saucers are real, and that they are space ships from another solar system. I think that they possibly are manned by intelligent observers who are members of a race that may have been investigating our earth for centuries...'*

Kane was sullen. This whole episode had tarnished Majestic and corroded his every fibre. He wound up the call. "To top it off, your fucking keeper has managed to discern the fourth-dimensional nature of the ancient sciences. He's a bomb with the fuse lit. If he shows his face again, reprimand him as normal, nothing more. I'll take care of the rest."

46

ORBIT OF LIGHT

NEAR LUGANO, SWITZERLAND

Mac was hooked. The Dimension of the Orbit of Light – a dimensional gateway for the mind. It was certainly an explanation for my strange hallucinations.

Philip spoke of the Pyramid Texts and their mention of the Afterlife, known as the Field of Mfkzt. Anubis the jackal-god symbolically presided over funeral rites and was known as the 'Guardian of the Secret'. On a stone relief from the 19th dynasty a pharaoh presents him with a conical loaf of Mfkzt to unlock the dimension of the Light Body. In Serabit, steles depict two different pharaohs, Tuthmosis and Amenhotep, presenting a conical loaf to the gods Amunre and Sopdu respectively. The inscription explains that both Pharaohs were given eternal life.

"The alchemists of the middle ages tried to unlock the secrets of Mfkzt, which they knew as manna, the sacred bread of the ancient Hebrews. The alchemist Nicolas Flamel honoured it as the legendary Philosophers Stone, able to confer a form of immortality. Today, only a few remnant traditions teach The Sacred Path, to attain what Christians call the Resurrection," Philip declared.

He then asked me a ridiculous question. "Who are you Aiden?"

"I asked you the same question remember," was my disinterested reply.

"Yes, you did and I told you what you wanted to know. But this time, I'm asking you."

"You already know who I am. You had my full credentials, remember."

"Just play along then. Tell me who you are."

The inane question was tiresome. "I'm Aiden Keyes."

"No Aiden. That's your name. Who are you?"

I shifted uncomfortably and looked at Mac for a clue. *What was he on about?* Mac just smirked.

"I'm not sure what you're asking."

"It's a simple enough question."

"You can see who I am, you're looking at me."

"I'm looking at your body. Do you think you're a physical body?"

The question was a riddle, but I didn't know how to reply. "Well yes, I guess."

"If I removed your arm or your leg, does that make 'you' any less you?"

"Not exactly…"

"Correct. Your physical self is just flesh and bone. You're far more than that aren't you?"

"Yes, of course. I guess I'm made up of my mind, my thoughts. I don't know." I was confused. "You'll need to explain."

"Your mind allows 'YOU' to think, correct? Your brain is the organ that allows YOU to cognise and perceive. It allows YOU to assess information, to reason, to retain knowledge."

"Yes, that's a fair assessment.

"Well, what is it that knows the knowledge?"

Was this a semantic trap of language or a logical sleight of hand? I admitted my ignorance. "I don't get it."

"All of us perceive, right. But we also perceive ourselves perceiving. We just don't know things, we know that we know. In all of us, there is a 'witness' that is able cognise. Reality exists with this eternal Witness, not with the thought itself. The Witness, the Higher Self and Pure Consciousness are all interchangeable."

"I know that I know things, but I'm still not sure what you mean," I said with a deepening frown.

"Well, you just said 'I know'. Who's 'I', Aiden? You agreed it's not the body, the brain or the mind. Your 'I' is the Witness, sometimes called the Higher Self. And therein lays the problem. People don't even know who they are anymore. Remember the old aphorism, *Know Thyself*. Most have no idea."

"So who do you think I am?" I asked defensively.

Philip shook his head. "Oh no, it doesn't work like that. It doesn't matter about me or anybody else, but it's important for you to know, don't you think."

"I've coped so far."

"Of course, but if you truly know who you are, it allows you to answer the big question. What it is that actually dies when we pass from this life.

"The Egyptians believed a type of portal divided this world from our existence beyond death. The classic tunnel of light described in so many near death experiences. Today, we have thousands of worldly subjects to amuse us, but the one that consumed the Egyptians was the science of immortality, the achievement of Enlightenment."

47

RETURN

VATICAN CITY

The men from Rome left Vienna after one night's stay. Angelo felt strangely alienated and appreciated the night's respite before he faced the belligerent Cardinal. Their flight was early and they were back at work at the usual time.

Both men had been summoned and at precisely 9:30 a.m. they stood before their inquisitor. Valla was perched high at his antique desk, stony-faced with irritation.

"We decided on an impromptu trip into the city," explained Comte. "I suppose we just got carried away."

The Cardinal was incredulous, "That's one interpretation. A less charitable version is you abandoned the Church, not giving a damn about your responsibilities."

Comte was eager to debate. He relished any opportunity to needle the Cardinal. Enmity visibly pulsed at Valla's temple. "There's another interpretation," Comte jousted. "The Church exists for one reason, to espouse the truth of God. What if our trip brought us closer to the truth?"

The Cardinal's cheeks flushed with his close companion, the

insatiable fiend called acrimony. "Perhaps you would like to elaborate?" he seethed.

Comte appraised Valla like opposing wrestlers. "What if our faith is missing the point of the Divine, missing the point of spirituality? What if the Bible has two quite distinct levels of interpretation? On the surface, a bunch of parables which zealots like you pronounce with warlike conviction, but underneath, a hidden doctrine for those capable of understanding without the intercession of priests."

"Preposterous," yelled Valla. "Baseless and utter rubbish!" The purple vein pulsing at his temple almost burst. Despite his rebuttal, Valla was well aware of Comte's assertion.

Angelo was sombre, cringing in silence as he prepared for Comte's deft manoeuvring. "You're forgetting something Your Eminence?"

"Forgetting what?" Valla asked tersely. His face furrowed into a burning scowl.

"Jesus said, *'Unto you it is given to know the mystery of the Kingdom of God; but unto those that are without, all things are done in parables'*. I simply ask Your Eminence, does the Church teach parables or does it teach the mysteries of the Kingdom of God?"

"We teach the Bible you fool. What in the devil's name are you doing in this House of God?"

If only he knew. Comte pasted a contorted smile designed to taunt, "But surely, Your Eminence, you would have me do the work of God."

A fleck of spit projected toward Comte as Valla screamed. "You work for the Church and you'll do as I tell you. Do you understand?"

Cool to the core Comte replied, "Jesus taught his disciples to seek interior knowledge by not listening to belligerent assholes. I have faith in that message. It was you who placed me in the archive and I'll seek knowledge according to Jesus." His voice distilled mockery. "Or are you suggesting I should put my faith in you?"

"Listen to me, you pathetic excuse of a man. You can go to hell if you wish, but I'll stop your influence on this young mind. Do you hear me?" Valla stared at Angelo as though he was battling for his soul. But Angelo noticed once again, reptilian eyes burning with enmity.

"I thank you for allowing me my right to choose Your Eminence. As for this young man, surely you would allow him the same right."

Comte pushed his advantage with one of his quotes, "Something else Jesus said, *'Beware that no one lead you astray, saying, 'Lo here!' or 'Lo there!' for the Son of Man is within you. Follow Him. Those who seek Him will find Him.'* Have you found Him, Your Eminence?"

Comte wasn't finished. He pushed Valla's button one more time. "I'm sure you're aware Christ taught that sin is an imbalance of the soul. So I will repeat your question of me. What are you doing in this House of God?"

Although the Cardinal wanted to crush Comte and humiliate him, he didn't have the energy. The Kingdom did lie *within*.

His lips bleated with manic fury. "How dare you. Get the fuck out! Get out!!" he screeched. "Both of you. Your days are numbered; I can assure you of that." Valla fumbled in his desk drawer and removed his medication.

The keeper had been a thorn in Valla's side ever since his return from Rwanda. Valla believed that Comte's outrage over the brutal genocide and that his rejection of authority was completely unjustified. He believed that Comte's ire was feigned, a sly subterfuge to gain Valla's confidence. Comte had been selected as Valla's personal secretary after he had recovered from his horrific injuries, but Valla thought he was the eyes and ears of Majestic, strategically positioned to infiltrate his office. Consequently, Valla had vigorously obstructed his appointment. He manoeuvred the grotesque individual into the archive of the Apostolic Penitentiary. It was a decision he now regretted. Comte had been more dangerous to him as the keeper than he had ever imagined.

Veles Kane was right. Valla had sold his soul to Majestic years ago. He was tired, and felt so debilitated by the iron grip that was choking the last of his independent decency.

"That went well," joked Comte.

Angelo was still petrified by the Cardinal's enraged onslaught. Valla had threatened to end Comte's tenure and maybe even his own. Despite a weakening resolve, Angelo still held a tenuous loyalty to the Church. *Perhaps the Church is my psychological security blanket, he thought. With everything that's happened, it shouldn't be. Somehow Comte doesn't seem to have a care in the world.*

"It's all lies," announced Comte as he hobbled back to the comfortable seclusion of his anteroom. "Valla knows they've been suppressing the truth for centuries. The Templars, the Cathars, the Freemasons and all the rest have consistently rejected the orthodoxy's false hierarchy and their suppression of the Sacred Feminine."

Angelo's ears suddenly tuned like an antenna. "What do you mean, the Sacred Feminine?"

"You know how it is. The Church gets into an almighty twist over the role of women. It's all garbage. The feminine principle has been deliberately repressed from its very beginning. Jesus always held women in equal regard to men and considered the Magdalene the truest of all his disciples. He endowed her with the most subtle of his teachings."

Angelo almost cringed at his own words of heresy. "I've heard some say Jesus didn't die on the cross. They reckon he was revived and even had children with Mary Magdalene."

"Yeah, so I've heard," replied Comte with complete disinterest. "There's a fair bit of circumstantial evidence which points in that direction. One thing I'm certain about though is the *Pistis Sophia* text. It explains how Jesus taught the liberation of the Divine

Feminine. The disciples, Peter and Andrew, preferred a much narrower interpretation of his teaching. Jesus specifically warned them against a literal approach, saying it led to chauvinism and ignorance. He was right. Look at this place, Angelo. Thank God times are changing; people no longer believe that male priests and paternal politicians hold a monopoly on truth any more. They've destroyed the public's trust."

"I know; I'm beginning to wonder what I'm doing here."

Comte stole a long deep breath. "There's a new force gathering and the restoration of the feminine principle is part of the process. The distorted past will eventually explode in the face of the foolish and the bigoted, especially the Valla's of this world."

48

THREAT OF DEATH

VATICAN CITY

The Cardinal had proclaimed his threatening edict, but the day drifted by without incident. Comte was completing his final activity when a message was flagged to his inbox. He clicked the mouse to reveal it.

His Eminence will keep his word.
Removal before sunrise.
Rendezvous at Mausoleum of Augustus.
1.30 a.m. tonight.

The keeper scrutinised the wording, paused and reflected for several moments. He tapped the delete key. That tap not only deleted the message, but also erased all saved documents, even his password protected files. His years of work were eliminated in seconds. The hard drive completed its specially programmed termination. He heard it whirl, its spin causing a shimmer of heat to rise and dissipate. The machine was rendered useless. Any forensic examination of its digital footprints would now be futile.

His brave assault on Cardinal Valla had sealed his destiny and the obliteration of his files had ensured the point of no return. Comte gathered his papers and placed them in a large brown envelope. These would probably be the last contribution he would make to his benefactors. Valla had delivered his ultimatum and Comte was determined to take it seriously. Maybe the message was a ploy to lure him, but he knew it would always come to this, so the decision was not difficult. His work in within the Vatican was done. His only regret was Angelo. Any discussion about the note might put the young man in further danger.

"You're right you know," remarked Angelo as he casually walked into the anteroom moments later. Comte was happy to see him. It would be the last time.

"I'm right about what?"

"I never believed we could acquire knowledge of spiritual things without the grace of the Church, but I've realised this was part of my conditioning."

Comte was blunt. "Brainwashing, I'd say."

"Maybe. Anyway, I've spent the day thinking. I've always struggled with the idea of God being within us, but I read the quote by Jesus in John 10.

Comte couldn't resist and quoted the passage. *"Is it not written in your own law that God said, You are gods."*

"You amaze me Comte, how do you remember scripture so well."

"Forget that, I'm just pleased you can now 'see'."

"There's also Psalms 82. *'I have said, Ye are gods; and all of you are children of the most High.'* It's what you said the other day. There is an inner message, a Secret Doctrine."

Comte was pleased with Angelo's progress. He felt an inner satisfaction that he had been able to help the young man. "Of course, so what does it mean?"

"Jesus was saying that we are and have always been part of God. Who we really are is identical with God. He showed us the way back home, beyond our earthly bodies."

"And that's the same message revealed in all religions. The problem is that it has been lost to religious ritual and doctrine."

Angelo was preoccupied. "Do you know much about the Third Eye?"

The question triggered admiration from Comte. It was what he had sought from the young man. Unknown to Angelo, the modus operandi of all hidden orders was to never reveal anything to the aspirant beyond their mental and moral capacity, or their psychological interest. The capacity for comprehension was linked to psychological intention. Angelo had now crossed that threshold.

Comte gave Angelo a parting gift. He chose to divulge a lasting testament about a most important insight.

The Third Eye is the sixth primary chakra within the body and acts as a consciousness gateway to the spiritual. It is called the 'still point', the 'mount of transfiguration'. Located near the pineal gland it is activated by the interaction of the pineal and pituitary glands. As a cultural practice, the Hindu tradition is to place a spot on the forehead to signify the Third Eye.

Not generally known, the sixth chakra actually interacts with the Earth's 'heartbeat'. A frequency of approximately 7.8 cycles per second travels in an ionised layer around the globe. Known as the Schumann resonance, it has a wavelength of approximately 25,000 miles. Every time it changes phase and contracts, it focuses over the Giza Plateau. With only a single wave existing at one time, it beats electromagnetically like a giant cosmic heart. With its capstone in place, the Great Pyramid of Giza acted as a giant resonator. Above the Kings Chamber are five slabs which allowed the room to be 'tuned'. The pyramid is a giant chronometer tracking the alignments of the planets against the evolution of humanity. It informed the Order of Melchizedek of humanity's progress, allowing for their occasional intervention.

When high states of consciousness are achieved, the Third Eye opens. The sixth chakra becomes active. This activation is a key evolutionary step for any person seeking ultimate freedom.

In the second shrine of Tutankhamen there are hieroglyphs that say, '...*when the Star of the Soul comes...*' The Star of the Soul is the sixth of the seven chakra experiences, the Third Eye.

Condemned as an occult or a black art, knowledge of the Third Eye was usually hidden for fear of persecution. Matthew 6:22-23 tells how Jesus transmitted the knowledge.

'*...the light of the body is the eye; if therefore thine eye be single, thy whole body shall be full of light. But if thine eye be evil, thy whole body shall be full of darkness. If therefore the light that is in thee be darkness, how great is that darkness.*'

This is one of the key messages of the Bible and one of the most guarded of the secret fraternities. It's how we can evolve to become one with the Divine Principle. Jesus's words have not been understood. But to the adept the words, 'thine eye be single' is clear. The single eye is the sixth chakra. The Templars and many others, particularly in the Far East, had learned how to open the Third Eye to penetrate the suprasensible realms, realms beyond the sensory stimulus of the physical. Of course, the adept also knew 'thine eye be evil' meant that access was closed to most.

Comte's gentle smile reflected his inner peace. "We are often fooled by what we see in the physical world. Those who access the Third Eye are not deceived by mere appearances. They achieve the venerated Second Sight. They are spiritually guided through the difficulties of life, back to the source of all that is and all that ever was, back to God and the eternal Christ within. Perhaps it's time for us to follow."

With those words, Comte camouflaged his emotion and bid

Angelo goodnight. Comte's time had come. He would meet his rendezvous with destiny.

————— ✸ —————

The approach to the Mausoleum of Augustus required crossing the River Tiber. Comte was wary of the rendezvous. The Mausoleum entrance would be dark and secluded. He feared being followed and decided to take the roundabout route crossing the Tiber via the Ponte Margherita. Late night lovers passed him with faces lit with the flames of passion. They only had eyes for each other, but Comte remained cautious, scanning the scene ahead and looking over his shoulder at regular intervals.

The sky was gloomy, the low cloud moving slow. Misty rain started to drift downward, turning the night air opaque in the diffuse streetlight. He loped along the esplanade skirting the riverbank and neared the Mausoleum from the rear. Spent raindrops splashed the pathway from the overhanging trees, driblets of water dampening his head and shoulders. He shuffled past the Ara Pacis Augustae and glimpsed at his watch. 1:26.

The moment of truth.

He crossed the roadway and settled in the dark recesses of the San Rocco Church. Comte was ready for his fate. He could visualise death by knife blade or bullet, but instead he promptly invoked faith in his benefactors.

He scoped the Mausoleum. Sure enough, he spotted an obscure, motionless figure in a hooded coat standing erect against the backdrop of the gated entrance. Comte looked nervously at his watch. 1:34. His choice was now. Make contact or disappear into the night. The thought flowed through him like a streak of lightening. As the light rain sheathed the mausoleum in a frothy mist, he closed his eyes and made his leap of faith.

He straightened his back and peeled himself away from the night shadows, his hobbled footfalls echoing on the wet cobblestones as he dispersed into the light rain. The figure turned and spotted him. Comte's blood chilled as he approached and prepared for the consequences. *Was this a covert devil ready to strike him down?*

The figure squared up and calmly removed the dampened hood, revealing a stunningly beautiful woman with a curtain of long blond hair spilling over her shoulders.

49

ESCAPE

ROME, ITALY

Comte was pleasantly surprised. The choice of contact was a relief. He immediately recognised Keisha, the woman Angelo had met in the library, the woman who had warned they were not safe and the woman whose skill with ancient languages had hardened his resolve. He had no idea she was an active field operative.

Comte offered his deformed hand. Keisha had never recoiled from his disfigurement and cupped the stump of his hand in both of hers. She smiled with unreserved admiration.

"The time has come Comte."

"Yes, I don't have the stomach for them anymore. Angelo told me about your meeting in the library. He was quite smitten by you."

"Was he now? We'll help him if he wants it. But you know the score, that's up to him."

"Yeah, I know, but I feel as though I'm deserting him."

"He'll be OK."

"He's probably safer with me gone. How long have they been onto me?"

"The cipher override program was activated five days ago. Your every key stroke was captured by a network outside the Vatican, but also by ours. As planned, it allowed our network to establish a wormhole into theirs. We've got some good stuff and with your hard drive destroyed there's no record we've been into their mainframe. Come on, we need to get you out of here. My car's around the corner."

Comte didn't hesitate.

The unlikely couple ventured into the Via di Ripetta. Keisha walked in crisp resounding steps as the keeper doggedly hobbled alongside. Comte was taken by another surprise. A scintilla silver Aston Martin AMV8 crouched menacingly at the curb, its curvaceous form glistening in the misty rain. Smiling to himself, Comte raked his eyes over the sleek exterior. *Impressive.*

Lights flashed as Keisha squeezed the remote. Opening the passenger door, Comte slipped into the sculptured leather seat and surveyed the sumptuous interior. He allowed himself a seductive thought. *Classy, for a classy woman.*

Keisha depressed the crystal starter button that housed an etched motif of the Aston logo. The ignition changed from red to blue and the powerful V8 exploded into life. Seatbelts snapped in place, Keisha peeled away from the curb and accelerated gently hoping to leak out of the city unnoticed.

Momentarily, Keisha shifted her gaze from the road to Comte, a look of concern visible in her unblemished face. "They planned to kill you tonight and leave your body in the Piazza San Pietro."

"Who, Valla? It's the sort of stunt he'd pull."

"Not exactly him. Our wormhole into the network exposed his associates, a group called Majestic."

"Majestic? Never heard of them."

"Not many have. They're the best as far as spooks go. They were commissioned as covert operators within the CIA. Eisenhower installed them after the war to manage operations that were too hot for the regular agencies. They've planted a mole within the Vatican, the trouble is no-one knows who he is."

"Got to be Valla!

"He's certainly that, but he's lost their confidence. We're sure this mole is someone else."

Comte was more amused than alarmed. "I thought the papers on my desk looked disturbed when I got back from Vienna."

Keisha slotted the gear lever into the metal gate as she steered around the Piazza del Popolo. The Aston responded impeccably, weaving past slower vehicles with ease.

"What did I do to deserve all this?"

"You've created cracks at exactly the same time when they're paranoid about a new archaeological discovery. When these cracks get out it could actually undo an agreement struck by Eisenhower back in the fifties." Keisha adjusted the rear view mirror. "God, we don't need this!"

"What's up?"

Her face was laced with concern. "They're behind us. God knows how?"

Comte half turned and peered through the steeply raked rear window. A black Modena 360 Ferrari followed. Without any warning, a burst of machine gun fire clattered onto the pristine paintwork of the Aston.

"Jesus!"

"It's OK Comte, we're bullet proof." Keisha fused her grip to the steering wheel and floored the accelerator. "Next time though, they'll take out the tyres. We'll have to abort."

Abort? How was that possible?

Another burst of gunfire was heard pinging off the paintwork. Threading the Aston between narrow streets and laneways, Keisha drove with consummate precision, pushing the vehicle to the limits of its adhesion. The Modena struggled to keep pace as it slithered around the corners at a ferocious speed. The Aston had been specially fitted with massive zero rated tyres to enhance grip, giving it the edge required. Re-emerging on the Via Flaminia, Keisha was ready for action.

Basked by the coloured dashboard lights, Comte glanced at Keisha's concentrated features and was comforted by her calm. She executed a skill and confidence that Comte found comforting. With the casual press of a button a head-up display illuminated on the lower part of the windscreen. It was a countdown timer, flashing 0:27. Then 0:26. 0:25.

Keisha remained cool amidst the barrage of fire and the bellowing V8, now red lining at 7,600 RPM. "Twenty-four seconds."

Twenty-four seconds? "Until what?"

"'Til we're out of here."

With a rapiered look, Keisha hit the handbrake and floored the accelerator. The Aston curled, darting off the main thoroughfare. The Ferrari scrapped the curb in the manoeuvre, but continued to shadow. Nervous excitement wrenched at Comte's twisted face as his head was thrown sideways. Ecstatic at the commotion, the trace of a contented smile forced its way through his deformity.

Without warning, a blue Alfa Romeo blindly pulled out in front of the Aston. Tyres screeched as the ABS engaged, the harness slamming hard into Comte's chest. The Ferrari took evasive action swerving to the left. Keisha apexed right, tyres grabbing the shoulder of the road, inches from the guardrail. The Ferrari had gained precious metres. Keisha manoeuvred to the front of the Alfa, another round of fire causing her to scrape metal. Sparks tore from the car's elegant flank. A sudden twist of the steering wheel and a slam into a lower gear pitched the Aston ahead. The movement was crisp and precise. The Modena chased in close pursuit anticipating the final kill.

0:05 seconds. Comte's muscles tensed as he braced himself for the unexpected.

One and a half kilometres behind, a black Sikorsky RAH-66 Comanche Stealth helicopter gained fast. Blue-Edge rotor blades kept its approach silent. Low voltage radar hidden in the bumper of the Aston Martin maintained precise coordinates on the pursuing Ferrari, now only fifteen metres behind. Without warning a GPS guided missile launched in a flash of fire, tracking the vehicle.

0:03 ... 0:02 ... 0:01 ...

A brilliant flash of luminescence.

An explosion of finality.

The Ferrari erupted into a massive fireball hurling it into the air. The flames following the shockwave coursed through the Aston as shattered glass from the adjacent buildings pinged off the bodywork. The enveloping conflagration disappeared as Keisha held nerve, the road ahead opening up into a valley of escape. Sharpened by exhilaration, Comte was thrilled that he had crossed another threshold. He smiled with delight. The feeble attempt at his death left with him with a contemptuous scorn for those who would seek to damage him.

Nothing would stop him from his new life with Elysius.

Not now, not ever.

<hr>

Keisha curled the hint of a satisfied smile. "Sorry about that. I told you they were the best. Let's revise that to second best."

Comte was intoxicated, not by his escape, but by the determined efficiency of the feisty woman beside him. And by those for whom she worked. It wasn't every day a pursuing vehicle was taken out by guided missile fire from god-knows-what in the middle of Rome.

Comte finally spoke, "I know passing copies of old manuscripts would piss off the Vatican, but this is a little more attention than I expected."

"The men in scarlet don't mess around. Neither do those who

control them. It's more than that though, Majestic is exposed and they're fighting for their survival. What you've done threatens their business and the politics of organised religion. We both know about Valla's enmity toward you, but Majestic decided to take action before he got suspicious. That mole I mentioned is deeply entrenched. Someone's been spying on you."

Comte had been careful to cover his tracks in passing documentation, but knew he had been less than careful in printing off his own reading material. He had never trusted Valla, but the idea that someone else knew his every move sat uncomfortably.

Blue and red sirens flashed a kilometre ahead. An avalanche of Polizia sped toward the impact site. Taking a sharp right-hander, Keisha accelerated up a quiet road. The bitumen unfurled for two or three kilometres before the Aston slowed and approached a state-of-the-art Volvo FH16 Globetrotter semi-trailer. The rear roller door lifted and two ramps electronically extended to the ground. Keisha manoeuvred the Aston into the trailer and killed the engine. The ramps retracted and the rear door closed.

The pair squeezed out of the car and then through an entrance to a rest area within the trailer.

"I suggest you relax and maybe get some sleep. The driver's been briefed on our destination; we'll be there destination in a few hours."

Comte was still riding a surge of adrenalin. *Car chases, explosions, unknown destinations.* It had been an exceptional night.

"Where're you taking me?"

"Elysius has a lodge where you'll be safe. You'll be able to ask all the questions you like when we get there."

Comte knew he would need to wait for answers. He had placed his life in these people's hands and they had delivered – more than he had believed possible. Questions formed and slowly dissipated. The exhilaration of the day had left him exhausted. It wasn't long before he found sleep.

— ◦◦◦ —

Sirmione is located on a narrow peninsula stretching about four kilometres into the crystal waters of Lago di Garda in northern Italy, near the famous city of Verona. This fortified medieval centre was defended by the Scaligera fortress, strategically positioned on the only point of access by land. Today, the castle is the most complete and best preserved in Italy. Surrounded by water and only assessable by the drawbridge, its historic crenulated towers stand as sentinels to the power of Mastino I della Scali, Lord of Verona, who commissioned the construction in 1259. Today, olive trees, willows, cypress groves and lemon trees garland the footpath from the fortress to the Grottoes of Catullo. Dating from the Imperial age of Rome, the ruins of this regal residential villa are situated on the northernmost tip of the peninsula, the sharp smell of sulphur being a fetid reminder of the thermal baths once frequented by Rome's rich and famous.

Situated near the edge of a thick olive grove with picturesque views of the sapphire lake, lay a medieval church. Now used as an Elysius lodge, it transmits and receives encrypted messages from other lodges around the world. With close links to the Knights of Malta and a few strategic European and American military officials, politicians and industrialists, Elysius does what it can to counter those under the influence of Belial.

Toward mid morning, Keisha Petersen led Comte into a meeting room within the medieval building. The whole episode delighted Comte as he basked in the clandestine nuances of this lovely woman.

"Ah, the remarkable Comte." A young man dressed in casual garb greeted him. Tall with chiselled features, his handsome looks exuded an elegant confidence. "My name is Jared. I must apologise for the uncouth episode in Rome last night. Fortunately, Keisha was available to facilitate your departure. She's one of our best."

"Knows how to drive a car pretty well, I'd say," Comte replied.

Jared tried to unsettle Keisha's controlled composure. "So you've noticed her talents. Don't worry Comte, I've tried many times, but Keisha's only interested in her work. Aren't you Keisha?"

Keisha looked away, bored with the innuendo. "Some things are far more important Jared. Listen, I have a hair appointment and more work to do with the Baalbek translations, so I have to go. Take care Comte, you're in safe hands. At least that's the line Jared has always used to try and convince me."

Keisha flashed a disinterested look at Jared and moved to farewell Comte. She shook his deformed hand, lightly clasping all three fingers.

"Thanks for getting me here safely, I'm indebted to you."

"The pleasure was mine. Take care, Comte."

50

BRIEFING

NEAR LUGANO, SWITZERLAND

Philip's explanation of the strange white powder had explained much. My experience now had some meaning, maybe some significance, especially if my mind had somehow witnessed another reality. The full significance of the experience still eluded me, but I did feel some sense of closure.

I still deserved answers about Keisha's involvement and Philip promised that she would explain in person later that day. I couldn't wait to hear her defence.

Mac and I were enjoying a late afternoon tea in Philip's office when he punched the intercom. "Send her in."

The door opened with a confident air. "Hi Gramps." Keisha wrapped her arms around Philip in a huge hug. "Good to see you again, Alex."

Her eyes shifted to mine as she humbly approached. "Aiden, I hope you're OK."

I was gob smacked. *Philip was her Grandfather? She knew Mac?*

It had only been three or four days, but gone was the sophisticated air of the international fashion model. Her long blonde hair had been expertly cropped into a very short 'bed hair' look. The satin spiky crown enhanced her high cheekbones and piercing blue eyes. Dressed in tight salmon t-shirt and blue denim, she revealed an Olympic physique transforming her lithe body from sensual to downright sexy.

Some women are prone to use the language of their sex to gain advantage, but Keisha displayed an expression of genuine concern, a display that belied her appearance. I should have acknowledged her thoughtfulness, but I'd been played like a pawn in a chess tournament and didn't see anything admirable in her subterfuge.

I turned away and lashed out, "You bastard Mac. *'I really need to meet this woman eh.'* Very funny."

Initially amused at my predicament, Mac's cheeky grin soured to a grimace. He knew I was pissed. My expression was sullen when I spat at Keisha. "And you're into games as well are you?"

Keisha retorted, "I don't play games Aiden. You should know that by now. After what happened to Jai, we knew you were in trouble. So we did what we did. If you've got a problem with that then get over it."

"I'll look after myself, thanks."

"Oh, for goodness sake, don't be so precious. I'm sure you can look after yourself, but we wanted to protect your discovery. As soon as I saw your photographs, I knew there would be a huge cover-up. That's when I got Philip involved. You know the rest, so relax."

I'd just been censured. Her explanation was credible, but I was still pissed off. I knew Mac's reputation with women well, especially after suitable lubrication with alcohol. There was no way he wouldn't have tried it on with Keisha. What he lacked in social etiquette with women, he made up with tall stories, incisive intellect and a roguish charm.

I was conflicted because in reality, why should I care? But I did, and that caused me to question her. "So what about you two?"

"We needed a systems analyst to create LITAN. Who better than Alex?"

Mac knew what I was thinking. "You have to admit, she IS worth meeting, but she doesn't like me that much."

Knowing Mac, he probably meant more than he was saying. I raised my middle figure in a gesture of 'Fuck you'.

I stared hard at Keisha. "You should have confided in me. You've had an agenda ever since you wanted me to stay at your so-called friend's apartment in Canberra. I mean what was that all about?"

Philip intruded, "A precaution and it was my idea. That apartment has a secure phone link and we wanted to lead you to Otto. We were buying time. LITAN was still processing your photographs and until we knew what got your field assistant killed we wanted you under wraps. As I told you, we have an operative within Majestic and it was clear they knew about Jai's death. We needed to know why."

"Great. So you play me and I finish up putting Mac at risk. That makes me feel a whole lot better."

"We're OK aren't we?" Mac observed.

I turned my attention to Keisha. "So I'm supposed to be indebted to you for your precautions, am I?"

"Not at all, Aiden. We're indebted to you for your discovery. I told you I was interested in the 'big' questions."

Philip hastily offered a diversion, "Perhaps you should give Aiden an update on his photographs."

Keisha readily agreed, "Good idea, it's time for that briefing you were after."

We followed Keisha into the adjoining conference room. Mac nudged me and with a saucy smirk whispered, "You wanted a briefing, eh?" I was in no mood for below the waist comments, so I ignored him. He could go to hell.

I sat next to Mac at a boardroom table as Philip fired a picture onto the large plasma screen with his remote. I recognised the photo as one that Jai had taken in Baalbek.

Keisha provided the commentary. "LITAN's given some interesting clues. The pictograms are early Akkadian. It tells of man reconnecting with the old-ones. Their abode is no longer accessible to us, but this cuneiform text here says they will return. Let's not forget that Christians, Buddhists, Hindus, Moslems and Jews are all waiting for some type of return or a day of eternal judgement. The uniformity of their belief is no accident. The cause for all their common views is the same."

The proposition was certainly controversial. "So you're saying that the end of the world, the coming messiah stuff is somehow connected to Baalbek."

Philip changed images. Another photo taken by Jai.

"It would seem so Aiden. I've told you about the Nephilim who 'came down'. The Sumerians told a story of a celestial body which entered the solar system in the beginning and created Earth. They called it Nibiru. The text here refers to this story, but it goes much further and provides a date for Nibiru's next entry into our solar system. It's a rather complicated text, but it seems to correspond with the end date of the Mayan calendar – 2012. Of course, this will all be security classified by the authorities."

Another image. This one I had taken.

"What's of interest is this text here. Roughly translated it means 'creators from heaven' or if you like 'gods who came down'. This is all about the Nephilim returning."

It was interesting speculation, but I was far from convinced. "It's just a story Keisha. You can't accept it as fact."

Philip intervened. "You may be right Aiden, but astrophysicists have been searching the inner galaxy for Planet X for years now. All indicators suggest it exists, but proof remains elusive. The Sumerians knew of it as Nibiru and if this is correct, Planet X should be returning to our system in the near future. If they were right about a planet entering the solar system and causing some cataclysmic event that created Earth, then why can't they be right about the gods? Imagine the ramifications."

"Fucking mind-blowing. That's what I say."

Typical Mac.

Fidgeting with the remote, Philip flicked through several more photographs. LITAN had translated each in turn and Keisha outlined her theory.

"According to the text those who are spiritually capable will be offered some type of 'immortality'. We think this is why the Templars were obsessed with the 'Cup of Immortality' in the Grail legends. Like Buddhists, they believed that it can only be achieved in the realm of pure spirit. Manna helped the ancients in their endeavour.

"I know your thoughts about the Bible, Aiden, but it does help to explain some of these ideas. In Revelation 2:17 it says: *'To him that overcometh will I give to eat of the hidden manna, and will give him a white stone, and in the stone a new name is written, which no man knoweth saving he that receiveth it.'*

"We believe that this unique knowledge was passed down at a time when Nibiru was close to Earth, thousands of years ago."

Philip now brought up a curious image of a skull. "I want to bring your attention to this phenomenon. I think it may link into Keisha's work with LITAN and your discovery. This skull is held in the Gold Museum in Lima, Peru."

The skull was remarkable, massively elongated with an enormous brain cavity, quite different to any ordinary human. Another skull from a museum at Ica, Peru was similar. "These are not aberrations; they're a genuine genetic variation. Keisha believes them to be Nephilim."

Keisha nodded, "I do. These skulls were uncovered near the Nasca lines in Peru. The 'official' line on these skull deformations is a concocted story of ritual head binding. This is a cover story dreamed up by the Belial propaganda machine, then inserted by another unnamed source into the media. However, we believe the head-binding was a crude attempt to duplicate something they had actually witnessed. Elongated skulls have been found in a number of places around the globe."

She instructed Philip, "Show Aiden the others from Palenque in Mexico."

Additional images appeared on screen. I was aware of these bizarre skulls and there had been various explanations given for the elongation. Essentially they had been described as some form of deformity. The opportunity had never presented itself where I could examine them, so I allowed Keisha's comment to pass. Nephilim maybe, but that was a long draw of the bow as far as I was concerned.

"They remind me of images of the early Egyptian Pharaohs," remarked Mac.

Philip picked up on his comment. "Spot on Alex. Check out this image. It's Akhenaton and his family. Note the extremely elongated skulls and head-wear. Keisha's convinced they were more than just human."

To me her conclusion was questionable. "Wouldn't you say the artisan has depicted them in the typical art-style of the time?"

Keisha was testy in defence of her theory. "I believe this family was a hybrid species of human-alien. Speculative theories about head-binding don't make sense. Nothing can account for these radical aberrations to skull shape. They, and those like them, were the 'gods' worshipped by early human cultures all around the world. They were the progeny of the Lemurian, Atlantean and Sumerian cultures. You just don't want to see it, do you Aiden?"

"No I don't see it, frankly. So-called gods coming to Earth from some far-flung planet and breeding with what – the Neanderthal? It's absurd; so far-fetched that the notion would get zero credibility with colleagues within my profession."

Mac put me in my place, "And I thought the care factor about your colleagues was zero."

"University academics!" scoffed Philip. "Now they're the ultimate cover story. They've been fed crap by the military-industrial complex since the 1940s, when everything of deep scientific value was security classified. I agree with Mac, since when did the credibility of your colleagues count."

"It doesn't, but this is not proof."

"We won't need proof if Nibiru returns. Will we?"

This was an argument I wasn't going to win.

"Have you asked Aiden about your proposal Philip?"

"Not yet. Perhaps you'd like to ask."

"Ask me what?"

"We want you to help us with a mystery in Morocco. A recently discovered diary written by a crusading Templar knight has been found in a secluded vault below St. Stephens Cathedral in Vienna. It speaks of three knights transporting an ossuary from near the site of the Temple Mount, across North Africa to the mountains in the west. On its own, it's an intriguing story, but there's a second consideration. We have a long admired convert to our cause from the Vatican who's been supplying LITAN with some useful material from within the secret archives. One of his dossiers indicates that there was a basilica built within a massive cave in the Atlas Mountains in the late 13th century. A papal letter written in 1311 by Pope Clement V suggests the Knights Templar built it to hide their knowledge of man's genesis. It was used as evidence against them and inspired the Papal Bull known as Vox In Excelso. Suspicion of its existence persisted and it was tagged the Basilica of the Eastern Star.

"To top this off, Philip discovered a fortnight ago that pressure was applied to the Moroccan government to close a cave uncovered last year by an itinerant goat-herder. There was a short article in Le

Reporter, a Casablanca weekly, about the goat-herder who mysteriously died two days after his find. The death has an uncanny resemblance to what happened to Jai, stabbed in both the carotid artery and the heart. We think his death might have a tenuous link to the Basilica."

"If what you say is right, wouldn't the Templar evidence of man's origins have been removed?"

Philip responded, "Almost certain, but we've only just received the intelligence and we need to check out the story. You would be a great help. Keisha and Alex will join you of course. Their expertise may well be required."

How could I refuse? I looked at Keisha and was given reassurance by her sparkling eyes. I could see the genetic link to Philip – elegant long fingers, perfect complexion and eyes of deep blue pools. Expectation was etched into her brow.

Naturally I accepted.

51

HEAVEN ON EARTH

IL GALLO LUNGO, TYRRHENIAN SEA, ITALY

The message on his encrypted phone had brought the Cardinal close to spontaneous combustion. Kane had requested his attendance at an overnight stay in Majestic's hideaway on Il Gallo Lungo. It was clear intimidation, but he couldn't refuse. He threw down his medication, soothed by a glass of cognac. He needed to iron out the stomach knot of simmering frustration. To make things worse, Kane's other guests were Ariel Goldstein and Ernst Volker. Majestic's men!

Valla was further incensed when he was disrespectfully greeted upon his deliberate late arrival, just as dinner was ready to be served. He made a feeble attempt to listen attentively to Kane's social diatribe. He was bored with the man's crass attempt at being the host. He had no politesse. After dinner Kane got down to business and baited Valla immediately.

The Cardinal finally snapped. "How dare you accuse me of incompetence? I did exactly as you asked. If you blame me for this you can go to hell."

Kane's composure remained icy. "I'm saying the bastard was

tipped-off, that's all. We suspect it was Elysius."

Valla fidgeted with the pectoral cross hanging from his neck. "Yeah, yeah sure. I thought you were the best. What a joke!"

"They've got friends in high places, even in Rome. Tell me it's not you."

Old fears kindled Valla's nerves. "Listen; don't lay your incompetence on me."

The Cardinal was feeling nauseous. He hated the name Elysius. Centuries after the visible remnants of the Templars had been extinguished their legacy still had the capacity to obstruct the objectives of the Church.

Kane's mouth hardened. "We'll deal with your keeper's escape, mark my words. The problem is he printed off a portfolio and took it with him. Something explosive."

Disdain spread across Valla's face. "What folio?" he drawled.

"It was a transcription from a very old Sumerian text. It's classified Security-12. Understand the problem now?"

Kane played the security card often. Releasing classification 12 information meant immediate elimination, but Valla felt immune to the threat. Hearing it again verified his view that Kane was a terminal bore.

Kane's tone became grave. "After Leonard Woolley unearthed all those tablets in Mesopotamia, it became obvious that the story of the biblical flood had come from this area. Most disturbing though were references to the Annunaki."

"Demons!" scoffed the Cardinal.

"I wish you would shut up about your fucking demons. That's all you ever go on about. I'm talking about EBEs. Extraterrestrial Biological Entities, although fortunately for us, you people continually mythologise them as demons." Kane deferred to Ernst Volker, "The Cardinal's heard of the Order of Melchizedek, though."

Valla tried to hide his reticence. "They're mentioned in the Bible, but we don't really dwell on them."

"I know and that's the problem. Your Jesus was actually anointed by the Order of Melchizedek and from the Egyptian King List they were called the Lords of Light. They apparently arrived tens of thousands of years before the construction of the pyramids in Egypt, China and other places around the world."

The Cardinal was incredulous. "Arrived from where? Disneyland?"

Valla was being deliberately disagreeable and Kane decided to dress him down. "Listen to me, when a man's hanging by a thread, it's good to know he has a friend. You'd be wise to listen and take heed."

Goldstein resisted a smirk. *Kane really was a pompous shirt-tosser.*

Valla loved a good stoush and his years within the Church had taught him to conceal resentment. But he had slipped up. He was getting too old for the intellectual claptrap championed by the likes of Kane, so he answered with subtle condescension. "Enlighten us then."

Veles Kane decided to incense. "In case you didn't hear the first time, this is classification 12."

If the discussion went public, Kane decided Valla would find himself swinging under a bridge somewhere. *Maybe Agostino could organise it at Blackfriars Bridge in London,* he mused.

The Cardinal understood and kept his counsel.

Kane gave an account of data held on Comte's hard drive about the ancient 'Lords of Light'. He had gathered the anthropological clues of their arrival found in the millennia old Lascaux cave paintings in France. Comte had also researched the Dogon tribe of Africa. This tribe recorded the arrival of the Nommo at roughly the same time. He had also printed material about the contact made between the ancient Tibetan culture of 10,000 BCE and the indigenous successors of the Shining Ones, anthropological descendants of the Lords of Light. This contact gave rise to the advanced knowledge of consciousness understood by various monks in the Far East. Knowledge that Kane himself was trying to extract from the Tibetan. The German Esoteric Bureau had desperately tried as well in the 1930s and 1940s.

Valla cringed. Under fear of death his mother had been recruited into the same Bureau.

Kane further explained that the continent of Lemuria was devastated by geophysical disturbance and subsequent inundation. Remnant survivors of the catastrophe scattered to various parts of the globe, including Europe, South America, India and the Caucasus. Around 5,000 BCE, the Sumerian civilisation was seeded after further extraterrestrial contact, and some seven hundred years later pre-dynastic Egypt was ruled by Isis and Osiris. The Pyramids of Giza and Shensi in China were constructed as consciousness amplification chambers, tracking and facilitating evolutionary upshift.

Kane's discourse created an uncomfortable silence. All of this information would change society's development if Comte was able to disseminate the material he had collected. The elites would lose control of the global flock.

Comte had to be found and silenced.

52

THE BASILICA

ATLAS MOUNTAINS, MOROCCO

Our cover was to be trekkers on a hiking holiday. The Atlas Mountains were a popular destination for tourists and Philip had arranged for a contact to meet us in the small town of Asni. He would act as our guide. From Asni, it would be necessary to travel to the village of Imlil, built on a cone shaped rise at the base of Jebel Toubkal, the usual starting point for climbing the highest mountain in North Africa. We grabbed a taxi at the Marrakech airport for the fifty minute drive to the magnificent Kasbah Tamadot, an elegant resort hotel perched on a hilltop just outside the small town of Asni.

Sweeping through the carved gated entrance, Mac's alcoholic predilection kicked in and he paid off the driver before the car had even braked to a halt. The lavish hideaway was in complete contrast with the rugged backdrop of the surrounding mountains. Our rooms were richly decorated in classic Moroccan style.

We had arranged an overnight stay to familiarise ourselves, with Mac needing instant gratification by raiding all our mini-bars. He contemplated the coming expedition from his balcony until the dozen or so miniature bottles were consumed. Meanwhile, Keisha enjoyed a beauty session at the spa and I swam a hundred laps. It helped me unwind. I still harboured annoyance about Keisha's deceit. I was indignant with Mac as well, but that was his style, he would only have seen humour in the deception.

At dinner, I tried to be civil with them both, asking Keisha about the obvious fondness for her grandfather. I learned that her parents were killed in a plane crash when she was young and that she had been raised by Philip. When she graduated from school she was given the freedom to travel, so with her girlfriend she backpacked through Eastern Europe and the Middle East for a year. She was fascinated with history and developed a fierce passion for all things ancient. University beckoned and she focused on something new, the sciences had great appeal, but in time her direction changed. She spent a summer holiday as a volunteer at the British Museum. She helped catalogue a multitude of cuneiform tablets with a specialist translator as her mentor. The bug hit and her interest was transformed. Within ten years, she was considered the foremost expert on ancient near eastern languages.

"Philip was always there when I needed him. He's my only family, but he wanted me to experience the freedom to find myself. He held a loose rein on me for which I am eternally grateful, but when I completed my Masters I spent a year with him and helped in his work. I believe in his mission, so I'm always available if I can help."

Mac ratified her appraisal. "I have to agree. Philip's a pretty ethical guy and LITAN gave me a new challenge just when I needed it." Mac grinned as he gave added impetus to his deception. "After all I really needed to meet this woman."

Keisha reprimanded him. "Come on Mac. Let's give Aiden a break. There's no need to soil the discussion."

I was grateful for her thoughtfulness, but wondered what she meant. The thought of Mac and Keisha together didn't sit right. I knew Mac too well.

I realised I was bothered because she had got into my head. I was tantalised. Thoughts I would keep to myself.

Late the following morning, we checked out and walked into the town. We found our rendezvous point, a local establishment with a small selection of food simmering in charcoal braziers. A couple of Berber women in long brown cloaks and white headscarves wandered past with loads of undergrowth strapped to their backs. Keisha was immediately surrounded by hawkers offering a bizarre assortment of goods. They certainly knew how to hassle and within moments, Mac lost patience and offered Keisha a needy escape route.

"God, I need a drink. This is doing my head in."

Moroccans are not too fond of alcohol and Mac's comment allowed Keisha to carve her way into the premises. Asni is familiar with tourists coming and going, and within moments Keisha was attracting the unwelcome attention of our waiter. She was modestly dressed in appreciation for local custom, but the waiter had mentally undressed her at his every approach to our table.

Keisha ran her fingers through her spiky blonde crop. "I wish he'd keep that filthy grin to himself."

The waiter's behaviour made me angrier by the minute. It smacked of sexual harassment. I couldn't hold back any longer. As he delivered our order, he once again appraised Keisha with bestial perversion.

I snapped. "Listen you! What's your problem?"

The waiter's swarthy face turned toward me. His insolent stare hardened. "You Americans? Think you own everything," he ruminated.

I felt the tension and was ready to attack at his slightest provocation. "So you do have a problem?"

He weighed the situation carefully and backed off. He had made a wise decision.

"No problem."

I could feel my blood pressure boil. "Good, so keep your filthy eyes off the lady, understand. If you're a man of faith, you should know about showing respect."

His eyes threw daggers as he clumsily placed Keisha's order in front of her. I could feel his vitriol. I was ready to take him out, but he turned and passed a final judgement.

"You Westerners – all crazy people."

Within a few moments, a man of distinct Arab extraction ambled toward our table. He was short and wafer thin with lanky black hair surrounding a balding crown. His hair was tied into a small ponytail that tickled a small and aged tattoo at the nape of his neck. His face was like tanned leather decorated with a deep scar across his right cheek. Dark brown pupils, yellow sclera. Hands calloused and weathered. Dressed in mid-sixties hippy style, baggy black cotton pants, loose white linen shirt and leather sandals. Voice like dry grit.

"I understand you three Canadians ordered a guide to trek the mountain. Caves near Tacheddirt. My name is Anwar and we're ready to go. Come on, grab your gear."

Keisha nodded. The appearance and reference to Canadians confirmed that this man was our contact.

Philip had provided a briefing into Anwar's background. His father had married a young Palestinian woman in 1962 when serving as a military aide to Egyptian president, Gamal Abed Al Nasser. When the president died of a heart attack in 1970, his father helped the new president, Anuar Al Sadat, instigate the Yom Kippur war against Israel in 1973. A close friendship formed. Anwar had enjoyed a privileged childhood. When his mother passed away from a congenital illness, he was sent to boarding school in the United States. He was noticed by Elysius when he completed his final studies at the Mohammed V University in Rabat in 1987. His thesis was an insight into the mythology of West Africa and he had travelled extensively throughout the continent since his study. Anwar never returned to Egypt. His father was discarded by President Hosni Mubarak after Sadat's assassination in 1981 and died during Anwar's last year at University. He had eagerly agreed to help with our endeavour.

Philip had never met Anwar and provided no intelligence about his personality, but it was clear from the man's body language that he didn't suffer fools. I picked up an impulsive and brutish demeanour that made me wary.

"There's no time to delay. Our transport is waiting. Miss it and you'll wait till tomorrow," he rasped.

Mac wasn't about to budge. He was waiting for another beer. "How about we have one for the road? Here, take a seat."

Anwar glared, was about to say something, but instead walked straight out. Keisha had had enough of the sleazy waiter and was eager to leave. Mac decided not to argue, so we followed.

Loaded with our backpacks, we squeezed into the back of a pick-up truck with a group of villagers for the journey to Imlil. All that Anwar had to say in defence of our appalling transport was that we needed to mingle and attract no attention. The loaded pick-up belched a black fog as it snaked along the yawning gorge, hungry for another victim. Pot-holed from neglect, the tight hair-pin road had been washed away in various sections, causing the driver to churn the pick-up through three-point turns, leaving us aghast by the three hundred metre chasm.

I was thankful when our feet touched the ground at Imlil later that afternoon. Anwar had arranged modest accommodation at a tavern, a short distance from his lodgings with a friend. The plan was to hike to Tacheddirt the following day. The best route was via the small village of Ikkiss, a total distance of some fifteen kilometres.

"This'll do," said Mac, pointing to a seedy looking bar with a couple of western backpackers sitting outside. He looked directly at Anwar. "Come on, I'll get you a drink. You can tell us about our journey tomorrow."

Anwar held a poker face. "I don't drink."

"Then get something else off the damn menu instead. We want to know how we're getting to the Basilica," Mac said, his face flushed with irritation.

"That will be up to you my friend. The deeper caves have never been of interest and there's no pathway in. I know a way, that's all. You three can take the risks."

What risks? We knew the authorities had closed the cave in question, but we needed Anwar's assistance in leading us to the correct location. There were dozens of caves in the area and his theory was that if the Basilica had remained hidden for centuries, then the more obscure caves would be the obvious place to explore. It made sense.

Keisha had been studying Anwar intently. She appeared cold, almost disinterested, but I knew she was assessing the implications of his comments.

She bristled. "What particular risks do you have in mind?"

Anwar's eyes held steady, but were poised ready for debate. "There are always risks in exploring caves," was his lame reply. "But with Dr Keyes's experience with caving, we should all be fine."

I wasn't happy about having responsibility laid on my shoulders, but I held my thoughts. Keisha accepted his answer without further enquiry. However, she did seek more information about Anwar's thesis. "My grandfather tells me you have some theories about the indigenous tribes of Africa. I'd be very interested if you'd share them."

Anwar was clearly hesitant. "There's nothing to tell."

Mac prompted, "Come on man, if you don't help the lady, we might have to stay and drink out the bar."

"I told you I don't drink and I don't spend time with drunks."

Mac was testy, his blood simmering to the boil. "Drunks don't do it for me either, especially mouthy ones who can't hold their liquor. However, you were politely asked a question and the very least you can do is answer the lady."

The atmosphere was thickening. I could sense that Keisha was trying to get to something, and she opened the way for Anwar. "I understand there are various tribes who claim their ancestors came from the Imanujela. Do you know anything about them?"

Keisha noticed me frown, so she explained. "The word Imanujela is linguistically linked to the Hebrew Immanuel, which means 'Lord who has come'."

Anwar finally spoke. "It's all just speculation."

Mac grimaced, "Not very helpful are you? Were you born like that or did you just develop the skill over time?"

Anwar slid an uneasy glance at Mac, so I interjected, "He'll keep Mac. I'm sure Keisha knows more than him anyway."

Unfazed by the standoff, Keisha took centre stage. "Perhaps Anwar, I should tell you what I do know. 'Zulu' means 'people of the sky'. Their stories claim that 'isikati', the Earth, was a sphere moving around the Sun and was connected to space, 'umkati'. The shamans say the Imanujela were controlled by spirit beings named Chitauli who travelled through the air in 'great bowls'. They held an enmity toward the people and purposely dividing their language."

She compared this to Yahweh who deliberately confounded the people's language in the Bible's Tower of Babel story. Same story, different culture.

Anwar seemed agitated by the conversation and ended the discussion. "Good, nothing more I can add. I suggest you get some rest; we leave at seven in the morning. I'll meet you at your tavern."

As he walked out, Mac laid down his cards. "I don't like the rude bastard. He knows more than he's letting on."

Keisha dipped her eyes, her mind collating her thoughts. I sensed some unspoken agreement with Mac's opinion.

"Perhaps he's just uncomfortable with foreigners," I conceded.

"He's a born again hippy who doesn't drink and I bet he's never smoked pot. And 'we can take the risks'. What's that supposed to mean. Fuck him."

Suddenly, Keisha lashed out. "Just give your jaw a rest Alex. You're full of shit."

She threw back her chair and stormed out of the bar. Instead of resting, Mac's jaw dropped in astonishment. I hadn't seen Keisha so temperamental. Her mood was an unbecoming 'princess' complex. Mac was ready to order again, but I dropped some cash on our table and grabbed him by his arm.

Outside, Keisha was once again aggravated by the rapacious hustlers. As we approached, she aggressively cut her way past. "Come on, tomorrow's going to be a long day."

We walked the short distance with her to our overnight quarters in uncomfortable silence. This was out of the ordinary, especially for Keisha. I assumed it had something to do with Mac and therefore it was none of my business. Her demeanour was remote.

Something was stirring, something quite dangerous.

53

EMISSARY

SIRMIONE, LAGO DE GARDA, NORTHERN ITALY

Jared poured a measure of fine liqueur. "Childeric sends his regards. He tells me you enjoy grappa."

"I'm quite partial."

Comte had taken the last couple of days to relax, taking his time to mingle with the locals and tourists alike. Whenever he walked through the narrow streets eyes averted away from him. But that was just fine. He was joyful for his newfound secular freedom. He had joined Jared on the terrace overlooking the calm waters of the Lake Garda, the scent of fresh pine filling the air. He savoured the powerful liqueur.

"Comte, now that you're free of restriction, we'd like to offer you a new challenge."

"If it's as good as this fine grappa I may well be interested," Comte chortled.

"You're under no obligation, I can assure you."

"I'm aware of that. I never do anything I don't want to."

"Good. I need to brief you on what we have in mind. It's going to be pretty relaxed and for the most part it'll involve the reading of ancient manuscripts. We're looking for your unique perspective. You've accessed many of the hidden records in the Vatican and we want you to cross-reference our documents with what you've provided us. Would that be of interest?"

"Of course, anything to help."

"We have a unique data system called LITAN which will be useful to you. You'll be able to upload and cross-reference material that hasn't yet been touched. It'll make life a lot easier."

Comte nodded as he sipped on his grappa.

"You'll be given access to many of the texts that explain pre-biblical history. Have you heard of a poetic opus called The Shahnameh."

"No, I haven't come across that one at all. What's it about?"

'It was written around 1000 AD and tells of the history of Greater Iran from the creation of the earth until the Islamic conquest of Persia in the 7th century. The text describes the birth of a child to a king called Sam. Sam refers to his son Zal as a 'demon child', a child of the Watchers. The poem says,

> 'No human being of this earth
> Could give such a monster birth,
> He must be of the Demon race,
> Though human still in form and face.'

The genealogical legacy of Zal is the membership of today's Illuminati. As you know, they hold the world in bondage through global debt slavery and suppression of key scientific knowledge."

"I'm familiar with The Watchers. They were linked to the Lords of El. Yahweh was one of them."

"That's right. Yahweh, a being in the Bible that today is falsely worshipped by many as the one and only God of the entire Universe. Complete nonsense."

Comte relished the opportunity to talk about a complex

historical issue that had altered theology and influenced religions over the centuries. "People still get confused. They think the Lords of El were God, the creative principle. A complete absurdity," he scoffed. "The Lords presented themselves as being the most high, but in fact they had deliberately deceived the primitive cultures who came to worship them as gods."

"Yes, as you know Comte, a great deal of the Old Testament is based on the Sumerian and Mesopotamian texts. Some of the malevolent Lords of El, Yahweh in particular, intervened in man's technical achievements including the deliberate fragmentation of language in the infamous Tower of Babel episode. Hence, bad speech became known as 'babble'. It was a ploy to slow the technological and spiritual advancement of the Cro-Magnon race. Orthodox religion has continued to play the same role, preventing us from evolving. Being told that we were born into sin has only held us back, atrophying the Third Eye."

Comte nodded and silently reflected on Genesis, chapter 11. He recalled the phrase 'let us go down and confound their language.' Yahweh wasn't the only 'god' to come down.

Jared tempted Comte further. "We also want to provide you access to the Dead Sea Scrolls."

Comte was petulant. "The deceitful bastards sat on those texts for decades before they were released. Absolutely criminal."

"They had a reason for that. Have you ever wondered why over the centuries, religions of all faiths seem to be constantly involved in every kind of intolerance and violence? Either that or they turn a blind eye. Within the scrolls, a text called 'The War of the Sons of Light and the Sons of Darkness' exposes Belial as those who have corrupted humanity."

Cold rage quivered through Comte's slashed naval passage. "No question about it. When I was in Rwanda, which is mostly Catholic, I was appalled that the Church said and did nothing about the massacres. Even the local churchmen incited violence. One even called his mother a Tutsi cockroach. When the evil bastard was smuggled out of the country by French priests, he was allowed to resume his pastoral duties in France. I don't recall the Vatican condemning these events at all. I hated the hypocrisy."

"I'm surprised you stayed committed to the Church."

"Oh no Jared, I didn't. I was committed to using the Church's resources. I wanted to use whatever I could to wake everybody up from their contemptible slumber. And Elysius offered me that opportunity."

"Then you can help us even more. We need to work on several fronts, Comte. Religions, political institutions and military establishments have all been infiltrated by Belial. They are the number of the beast – 666. You'll know the verse in 2 Chronicles 9 when Solomon fell from his ordained mission and became ensnared in material pleasures."

"I know the passage, yes."

"It's why Elysius continues to remain outside the global power-structure. The corrupters are still amongst us Comte and they're leading the world into decadent materialism and fundamentalist religion. They deny the higher spiritual world because they are all tools of the regressive forces."

Comte nodded in agreement. It was refreshing to talk to someone who was like-minded. "What saddens me is how the corruption is denied. Even back in the days of King Solomon, power and wealth took precedence. The man had been given wonderful knowledge and yet he chose the easy path. He had received the star-map, the Key of Solomon which mapped our celestial origins and he could have taught the Sacred Path of higher consciousness and salvation, yet he ignored it. He chose what our business leaders and politicians choose, self-serving privilege and opulence. The Key linked all the ancient civilisations and religions with their star-god contact. But as always seems to happen, the secrets became condemned as demonic and much later, they were ironically perceived to be angelic, to ensure the truth was only ever known by the unrepresentative elite."

"Yes, you have to wonder how history would have panned out if Solomon had taken a different course. Yet, the secret stands in the human landscape if one knows where to look. As you would know Comte, the design of Washington DC is deliberately based on precise sacred geometry known since the time of King Solomon, a geometry bequeathed to the Knights Templar and, then much later, to the Scottish Rite of Freemasons. If people knew the 4th of July is the only day that the sacred cross of the sky rises with the Sun when viewed from Washington's Grand Causeway, they would know the true influence of the first U.S. president, George Washington. His Masonic high rank shaped a city in his name and founded nation."

Jared could feel Comte's passion. "It's odd isn't it? Christians are awaiting the Second Coming, the Jews are awaiting the birth of their Messiah and Islam is awaiting Judgement Day. Yet, the neo-Templar Orders, the Buddhists, the Advaitists and the Gnostics wait for nothing. They know Christ never left the world. Jesus may have died, but the Christ that dwelt within him is eternal. Christ is the state of transcendental consciousness that has always been and will always be present to those with eyes that truly see."

"That's true," agreed Comte. He repeated his favourite quote, the one from Luke that he had previously stated to Angelo. *"The kingdom of God does not come visibly, nor will people say, here it is, or, there it is, for behold, the kingdom of God is within you."*

"Exactly! If they could raise their consciousness, they would know the truth. Right now though, you should grab your belongings. We've arranged a new identity for you, passport, credit cards; all the things you need to start a new life. When you're ready we're taking a relaxed drive to Monaco. It'll be your new home."

54

JOURNEY TO THE UNDERGROUND

ATLAS MOUNTAINS, MOROCCO

Anwar was punctual and eager to leave. The cool morning air was rivalled by Keisha's frosty demeanour and Mac's prickly mistrust. To make things worse, Anwar's condescending tone was annoying us all.

I harboured a gnawing anxiety as we headed up a sparsely wooded incline away from the town. I had no idea what had prompted Keisha's outburst with Mac the previous night and was dismayed by the colour of everyone's mood.

Within forty minutes, the weight of our backpacks slowed our pace. We walked solidly over the bleak mountain pass, finally reaching the terraced slopes of the Berber village of Ikkis. Those hours were strained. Mac's displeasure was displayed by agitated mumblings over the slightest issue, sometimes even resorting to talking to nobody but himself. Keisha was ensconced in a shield of silence. Anwar offered no compromise, pushing us without a break, eager to collect his payment. I was beginning to wonder why the hell I was here. I had experienced all Mac's moods over the years so he didn't bother me too much.

It was Keisha who confounded me. I was still captivated by her, but today, I noticed large doses of Little Miss Independent. She had controlled the spoiled brat until now, but my confusion was what had brought it to the surface. Not that she was being demonstrative. It was the 'don't screw with me' attitude that was getting under my skin.

Keisha was wrapped in her own cocoon. The trek was helping her process. She thought of Aiden's admirable outburst toward the sleazy waiter. His manly posturing made her smile. She respected his dogged determination and empathised with how he had felt deceived by her. He had been right to feel angry, but there had seemed to be no other way. She fancied he would eventually understand her motive. She was being drawn to him; even his appearance grew more handsome by the day. His powerful, lithe physique and sorrowful hooded eyes magnetised her. But she would always hold firm to her obligations. Her involvement in Elysius made the luxury of a relationship almost impossible. She had no desire to draw him into her treacherous world, and yet, he had already crossed the Rubicon. He had been a victim of his own circumstances and was determined to master his destiny. She hoped neither of them would regret it and pushed steadily on, wrapped in her silent armour.

The archaic town of Tacheddirt is the highest settlement in the Rhirhaia Valley. We slowly followed Anwar up the only access, a winding footpath of around three kilometres, leading to a cluster of rectangular mud brick dwellings spilling down the mountainside.

It was mid afternoon and we took a much needed break. The primitive façade of the town offered little welcome. Fortunately, Anwar's familiarity with a toothless old man enabled us to have some rudimentary communication. He organised a meal from the woodfired kitchen of the only establishment available. Contrary to the food's uncouth presentation, it was surprisingly satisfying. Discussion was limited. The tone of the day had remained unchanged, grunts from Mac and a steely resolve from Keisha. As soon as our plates were scrapped clean, I threw my pack across my shoulders and made a move. I'd had enough.

We headed east, further up the valley, until we came to a spectacular precipice. Mac's couple of beers had energised him and I enjoyed some light banter during this part of our journey. Keisha trekked up ahead, the edge to her body language honed sharp as a blade.

After another couple of hours, we overlooked a mountain range that disappeared into a stunning blue and white haze. I stood for a few moments catching my breath, taking in the spectacular view and feeling the sunlight prickle my skin. Skirting the mountainside through some rough terrain, we hiked for another half an hour. Ahead, the slope reared upward with huge boulder-like formations blocking our path. Anwar guided us through the maze, as the mountains closed all around.

After clambering over and under rock formations on all sides, several openings into the rock face became visible. Anwar studied the brooding purple sky that was quickly bearing down and offered caution. Even in the height of summer, thunder and hailstorms can move in on a cloudless day within minutes. We heeded the warning and gathered pace to reach shelter. We made the cover of the closest cavern just before lightening tore open the darkening clouds. Thick sheets of rain pelted down putting a further dampener on Keisha's mood.

Wearily, I sheltered under the escarpment and asked Anwar what might lie ahead. He claimed that this particular cavern went into the mountain for a distance of around a hundred metres, but there were several others further along that to his knowledge had never fully been explored. If the Basilica existed, he thought that one of the other caves would most likely be its hiding place.

The rain ceased after only a few minutes, so we settled in and set up camp. Anwar remained introverted and erected his tent some distance away from us. I didn't blame him; he hadn't received any appreciation all day, so I figured he was entitled to keep his distance. Keisha was still touchy, so I broached my concern.

"What's been bugging you all day?"

"A dark omen. Something bad," she lamented.

"I'm serious. Can't you loosen up?"

"I am serious."

Best to play along I thought, "OK, so what omen?"

Her reply was curt. "Don't push it Aiden."

"Alright I won't, but the least you can do is relax a little. You've been a bitch all day."

"You ain't seen nothin' yet."

I shrugged. She could wallow in her own black mood. I could do without the headache.

In truth, Keisha had been weighing her options. I soon discovered her concern. After we were all settled, Anwar set off to scour the overhanging escarpment for dry firewood. Within moments of him being out of sight, Keisha edged her way to his solitary camp and was carefully combing through his belongings. I was astounded by her brashness. I had put off a confrontation earlier, but this was the last straw.

"What the hell are you doing?"

"Saving our skins, that's what."

"From what exactly?"

"Don't know, but that faded tattoo on his neck has been bothering me ever since we met him. I captured a photo of it on my cell phone as best I could when we were in the pickup truck yesterday. I transmitted it to Philip. He's run it though LITAN and it appears to be an initiation mark."

"So he's got a tattoo. So what? I don't see the problem."

"The main feature is the NASA symbol. That didn't concern me, but the marks at each end did. They're Akkadian characters."

"I haven't noticed."

"I know, but Aiden, they're the mark of initiates into the Martyrs of New Babylon. On their own, they have little importance, but Majestic has recruited them into their ranks. That spells trouble."

"I hope Philip's intelligence is right."

"He's rarely wrong Aiden."

"So 'rarely wrong' has caused you to stew all day because you think Anwar's with Majestic? Should we be worried?"

"Philip is, and if he is, I am. He thought Anwar would be ideal for this mission due to his knowledge of West African mythology, plus the fact that he's a local who knows the area. He didn't expect this and has told us to be careful."

"So have you found anything?"

"Nothing."

"What does Philip have in mind?"

"There's nothing to worry about. Just don't go saying anything to Mac. Otherwise he's likely to put Anwar in a choke-hold."

I took her advice, but thought the cloak and dagger stuff was a lame excuse for Keisha's capricious behaviour. We strayed back toward Mac who was now settled in with the bottle of Famous Grouse he had carried in his pack all day. "I still don't like the little bastard. Let me piss in his stew when it's ready. See how he likes alcohol then."

Mac had relieved the tension. We all laughed heartily and watched as Anwar returned with an armful of dried twigs and branches. I noticed his pack still glued to his back. *Why take the pack with him?*

Keisha and I approached as Anwar prepared a cooking fire. I decided to edge open the closet of Anwar's antagonism. I asked more of what he knew about this location. Surprisingly, he freely expressed himself. He said that this section of mountain range had been lifted due to continental shift rather late in the geological past. The local Berbers valued the area as one of mystical significance.

Mac had slumbered over and commented, "That makes sense. This area is probably an electro-magnetic vortex. Religious temples were often built on these focal points because of their effect on human perception. The subtle web of electromagnetic energy affects the density of the 'veil'."

Anwar weighed Mac's proposition. Maybe he had realised there was more to Mac than his propensity to drink, but his tone conceded nothing.

"Veil?" he mocked.

"Yes. The thinner the veil, the easier to achieve higher consciousness."

Anwar frowned and slipped in with his own observation. "So you think the Templars built a Basilica here to achieve higher consciousness?" He looked at me and mocked, "That's why I don't drink."

Mac ignored the jibe, but wasn't about to let the matter drop. "Maybe we'll find out tomorrow."

"Maybe there's nothing to find," Anwar shot back.

"What makes you so sure?"

"Nothing at all."

"Come on, share it," pushed Mac.

"There's nothing to share. Maybe it's not your destiny to find it. Maybe it is, God willing."

I smelt the odour of Keisha's concern.

Mac kept pushing. "You might think I'm stupid, but that would be a big mistake."

Anwar's scar on his right cheek twitched as he glared at Mac.

Keisha joined in. "You're right Mac, but Anwar knows full well what our destiny is. Don't you Anwar?"

A direct challenge, but the man kept his brittle composure. "I'm here to help you find what you're looking for. And I hope you do."

"So do we?"

I knew the stakes had been raised. "We'll all find out soon enough, so how about we have some calm."

Keisha eyes squinted at me with fury. "Aiden, you keep a lid on it as well."

I was annoyed by her hostility. I had finally had enough.

"How about saving your tantrums for someone who gives a damn?"

I expected further abuse or reprimand, but she calmly removed herself and retired to her tent. Anwar also left, encasing himself in taciturn solitude.

Mac always surprised me when I least expected. He grabbed another bottle of scotch from his pack.

"What possessed you to carry that around all day?"

Mac plastered a grin. "Actually, you've been carrying this one for me. I took it out of your pack earlier when you were flapping your jaw with Keisha."

We both cut loose with a bout of wild laughter. Another release, thanks to Mac.

I nodded towards Anwar's tent. "What do you make of that little slime?"

"Don't know yet, but he's giving me indigestion."

Mac lit one of his stinking cigarettes and diverted his comments back to electromagnetic energy. He provided an engrossing insight. The ancients apparently tuned their megalithic constructions to the energy lines that travel below the surface of the planet. The early Christians destroyed many of these 'pagan' temples and then built a church over the same site. Even the ancient Chinese geomancers understood these ley-lines. The intersection of a yin and yang line was always considered the most suitable location for a meditation temple. It was the original practice of feng shui before it became a Western fad.

Ancient stone piles also mark ley-line intersection. Thousands of them all over the world were used as crude amplifying antennae. The two biggest vortices, the Great Pyramid at Giza and Glastonbury Tor in England have subtle interstellar electromagnetic energies. There are many significant sites, Stonehenge and Avebury being the most well known in England. The Druids practised the traditional ways by attempting to balance and amplify these energies in an effort to tune human consciousness with the Earth.

Mac elaborated. "It's just plain physics, there's nothing supernatural about it. The intersections create standing columnar waves. Funny how Moses received his commandments on Mount Sinai, don't you think? It's another major ley-line juncture."

Mac took a deep drag, sucking in his poison. "People who don't know me well have always labelled me a substance abuser, but they're full of shit," he scowled. "I've taken a great interest in Keisha's theories since I was involved with LITAN and she's opened my eyes to biblical history."

"She knows her stuff that's for sure."

"She told me about the Book of Ezekiel which describes an anointed being, a cherub, walking amidst the Stones of Fire. Like Keisha I wondered what it all meant. What do you think these God-made 'Stones of Fire' are Aiden?"

"Don't ask me. You're telling the story."

Mac pointed to the sky. "They're up there, the stars and the planets, as seen from Earth. Throughout scripture, the Bible speaks of the first dwelling places of some of the sons of the gods. They existed even before Adam was created in Genesis. It seems there was a planetary calamity involving Mars that destroyed a previous civilisation causing another planet to disintegrate entirely. It finished up as the asteroid belt. Even the Biblical Jeremiah was told about cities that were destroyed long before modern humans were created.

"So you've discussed all this with Keisha?"

"Of course, she's a remarkable woman."

It was time to end the discussion. I didn't want to hear anymore. The thought of Keisha and Mac together was more than I could bear.

55

CROSSING THE THRESHOLD

PORTOFINO, ITALY

Perhaps it's time to follow. Those words were the last Angelo heard Comte speak. Angelo knew his best friend had gone for good. It was no surprise, Comte's demeanour at their last meeting had already warned him. He hoped that one day they would meet again.

His physical condition had improved greatly and Cardinal Valla appeared less intense, less agitated, almost relaxed.

Angelo was preparing the final draft of a speech when a surprising message popped up over his work. It flashed three times and disappeared as quickly as it had appeared. The words marked him.

Leave now, never return.
Seek the Divine Feminine.
Go to Mooring at Portofino Quay.

Angelo eyes darted to his side. Valla's personal secretary was busy with his papers and had not noticed the flashing message. He considered the words. The Divine Feminine? They suggested knowledge of the conversation between himself and Comte. *Is this Comte making contact?*

A rash of thoughts flooded his mind. If Comte had been living on borrowed time, maybe he was too. *Should I heed the warning?* The answer was a resounding yes. Angelo quickly typed the remainder of the speech and placed it in his out tray. With the work done, Cardinal Valla would not miss him, at least not for a little while.

Angelo read a deeper meaning between the lines of his clandestine message. There was much more to discover in life and the time was now. He hurried to his boarding room on the Via del Corridori and packed his meagre possessions. He threw aside his ecclesiastical garb, a uniform he would no longer need. Dressed in jeans, sneakers and light jacket, Angelo stepped into the world beyond.

Like Comte he would never return.

The meditative effect of Portofino soothed Angelo's anxiety. It was a mesmerising pearl. The haven of uncommon beauty stretched in an arch around the glorious bay and was sunk in the perennial green which covered the adjacent hillsides.

The aroma of cypress and juniper mingled with the salty fragrance of the sea. Angelo was inspired by the precious, secluded atmosphere of the exclusive village. It was privileged, cosy and unobtrusive – all melting into the delicate blue of the Ligurian Sea. It was heaven on earth.

Like a carefree tourist, he casually meandered past the pastel houses hugging the foreshore, past the small boats drawn out of the water onto the edge of the Piazzetta, past the exclusive boutiques, restaurants and bars and then wandered along the quay. The bay was peppered with craft of all kinds, including some belonging to the very rich. A modest, but stylish timber hulled yacht with classic curved lines basked at the end of the quay, waiting for its human cargo. Angelo cautiously approached a suntanned and scantily clad woman stretched out on the deck. She was lazily skimming the pages of a glossy magazine.

"Hello there. Is the captain of this craft waiting for anyone?"

The woman looked up and slowly checked out the young man. He was indeed good looking and athletic. "Well, I'm the skipper and if you're Angelo, then the answer is yes."

Angelo stalled. He was not expecting a woman, and certainly not one so attractive. She was slim and of medium height with brooding cocoa eyes, short lustrous hair the colour of midnight and a body that stirred him.

"I'm Angelo."

"Hi! People call me Blaze, so if you can show some ID you're welcome aboard."

Angelo reached for his wallet and flashed his Vatican security pass.

"Do you know who sent for me?"

"All I know is that it was a friend of yours. I was told to guarantee your safety. Apparently, he'll meet you at our destination."

Despite misgivings, Angelo threw his bag aboard. He felt uneasy. He guessed Blaze was in her late twenties and his discomfort was heightened by her bikini. It left nothing to the imagination. Her breasts were full and rounded, covered by the barest triangle of cloth. She wore a thong that exposed her smooth tight buttocks. They were cut so brief that when she stood to help him aboard he couldn't help but stare. He was embarrassingly aroused. To dampen the stirring within his loins, he faced the sea and stared into the distance.

He had never been around women and his uneasiness was enhanced by his father's words. *Be careful with beautiful women.* Yes, he remembered how recently those words had resurfaced when he met Keisha in the Old Study Room. But Keisha had been no threat. Maybe Blaze wasn't either.

The skipper made no display of sexual guile. She immediately set about releasing the yacht from its mooring and within minutes, the craft was motoring away on the glassy turquoise waters of the bay. Like a giant azure jewel, the calm ocean glinted in the sunlight as Angelo was drawn to his fate. The young man glanced surreptitiously at the bared woman and surveyed her longingly. He felt himself go hard.

Blaze concentrated on her mission. Deliver Angelo to Monaco along the Riviera coast without raising suspicion. The yacht was not ocean-going, but was more than capable of traversing the coastal waters of the Mediterranean. Portofino disappeared when they passed the headland and Blaze set a course not too distant from the shoreline.

Like many women who soaked up the sun along the Italian and French Riviera, she had dressed to blend in. Many would lay on the beach or onboard their boats either naked or at the very least scantily clad. But she noticed this caused her young passenger distress.

Blaze allowed Angelo his space. He had slipped below deck to unpack and some time later, re-emerged. Angelo stood at the fore of the yacht watching a flock of seabirds skimming and darting off in the distance. *How different this was to the regimentation of life in Vatican and the University,* he thought. Blaze approached to offer refreshments and once again noticed his vexation.

She decided to be frank. "I'm sorry my bikini offends you. Now that we're away I'll go and cover up."

Angelo remembered the message – Seek the Divine Feminine. Her suggestion to cover up embarrassed him further. "I'm sorry, it's just that I've never been around women and I really wish that I had. Please stay as you are. I'm beginning a new life and I have to get used to it."

Blaze noticed the swell within his jeans. The young man's muscular frame and boyish good looks had also aroused her. She approached him and placed her hand over his growing bulge. With compassion for his need, and also for her own, she offered, "I can relieve this if you wish."

Without waiting she attacked the belt of his jeans. Angelo was overcome with her forthrightness, but he readily responded by pulling her bikini top over her head. He cupped her full breasts within his eager soft hands. He breathed heavy, his thumbs caressing her firm pink nipples. She was indeed divine.

Blaze quickly lowered his pants and gently held his ripe testicles, lifting them slightly as though measuring the volume of their expectant release. She dropped to her knees and gripped his substantial shaft. It was rock hard and stood proud like a helmeted Imperial guard. Hungrily, she swept her moist tongue up its entire length, lingering to lap at its velvety tip.

Blaze looked up at Angelo, and he sunk into her liquid dark eyes, as her intense oral interrogation was reprised. Lack of intimacy had not prepared Angelo for the sweet experience. Instead of savouring his pleasure and restraining the rising tide, he erupted. He gripped the guardrail and squeezed. Blaze felt his engorged organ pulse and suddenly his warm, creamy fluid erupted. She held firm and readily stroked his swollen appendage causing him to pump his prolific seed in several more powerful jets over her breasts. Finally spent, she licked his manly fullness as it slowly melted into her palm.

Blaze stood to kiss him. As her dripping nakedness pressed against his body and their lips met, Angelo panicked. It was like a million synapses within his brain had lost their wiring. Anxiety flared. He pulled away, grabbed his jeans and fled to the deck below.

56

MOMENT OF TRUTH

ATLAS MOUNTAINS, MOROCCO

The bolt cutters chewed through the chain with little resistance. This was the fourth cavern we had entered. Berber folklore claimed that several caves extended for many kilometres under the mountain. The three previous caves had only extended about a hundred metres or so, but with this assault we had already traversed twice that distance. It was here that we encountered the fence, raising our confidence that we had found the right place.

Nature had carved a small amphitheatre about five metres wide and ten metres high, a stage with its curtain now drawn to perform our next act.

Mac allowed Anwar first entry. Keisha quickly followed with me being the last to clamber through. The air was still thick with mistrust and Keisha had been like a hawk watching Anwar's every move. So had I. It wasn't that I was particularly worried about him; I focused on him more out of respect for Keisha's concern. If he presented any danger, I had no qualms about taking him down. None of us like the wretch anyway.

We kept moving, climbing over, ducking under and pacing

further into the mountain. Piercing the claustrophobic earthen confines our torches displayed monstrous shadows against the rough hewn walls and ribbed vaulting.

We had progressed about four hundred metres through winding, undulating passages before reaching a dead end. This cave, like the previous ones, was dry with no seepage of moisture, so it was not the typical stalagmite, stalactite cavern. There had been a multitude of narrow side openings along the way, but we had followed the most obvious course. Now we weren't so sure.

I sprayed light around the modest space and noticed a small vent-like fissure. The aperture was only centimetres high and about a half metre above ground level. Mac bent down to shine his torch into the gap, but his footing slipped on a sloping rock causing him to lose balance. It was then that he noticed it. A sliver of light speared into the narrow space about ten or fifteen metres ahead. Mac didn't hesitate. Lying on his stomach, he squeezed his way through the vent. Within a body length, the aperture expanded into a space suitable for crouching. Mac called out for us to follow.

I allowed Keisha to crawl through and then followed. We cautiously moved forward, bent at the waist and found Mac about ten paces ahead standing full height. He was looking upward into a small shaft cut through the mountain rock. "Where's Anwar?" queried Mac.

"Shit, good question." Without delay, Keisha turned and shuffled back toward the aperture.

Mac was enthralled by the shaft. It flooded our space with natural sunlight. He was standing at the opening of another passage way and it was clear by its shaped uniformity that this was the original entrance to our present position. We had come the wrong way. "That shaft is some piece of workmanship. It looks like something the Egyptians or Aztecs would have made. It's almost a perfect arch."

Someone at sometime in the past had cut the opening from the outside, deep into the mountain. It had been done with almost industrial precision. We were on the right path.

I had allowed the excitement of the moment to catch me off guard. I was troubled about Keisha and told Mac I was going after her. I struggled to squeeze back through the passage, somehow it seemed narrower and my heartbeat quickened when I heard the sounds of struggle ahead. Keisha was obviously in trouble. As I reached the aperture and slid into the open, I was struck by a grisly scene.

With wildcat agility, Keisha positioned herself slightly behind Anwar, placing her left forearm against the nape of his neck. Simultaneously, her right hand angled across his forehead. Anwar had no time to break free. In a split-second, Keisha gripped hard and pirouetted, twisting his head and snapping it back against her rigid forearm.

The sickening crack of his spinal cord echoed around the chamber. Her athletic frame flung the body to the ground like an empty sack. She hung her head in shocked resignation, pushing her hands against the cave wall, coming to grips with what had just happened. Her breath laboured over the exertion.

This beguiling woman had just killed a man before my very eyes. It was no clumsy effort. It was quick and clean, with the practised dexterity of a trained assassin.

Detached and pinched with worry, she spoke, "It had to be done."

A minefield of responses split my thoughts. She had told me that Anwar was a potential danger, but I felt a flush of conflict. Keisha was also dangerous – kinetic virulence wrapped in the flesh of sensuality.

"You didn't like him, so you killed him?"

"Don't be an idiot Aiden. What do you see over there?" She shone her torch along the cave wall. I moved close and understood – Semtex 10 – enough explosive to bring down the cave.

"You suspected this?"

"He always kept his backpack close. Too close for my comfort. When he thought he had a chance, he acted. I shouldn't have waited for him to enter before us. God, I'm stupid."

"Slipped up did you? Come on, this was your plan wasn't it, or was it Philip's?" I asked provocatively.

"Sure, it's what I do for fun. Listen, he was the one who slipped up." Her response was malignant with scorn.

I felt foolish. Keisha had been right about Anwar. It was me who had slipped up. She reached for the dead man's backpack. His cell phone was acting as a timer. 18.39 and counting.

"The bastard's created a real problem. Eighteen and a half minutes. It's taken over forty to get this far, so there's no way we can get all the way out. Like I said, it had to be done."

"Maybe we can diffuse the explosive."

"It could be booby-trapped. Come on, let's catch up with Mac. We don't have much time."

She was right. I wouldn't know where to start. A vibration trigger would end it here and now. Keisha crouched forward and hurriedly edged her way through the aperture. We pressed forward with urgency and found Mac a further seventy metres ahead.

"Where's Anwar," he queried.

Keisha was blunt. "He's dead."

She belligerently steamed ahead carrying her frame with poise, but her vitality was jaded. Her confident air had been subtly maimed.

I clarified, "Keisha discovered Anwar was a Belial operative, something to do with that tattoo on his neck, so she snapped it like a twig."

"What? She did what?"

"I guess she thought she had no choice."

Mac spoke from the penumbra of light. "What haven't you told me?"

"The bastard's laid explosives back there and this cave is going to blow."

"See what sobriety does – the slimy little prick," Mac seethed.

"I know. This is all going to go up in a few minutes, so let's catch up with Keisha."

We moved with speed. The passageway curved slightly to the right and allowed movement without bending our torsos. Out of the greying gloom, the passageway spread out, lit again by a beam of piercing light. Up ahead, the area opened out to a massive space about a thousand square metres in size.

Keisha almost ran, pointing to a massive edifice. "We've found it," she beamed. "Welcome to the Basilica of the Eastern Star."

The walls were carved out of the natural stone, creating an arched portal. Protecting each side of the entrance, finely carved effigies of a dozen knights stood proud. Although quite different in architectural style, the rock-cut facade reminded me of the Al Khazneh at Petra.

We entered the portal and moved into the nave. The Basilica was bland and austere, different to the Byzantine and Gothic structures in Europe. The arched stanchions of the building rose ten metres high where they were engineered into the natural geology of the cave. The ceiling towered like a dome into the throat of the mountain. Fluted pillars rose into vast rib vaulting which clutched the natural rock ceiling. I hoped they were more than pure decoration. *If the explosive blew, would they hold the cavernous ceiling?* At our feet, the stone floor was interspersed with intricate and colourful mosaics, but the overall scene was of understated grace and overwhelming volume. Everything felt enormous.

Beyond the small quire and above the altar was a large circular leadlight window, illuminated by another shaft of penetrating light from beyond. The massive window was comprised of nine segments, each adorned with the figure of a knight. The segments met at the circular core featuring an image of the Risen Christ.

On either side of the altar were a set of three arched windows, each decorated with images of two disciples, making a total of twelve. A deep blue stained illumination fell upon the altar from the windows.

In an eerie, almost supernatural way, the Basilica was extremely beautiful. Considering the history of Morocco, Mac suspected the mosaics were most likely twelfth or thirteenth century Moorish. Gracing each side of the altar, two white conical spires some five metres in height stood like ghostly apparitions. Carved around their base were sheaths of grain used in the production of bread and above them were bees, like those used as symbols by Egyptian priesthood.

And then it happened. A deep death rumble rocked the foundation of the Basilica. Although muffled, the explosion was powerful enough to expel a plume of dust from the spires. A shock-wave punched me in the chest. Grains of silt dropped from the rock ceiling, raining down in a strafe of perpendicular showers. Fortunately, the cavern roof held above the altar, however, two of the decorative fluted pillars at the entrance buckled and crashed to the floor, carved stone shattering into hundreds of pieces.

The air choked with dust. Fortunately, the nave had taken the most damage. The protective knights of eight centuries past had fallen to the ground, smashed by the tonnes of rock and stone from the collapsed portico. Keisha had been vindicated. Anwar had been a harbinger of death. The Basilica was now lost, our only consolation being the light still filtering in from the outside world.

Mac sat on the floor. "Well that was lame. The moronic half-wit couldn't even get that right."

Keisha was also composed. "The Templars didn't enter the way we did. They followed those light shafts." She pointed to the stained glass that illuminated the altar. "You'll see when the dust settles, but beyond those windows there're more light shafts. There must be another entrance."

We searched for clues within the Basilica. *Did it hold the secret mentioned in the diary found in Vienna?* Within the sanctuary, directly in front of the altar, a large mosaic calendrical disc was set precisely where the light beams crossed.

Keisha examined the markings at the disc's centre. "I know this symbol. It's on the Temple of Hathor at Denderah."

Mac leant forward. "Egyptian? Here?"

"No doubt. See this marking. It's a pictorial representation of Thoth. And around the edge is the Zodiacal constellations laid out as a calendar. I'm not sure, but it could be from the era of the Companions of Horus."

Templar artisans had carved these pre-Pharaohic rulers into the disc, each Companion holding a cross.

"What's with the cross?" I asked

Keisha elaborated. "Actually, it's an Ankh. The Egyptians used the symbol long before the Christian era. It symbolises Enlightenment."

We all fell silent as Mac shined his torch onto the huge disc, focusing on the very centre. An exquisite set of symbols was revealed. "Keisha, I reckon this is the Hiram Key."

"Yes, you're right. Hiram Abif is the most important figure in Freemasonry. He was murdered for not revealing the Great Secret. His key represents 'Jacob's Ladder' mentioned in Genesis 28 where beings were seen ascending and descending between Earth and Heaven."

Mac countered, "I'm convinced the imagery here is similar to the First Degree Tracing Board of the Freemasons. It's an important part of instructing their initiates into the Mysteries. It traces the origin of three sun-like stars with inhabited planets, a map if you like, with a secret known by the elect for millennia. The map gives the chronology of human contact. Various presidents including Washington, Jackson, Taft, Truman and Ford all knew about it and decided to bury the knowledge."

Mac struck the disc with the back of his torch. There was a subtle change in sound. "I reckon it's hollow." He rose to his feet.

I took several photographs before Mac returned with a large iron candle stand. Without regard for the historical value of the beautiful disc, he smashed the stand down hard. After several more poundings, it finally cracked and then with one last strike the disc shattered inward.

57

TREPIDATION

LIGURIAN SEA, ITALY

Like her name, Blaze still burned with sexual heat. She empathised with Angelo's embarrassment. He had not yet developed his skills with women, so she left him below deck to compose himself.

He had been alone for fifteen minutes or so, lying on his bunk staring into the ceiling. He was confused and had no understanding why vile images were invading his thoughts. Blaze had been wonderful, blissfully divine. She had indeed relieved him, but coming over her had triggered an unnatural fear, so intense it constricted his airways. He almost choked. The reaction hadn't been triggered by guilt. In fact, at the very moment of orgasm he had scaled an ecstatic fervency where guilt had no home. It had been so much more satisfying than his solitary masturbation. No, this was fear beyond reason, something buried deep within his psyche.

He reflected on the memories reborn after his recent attack in Rome on the Via di Porta Santo Spirto. But now a new memory tumbled through – a flashback – a half-naked man holding his erect penis and pushing it towards Angelo's innocent face. He had just started school. He remembered how he had run away and how his refusal had resulted in a callous beating. Worse still, that episode was repeated over and over. The man came to him almost every night. He had eventually complied; it liberated him from the beatings. *Was this real?* He fought hard for the memory to fade, but the fear of what the memories meant raged with wild abandon.

Blaze set the auto-pilot. The boat was about three kilometres from shore and she was still embraced by her yearning. She needed the fire quenched. Her body ached for Angelo's magnificence to be deep inside her. But she also had compassion. She didn't want the young man's first sexual encounter to be a humiliation, so she decided to encourage him, to demonstrate to him what it was like to pleasure a woman. She had unashamedly remained topless whilst on deck and now removed her thong. Her body was bronzed all over and literally glowed with the heat of her desire.

Blaze slipped below deck and stood before Angelo in her arresting naked glory.

"I need you to relieve me Angelo. Would you?" She ran her hands over her thighs and felt herself moisten.

The celibate young man stared at her confident nakedness. He forced himself to breathe steadily trying to fight back an intensifying nausea. She was a sensual goddess and he longed to make love to her. He felt himself rouse, but he also tasted acidic bile rising in his throat. He bolted from his bunk and climbed onto the deck projecting the queasy contents of his stomach into the ocean just as he reached the guard rail.

Blaze fumed. Angelo's reaction had been unexpected. She lay down on her bunk and realised that only she would be able to douse the flame smouldering within. She couldn't wait. She slipped her hand between her open legs and caressed her sweet, damp folds. Her breathing quickened and with each unbridled stroke her lamentations became more audible. Angelo listened from above as Blaze slowly fashioned her boiterous crescendo.

58

MACHINATIONS

IL GALLO LUNGO, TYRRHENIAN SEA, ITALY

The previous evening's discourse had been interesting because of its peculiarity, but as far as Valla was concerned, talk of extra-terrestrial biological entities was fanciful and clearly demonic. In his rigid, dogmatic world there were angels and demons, spiritual entities that either helped or harmed mankind. Nothing more. To accept anything else was against everything he stood for. He remembered those days long ago when his mother spoke to the angels. As a child, he had prayed daily to be like her. But as he matured, he begged God to spare him from her demonic possession.

Goldstein also had difficulty with the idea of contact between humans and EBEs. It all sounded like a classic B-grade movie from the 60s. He figured Kane was espousing the most pathetic of all conspiracy theories. Little did Goldstein realise that Majestic had maintained a media conditioning programme since the late 1950s to hide extraterrestrial contact in plain sight, by covertly making it a source of cheap entertainment. This ingenious method allowed governments to discredit genuine research as being a product of media fantasy.

Volker, on the other hand, knew that Kane was one of the most erudite and intelligent within Majestic. He was a cruel, evil genius. Kane worked for the elite and was no fool. To the contrary, he had graduated with honours at Stanford and understood the machinations of those who controlled him. He was one of their master manipulators.

Majestic had their stooges and Volker considered that the Vatican Secretary of State was one of them. He was clearly a tough old bastard, but it was clear that Valla needed to defer authority whenever Kane was around.

Volker understood how the manipulators did their best to extend the Dark Age. He reflected on the Dead Sea Scrolls that were discovered in 1947. The École Biblique, founded by a Dominican priest in 1890, finally yielded to public outrage and released the scrolls after concealing them for decades. Divine Providence had seemed to protect the Qumran and Nag Hammadi texts from ultimate destruction, and now at last, modern scholars are able to examine and comprehend their explosive contents. Volker had been fortunate to interview one of those scholars, and to have read the translations.

He remembered Scroll 1QM 13:2. It told of a battle between the hosts of God and the wicked spirits of Belial. These spirits were specifically identified as 'angels of destruction' belonging to the sons of darkness. The troops of Belial consisted of both humans and spiritual beings of darkness. The ensuring battle, mentioned within the scroll, was between these forces and those of the Archangel Michael. The Knights Templar and other Gnostic groups knew that the hosts of the Archangel were none other than the Order of Melchizedek.

Volker held his inner thoughts close. Inwardly, he admired the antagonistic keeper of the archive who had been the object of derision. The man had courage and superhuman tenacity. However, he knew the keeper had already been sentenced. *And the Cardinal?*

Volker was sure that his destiny was also held in the hands of Veles Kane.

Gathered together for another Kane assault, the men sat on the terrace overlooking the calm waters of the Tyrrhenian Sea. They had enjoyed a sumptuous breakfast served politely by Kane's house staff. The Cardinal was at last prepared to acknowledge praise for the respectful service, something the master of the house completely lacked.

Kane stolidly pronounced, "I'm afraid as much as we have had our successes, with the passage of time we will need to disseminate some of the crumbs of human history. Of course, it will be planned and controlled. The populace is already being conditioned. The release of big budget sci-fi movies over the last couple of decades has slowly softened them, and our contrived mass conditioning will continue to evolve according to suitable time frames. We will start to reveal some of the previous life on Mars – microbes and so on. We've already admitted there was water on the planet. But we'll keep the major revelations well away from them."

Ernst Volker commented, "I agree it's becoming more difficult. The photos taken by the Viking space probe must have caused concern, particularly with the latest developments in digital technology."

"Yes, the pyramids and the face on Mars have been major embarrassments. Fortunately, NASA threw a smokescreen over most of those the images, but fragments of information about what those photos captured remain. It won't be too long before they work out that the geometry from those decayed pyramids match the geometry of the Solomon Key. It gives the precise coordinates of the planet where the inhabitants of Mars came from."

Volker gave a glimpse into his own esoteric knowledge. "You mean the planet that orbits the Star of Ra, honoured by the Egyptians."

Kane tried to hide his admiration of Volker's comment. "Of course," he said flatly.

Kane revealed more classification-12 information. Around forty thousand years ago, a celestial body that passes through our solar system every 3,600 years was discovered. As it entered the planetary regions of Mars, the inhabitants of that planet refined their dreadful calculations. The celestial body was expected to come close, but their refined calculations established it would be too close. It would strip Mars of its atmosphere. Like the Noah from our biblical stories, a few chosen ones from that ancient civilisation built a craft, an 'ark' capable of making the journey to Earth, a world then inhabited by primitive Neanderthals. Twenty-four males and twenty-four females made the journey from their fugacious homeland. The arrival was recorded by our ancient cultures. The most prominent example is the two sets of twenty-four figures flanked by a central figure at the Inca 'Gate of the Sun' at Tiahuanaco in Peru. Even in ancient Irish lore, the first inhabitants of Ireland were called the Race of Partholon, a race from the Other World, who landed in Ireland on the first day of May, the day called Beltane.

Goldstein saw the whole story as a bedtime fairytale suitable for children. The seriousness of Kane's communication was not enough to temper his banal humour. "Did they arrive with a maypole?"

"Well may you jest Goldstein. Fortunately, you're not here for your intellect, but it happens to be the real reason the day was celebrated. There are other examples across the globe. In Persian legend, the celestial being, Oromazes made twenty-four pairs of gods and placed them in an 'egg'. Even Andean culture recorded these gods coming to Earth. Ancient Egyptian texts refer to the Neteru and much later, the Sumerian Annunaki and the biblical Nephilim interceded to breed a new race of hominid, the Cro-Magnon, the modern human. I'm only telling a clown like you, so that Ernst and the Cardinal know what we need to extract from the Tibetan. He knows the history. Their sacred book, the Kantyua which was dictated by Buddha, describes extraterrestrial contact. The Tibetan also knows how to exist beyond the physical world, learned long ago from those who came and taught the Ancients."

The Cardinal shook his head. "Your talk is nothing but foul atheism. Pagans all over the world worshipped demons. Any other speculation is heresy."

Volker thought the Cardinal was more influenced by who was telling the story, rather than by the facts within the story. He put forward a proposition. "Your Eminence, with due respect to your faith, you would be aware that evidence of water has been found on Mars and science is confident of discovering fossilised microbes among samples yet to be obtained."

Valla's attitude thawed. "I have no problem with what you say. After all, God works in mysterious ways. However, talk of extraterrestrials coming to Earth to breed with ape men goes against the teachings of Genesis and therefore the Church."

On behalf of Majestic, Volker had studied the ancient texts with particular interest to the Sumerian and Akkadian clay tablets that recorded much of the Genesis story. Capturing Volker's interest, the tablets had described much about man's creation and the significance of the gods who had arrived on Earth. He decided to challenge the Cardinal's so-called teachings of Genesis.

"Your Eminence, I don't wish to aggrieve you, but does the Church really teach Genesis correctly or has it manipulated that very first book of the Bible into a complete fiction. If it is understood just as it is written, then I would say the story is completely different to what we are all taught by the Church."

The thickening vein pulsating in Valla's temple was a portent to Volker's accusation. "I take it you're a heathen as well. Your remarks are a vile stain on God."

Volker persisted. "You miss the point Your Eminence and I think deliberately so. When God said 'Let us make man', the gods made mankind male and female. Seems fair enough, otherwise how could the species procreate? But after bringing this hominid species into existence, it was noticed by the Lord God that there was no man. Odd, don't you think. This wasn't God. This was a being called Lord God who created the man we call Adam. I see this as a conundrum, Your Eminence, a conundrum which you and the Church have conveniently ignored. But the answer lies within the cuneiform tablets written by the Sumerians and Akkadians, long before the book known as Genesis was ever written. Prior to creating a man who could till the ground, the gods had created the more primitive hominid species. Adam was the man who is signified as the first Cro-Magnon, the first modern human who was a product of genetic manipulation by the Lord God, someone the Sumerians knew came from the heavens with others to rule over the Earth – a being they called Enki. Perhaps you can tell me Cardinal, who or what was doing the gene splicing?"

Kane appreciated Volker's sharp mind and leered at Valla. He noticed him inwardly squirm.

Excellent!

59

OSSUARY

ATLAS MOUNTAINS, MOROCCO

Expectation turned to disappointment. The mosaic disc collapsed into an empty cavity.

"Maybe it's a decoy," said Mac. "They didn't go to all this effort for nothing."

We had wasted precious time. Mac quickly moved behind the altar and began searching the apse. He found another mosaic insert, a white background emboldened with a Templar cross. Once again Mac tapped it with the base of his torch. It sounded solid. "No cavity here."

From his kneeling position, he moved closer to the altar. A block of stone about one metre long and a half metre wide acted as a plinth for the altar table. As he had glanced toward us, he noticed an insert of stone was embedded into the plinth just below the overlapping top. It fitted perfectly into a round cavity about the size of a fist.

Simultaneously, as Keisha inspected the stained glass glow that splashed upon the altar, she ran her hand across the surface, pushing aside the grime of past ages and the granules of silt that had rained down from above. Her touch caressed a round imperfection toward the outer edge. It was a stone disc inlayed into the stone. "I may have found something here."

Mac was quick to realise the significance. He quickly felt along the opposite end of the altar. Another round insert revealed itself.

"Let's find out what we've got. Aiden, stand here."

He dropped to his knees as Keisha and I moved into position at opposite ends. "You two press down on those as hard as you can when I say."

In unison we pressed on the inserts, as Mac pushed his into the plinth. Nothing happened at first, but with matching pressure the stone inserts started to move into the stone. Slowly the altar top twisted, rotating in a slight arc. A narrow opening in the top of the plinth was revealed, enough for Mac to run his fingers under the edge. He found a wooden lever that he had to force. A mechanism within the plinth activated. We heard the movement of further levers, but the altar remained as it was.

"Another decoy perhaps?" I asked.

"Don't think so," replied Mac.

Keisha moved away and scanned the apse for a further sign. She moved to one of the conical spires majestically standing next to the altar. And then Keisha spotted it. Carved around the base were sheaths of grain and one sheath had disappeared within the spire's core.

The recess was narrow and opened to a space within. I knelt on the floor and shoved my arm inside. I felt nothing. Reaching up higher, I touched what felt like a stone peg. I couldn't get a hold, so lying on my back I reached further up. I pushed hard on the protrusion and it shifted, activating another mechanism. The spire at the other end of the altar shifted slightly; stopped and then continued to move aside from its resting position. It slid about a metre across the floor. Mac and Keisha ran to it, discovering another hollow space, this time under where the cone had stood.

"Aiden, we've got it."

I moved to join them, but as soon as the pressure of my palm was released the spire began to move back into its original position.

"Stay where you are. Don't move!" yelled Mac.

My arm was about to burst, the pressure I needed to apply to hold the spire in place was excruciating. "Hurry up Mac. I can't hold it much longer."

"There's something in here."

Sitting in the hollow space was a stone ossuary and a solid metal chest. Mac had the pleasure of lifting them from their hiding place. "Got 'em."

I released my palm. At once, the mechanism's gears went into reverse. The spire repositioned, the sheath of grain reappeared on the base of the other spire and the altar top slide back into place. It was as though nothing had changed.

A great deal of medieval effort had been exerted to hide the ossuary and its contents, but it may have been discovered long ago and emptied of its contents. The style of ossuary suggested it was typically Hebrew, from the second temple period, 1st or 2nd century BC. Its dimensions were approximately 50 by 25 by 30 centimetres. Ossuaries like this were used to store the bones of the dead after the body was allowed to decay within a burial tomb.

The copper chest, decorated with a Templar cross was tarnished by the ages. A latch had clamped the lid in place. The edge of the lid was fused with wax, completely sealing it against the outside air. It was not easily opened. Mac used the bolt cutters to cut through the latch and I chipped the wax edges with my Swiss Army knife. Finally, we had the leverage required.

Mystery was laid bare for the first time in centuries. Two linen packages were exposed. Mac grabbed the largest and unfolded a thickly bound, leather book. The Templar Cross and a knight's sword emblazoned the cover. The paper pages appeared to be made from fibrous vegetable matter, maybe flax, typical of 12th century paper making in Moorish Spain. Intricately embossed, they were filled with rich colour. Like the Book of Kells at Trinity College in Dublin, the delicate artistry was masterful. The text was in Latin.

The other package was small. Keisha unravelled a small glass vial sealed with wax. Inside the dirty vial was a whitish powder.

"What's the bet it's the same as you found in Baalbek," exclaimed Mac.

Keisha cautioned, "The Templars certainly used it. We'll need to get it tested."

She turned to the ossuary. It was completely bare of any markings or identification. I loosened the lid which came away with ease. Once again there was a linen wrap within. Keisha peeled the disintegrating linen away, revealing human bones and a skull. It was then that we saw it. A gold ring inlaid with a green gemstone. Inscribed upon the ring was the unmistakable seal of Solomon.

Could it be?

This was a unique specimen. They were the bones of a tall individual, their patina indicating an age well beyond Christian time-frames. I would need to examine them in detail, but this was definitely a very old specimen of a person at least two metres in height. The pelvis formed a rough cone shape and was not nearly large enough to pass a newborn, so I had no hesitation in determining the specimen was male.

It was an exhilarating discovery, but the time had come to find a way of escape.

Keisha and I began searching the perimeter of the Basilica.

Mac continued to examine the mosaic floor patterns and with his iron candle holder, he scoured each pattern banging the holder down onto the mosaics. We found no niches or crevices in the perimeter and eventually found Mac standing below the stained glass windows.

Banging his candle holder onto a non-descriptive mosaic, he screamed out. "This one's hollow."

Once again, he smashed hard and after several more poundings the mosaic fell inward. Sure enough, steps led below leading to the cave floor that slid under the flagstones of the Basilica.

"Fucking sweet!" chuckled Mac.

We left the stone ossuary behind. It was just too heavy. We were careful not to contaminate the bones. I removed a large plastic bag from my backpack and slipped on a pair of surgical gloves – my usual expedition essentials. There was no way we could take the whole skeleton, but the skull, femur and radius bones were carefully inserted into the plastic for further investigation. This would help with determination of height and be suitable for DNA analysis. The gold ring was also removed.

With the other Templar booty, we descended the steps. Two metres down, the cave floor slipped under the thick walls of the Basilica and opened into another cavern. We moved forward some fifty or sixty metres where the cavern narrowed and curved sharply to the right. Up ahead was a three metre wide wall of gravelly mud brick, centuries old, but a barrier to our escape. We were trapped.

Mac quickly raced back the way we had come and soon returned with his iron candle stand. Once again, it was used to good effect. He smashed it against the large mud bricks.

It was hard work, but he made progress, the mud and gravel finally breaking and giving way. Grabbing bricks with our hands, we loosened and pulled them away to create a crawl space. On the other side, the mud brick wall had been plastered with bare earth creating the illusion of a natural cave wall. Being only three metres wide, it was the perfect camouflage.

Once through, we were elated by the sliver of blue visible through a narrow mouth of sparse vegetation. Keisha was right. There was another entrance after all. We were free.

The woman was an enigma. There was more strength to her foundation than I had ever imagined. She was a woman who killed with consummate ease yet was the epitome of innocent femininity.

I mused over the transformation.

Elegant and sophisticated to athletic and agile, always sexy and sensual. Beautiful blond hair cascading long one moment to cropped raunchy spikes the next. Well-tailored pants and fashionable low-cut blouse to t-shirt and jeans. Compassionate, yet ruthless. Open, yet secretive. Mostly agreeable, yet prone to petulance.

She was a riddle I was determined to unravel.

60

NEW HOME

MONACO

Monaco. Not the location Comte had expected to reside. He was currently domiciled at the sumptuous Hotel Metropole Monte Carlo, exquisitely adorned with ceiling frescoes, glass domes, marble and crystal. Registered in the assumed name of Teo Casari he had been given celebrity treatment when he arrived with Jared. It was a lifestyle he could get used to.

Lazing by the pool he waited for further instruction. He was invigorating his exhausted body and mind from his years of work. But Comte had the usual problem to contend with, the other guests were horrified by his deformity. He was even asked by a hotel staffer to remove himself from the pool area. Totally free of the moral precepts of the past, Comte took delight in raising his middle finger.

To familiarise himself, Comte had already walked the La Condamine quarter admiring the elegant yachts and luxurious ocean cruisers within the bay. He cast his mind to Jared's remarks regarding this small principality and Elysius's connection.

It was in 1215 that the Genoese laid the foundations of the Fortress of Monaco on what is now known as Le Rocher – the

Rock. Unknown to Francois Grimaldi and his Guelph supporters who seized the fortress in 1297, Elysius's predecessors had built a large vault deep within the Rock. Separate to the Fortress, the vault had later served as one of the key repositories for Elysius's ancient manuscripts. They were retrieved from imminent destruction after a brave renegade smuggled them out of the Vatican during the mid-seventeenth century. Louis XII of France had granted Monaco protected Principality status, but this annexure was now threatened by the Church. Orders were issued to return the smuggled documents to Rome. The offer was rejected, but only after they had been moved once again for further safekeeping. In compensation for the loss, Louis XIV gave the Embassy of France to the Holy See in 1698. The issue was forgotten and so were the manuscripts. They were eventually returned to Le Rocher at the time of the French Revolution, remaining there ever since.

The old city is now famous for the Fortress which is still the palatial home of the House of Grimaldi. Just two blocks away, Comte would have the pleasure of analysing these rare works.

The keeper's scholastic and analytical abilities had been carefully observed by Elysius. Most of all, it was his willingness to spread the knowledge that was appealing. It was proposed that he catalogue and upload all the Le Rocher texts onto LITAN and assist with scriptural interpretation. He would be granted unrestricted access and the good fortune to retain an assistant. Comte couldn't resist and had naturally asked for Angelo. The disfigured keeper almost pinched himself, he had been bestowed a lifestyle that was unimaginable compared to his virtual internment within the Holy City.

Comte had been instructed to relax, but was also alerted. If he was approached, he was to ignore any advance until his new identity papers were ready. For safety reasons, only he should make contact and that would be to a man in his mid-thirties who would be wearing dark casual pants, open neck white shirt and light blue cashmere sweater. At the time indicated, Comte shuffled into the bar, scanned the room casually and spotted Rene Anjou, his Monaco connection.

The man's hair was thick light brown, cut short at the back and right side, and then swept upward to the front and across to the left. It was neatly groomed with product. Rene extended his hand and Comte met his palm. His two fingers wrapped to form a half grip. Rene projected a contemporary and pleasant presence, a sign of respect for the strange man who had provided Elysius a trickle of valuable documents that flowed into a torrent.

He wasted no time. "I have a car waiting. Let's have some dinner."

A chauffeured black limousine was driven the short distance to what the initiated call Louis Quinze, an extravagant and showy restaurant at the Hôtel de Paris on Place du Casino. Catering to an exclusive clientele, the maître d'hôtel showered Rene with cheerful familiarity. Even Comte was greeted as a valued guest, with no disgust or chagrin toward his disfigurement. *They conceal their prejudices well,* mused Comte as he was led to a dining area adorned with gilt, large mirrors and grand chandelier. The two men were led to a private booth reserved specially for them.

"We could have stayed at the Metropole for dinner," offered Comte.

"Of course, they serve a wonderful menu, but I grew up in Nice with one of the chefs here. I'm always looked after and besides, we'll have privacy."

"All the better then."

"From what I've heard about you Comte, you're going to enjoy your work here," promised Rene.

"Time I had a new challenge," he replied, "although today I thought back to when Elysius first made contact with me. It was two years ago next week."

"Then let's celebrate the anniversary and I'll tell you what we have waiting for you."

Rene promptly ordered a bottle of 1982 Chateau Lefleur.

Comte like what he heard. "Sounds interesting. You know, I was never told how the Order chose me. Do you know?"

"Just over two years ago, we had concerns about the Vatican Secretary of State, Antonio Cardinal Valla. He has regular contact with Veles Kane, a hard-nosed Majestic operative who runs his own network of conspirators. We researched his connection to Valla and found that some thirty years apart they were both students at Harvard, and both were members of a fraternity known as The Skull and Bones. Most members of this fraternity rise to high position and make use of each other for their connections. Presidents, international bankers, CEOs of global companies and even your famous Cardinal are linked in a sinister plan for global control, the control of information, the control of credit and to withhold the most important discoveries of our civilisation. My job is to help Elysius break this impasse. Otherwise humans will be just another evolutionary failure, cut-off from their greater brethren. Consequently, we installed a worm-hole into the Vatican computer network, both LAN and mini-server. Spyware technology that was invisible until some months back."

Comte's face twisted into a grin. "Love it. Bet they were pissed off."

"Don't think so. It was never discovered. When they installed new detection software, our program self-destructed and deleted all evidence of its existence right back to the original digital fingerprint. We've reconfigured our program since then and now we're back in. Of course, one of the first things of interest with our first worm-hole exercise was your dossier."

"I was compiling it for my own interest. After my injuries and what happened to those poor souls in Rwanda, I lost all faith in what I found to be utter fiction. I discovered that the fiction hides a greater truth. But Elysius knows all that, so I can't see why my dossier was of so much interest."

"It left a great impression because much of it came from source documents that only you could access. We've been indebted to you ever since. As agreed your work will soon be disseminated. The veil of religious deceit will be lifted, I assure you. It's the only way the world will find peace."

"I certainly agree with religion being deceitful, but world peace is drawing a long bow, isn't it."

"Perhaps, but it'll be a step in the right direction." Rene read the menu with a connoisseur's eye and offered a suggestion. "I can recommend the degustation menu with the accompanying wines, if you would like. It's sex on a plate."

"It's decided then. In my condition, it's the only sex I'll ever get." Both men laughed. "On a more serious note, Jared told me about the manuscripts retrieved from the Vatican in the seventeenth century. I'm curious to know which ones they are."

Rene smirked. "You mean Jared didn't tell you?"

"Perhaps he was leaving that to you."

"Well, I think you're going to enjoy this. The Vatican freely admits all the authentic texts prior to the 8th century have disappeared. Now where do you suppose they might be?"

The implacable Comte was amused. "You're kidding me. Jared said they were texts the Church wanted destroyed. I had no idea they were all the pre-8th century ones."

"Now you know. They've been in storage for centuries and we've been in need of a specialist to help sort and catalogue them. More importantly, we need them interpreted for complex spiritual and scientific content. There are several thousand and they're at your complete disposal. But the best surprise for you is what Keisha was able to determine from her very quick appraisal of them."

"Keisha's been through them?"

"Only a quick glance, but enough to know that there are texts paralleling the most controversial stories translated from the ancient

Sumerian tablets. As you know, much of the Torah has its origins from those tablets. At her request, all translated cuneiform tablets are now being uploaded to LITAN. It's a massive job; the British Museum alone has over 140,000 remnants and most of them still need translation."

Comte was ecstatic. He finally belonged. His search for purpose had been realised. "I have some great research ahead then."

Rene offered Comte an insight. "Keisha has an interesting view. She says that most religious scholars look at the Hebrew and other biblical texts as being either factual or an allegory, whereas those very same scholars regard all texts that precede the Hebrew as myth and plain fantasy. Keisha thinks the assumption is absurd."

The two men were interrupted by an immaculate waiter seeking their dinner order. Once provided, Comte passed a view he had long held.

"I agree with Keisha. I believe Eli Rosen also had the view that the cuneiform translations should be read on face value. And why not? A great deal of Genesis has its origins in those earlier Sumerian texts."

"Glad to hear you're on Keisha's wavelength." Rene's tone then moved to caution. "Comte, before you gain access to all this, I have something vital to ask."

"Sounds ominous."

"It is. I don't really know how to approach the subject, so I'll just come out with it. Our entrée into the Vatican computers has confirmed your activities were not only being monitored, but were being transmitted to an unknown destination. We suspect Majestic, but that's not conclusive."

Comte shrugged, not particularly concerned with cloak and dagger mystery.

"How well do you know Angelo DeMarco?"

Comte's face burned with grotesque petulance. "Mr Anjou,

don't even think about it! I'd trust Angelo with my life."

"I understand. We've checked him out and he seems to be what he appears, but I had to ask the question, especially with him coming here to join you. I hope you understand."

"No harm done. I realise you have a job to do. But really…"

Rene was satisfied. The thought needed airing and he could now make his report. It was time to lower the temperature and get to know the quixotic Comte.

61

DISCLOSURE

—————

IL GALLO LUNGO, TYRRHENIAN SEA, ITALY

Albrecht's cell phone cut the air like a scalpel. It was Hawass. "The Tibetan's ready to talk."

Cardinal Valla excused himself. He wanted to return to Rome, but Kane would have none of it. "You're going nowhere. You may actually learn something."

Valla didn't have the stomach for torture or to see a holy man subdued. The monk clearly wasn't a man of God, but Valla considered he was holy by Tibetan standards and what he had witnessed days ago was a scene unworthy of his presence. Kane and his henchmen could deal with it. "I have important work to do in Rome."

Kane forced his point, "I said you're coming with me."

Valla was sickened with his predicament. He only wanted to serve God. The price of Kane's bidding was beginning to tire him. However, he quietly acquiesced and walked across the sun drenched terrace with the others. He followed them to the interrogation room. The air was rank, filled with the stink of body odour and the stench of burnt flesh.

Kane was incensed. Strapped to a metal chair bolted to the

cement floor, the Tibetan had been stripped naked and horribly burned. The left side of his face was blackened and blistered with a bloody mass of congealed ooze. His eye had been incinerated within its socket and his left ear had been burned to charcoal, the aperture closed over with melted flesh. His genitalia had also been burned; his fleshy protrusion and his urinary tract now rendered useless. Kane hurled screaming abuse at Hawass. "You fucking animal. Get out you great lump of shit!"

Hawass objected, "He refused to talk. Nobody refuses Hawass. He passed no sound for four days until ten minutes ago."

"I don't care. You're putrid scum Hawass, so get the fuck out. NOW."

The beast left the room. The fact the Tibetan had been burned by Kane was lost in the moment. The irony did not escape Goldstein. He, too, was disgusted at the obscenity and could not comprehend how the Tibetan had made no sound. The pain must have been unbearable.

Goldstein spoke two words that clawed at Kane's conscience. "Class act."

Kane ignored the sarcasm.

The Tibetan slowly raised his head. He sighed deeply, allowing his lungs to breathe a moment of life. He quietly spoke in clear English, a complete surprise to the men present. "I have decided to talk. You seek the knowledge of the device. Is this so?"

Kane calmed, "It is. If you hadn't been a fool, none of this would have been necessary."

The Tibetan's persona was serene. His features filled with light and the inflamed melted flesh visibly cooled. Peace and tranquillity permeated the space around him. The stench in the air dissipated to the sweet scent of bouquets. Valla diagnosed the sign of demonic possession and clutched his pectoral cross for protection.

"You are mistaken. It was very necessary. I have never had need of the tetrahedral. The Old Ones used it sometimes, if they struggled to reach Jhana. There's no reason to tell you how to use it because you cannot."

"What's this? You just said you'd tell me."

"I said I have decided to talk. You see, the knowledge you seek cannot help you reach your objective. What you desire will not be yours. The keys to enlightenment are earned. They are not obtained by brutality. Your own hatred, greed and delusion for the control of others prevent you. The Path is shut. You cannot open the door because of who you are.

"Your Mr Hawass was most disturbed because I didn't give him satisfaction. He sought the screams of a monk. The poor man didn't realise I wasn't here."

Kane's expression hardened. "You're delusional. You're here alright and you WILL die if you don't give me what I want."

The Tibetan ignored the statement and piercingly appraised each of the four men with a laser-like stare. He may have had only one eye that functioned, but it penetrated with a fierce psychic intensity. The men were rendered speechless by the authority of the assessment.

At last the monk spoke. "Veles Kane – bureaucratic, sadistic, choleric and vain. Ariel Goldstein – assassin, structured, conditioned and narrow. Antonio Valla – zealot, obsessive, pompous and deluded. Volker – learned, latent, abstract and servile," the monk pronounced. "I have put my time here to good use. I reached into your unconscious last time you all visited and you told me much.

"Ariel Goldstein. You will deliver me from this wrecked body. It has served its purpose. That is your duty to perform and when released from this vessel I will have no need to incarnate into human form again. That is my destiny and my presence here is the last duty I need to perform in this world. You however, will be cast into a hell of your own making within a month, to wander the dark realms of existence until you recognise the light you have chosen to ignore. I bless you in your future suffering that you unconsciously choose by your intentions.

"Antonio Cardinal Valla. What a price you paid to be dressed in scarlet. Your delusions possess you and hold you captive. You acquiesce to your controllers, the demons and the manipulators of this world. You have lost your way and your soul. You cannot understand the true message of your scriptures. You dwell in the dense ether of your own creation. In my meditations, I have read the Akashic records and seen your life. Your mother observes your suffering. She dwells within the light and cannot speak to you through your opaque shroud of deceit. Your attachments hold you back. Only you can find release. The eternity you seek is hidden until you rise in consciousness."

The observers were held speechless. Words would not form. The Tibetan's gaze fell upon Volker. The monk's iron stare softened.

"Ersnt Volker. Your intelligence has kept you true. Stay on the path."

The fire in the Tibetan's gaze intensified when he looked toward the Intelligence Director of Global Studies. "Veles Kane. You dress like the successful business man. You move with the flair of confident self awareness. How you have risen in your chosen profession. You think you wield power and so you prance. You are beguiled. You are nothing but a pompous puppet doing the will of the dark forces that pull your strings – a plaything of the malevolent.

"You know the history of mankind and how we have evolved, and yet you and your masters seek to hold that knowledge secret. Your purpose is to manipulate the masses into total serfdom. Consequently, you work against the evolution of humankind itself. This device helps those already on the path to rise further in consciousness. Your controllers are the fallen and whilst you remain attached to them, nothing can help you rise. The tetrahedral is useless to you.

"Before I am cast from this body, I will tell you a story of another Tibetan. He has always described himself as a brother who has travelled a little longer along the Path than most. He is a spiritual guide and teacher for mankind.

"This being led my meditations to the one who is here to influence the spiritual evolution of our planet and to prepare for the return of his brethren. He holds no public position, but serves a small collective called the Council of Change for Evolutionary Consciousness. He is recorded in history throughout the ages, as are others on all continents, known by many religions and names. He stands ready to help mankind understand the Truth of our existence. As the planetary home of our ancestors enters the regions of our solar system once more, those who have travelled the path of light will be aided in the battle against ignorance. There will be an in-gathering of the few who are ready.

"He has recently returned for this purpose and stands ready to perform his duty to help his fellow beings. He cannot be held back from his task. Should his physical form be destroyed, he will continue his work to destroy the blatant lies of the past. Liberation for the worthy cannot be stopped by the regressive powers that hold the world in bondage. You can prance with your vanity all you like Veles Kane, but your days are numbered. Your epitaph has already been written. I suggest you prepare for your sordid destiny. You will know only the grey forms of darkness."

The monk silenced. His eye glazed over, exhaled his breath and dropped his head to his chest. He was done.

The monk's words touched them all except Kane. He was the first to respond. He had quickly found his voice. "The bastard's right about one thing. Do him now, Goldstein. I want to see him fall." Goldstein hesitated, held back by words that had stung him. "I said, do him. Otherwise you can get the Hawass treatment yourself. And don't think for one minute I don't fucking mean it."

Goldstein recognised that Kane had snapped. He decided not to test him further and dejectedly reached into his jacket. He removed his Heckler and Koch. He raised the gun and fired. The Tibetan's brains splashed against the wall behind him.

Volker turned away in disgust as the Cardinal whimpered, images of his mother's death released from the deep recesses of his mind.

62

REFLECTION

MARRAKECH, MOROCCO

A check of our coordinates, a call to Philip and a two-hour wait. Our problem was two-fold, to avoid local suspicion about our 'missing' guide and to have access to the contents of the ossuary. An honest disclosure of the find would bring too many questions. We had arrived in the country as tourists and would need to leave via the traditional custom requirements. But Keisha had another surprise for us. An encrypted satellite call immediately set Elysius into action and by late afternoon, a Bell 206L Long Ranger helicopter was hovering at the mountainside. It made for an easy departure.

We approached Marrakech as the sun finally slipped below the horizon. The old city basked in a deep ochreous glow. Accommodation had been arranged at the La Sultana Marrakech, a small luxury hotel on the rue de La Kasbah. Philip advised that he would have to arrange a diplomatic solution and that a private flight was on standby.

After completing registration at our hotel and securing our possessions in the hotel safe, we were all lured to the Djemâa el Fna, the mysterious, but wildly exuberant marketplace within the

labyrinthine medina within the city centre. It pulsed with bur-
lesque charm – storytellers, acrobats, snake charmers and musicians
with their Gnaouan drums. A mix of Berber, Arab and African,
Marrakech is the soul of Morocco – a city of salmon pink com-
plementing the red earth that gave it birth. On the crossroads of
the ancient caravan routes from Timbuktu, I wondered about the
medieval Knights Templar and their connections with this amazing
place, so far away from their native homelands.

Aromas from the outdoor food stalls with vendors whipping up
an array of fish, meat and salads captivated out taste buds. Delicacies
like lamb and beef in earthenware tagines had stood on hot ashes
all day and we salivated over the aromatic flavours. Our senses were
enhanced by the hawkers and hustlers selling everything from cook-
ery pots to pig-blood cakes.

The helter-skelter of the city was exuberant. Pedestrians com-
peted with donkey carts, mopeds and dilapidated sedans. The
insouciant movement of people and the conduct of their affairs was
a reflection of past centuries. Even the more refined parts of the city
had a rugged edge, a quality unique to this intoxicating city.

We enjoyed a hearty meal of slow cooked lamb and artichoke
with spiced vegetables at a restaurant near the marketplace where
Mac could indulge. We discussed the events leading up to our find.
Keisha rationalised her actions.

Keisha opened up. "I want to apologise to you both. I should
have told you what was going through my mind. I'm sorry," she said
quietly.

Mac threw down his whiskey. "I couldn't stomach the tenden-
tious arsehole anyway, so no apologies required."

Keisha glanced in my direction, "Sorry I was being the bitch, but
I knew what I had to deal with and I wasn't looking forward to it."

"You don't need to make decisions for us, but I'll admit you were
right, so let's forget it. We're here for a reason and we found what we

came for. Let's hope we can all get out of here without any further trouble."

"Don't worry. Philip will come through, he always does." Keisha was desperate to begin the translation of the Templar book and for my sake had already phoned Philip to set up the lab.

"I'm not worried Keisha. I just want to be the first to examine those bones, that's all."

My feelings had cooled towards her and decided that I would no longer see her through dewy eyes. She was a professional in more ways than one and it was something I intended to remember.

She softened the distance between us by discussing the medieval diary discovered in the bowels of St Stephens Cathedral. It was obviously authentic. This and the 14th century papal letter of Pope Clement V indicating the Basilica held the secret to man's genesis was persuasive enough to conclude that the book, the vial of powder and the skeleton may hold a captivating secret.

Back at the hotel, Keisha retired to her room. She ran a hot bath to soak away her anguish. Accepting Aiden's disappointment in her was difficult. Normally, she would have brushed it off as petty male ego, but there were genuine emotions stirring within her. She remembered that interview on television when she had seen him for the first time, that ruggedly masculine figure with the conspicuous boyish charm. She liked him. More than that, she wanted to be with him. There was a sublime masculine allure to the man. She had fantasised having his strong hands on her toned body, her soft lips hard upon his.

Keisha ducked under the water and emerged from the bath refreshed and her mind set. Yes, she liked him and wanted to be with him. But just like him, she wouldn't compromise.

I joined Mac at the bar for a night-cap. Within a couple of minutes, he was openly surveying a stylish woman reading some documents in the lounge. I figured I was going to be in the way, so I threw down my drink and made a hasty exit.

Philip organisational skills had been exemplary. Through his Spanish Embassy contacts, diplomatic immunity was quickly negotiated for Keisha with the Moroccan Foreign Office. This would allow her to return with the contents of the ossuary, no questions asked. Mac and I would go through customs as normal, but could leave on the same flight.

Within fourteen hours of rescue, Keisha and I were flying across the Mediterranean. As for Mac, he changed his plans at the last minute. He was ensconced in a room with the woman he met last night. She was a Parisian who was in Marrakech for a trade convention at the Palais des Congres. Mac had entertained her with his sardonic humour, his acceptable French and a couple of bottles of Dom Pérignon. Mac was going to accompany her at the convention. I laughed at his prospects, but he reckoned that I would be busy analysing the bone specimens and Keisha would have her work cut out with the Templar book, so he deserved some R&R.

Keisha was more concerned with Anwar's treachery. His disappearance would soon cause an investigation and Keisha warned Mac about his safety. She wanted him to return with us, but Mac said he was flying to Paris to continue his tryst and would see us in a few days. We both knew Mac well enough to know there was no point persuading him otherwise. He was on a mission and wouldn't be distracted.

63

REUNION

MONACO

After her isolated gratification, Blaze dressed in three-quarter jeans and buttoned shirt, and silently carried out her mission. She wanted to understand Angelo's personal torments, but allowed him plenty of space, speaking only when necessary. At least the silence was tolerable. Time dragged awkwardly and with relief, she finally delivered the young man to Monaco late the following day.

Seek the Divine Feminine. That was the message. Angelo had found the divine in the image of Blaze, but his rite of passage was poisoned with putrid, festering thoughts. They fought for expression within the deep recesses of his mind. Memories long since buried were constantly seeping into disturbing and repulsive flashes of recognition.

Spray pounded off the wooden hull as the yacht sliced through the coastal waves. The salty air and open sea had given Angelo time to reflect on his childhood and the consequent attachment to his faith. He realised that his mind held no memory of his young life. It was a wasteland that had absorbed itself into the desperation of a faith now shattered. Comte had changed everything. And this journey was the culmination of this change. It had been fuelled with horrid memories which required the soothing balm of spiritual understanding.

He wished he could explain himself to Blaze. Her motive to satisfy had been genuine and without malice. Her desire had been to give and receive pleasure for pleasure's sake alone. His response was an embarrassment he could never forgive.

Blaze moored the yacht with dexterous poise. Two men waited patiently onshore for her human cargo. She witnessed Angelo's expression when he waved to the disfigured Comte. It was an expression of resounding joy, of love even. Blaze had known love and knew how to recognise it. She reconciled her hot anger from the day before. *'God, I'm an idiot. He prefers the cripple.'*

For Angelo it was a pleasing reunion with the only person who had opened his mind. Before Comte, it had been resolutely closed by his theological studies. Comte was a lighthouse in stormy waters

Angelo's overnight torment revealed there was much in his subconscious that needed deliverance. There was a grisly cell where his memories were trapped, but Blaze had opened the prison door just enough to frighten him. His blighted cognizance fought hard to keep it contained. As he disembarked, he held out his hand to Blaze in thanks for the safe passage. The only word that passed his lips was 'sorry'. She nodded with understanding.

Rene stood back and evaluated the young traveller as he warmly greeted Comte. Elysius had wanted Angelo's history confirmed and Rene had discovered that soon after the death of his mother, at the age of five, his father had sent him to religious boarding school. As was the case with all students, he was given a strict education and had been exemplary in his studies. Upon graduation, he had entered the university in Rome. Angelo had been immediately acquired to work as an assistant within the Palazzo del Governatorato. Only recently, he was transferred to the Medieval Palace to act as an administrative assistant to the Vatican Secretary of State. Comte had vouched for Angelo and Rene had found nothing in the young man's past to contradict Comte's assessment.

Angelo was excited about their opportunity. Books and manuscripts retrieved from destruction – the pre 8th century texts of the Vatican –what a find! And he would be working with his esteemed friend. That's what he needed now – stability and the chance to find peace.

Rene had organised a shared two bedroom apartment for the two men in the Fontvieille district not far from their work at Le Rocher. The arrangements with Elysius meant they would be paid handsomely for their work and have the freedom to enjoy a life away from ritual confinement. Comte was keen to examine the old Vatican texts and promised Angelo that he could catalogue anything relating to the Divine Feminine. Angelo would be able to self-discover, without doctrinaire coercion of what and how he should think.

Comte had already told him about the heresy of the Templars, how they had denied the Virgin Birth and the death of Jesus on the cross. It seems they also held the belief that Jesus married Mary Magdalene, his most beloved disciple.

Her portrayal as a harlot whose life was transformed by the grace and forgiveness of Jesus had its origins in Homily 33 delivered by Pope Gregory I in 591 AD. Ashamedly, it took until 1969 for the Church to officially repeal the label.

Perhaps the texts now at their disposal would reveal why this particular pope had labelled her so appallingly. Perhaps they would reveal the reason why Gregory was such a misogynist. *Had he distorted the truth in an effort to strengthen Church patriarchy?* If so, he had done well. Even now, women were banned from holding exalted position within the Church establishment. Sadly, the stain of Gregory's sermon still festers.

Angelo hoped that the opportunity to study, record and catalogue may reveal actual witness documents to these disgraceful pronouncements. He had already learned something about the enigma of Mary Magdalene. A copy of the Gospel of Mary given to him by Comte had been a special revelation. Jesus had spoken to her about how the mind governed the progress of the soul. The most famous disciples, Peter and Andrew, had both challenged Mary over this claiming the teaching was a heresy. They didn't believe that Jesus would give special knowledge to a woman.

The confrontation was evidence to Mary of Peter's chauvinistic narrow mindedness and superficiality. Angelo discovered the confrontation had been well documented in a number of texts. Sadly, it was Peter's teachings that had become dominant force in modern religion, despite Jesus's warning against narrow literalism.

In the *Pistis Sophia*, Jesus is presented as the liberator of the Divine Feminine. She is raised from the bondage of the material world and restored to her divine status. The Holy Spirit is associated with attributes such as consolation, forgiveness and empathy. But of course, this stands in stark contrast to religion, often justifying violence against those who do not accept orthodoxy. Angelo realised that the battle between Mary and Peter was still reflected in religion to this very day.

However, old Gnostic traditions have persisted. Many now believe that Mary was in fact the conjugal companion of Jesus. A papyrus codex discovered in an earthen jar near the little village of Nag Hammadi in Upper Egypt in 1945 had been concealed for more than 1,600 years. The codex was the Gospel of Philip. Comte allowed Angelo the opportunity to read a copy held in Le Rocher. In relation to Jesus and the Magdalene, it said that Jesus... *'Used to kiss her often on the....'*

Exactly where Jesus kissed her is missing in the aged text, but according to this scripture, the fact remains he kissed her often. Angelo discovered what Christianity feared about Mary. The idea that the Resurrection of Christ might be undermined terrified the religious authorities. Angelo was able to confirm that Gnostic Christians believed in Resurrection, but only of the soul, never the physical body.

Continuity of the soul is taught in many religions, however modern Christianity stands alone in insisting on the resurrection of the body. Even James, the brother of Jesus, regarded the Apostle Paul's idea of bodily resurrection a complete nonsense. And to confuse the matter further, if Paul ever did espouse the idea of bodily resurrection, he seems to have retracted it in 1st Corinthians 15:44, *'It is sown a natural body, it is raised a spiritual body'*.

Philip's Gospel intrigued Angelo. It was clear that Jesus loved Mary more than he loved all the other disciples. It even said that Mary Magdalene was Jesus's *'koinonos'*, suggesting that she was indeed his spouse.

64

DNA

NEAR LUGANO, SWITZERLAND

The basement laboratory at Philip's estate was world class, but the results were unsettling. Routine measurements of the femur and the radius bones confirmed a specimen which in life stood 1.95 metres in height, tall by any standard. Geochronology dated the skeleton at between 2,800 and 3,200 years old. The skull was clearly human. The cranial cavity was only slightly larger than the average male.

Together with a skilled forensic pathologist we extracted the DNA.

The bone specimen was unique. The karyogram revealed only 44 chromosomes divided in 22 pairs. All humans have 46, divided into 23 pairs. Primates have 48 chromosomes, divided into 24 pairs. The results were triple checked using different samples and they were confirmed every time. Our specimen appeared like a modern human, and yet it wasn't. I was under no illusion, this was a new species and yet, it was estimated to be around 3,000 years old. The evidence was electrifying, but surely impossible.

The 22nd chromosome was an enigma. It was fused to the sex chromosome. This specimen was either a human with some sort of genetic defect or it was not human at all. There was no doubt it was a tall, male human-looking being with a brain capacity slightly larger than a common man and DNA that almost matched our own. Yet he was as different as a primate in his chromosomal identity.

With wishful thinking, Keisha had nicknamed our specimen Solomon, based purely on its age and the story of the Knights who had carried the ossuary from the Holy Land. I joined Keisha in Philip's office to discuss what we knew.

"That biblical passage I read you refers to beings before the creation of Adam and Eve, so maybe he's the link to us, the one before the Cro-Magnon."

"If the chromosomes weren't so different you may well be right, but the specimen is too young. I don't know what to make of it all."

"Me neither, but there's room for another hypothesis?" Keisha advanced her theory. "What if this specimen is the progeny of one of 'those who came down'? The Nephilim mentioned in the Bible. Perhaps the ancestors of this specimen bred with the earthly hominoids to create the Cro-Magnon. He's exactly like us, but isn't us. A tall male with a slightly larger brain size. I reckon we have one of the Nephilim or even one of the Elohim."

"You'd like that to be true wouldn't you? He's too young for a start. This is evidence of a strange or mutated species, that's all."

Keisha was persistent. "Maybe not so strange when you consider the written record. I've made some progress on the Templar book by checking the detail for a more exacting exegesis. It tells the story of a small group of persecuted Gnostic Jews who protected the relics of the one they called El Shaddai, translated in modern bibles as the Lord. The relics were given to the Templar Knights to protect them from the heathen infidel. When Jerusalem fell, the ossuary and its contents were taken to safety.

"El means deity and was often expanded to Elohim. El Shaddai means 'Most High'. It explains why the bones were so revered and why they were held in a cave below the Temple site at Jerusalem. More to the point, our Templar author writes that the Gnostic protectors of our specimen believed him to have arrived in *'a fiery cloud'."*

"That's all very interesting Keisha, but the specimen died around 1,200 BCE. Cro-Magnon has been around for maybe 50,000 years."

"You're missing the point Aiden. If beings came to Earth to create man, it doesn't mean they came thousands of years ago and never came back. What if the 'Most High', the El Shaddai has continued to visit over the millennia? What if some of them never left?"

"Your suggesting this specimen is extraterrestrial?"

"Yes. Well, I don't know. Maybe."

My blood chilled at the thought. I knew of her reputation in academia – unconventional, prone to eccentricity and uncompromising. She followed the data, no matter how controversial the conclusions. She was certainly living up to her reputation. I had no explanation at all for the DNA results and could offer nothing to challenge her.

"Does the Templar book tell us who the knights were?"

"It names them, but they're obscure. There's no reference to them in any historical record other than this, so who knows? It seems they just disappeared. But they left something very special."

"You really think the specimen is one of the Nephilim don't you?"

"He's sure different to us. What if the old Sumerian texts are correct? The gods came down to Earth and genetically engineered an existing species of hominoid to create us. He could well be a missing link to Cro-Magnon."

"I'll promise to keep an open mind, but that's all."

"I'd appreciate that Aiden." Keisha broke open the crust of her armour. "I'm not an ogre you know. You might find I'm more acceptable to your ideas than you think."

She reached out and placed her hand on mine, a truce to the distance that had developed between us. "Come on; let's see whether Philip has made progress on that vial of powder."

65

REVELATION

MONACO

The sun's florid rise greeted Comte as he commenced his dawn stroll. From the apartment on the Avenue des Papalins, he skirted the Fontvieille marina, hobbled past the Palais Princier de Monaco and followed the Ruelle Saint-Barbe behind the Cathedrale de Monaco. He had come this way for the last two mornings and savoured the fresh sea air which replenished his lungs. He felt revived and decided he would persist with this new regimen.

He was glad to be rid of the pompous hypocrisy of the Vatican. Comte had been reborn, but struggled with the concept of a new name. Teo Casari seemed so foreign. It made him feel like a 1950's movie star. Elysius felt it was necessary for his safety and it had been decided that Angelo needed a new identity as well. His papers were being delivered by Rene later today.

With a tinge of regret, Comte's solitude was broken. Angelo had caught up with him. They followed the high ridge that overlooked the mirrored sea. The Rock was aptly named. The monolith stood 141 metres high and Comte lingered at its highest point. They sat on the edge of the cliff face in quiet contemplation. Comte felt that

Angelo was on the cusp of a comment and motioned him to speak. Like most students eager to learn, Angelo was exuberant about his recent understanding of the Gnostic Gospels. They spoke at length, shedding light on some of the most obscure scriptures. Comte sensed an unusual aura surrounding Angelo, something askew with the normal emanations he had always felt from his young friend. He ignored the feeling and further encouraged Angelo with his study.

Later that morning, Angelo continued his research. Mary Magdalene, Mary Salome and Mary Jacobe were considered the first witnesses to the empty tomb of Jesus. After the crucifixion, the three Mary's set sail from Alexandria with Joseph of Arimathea. They arrived at a fortress named Oppidum-Râ. The location was known as Notre-Dame-de-Ratis-Râ, becoming known as Ratis, meaning boat. In 1838, the name was changed to Les Saintes Maries-del-la-Mer. The town's church even contains a painting by Henri de Guadermaris depicting Mary's arrival.

Gnostic sources claimed that Mary Magdalene was three months pregnant at the time of the Crucifixion. Angelo discovered that the idea of the Magdalene having a child was connected to an odd event that occurred in 633 AD. A mysterious boat had drifted into the estuary at Boulogne-sur-Mer in northern France. The boat had no oars, sails or sailors, but contained a luminous metre high statue of a Black Madonna with a child, together with a copy of the Gospels written in Syriac. The arrival caused much controversy around the region, and well beyond.

The Black Madonna, known as *Our Lady of the Holy Blood*, had evidently influenced the Knights Templar because she became the insignia to the Boulogne Cathedral. Even one of the most beautiful structures in the world, Chartres Cathedral, contains a crypt venerating the Black Madonna as do many others throughout France.

The story of the Black Madonna raised many questions in religious circles over the centuries. Long ago, it had been customary to portray Mary Magdalene in a red robe, similar to those worn by the Cardinals. The colour red designated the rank of High Priestess in the Order of Ephesus. Mary's clerical status was depicted in the famous 1465 fresco, *Saint Mary* in the Gothic cathedral of Arezzo near Florence. The fresco shows her wearing the red robe. She was similarly clothed in Botticelli's *Mary at the Foot of the Cross*. The very concept of a woman, let alone Mary, holding clerical rank terrified the patriarchal Church. Even worse was the idea that the Magdalene held the bloodline of dynastic succession within her womb.

Consequently, the Magdalene was strategically labelled a scarlet woman. Nevertheless, those acquainted with the truth of Messianic succession idolised Mary Magdalene as the Black Madonna. This deliberately distinguished her from Mary, the mother of Jesus, who the Church had designated as the White Madonna. The orthodoxy elevated the religious significance of mother Mary to bury the significance of the Magdalene. It was no accident by Pope Gregory that a scarlet woman became synonymous with a whore.

The Church's use of the White Madonna, frequently shown as holding the infant Jesus was a deft manoeuvre. The symbol is based on the much older Egyptian symbol of Isis, the 'Universal Mother'. Isis was often portrayed holding her child Horus. France's patron goddess, *Notre Dame de Lumiere*, 'Our Lady of the Light' is also based on the Universal Mother. To Angelo's surprise, the battle between the orthodoxy and Mary Magdalene as she fled into exile with the Messianic bloodline inside her womb is described in the Bible itself, Revelation 12. He read the following translation:

And a great sign appeared in heaven, a woman clothed with the sun, with the moon under her feet, and with a crown-like tiara of twelve stars on her head.

She was pregnant and she cried out in her birth pangs, in the anguish of her delivery.

Then another ominous sign ... behold a huge, fiery-red dragon, with seven heads and ten horns, and seven kingly crowns upon his heads.

...and the dragon stationed himself in front of the woman who was about to be delivered, so that he might devour her child as soon as she brought it forth.

And she brought forth a male Child, One Who is destined to rule all the nations ... and her Child was caught up to God and to His throne.

And the woman fled into the wilderness, where she has a retreat prepared for her by God.

Then war broke out in heaven, Michael and his angels going forth to battle with the dragon...

But they were defeated and there was no room found for them in heaven any longer.

...And when the dragon saw that he was cast down to the earth, he went in pursuit of the woman who had given birth to the male Child.

...then the dragon was furious at the woman, and he went away to wage war on the remainder of her descendents who obey God's commandments and who have the testimony of Jesus Christ – and adhere to it and bear witness to him.

Angelo recognised the woman as Mary Magdalene and the dragon that waged war upon her as the Church. It truly was a revelation.

He spoke to Comte, "I'm amazed what I've found out about Mary Magdalene. She's more important to history than I thought."

"And what do you make of it all, Angelo? You're free to express your thoughts now without having to pander to that control freak, Valla, so tell me."

"I think the Magdalene is a representation of the Divine Feminine. It seems she carried the blood of Jesus within her womb. She was carrying a child when she fled to France. I'm curious now as to what happened to her offspring."

"Seek and ye shall find. Remember."

'Yes, I know. Thanks for showing the way."

"Rubbish, you were ready that's all."

"I've rediscovered the meaning of Revelation 12. I reckon it's all about the Magdalene."

"Truth is always revealed when you're ready, Angelo. You've read through the layers to find it."

"I also found that the image of the Madonna and child is a replica of Isis and Horus, another Universal Mother. I also want to find out more about Eve. Surely she's a representation of the Universal Mother as well."

"You're right Angelo, but like the Magdalene, the Church has tarnished Eve with original sin, another stupid notion that has no basis in fact."

There was a deeper truth Comte was confident the young man would soon discover. A treasure beyond measure. The Divine Feminine also refers to an interior process of transformation which allows the raising of consciousness into the realm of spirit, protecting the evolution of the soul.

In this way Jesus could say; '...the light of the body is the eye; if therefore thine eye be single, thy whole body shall be full of light. But if thine eye be evil, thy whole body shall be full of darkness. If therefore the light that is in thee be darkness, how great is that darkness.'

Comte knew that Angelo would soon be brought to the threshold of this revelation. His friend's spiritual liberation would soon begin.

66

COMMUNIQUÉ

NEAR LUGANO, SWITZERLAND

Philip confirmed Mac's speculative assertion at the Basilica. The powder was indeed an ORME, an exotic orbitally rearranged molecular element.

Keisha gave an insight into what was historically known about this strange substance. She claimed it was kept in the Ark of the Covenant and in 1127, Bernard de Clairvaux, patron of the Templars, returned the long lost Temple artefacts of Jerusalem to France.

Several decades later the Templars commissioned the construction of Chartres Cathedral, the last known location of the Ark. A relief was inscribed on an entrance pillar declaring, 'The Ark of the Covenant was yielded from here'. The powder found inside the Ark, combined with its ability to store huge amounts of electricity, was found to create a superconductive Meissner field, a gateway to another realm.

Philip acknowledged Keisha's assessment. He described how the powder allowed the Egyptian Pharaohs and other accomplished seekers access to the spiritual domain.

"The sample is molecularly similar to your find in Baalbek. Why it was with the skeleton is just speculation. I know where Keisha's going with her theories. What about you Aiden?"

"Well I'm not quite as bold. We have a new species, not human, hominoid or primate. I have no idea what to make of it. I admit Keisha's theory seems reasonable, but it offers nothing by way of fact. It's abstract in the extreme."

Keisha countered, "You're right of course, but it would explain a great deal. The ancient texts would come to life. They would have a new coherence."

For a brief period we discussed the peculiar chromosomal results of our specimen. Philip seemed preoccupied with his thoughts and Keisha asked about his concern.

"I received some intelligence this morning which needs follow up. I don't know whether to ask you both for another favour."

Whenever Philip asked me a question, I found I was constantly being pushed beyond my comfort zone. Keisha summed up my thoughts. "Ask Philip. We can always say no."

"It's rather odd intelligence, so it may come to nothing. We've received a communiqué about the murder of a Tibetan monk. Majestic had him cruelly interrogated about his knowledge of a tetrahedral device that supposedly helps in penetrating the supersensible world. The monk suffered terribly, but our infiltrator, Ernst Volker, claimed he experienced no pain."

"Like the monk in your photograph Keisha."

"My thoughts exactly. What's odd about the intelligence Philip?"

"Before he was killed the monk told of a man he meditated upon. All he said was that the man held no public position, but stood ready to help mankind understand the Truth. The monk uttered these words."

Philip replayed the audio forwarded from Ernst Volker's data card. The voice of the Tibetan came to life. *As the planetary home of our creators enters the regions of our solar system once more, those who have travelled the path of light will be aided in the battle against ignorance. There will be an in-gathering of the few who are ready. He has recently returned for this purpose and stands ready to perform his duty to help his fellow beings. He cannot be held back from his task. Should his physical form be destroyed, he will continue his work to destroy the blatant lies of the past. Liberation for the worthy cannot be stopped by the regressive powers that hold the world in bondage.'*

"We need to find him Philip. Who is he?" Keisha asked.

"Not sure. All we know is that he belongs to a group known as the Council of Change for Evolutionary Consciousness. With your translations from the Baalbek discovery and the monk's comment about 'the planetary home of our creators', I think this man may be invaluable."

Keisha's brow crinkled. "I know Ernst. He's studied the ancient texts and knows his stuff. He would've evaluated the monk's words. If he thinks there's value in the intelligence, then it has to be followed up."

"My thoughts as well. I just hope he doesn't become compromised like our friend Comte. For now, it seems Majestic is more interested in finding Comte than anything the monk said, so we may have a window of opportunity."

I was oblivious. "Who's Comte?"

Keisha clarified, "A remarkable man who has served us from within the Vatican, but he's been betrayed and Majestic are out to silence him. Fortunately, we got him away safe and sound."

I read the delight in Keisha's tone. I took a leap. "It was you that got him away, wasn't it."

"I helped him out as he helped us,' she shrugged

I assessed Keisha with fresh eyes. She was right once again. She wasn't an ogre. Whilst she was capable of killing, she was also deeply compassionate for those in need. I turned to Philip and asked, "How do we find the man from this Council of Change."

"Ernst ran a search through Majestic's database. It's a long shot, but I think it's worth following. A private company, Ulysses Marine Institute have a research vessel exploring the sea floor off Cyprus, at the site of the so-called 'Atlantis' discovery. Ernst has been intrigued by this site since it was first located, so it's an interesting coincidence. Ulysses is owned by a trust, the trustees being two well-known, independently wealthy entrepreneurs from the U.S. and the U.K. and another person who runs a small bookshop in Edinburgh, Scotland. This person wrote a treatise under a pseudonym and published it on the internet. It's a wonderful exposé into how the banks control modern society. The last chapter mentions that when the world collapses under the weight of greed and debt the Council of Change for Evolutionary Consciousness will show the way. Ernst couldn't find any other reference to the Council anywhere. They're an enigma."

"So, you think we need to meet a bookseller in Edinburgh. Who is this guy?"

"His name's Mitch Hamilton. He's not in Edinburgh; he's on the exploration ship, the Ulysses Enterprise, currently eighty kilometres off the south-eastern Cyprian coast. As trustee, it seems he wanted to be there."

"We can't be sure this is the same man that the monk mentioned," Keisha queried. "But it's a lead worth following."

Philip responded, "I've already contacted the ship. I sought Mr Hamilton's permission for a visit and he accepted. You can be there tomorrow if you're both happy to go."

I was cautious. "Do you know anything else about the man's background? We don't want to find ourselves with another Anwar."

Philip clarified, "That's true Aiden. I feel dreadful about that, but I know nothing more about Mitch Hamilton. I've tried to check his background, but can't even find a birth record for him. Prior to him opening his bookshop in 1999, there's not a shred of evidence that he even existed. It's as though he arrived from nowhere."

Keisha was more circumspect. "Well at least we know where he is right now, so tell him to expect company tomorrow."

The familiar dream took hold.

I heard a faint buzzing, like bees circling a hive. My skin crawled as I feared what might come next. I struggled to wake from the dream, but was trapped in an alternate reality. My body was inert, paralysed.

The grey silhouette of the sickly child returned. I demanded to know what it wanted, angry at the terrifying intrusion. It explained it was one of a multitude of species in the universe. He meant me no harm; instead he wanted to give me understanding.

The child explained there were off-world species who despite being vastly more technically advanced than humans, they had been retarded in their evolution. They had tampered with our junk DNA sequences causing acceleration of ageing to our species. It's why modern day humans rarely lived more than just eighty years.

But much more precious to this particular species was the extraction of our chakra energy. The child explained how they sought attachment to our thought forms. It gave them access to the roller-coaster ride of human emotions, long since extinguished from their civilisation, allowing them participation in wider manifestation. Living vicariously through certain human hosts, they sometimes manifested as unexplained phenomena. These malevolent beings frequently manifested as negative entities within their human hosts, hence, the Church diagnosis of demonic possession.

Why was I being told this? As I looked at the frail child, the answer came. Every species has a few special beings capable of transcending their genetic coding and social conditioning. In every species, there were the few who sought universal truth. This child was asking whether I was ready to understand.

67

SHAME

MONACO

Angelo thought of Blaze as he fell into sleep. Her bronzed olive skin contrasted with his pale office complexion. His hand lay over his erection as he gravitated toward dream. He recognised Blaze in the company of two beautiful women as she sailed her yacht into the bay at Les Saintes Maries-del-la-Mer. He likened her tanned image to the Black Madonna, as the Divine Feminine carrying the future hope of mankind within her.

Angelo slept fitfully. Mental clouds gathered. His dream drifted and images darkened his mind. He saw a man's face. Angelo was young, about eight, and was repulsed by the man's sly grin and the smell of expensive aftershave. He tried to run, but was caught and slapped senseless. The man's sadistic pleasure inflicted excruciating pain. Now he stood over him almost choking him. He gagged and received another blow to the head. Oral sex wasn't enough. He was forcibly turned over, his face pushed hard into the pillow, almost suffocating him. His pyjamas were stripped down to his ankles. *Get off me, get off!*

The lucidity of his sub-conscious clouded and his mind once

again faded to the three women sailing their wooden hulled yacht into the bay at Les Saintes Maries-del-la-Mer. Three individual personas radiated from the boat – beauty, compassion, maternity. He roused into a semi-somnambulistic state. His sheets were pasted with dry semen, but in this half awake state, he suffered an acute pain. It felt like the penetration of a thousand razor-blades.

Angelo peeled out of bed and staggered to the living room window. The firing pin of his psychosis was cocked. His mind craved self protection. He stood naked at the fifteenth storey living-room window and looked out over the illuminated marina. Unlike his nightmare, the lights would dim when dusk arrived. The city would slowly come to life and the moored yachts would once again bask in warm morning sun. Angelo reasoned that the sun would never again shine upon him.

He sobbed with pain. In an act of programmed automation, eyes glazed over by moist tears, Angelo unconsciously picked up the phone and keyed a string of numbers. He made the connection and placed the phone on the counter. His pain began to subside.

His body however, continued to burn with the fire of vengeance. He had an urge to pump iron, feel the blood of aggression surge through his veins. He fell to the floor and crunched a hundred sit-ups, quickly followed by a hundred push-ups. Finally, he lay on the floor sheened in beading sweat, struggling to catch his breath.

Angelo was on a roller–coaster of emotion, the pain still gripping his heart. The wound of his slippery memory had healed with a deep scar, bringing the sharpened image of his horror into focus. Just like in Rome, Angelo curled into a ball and hid within himself.

As the hours unfurled from their overnight slumber, Comte found the young man naked and vulnerable, lying clenched in the foetal position. He felt the emanations of his friend's aura. It was deep in turmoil, exuding darkness as Angelo burned in feverish sleep. Comte placed a light blanket over him. He had noticed an aural disturbance about the young man the morning before. Something was in disarray and Comte resolved to question Angelo about it when the time seemed appropriate.

He faintly heard the echoing silence of a still open phone connection. He checked the number dialled. None was displayed. He placed the phone to his ear, heard nothing and then disconnected the call.

Comte's morning stroll was reflective. He was concerned. He wondered whether Angelo was struggling with his decision to leave the Vatican. The boy had been deeply committed to his faith, so perhaps grief was taking hold.

As expected, Angelo met up with him mid-morning. He was jovial and keen to continue his study. Comte left his concern unstated, best to leave Angelo to his newfound motivation. He recognised concealed feelings from the young man, as though his outward happy expression was a fictitious mask. He had learnt long ago that appearance was often trickery, smoke and mirrors used to conceal an underlying truth. He resolved to keep an eye on his friend and broach the subject only if necessary.

Angelo's subtle torment reminded Comte of Cardinal Valla. He gleefully imagined the thunderous roar of Valla's anger when he discovered they had both vanished. There had been no official retirement or resignation, no discussion, no sympathetic departure and naturally – no guilt. Just the thought of Valla's vitriol made him tingle with mischievous delight.

Comte's purpose was clear. As Teo Casari, he had the opportunity to be one of the most dangerous men to ever work in ecclesiastical circles. The irony was irresistible. He would stop at nothing now to openly transmit the truth to anybody who would listen.

Angelo began to dig through some new material. It was an early copy of the Gospel of Thomas. Despite being older than the books of the New Testament, this Gospel was excluded from the Bible. It had been regarded as too inflammatory. Within its pages, Angelo learnt that spiritual progression is only possible by letting go of everything transitory. In Logion 22 of this Gospel, Jesus said that we enter the Kingdom of Heaven only when we have transcended the polarities of the physical world.

'....when they make the two one, the inner as the outer, the outer as the inner, the above as the below, the male as the female into a single one. Only then can we enter the Kingdom of God.'

Angelo knew the passage was profound. He was deeply moved and glimpsed its meaning. It described the merging of the Divine Feminine with the Divine Masculine. Through this union, as opposites become one, it was possible to enter the Kingdom.

He sought out Comte. As always the keeper decided to challenge him. "Are you familiar with the Greek Goddess Persephone?"

"Afraid not, but you'll tell me right?"

Comte smiled, "Only a bit. In Greek mythology, Hades carried Persephone off to the Underworld to be his bride. She was worshipped in the Eleusinian Mysteries as the Goddess of spring growth. Her mother, Dementer refused to let the earth bear fruit until her return, but because Persephone had tasted the food of Hades, she was forced to spend part of the year in the Underworld. It wasn't until she returned every spring that the earth was restored to its former health.

"From the beginning the Goddess principle was 'the' guiding light of mankind. But around 5,000 BCE the male gods gained ascendency. You've heard them all – Zeus, Yahweh, Thor – there's dozens of others, but time is long past for the female principle to finally stand together as a co-equal alongside the likes of Yahweh, the Lord God, Allah and all the others. Mankind is still caught in the winter of its history and each individual needs to seek out Persephone so that the planet can be spiritually restored.

"We not only need guidance from the Father, but also from the Divine Mother. Religion needs to change, Angelo. The feminist movements around the world have started what can't be stopped. Aren't you glad you're here instead of working for that bastard Valla?"

"I'm glad I followed you, but I've felt very uneasy since I left. I'm having nightmares and I don't know why."

Comte thought he may open up. "If you want to discuss it, you know you can."

Angelo's reaction was unexpected. "I'll work it out myself Comte. OK."

"I'm sure you will. Come on; let's get your new ID from Rene and enjoy the fruits of our labour. I want to try that restaurant near the marina."

68

ANCIENT CITY

MEDITERRANEAN SEA, OFF CYPRUS

The Robinson R44 helicopter appeared like an ink spot on the horizon. Mitch Hamilton scrutinised the approaching craft. Philip's call to the research vessel had already outlined the purpose of the visit. He had explained to Hamilton that Aiden was a well-known anthropologist and was keen to obtain information about the current status of the Institute's research into the 'Atlantis' site. Aiden sought new material for his next BBC television series and would be accompanied by his assistant, Keisha Petersen. The explanation was clever.

Hamilton had been happy to oblige and offered a berth for an overnight stay. He figured that if the BBC had the resources to get Aiden Keyes and his assistant to the vessel, it would be worthwhile having them there.

Hamilton made his way to the helipad rising from the stern of the Ulysses Enterprise. Built in 2003, the ship represented the latest generation of marine research vessels. With accommodation for up to forty people and a top speed of seventeen knots, it was equipped with state-of the-art technology. The vessel was able to stay at sea for extended periods, carrying out all types of marine research, ranging from plankton sampling to hydro-acoustic research and seismic operations.

On this occasion the vessel had a small crew. Apart from Hamilton and the captain, there were five others – four of whom were specialists in the use of two person submarines and remote operated submersibles. Two of the men were preparing the ROV for the first dive of the afternoon, making sure the underwater cameras were functioning with optimal performance.

Keisha and I stepped aboard and climbed down the helipad steps to the deck below. As our host approached, the Bell lifted from the platform, banked and headed back toward the Cyprian coast.

Hamilton held out his hand in welcome. He had a powerful grip, yet appeared relaxed and informal. He was tall with a robust, muscular frame and clear blue eyes that matched his pale complexion and short flaxen hair. I observed Keisha appraising his appearance and noticed her subtle approval. She took particular note of Mitch's accent. There wasn't one. It was universal with no defining intonation or tonality that suggested its heritage. One thing for sure, he wasn't Scottish.

Mitch promptly heralded us to our cabins below. They were well appointed and made ready for guests. My chill with Keisha had steadily thawed and I toyed with the idea that only one cabin would be made available. Sadly, that was not the case. Mitch was eager to join in with his crew at the ROV so we dumped our bags and followed him. He introduced his crew, each one of them giving Keisha the full eye treatment.

"We're about to launch our ROV into some very deep water for some sonar and audio-visual mapping, so if you'd like to follow me, we can view it from the operations room."

I was glad the crew would soon have eyes for their work. I wanted to confess our true motive to Mitch, but was also conscious that we should act out our roles. Besides I was interested in seeing the dive. "What are you going down to look at?"

"We want to get some clear close-up footage of the wall. It's about 1,500 metres below and extends for about three kilometres. It's a massive structure."

"This would be of definite interest to the BBC if it was presented correctly. Do you really think this is a remnant of the Atlantis?"

"One remnant yes, but this isn't the only one. There's much to be publicised and I hope that having you and the BBC on side would give the subject credibility. Sadly, when the media does report anything, it's usually dumbed down to entertainment value. That means it's all being kept under wraps."

We arrived in the operations room, an expanse of dedicated submariner technology. Mitch sat at the control panel and worked one of the computers as the visual feed began broadcasting images. The submersible was slowly being lowered; water lapping at the camera lens showing a clear view of the ocean surface before the submersible sank below.

Mitch manipulated the submersible's trajectory. The marine life became less visible as the ROV dived deeper into the murky grey, powerful arc lights illuminating the surroundings.

The ROV sank deeper still. The men were quiet as the structure creaked and groaned under the increasing pressure of the ocean. It was a long wait, but at 1,369 metres below the surface, the seafloor came into view. It swept away into a valley, the submersible following the subterranean ridgeline. A spectacular formation came into view. An unmistakable wall of stone traced the edge of the sunken valley. I was reminded of Sacsayhuaman near Cuzco in Peru, huge blocks of random stone perfectly aligned and fitting with mechanical precision. Equipment aboard the ROV scanned and calculated on their dimension and mass. Some of the stone blocks were calculated to weigh over 300 hundred tonnes at the surface. I was enthralled by the desolate scene, a watery grave for what was clearly the remnant of a previous civilisation.

Mitch finally delegated his work to one of the others. "I always like being involved, but these guys are the experts. We'll leave it to them, shall we?"

Keisha was eager. "There's some questions we'd like to ask if you have the time."

"Sure. Let's get something to eat first."

Finally we had the privacy with Mitch that we sought and I struggled with how to broach our deception. Without hesitation, Keisha solved the problem.

"Mitch, we need to be honest. Aiden is a bona fide BBC television presenter, but that's not the reason we're here. There's a lot more to it than that."

Mitch raised an eyebrow. "There often is."

Keisha was direct. "A Tibetan monk was murdered a couple of days ago. Before his death he mentioned the Council of Change for Evolutionary Consciousness. I know this might sound crazy, but he said something about the planetary home of intelligent beings entering our solar system."

Mitch eyes blazed back at Keisha. The corner of his mouth curled slightly. "Go on."

"This is of great interest because it confirms some ancient writings Aiden recently discovered. Sadly the Tibetan was not the only one to lose his life."

Mitch intervened. "Thank you for your frankness and in return I'll be candid with you. Don't worry; I know who you both are and why you're here."

Had we been set-up? Again? "Maybe you'd like to explain. How could you possibly know our purpose?" I asked ruefully.

"The moment the Tibetan passed, I knew."

It sounded like we were being played. "How did you know about the Tibetan. Is this a game?"

"No Aiden, definitely not a game. I have a gift that extends to a number beings that have been assisting humanity for a long time now. The Tibetan venerable you refer to is known as Khetsun. We are also in contact with others that are part of the hidden directorate."

"So you knew him?" I challenged.

"I knew him only after he died. You see, only his body died. Exalted ones are always with us and sometimes they choose to take form to help us. There are many names for these beings and their abilities. After all, every individual has their own gifts and weakness, all driven by the immutable law of cause and effect – karma if you like."

I felt uncomfortable with what I was being told. Surely it was impossible. "But how can you know these things?"

"I can describe it this way. If you want to listen to a radio signal, you tune into the transmitted radio waves by the use of a receiver. You hear the audio. Whenever anyone speaks, or acts or even thinks, an etheric energy wave is sent forth spreading outward across the cosmos. The cosmos contains everything that is, so it never loses information. My mental faculties act as a receiver to tune into those signals. For me, even a handshake is like turning the dial of a radio. It allows me to tune into your signal. Our meeting at the helipad also told me much about both of you."

"Now I've heard everything. You mean to say that you know all about us."

"No, I don't know all about you. But when I am completely open, I know enough to help others. It takes time to review a person's life. I know why you're here and what you're seeking."

Big call. "Sorry Mitch, as a scientist I need to test you on that statement."

"I don't doubt your scepticism, so I'm happy to tell you what I picked up. You've photographed an ancient site in Lebanon that tells the story of the Annunaki who came to earth. There are some who are resisting your discovery and the dissemination of your find. The pursuit of evidence has led you here. Some already know this, so that's not new, so I'll tell you something they don't know. Your dreams are leading you to a deeper understanding of the universe and some of the beings who occupy it. The sickly child you've been conversing with is here to help you Aiden. It wants to bring you the truth. Have I passed your test?"

I was numbed by Mitch's disclosure. My mind raced as I felt a tug deep in my chest. Then my eyes moistened as emotion took hold. How could he know these things? I needed time, space and mostly quiet solitude to assess what had just happened.

Keisha looked at me for some sort of confirmation. She saw the grudging acceptance in my expression.

"He's right isn't he?"

"Yes, I had that dream last night."

69

EVIL INTENT

MONACO

Albrecht spoke directly to Goldstein, "You have another elimination. One of my assets has called in. We've traced it to Monaco, an apartment on the Avenue des Papalins."

"As long as there's no gutting. It's totally unprofessional."

"You don't get it do you? I'll decide the method and in this case no message needs to be implied, so I'll leave the details to you. Your target is a hacked-up cripple, you can't miss him. Ugly bastard. He's in the company of my asset, Angelo DeMarco. Here's photographs of them."

"What's the story with DeMarco?"

"He's only recently been activated, so test the water with him. Mention me to gauge his reaction. He may still be useful."

Goldstein knew of the Majestic mind-control program. He had always been sickened by it. "How long's he been a sleeper?"

"We got him when he was six. He was fully compliant by twelve. By fifteen he had no memory of his experiences. He's been on hold ever since. Seven years."

"How he was made compliant?"

"He got the Mengele treatment."

Goldstein cringed. Not content with Josef Mengele's Monarch Project at Auschwitz, the U.S. secretly moved the Nazi butcher to head up the MK-Ultra mind control program for the CIA under Operation Paperclip. The events of this period of U.S. history shamed Goldstein. He realised that DeMarco's programming had been trauma-based, the most vile method of gaining control. Using this technique, the victim was exposed to massive psychological trauma, using extreme physical abuse and the most depraved sexual defilement, always beginning in childhood. The trauma fractured the psyche into alternate personalities which could then be programmed to perform any function that the controller wished to install. These personalities were brought to the surface using triggers such as sounds, codes or specific actions. The latest techniques were usually electronic-based, small computer chips wired directly to the brain and activated by the use of a laptop computer. Even sounds received through a mobile phone were frequently used.

"Who was his handler?"

Kane puffed with pride and declared, "Who do you think?"

Goldstein knew it. The man was a slimy paedophile. His only action in the field was to act as a stinking piece of filth. A real twisted piece of human waste. Goldstein didn't know how, but he resolved to either get out of Majestic's clutches or strangle the bastard.

"One more question. What trigger was used?"

"He was bashed by some muggers in Rome; nothing to cause major damage, but enough to bring him back into the fold."

Veles Kane had been Angelo's controller since the beginning. The sexual and physical abuse had finally ended at twelve, but by then Angelo had been moulded to act whenever required. Angelo had been tested rigorously and the techniques employed had worked to perfection. Kane had thought it necessary to activate Angelo's services and had organised his recent appointment to Antonio Cardinal Valla's office. Angelo had always passed on what he had learned from the Cardinal's dispatches. Over the weeks he had never missed. The beauty was that Angelo had become an automaton, programmed and unaware of his actions. But something had gone horribly wrong for Kane's operation. When the young man met Comte, his programming began to unwind, like a virus intent on destruction. The pre-determined bashing had acted like an anti-virus. It reprogrammed the old behaviour. When Angelo disappeared to follow Comte, Kane was unconcerned. Like a whale that needs to breathe by rising to the ocean surface, he knew Angelo would do the same. It was only a matter of time.

Angelo once again woke in the early hours. His dream had been filled with terrors of violation and suffocation. He visualised his father, so proud to be given the opportunity to place his young son in a respectable religious school. If only he had known.

The demons now possessing Angelo had always stayed beyond the shadows of his mind. But now they had awakened. His ejaculation over the beautiful Blaze had triggered the memory of his torment and horror. Angelo reflected on his beating in Rome. It was a reminder, an ultimatum. Of what, he couldn't figure.

Kane had taken the decision quickly and had organised the beating. It was a cunning display of his ruthlessness. It served two purposes. Angelo's intelligence of the Cardinal's office had been exemplary, but he had concealed knowledge of his contact with Comte. That was unforgivable. It needed to be met with the only course of action. Angelo's mind needed a further trigger. The beating set his psyche on the required course. He was unconsciously forced to comply with his programming.

Kane had also reasoned that the beating would act as a subtle warning to Valla. The Cardinal's duty certainly lay within the

Church, but also beyond it and Kane knew fear would extract Valla's tithe.

Over the years, a handful of Cardinals had made complaints to Valla about the irritable behaviour of the keeper and Kane had long wanted the archivist monitored. But Valla had always resisted, insisting the keeper's mind was as crippled as his body and that he was of little concern. Valla had always suspected Comte had been Kane's stooge and had shunned any suggestion about him. So, Kane finally played a hand that even the suspicious Cardinal could never have anticipated. A quiet and almost timid pontifical student applied for a position newly created within the Cardinal's office. Valla had interviewed him and was suitably pleased. Angelo DeMarco was shy and placid, a young man who Valla felt he could mould. Kane had reasoned that Angelo would encounter the deformed keeper sooner or later, and when he did, information about Comte's behaviour would be forthcoming.

But Angelo had been strangely silent. Comte's physical disability together with his cynical irreverence for authority had burrowed deep into Angelo's awareness. The psychological impact of the insidious keeper on the impressionable young man had somehow neutralised his programming. But after his beating, information flooded in about the keeper. What came through was disturbing. The description of Comte's mission to Vienna, and the discovery of a Templar diary suggested Comte had contacts within Elysius. The treasonous keeper had to be taken out.

Angelo had cleverly created access into Comte's computer hard drive using the Vatican's intranet. Its contents caused Kane more concern. Fortunately, Comte had never sent an email outside the Vatican enclave, but his drive was filled with an avalanche of damaging information. He had downloaded all his files onto a flash memory stick and the information it contained could be anywhere.

70

SYNCHRONICITY

MEDITERRANEAN SEA, OFF CYPRUS

Mitch had a warm and embracing authority. Rather than me testing him, his response had tested me. I hadn't mentioned my dreams to anyone. *How could he have known?* The revelation was forcing me to reconsider everything I thought I knew.

Keisha was equally surprised, but she noticed something in the exchange that gave her a lead. "I want to know about the Council of Change and your connection to it. Am I asking too much?"

Mitch was forthcoming. "Not at all, it's why you're here after all. The Council has deliberately stayed below the radar for a very long time. But we have intervened in different epochs from the Lemurian, the Atlantean, the Sumerian, the Egyptian, the Greco-Latin, the Mayan periods, and with the other cultures of the East and West. What people call the 'modern world' is now on the brink – environmentally, economically and spiritually. Aiden's television profile can be a real positive, so perhaps we can help each other."

"And how can I do that?" I quizzed.

"All things are connected and the time is right to reveal something that will change things. Come on, how about we have a coffee?"

Mitch practised his barista skill with the espresso machine and explained how the Council of Change for Evolutionary Consciousness was being directed from a realm outside our three dimensional world. Its mission was to induce a mass shift in consciousness.

According to Mitch, human evolution was about to be tweaked. It would begin with the destruction of corrupt and bankrupt souls; people who are intent on profit at the expense of humanity – the financial rent seekers who profit from creating war and international debt. The powerbrokers who keep the sovereign nations of the world in a stranglehold of debt will be swept away. Crippling usury will be abandoned.

The catalyst for this change was to be the introduction of free energy, available to all on the planet. Tesla energy technology would be gifted to all the nations by the Council. To top it off, Mitch claimed to be the Council's earthly representative.

"My goal is to prepare the world. Synchronicity has brought you here to help distribute the news. The convergence is coming."

My mind flared with nervous recognition. Baalbek had directed me to this moment. Meeting Keisha, Otto, Philip and our fortuitous find in Morocco had all been part of the synchronicity. But, I still couldn't understand my role.

I shook my head in disbelief. "You want me to present a television event where I disclose that our future is being directed from a different universal dimension by some unseen Council. Are you kidding?"

"The child in your dreams isn't kidding. He wants you to see and yet you ignore him. And deep down, you know that's not wise."

His words stopped me cold. "So I begin the series by saying my dreams have revealed beings from other worlds who are about to change our evolution, extraterrestrials who direct our course from the ether. It's complete nonsense to suggest such a thing."

Keisha's sabre-like glare cut through me. "Ignore him Mitch. He has trouble seeing through the looking-glass. I have a question though. Would the directors of your Council be the Elohim?"

Mitch's eyes widened, evidently impressed with Keisha's leap. "Elohim! I see you are well versed. Short answer is yes, although they've been known by many names over the course of human history."

"So who are you Mitch?"

Keisha's tone was matter-of-fact. The same tone as Philip had used when he posed the same question to me. *'Who are you?'* She had balls. I was keen to hear the response.

"I'm the same as you. I'm one of their offspring."

Keisha stared at Mitch, forensically scrutinising him. Her face betrayed no emotion. "Yes, you are the same as us, but there's no history of you before 1999. Why is that? Or is it because you weren't here?"

Big leap and once again, unconventional in the extreme. I had no idea of the implications of such a question. Actually it was more than that. It was the potential answer that troubled me more.

"I know what you're leading to Keisha, so I'll answer this way. I've always been here, but not as you may think. 1999 is no coincidence. But be careful what you ask. The answer may bring you responsibility. So in deference to popular culture, you get the choice between the blue and the red pill. You can choose the blue pill and I will give you a scripted response so that you can sleep easy tonight. Or you can choose the red, which will open a gateway to a hidden truth. But you're no stranger to truth Keisha, so let me know if you want to go deeper into the rabbit hole."

Without hesitation, Keisha shot back, "I'll take the red."

Mitch nodded and then asked me, "What about you, Aiden?"

Jai had died at the beginning of all this and there was no way back. "Count me in for the red as well."

"I like your answers. It shows we were meant to meet. Like I said, I'm one of their offspring, just like you, but there's a subtle difference. I'm a direct offspring. You, however, like all modern humans were created in their image. Finish your coffee; I'll be back in a few moments."

Mitch quickly left and returned in less than a minute. "I just needed a swab and test tube from the lab next door. Here Keisha, I want you to take a sample of my DNA. It'll be my gift to you in your search for Truth."

Keisha was unmoved, "Can I ask why?"

"When you leave, have the sample tested and the red pill will take effect."

"And we'll cop a painful truth?"

"Nothing painful, but yes, you'll cop the truth. You'll finally understand your theories. And I'll guarantee one thing; Aiden will want to present the results in his next series. Let's not spoil my gift. I'll be happy to discuss it all after the results come in."

We both had a multitude of further questions, but Mitch was adamant. The matter was closed.

Instead, he acted as a true host. We spent some more time watching the underwater show, the ROV capturing some incredible footage of the ancient wall, drilling samples to bring to the surface for analysis. Keisha and I discussed how the images could be used in my next series and I agreed that the footage would be a great segue into an exposé on ancient peoples. This was possibly a chance to challenge the dominant view and help scientists understand more about humankind's distant past.

As the crew prepared to bring the submersible aboard, Keisha and I went below to request transport for the next morning and to organise personnel for some further DNA tests.

I took the opportunity to log into my email account. I had to be back in London by the end of the month to start on my next series and I decided to confirm a meeting date. The send/receive bar immediately filled and deposited a message. My lightened mood turned to grief.

From: <Mac>
To: <Aiden>
Re: Be careful

My Parisian dreams are dashed. I passed out after too many drinks and found Jacquie in the bath next morning with her throat cut.

I should have listened to Keisha and left Marrakech when you did. She would still be alive if I had. The police took me in for 72 hours, but finally, they found the scum-bag who did it. He isn't talking.

I've taken it as a warning. Like you with Jai. Be careful and look after Keisha. I'm on my way to Philip. I'll wait for you. Talk then...

Mac

71

JUDAS

MONACO

The sands of time tumbled through the hourglass, from the blank amnesia of the past to the abrasive pain of recent recollection. The night horror was excruciating. Angelo fitted the jigsaw together, slowly picking the scab off his hidden memories. The shameful 'how' pieces had all been gathered together, but it was the 'why' pieces that still eluded him. He had traced his past and finally recognised the face behind the smell of aftershave. Uncle Veles, the epitome of evil. He and his sordid acquaintances had sought their sadistic pleasure almost nightly.

A vile resentment emerged – even toward his father. *Why did he forsake me?* Angelo's greatest resentment was held for God. God the Father – what a joke! His own father never knew, but God was all-seeing and did know. *How could He allow it?* A Heavenly Father not worthy of a son. Angelo was disgusted and ashamed. In recent years even the Church had been tainted by such scandal. Where was God in all of this? Angelo resolved that the door to his private hell would remain closed to the world. More than closed; locked. To everyone, even Comte.

Angelo tried filling his day with the minutiae of a few manuscripts. It helped him focus. Away from the darkness poised to
engulf him.

He had found an old document that recorded a confrontation
between Sylvester, Bishop of Rome in 318 AD, and a delegation of
the surviving descendents of Jesus. They had accused the Church of
poisoning His teachings. The Bishop's arrogant response however,
was to tell them that the power of salvation did not rest with Jesus,
but with Constantine, the present Emperor. Angelo was floored by
the hypocrisy.

He was further disturbed by records confirming that two
hundred years earlier, successive Emperors, Vespasian, Titus and
Domitian had attempted to exterminate the descendents of Jesus.
Each one of them issued proclamations to hunt down his heirs and
put them to the sword. They subsequently became known as the
'Desposyni', Heirs of the Lord.

If Jesus had direct descendents then this would indicate he had
been married, presumably to Mary Magdalene. Comte had told him
about a 13th century Cathar document which confirmed that Mary
Magdalene was his spouse. The evidence seemed conclusive. Maybe
it was the reason the Church annihilated the entire Cathar community in a barbaric episode that would echo down through the centuries, galvanising the Knights Templar and later the Scottish Rite
of Freemasons which profoundly influenced the Founding Fathers
of the New World.

Angelo wanted to spend the evening with Comte, hoping to
relieve his sordid anguish. But Comte had arranged a private evening meal with Rene. This was a night Angelo would face alone.

Angelo slept fitfully, but woke with an alertness he had not enjoyed
for weeks. He rose early to join Comte on his dawn walk and was
determined to seek wisdom from his mentor.

The sun had not yet commenced its sweep through the morning sky and the jubilant keeper had news to share. "Today's a great day, Angelo. We're finally ready to commence our work. We're going to blow their unholy fraud apart."

Comte's clumsy hobble almost propelled itself into a skip. Even the salty mediterranean air being sucked into his twisted nose cavity was audible. He was liberated and free – free to live life according to his own rules, free from control-hungry bigots like Cardinal Valla.

Angelo was reticent. "I thought we were going to catalogue all the old texts."

"We are, Angelo, we are. But it's time to tune the collective intellect. Selected texts are going to be released one by one. Together with what I've copied from the Archive, we're going to thaw out the frozen secrecy of the past. The documents held here in the Fortress are dynamite. I can't wait to see that sanctimonious jackass squirm."

Rene had confirmed Elysius's approval of Comte's plan at dinner. It was agreed that selected documents would be released on a programmed basis to prepare the way for full disclosure of humankind's genesis. In the past, Elysius's benefactors had funded several movies that promulgated certain aspects of the hidden knowledge, but they had not yet indulged in the most important elements of human inquiry. It was all part of the Great Unfolding, the infusion of higher knowledge through the channel of mass entertainment.

The young man's mind segued, trying to calculate the impact of this development. When Comte's course was set, he realised there was no way the resolute keeper would ever deviate.

As had become habit over past days, the two men strolled to the Rock and sat on the edge of the cliff in quiet contemplation. Comte was lost in exuberant thought about the new project, while Angelo was lost in consternation. Comte eventually clambered to his feet, eager to seize the day ahead. Angelo joined him, wondering how to deal with his inexplicable, vile past.

A stranger approached along the walkway at the edge of the cliff. Angelo's radar of perception bristled. He scrutinised the man with suspicion. The stranger spied Angelo like an eagle eyeing a rodent on the terrain below. There was something in the man's mien that disconcerted Angelo; it was the purpose in his stride and the subtle hostility of his focus.

The stranger suddenly stopped, half-turned and looked out over the sea. Comte's mind was full of possibility and he paid little attention. He shuffled ahead with confidence. But Angelo was wary, imperceptibly slowing his pace.

Old fear sparked his wracked nerves. A warning. Then it hit him. He must have been nine or ten. He had told a secret about a schoolmate and before the day was out, the boy was dead. The spectre of death once again spurred its way into him as he now recalled his latest secret, a series of numbers punched in automation two days ago.

Angelo was on the cusp of a comment, but Comte was a pace or two ahead. As he passed the stranger he greeted him with a nod. The man's face constricted and in a moment, he stretched out and grabbed Comte, twisting his right arm high up into his shoulder blades. The man's other hand savagely grabbed the keeper's throat.

The man spoke, his mint breath exhaling over Comte's nose cavity. "Back off DeMarco."

Angelo rooted himself to the ground. "Your Uncle Veles sends his regards. He wants to thank you."

Comte was swiftly swung off his feet and forced over the low wall. The grip around his neck was like a vice, his windpipe closed, choking him.

Black emotions cascaded over Angelo. Fresh tears welled, stinging him. Fear for his friend and anger at this violation surged through his body. "Let him go, he's done you no harm."

"True, but he's been a slippery bastard. Troublesome too."

Comte remembered his words to Rene. *Angelo is my only true friend and I would trust him with my life.* He gagged for sweet air, snorting life into his crooked nose cavity. His voice was cracked and raspy. "Who are you? What's Angelo got to do with this?"

The man momentarily relaxed the throat-hold and pulled Comte's deformed hand further up behind his back, tearing at the ligaments in his shoulder. "The name's Goldstein, but you can call me Ariel."

Angelo harnessed courage and moved, but Goldstein pushed Comte closer to the cliff. Angelo held back. "Nice lad isn't he? Always does as he's told. Although he was a little slow this time. His Uncle Veles has a cure for that."

Comte coughed up a gargled protest. "What are you on about?"

Goldstein skewered Angelo with a savage glance as he spouted in Comte's ear. "Didn't the boy tell you? What a shame. His arse was pumped for years to train him into a performing seal, and now he's earned his fish dinner. You're arse is always safe if you perform, isn't that right Angelo?"

Comte could see the bewilderment and indignant shame in Angelo's humid black eyes. He finally understood. Angelo's mind and body had been infected with abuse. He saw a broken man now exposed with nowhere to hide. Comte thought he had saved him from the Cardinal, but he now realised there had been other, far more sinister forces at work. Comte's expression conveyed no anger or resentment toward Angelo, only a deep affection for a mind torn between a perverted duty and a spiritual quest for truth.

Goldstein edged the keeper to the cliff face. Pebbles shifted underfoot, slipping over the edge to the heaving sea below. Comte was pushed forward, ever closer to his fate. He balanced on terra firma only with the aid of Goldstein.

Comte felt the need to leave a final gift.

"It's OK Angelo. You came here to find the Divine Feminine.

Believe in her like I believe in you."

The words offered restitution to a haunted soul. But Angelo only felt the filthy stain of evil that no bath would ever cleanse.

Goldstein grimaced at the sentiment. "Cut the pontifical platitudes you pathetic retard."

Comte strained to push back, but Goldstein twisted his arm higher, dislocating the shoulder blade with a dull crack. In agonising pain Comte declared, "The Lord made us pure in blood, but he who is pure in heart will return to the Lord." His words hung momentarily waiting for the final sordid act.

Goldstein's throat-hold squeezed tighter, but with the speed of a viper, Comte's clawed hand struck out and clamped Goldstein's wrist with the grip of an iron pincer. Without warning and with the agile power of a crocodile death-roll, he spiralled his wretched body off the cliff, Goldstein's wrist still locked firm against his throat. His bulging lower eye compassionately winked at Angelo in his final act. Comte and his attacker hurtled one hundred and forty metres to the rocks below, a convulsing wave capturing them into the metallic grey sea.

72

HELL'S FIRE

MONACO

Aggression pumped through Angelo's veins contaminating his heart with mournful dread. His entire body screamed. Comte had performed his final act and Angelo craved revenge. Overwhelmed by punishing grief, he slipped away and wandered the streets aimlessly. Every moment was a living hell. His eyes burned with murderous intent.

Comte had led him into a life of discovery, but it was deceit and brutality that had followed him. He knew he would never be free of it. He would never be as free or as empowered as Comte. The irrepressible Comte – he had faced his death with a joyous wink. It was so like him. Angelo had never known joy until he viewed a glimpse of it with his only mentor and friend.

Guilt wrenched his soul, guilt for Comte's death, guilt for his manic compliance, and guilt for his defilement. Like maggots gnawing at raw flesh, emotion stripped him bare. There was nothing about his life worthy of redemption. He had gambled Comte's life and lost. The eternal brutality of life tore him apart. There was nowhere to turn, nowhere to go, nowhere to hide. He could never hide from himself. To seek forgiveness would be a submissive sacrilege. He wasn't worthy. The pupil had turned on his master. The pain of a thousand sins consumed him. He heard the devil laugh.

⸺ ⊶⊷ ⸺

A bluish-white full moon hung low beneath a bank of wispy clouds when Angelo returned to Elysius's compound near the Fortress. He approached via the rear courtyard, careful not to draw attention, pacing the misshapen cobbles with skill. His guise of choirboy innocence grew gaunt in the pale light of dusk, as he resolved to staunch his wound. He would finally take control.

Rene was worried. He had called at the compound in the early afternoon to meet with Comte. It had been locked with no sign of either man. He assumed they had taken a long lunch, but when he called back two hours later, it remained unoccupied. The light of day had passed and with no answer at the apartment on the Avenue des Papalins, Rene made a final call. Once again, he entered the compound through the rear courtyard.

A dead, gnarled and twisted elm stood resolute in the centre of the yard. It had lived for well over a century and passed into death over the course of the last decade. Its eerie branches silhouetted against the vanilla canvass of the bright full moon. A forlorn and disturbing sight greeted Rene. A rope was dangling from the lowest branch, the noose short and tight around the neck of Angelo, his face drained to grey. The young man's dark eyes bulged and his purple tongue was swollen, distended against the corner of his open mouth. Rene was too late.

73

TRAGEDY

MEDITERRANEAN SEA, OFF CYPRUS

The air went still and then whipped into a frenzy. The crew never heard it approach. Out of nowhere, a Sikorsky H-60 Blackhawk helicopter with Blue Edge rotor technology hovered. Armed mayhem descended.

Four men abseiled from the chopper and once their military boots touched deck they opened fire. Bullets peppered the deck, bunching the crew together.

The muffled sound of the chopper seeped below deck. *Surely it wasn't ours.* Keisha had just stabbed the send button requesting an update for the morning. Our confusion evaporated with the staccato sound of gunfire.

Mitch and the crew were quickly bailed up by the four gunmen, eager to kill given the slightest excuse. Two men ducked under the wash of the rotors as the chopper touched the helipad. The first man was of moderate statue and dressed in fatigues. He had a choreographic gait and approached his armed protectors with graceful agility. He had the farcical look of a catwalk model gone soldier. The second man was a hulk. Also dressed in fatigues he stomped his way forward like a lopping bear. A greasy plait hung to his waist from the back of his pock-faced head.

The smaller man surveyed the crew, one of them standing tall like a lone skyscraper. He addressed them. "My name is Veles Kane. I'm not here to waste time. Mitchell Hamilton is on this ship and we won't leave until he comes forward. Where is he?"

No-one spoke.

The gunman to the right of Kane was given the nod. A bullet was fired into the head of a crewman within his sights. The body dropped like a wet sack.

The bear spread a slimy grin revealing chipped, nicotine stained teeth.

Kane scowled. "You don't want me to ask again, I'm not in the mood."

Mitch immediately spoke. "I'm the one you want. Leave these men alone."

"You should have spoken before, Mr. Hamilton. You would have saved your crew." Kane deferred to the bear. "Hawass. Cuff him and bring him to the bridge."

Kane moved away, opening some space between himself and his armed contingent. Hawass slapped a plastic tie around Mitch's wrist and pulled it tight. He pushed him forward to follow Kane. The still air was pierced by four more shots. The remaining crew fell to into death.

Mitch moved to take action but was too late. Hawass already had a gun aimed directly at him. There was no room to manoeuvre. Kane threw his hand in the air gesturing to his men to execute his orders. The four gunmen spread across the deck. Three of them had been given orders to search the ship and liquidate any other crew. The fourth was ordered to set explosive devices along the keel, pro-grammed to detonate from Kane's cell phone on departure. Only he had the ability to disengage the explosive using a secret pin code.

His plans didn't allow for that possibility.

Keisha and I heard the shots. The captain had been analysing some data from the ROV dive and he raced to the bridge to get a full view of the deck. He saw Mitch being led at gunpoint in our direction.

The captain reached for a keyring hanging below the navigation console. A firearm was locked in a drawer, but he was too late. A gunman smashed through the door and shot him through the head before the key had reached the lock. Mac's email had been prophetic.

Keisha's mien changed. Her blue eyes revealed a mind sharpened by threat as her body tensed. She quickly sprinted to the stairs that led below. "Quick, I need to get to my cabin. I need that DNA sample. I'll meet you at the two-man submarine. It's our only chance."

I followed her down one flight. "I'm not leaving you."

"Go. We don't have time to argue. Just be careful."

I reluctantly watched her slide down another flight as I moved toward the door that led to the deck. The latch tilted. Someone was entering. I turned and quickly followed Keisha.

Hawass pushed Mitch hard into the captain's chair. His hands were clamped behind him, the plastic tie cutting at his wrist. As Mitch fell back, he kicked his leg straight out with savage force, smashing his boot into the gun held by Hawass.

The gun released from the bear's grip and slid across the floor. The heavy push allowed him to use the chair as a springboard giving him the momentum to push forward into a standing position. Although he towered over his attackers, he adroitly sidestepped the lumbering swing of Hawass. The gun lay near the exit. Mitch scrambled toward his escape and kicked the gun into the corridor where it tumbled down the steps to the next level. He slipped out the way they had entered, kicking the door shut with his boot.

Hawass lumbered after Mitch and crashed through the doorway. Mitch was gone. Kane watched helplessly. His advantage was lost.

"I told you we'd meet at the two-man sub," Keisha protested. She ducked into her cabin, grabbing the zip-loc bag that held Mitch's DNA and stuffed it into her denim jeans.

"I know, but someone was coming through the door. Quick, there's a fire-axe at the end of the corridor. Let's go."

We hadn't been in this part of the ship and moved cautiously. Hushed footfalls fell on the shiny floor. I held the axe tight, ready to wield it at any provocation. The ROV was on standby on the upper deck at the stern and the two-man sub was on portside. We made our way to the upper deck and I checked that the area was clear. We made our move.

The sub stood proud on its moorings and beckoned from only eight metres away. Suddenly, warning shots peppered the air. No-one was visible, so we flattened ourselves on the deck. We had nowhere to hide.

I struggled to pull the axe under my body, hoping to hide it. No luck. More shots were fired, this time too close for comfort. Several rounds splintered the axe handle, slivers of wood shattering. One piece tore at Keisha's cheek, lodging just beneath her eye. A solitary gunman approached and jerked his assault rifle in a gesture to make us stand.

Keisha lifted herself off the deck, a trickle of blood running toward her chin. In an adrenaline fuelled lunge, I grabbed what was left of the axe. A shot was fired as a warning. The bullet pierced my shoulder, the axe clattering to the deck. For a fleeting moment I felt no pain, but then it burned like a red hot poker. My stupidity had put us further at risk.

The gunman was alone and the ship appeared deserted, yet when we were delivered to the bridge, two men smirked at our entrance.

Their intent was clear. There would be no survivors, once they got what they wanted. I weighed the possibility of grappling one of them to give Keisha a chance. I was sure we were facing a death sentence. Perhaps it was best to wait.

The gunman spoke, "Commander, I only found these two. Rather than kill first, I thought I would bring them to you. There was no woman logged on the manifest."

The smaller man questioned, "What about Hamilton?"

"Not sure sir."

"Continue your search then. He cannot be allowed to leave the ship alive."

The Commander casually levelled a Glock pistol in our direction. He spoke to his companion, the pock-faced hulk with the long greasy plait. He was a huge slab of ugly muscle. "Restrain the woman." He aimed the gun at my face. "You! Get over here."

I moved as directed, leaving Keisha exposed. Pock-face slapped her hard almost knocking her off her feet. He went to grab her, but he wasn't prepared for Keisha's agility. She pirouetted, hitting him in the jaw with a powerful roundhouse kick. It was like kicking an automobile. He didn't move. His only response was a plastic grin, bearing his stained teeth, the sole of her boot leaving a reddened stain in his heavily blemished face. The force of the kick had knocked Keisha to the floor. He bent down and pushed her face into the floor as he grabbed her arms and slapped a tie around one of her wrists. He then wrapped his huge paw around her neck and hoisted her to her feet. With brute strength he lifted her higher, allowing her to dangle above the floor. "Try that again bitch and I'll rip your neck off."

The beast lowered her and tied her wrists above her head with another plastic restraint, locking her hands through a rail running across the ceiling. He then tied her legs at the ankles.

The Commander appeared amused. "She's quite feisty Dr Keyes.

I like that in a woman. Especially ones who look like this."

The bastard knew my name. My shoulder was giving me hell and blood was saturating my shirt. I boiled with rage. "Leave her the fuck alone, you filthy maggot!"

"We'll look after her just fine. I must say Dr Keyes; this is quite an unexpected surprise. Two for one. Perhaps you should have walked away while you had the chance."

His accomplice moved in my direction with his plastic ties. The Commander ordered, "Dr Keyes will give his word to stay where he is. Won't you?" One move and she'll be mopping your brains off the floor. He raised the gun to my head.

"You obviously know us, but who the hell are you?"

The man bristled with pride, but Keisha cut in. "He's Veles Kane, numero uno of Majestic. He's the human waste behind Otto's death."

Kane squinted at Keisha and flashed recognition. "Yes of course, Keisha Petersen. I didn't recognise you, the blood on your face and all. What happened to your long golden locks?"

Keisha didn't answer, but the sting in her eyes intensified.

Kane and Keisha knew each other, and now Majestic were in control. Our only escape was going to be a battle to the end. The image of Otto's disembowelled corpse told me what we were dealing with.

Kane cut to the chase. "I don't believe in coincidence so you must be here for the same reason as me. Trouble is we lost him. So we can save time. I want to know about the Council of Change for Evolutionary Consciousness. Perhaps you can enlighten me?"

Keisha gritted through her teeth, "Don't say anything Aiden."

"Oh, but he will, Ms Petersen, he will. Hawass!"

So pock-face had a name. A chill ran though me at the sight of his plastic grin. Hawass removed a boning knife from a leather sheath attached to his belt. He got up close and stuck his nose against Keisha's cut cheek. He snorted in a deep breath. The ferrous scent of congealing blood made him salivate. He stuck out his drooling, furry tongue and slurped at the coagulation, lapping at her cheek like a tiger sipping at a water hole. His fetid breath made Keisha heave.

I went to move, but Kane steadied his pistol, pushing the barrel against my temple. Blood ran in rivulets down my arm, dripping onto the floor.

"You know what I want Dr Keyes. Hawass can be quite persuasive."

Keisha was defiant. "Tell this piece-of-shit nothing Aiden."

Mitch had escaped from their clutches and I wondered if he had already been found. *Could we play for time?* He was our only hope.

Keisha struggled with her footing and fell sideways, the weight of her body hanging from her tied wrists. Hawass steadied her and placed the razor sharp knife against her throat. As quick as a flash, the knife was expertly stroked downward, peeling her t-shirt away from her body. The blade cut through her bra and deftly scored her flesh from her chest to her navel. A fine line of blood oozed from the shallow cut.

Like an animal going for the kill, Hawass stripped the shirt apart, completely baring Keisha's torso. The pig's ravenous eyes devoured her image as he bent down and licked the seeping claret liquid from her taut stomach. Keisha struggled and squirmed, losing her balance once again, but Hawass continued his lascivious torment, tracing his foul tongue around her firm breasts. Keisha steeled her dignity by closing her eyes to the atrocity.

Kane gave me a cruel, satisfied glance. I felt impotent by my inaction. Keisha was being dehumanised by a leering piece of trash. I needed to act, but how?

Kane inched closer, the pistol still attached to my temple. "I think you should speak now, otherwise my friend will surgically remove each breast. Her womb will be next. She'll be conscious throughout, it's quite an art. I've seen him in action before."

Keisha struggled, the plastic ties at her wrists now cutting deep. Hawass continued his repugnant torment, slurping hungrily at Keisha's face. She flicked her head back and forth trying to rid herself of his attention, but Hawass grabbed her spiky hair and pulled her head back – hard. Holding her head still, he sloshed his tongue across her lips and up the side of her nose. She choked at the breathy stench. He then ran his filthy pointed fingernails through her cleavage, smearing her still seeping blood over her nipples. He sucked his fingers and mocked.

"Tasty."

He backed off and placed the blade on the underside of her breast. "Ready when you are boss."

Terror squeezed through me. I had no doubt this sadistic filth would carry out his threat. *What was the point of remaining silent?* The stakes were too high and I couldn't risk losing Keisha. Not like this.

I weighed my options. Hawass was made of brick, but his bulk would slow him down.

I screamed at him. "Leave her alone you sick fuck. I'll tell you what we know. Sit down and I'll speak."

My statement had its effect. The feral pig grinned, wiping bloody saliva across his face. He sat back in the captain's chair waiting for further instruction. I focussed my peripheral vision and screamed fanatically at Keisha. "TELL HIM, BITCH."

The virulence of my verbal attack surprised her, but it also perplexed Kane. For a split-second he glanced toward her, gauging her reaction. Through the brutalising pain of my damaged shoulder, I acted with speed, lifting my elbow and jack-hammering two lightening stabs into Kane's face. The cartilage of his nasal septum crunched as my elbow met his ethmoid bone. Blood splashed from his split nostrils as he fell backwards. The gun fired. I felt a bullet gash my side, a thin slice of flesh ripping beneath my shirt.

Hawass had already moved, but I had anticipated his reaction. The razor edge of his boning knife glistened with the stain of Keisha's blood as he leaned out of the chair. Kane was on the floor clutching his smashed face. A second bullet whizzed past my ankle as I gained my balance. I only had a moment to spare. I stomped on his hand with my heel, crushing his fingers against the gun. He groaned in pain and his grip released, dropping the gun to the floor beside him. His fingers wouldn't be holding anything again.

The blade closed on Keisha's throat. Hawass moved his arm, ready to slice across her neck. My knees buckled and I fell heavily on Kane, disgorging the air from his lungs, enough to immobilise him for the chance I needed. I gripped the gun in a clean sweep.

The knife began its cross movement. The nerves travelling through my shoulder didn't seem wired to my fingers, the trigger taking all my strength to engage.

The bullet hit the behemoth in his thick neck. Its momentum made him stagger, the blade cutting the air as it breezed past Keisha's throat. Like a solid oak, the man stood resolute readying for another slash.

I fired again, this time the bullet entering the brain through his jaundiced eye socket. A cloud of bone and brain blew away from the back of his skull. The hulk finally crashed to the floor.

Kane breathed deep and struggled to remove my weight. He shoved his thumb deep into my side wound. I struggled to stay conscious, but I summoned enough strength to roll off him.

I aimed the Glock. I saw a glimmer of fear that lived within him.

The twisted psychopath was unrepentant. "Go on gutless, I'm unarmed and no threat, so do it. You'll have to live with your conscience."

I smiled back. "My conscience will be just fine. This is for Otto.

Then I'll gut you."

I slowly pulled the trigger.

———— ❊ ————

Veles Kane slid into a dark abyss, drawn to his continuing existence according to karma, the immutable law of cause and effect. He landed heavily on solid ground that rose up to meet him. The air was thick, a dark grey fog swirling. A confused and bedraggled shadow shuffled toward him, mumbling insanities. Kane tried to speak, but no voice came.

He approached and then recoiled in horror. As the shadow gave way to etheric structure, he recognised it as Hawass. His form was slashed, flayed into a thousand ribbons, oozing bitumen-like, hot black blood from every crevice. The emotional body was gone. Now he existed in a place of universal suffering. He had no eyes and howled like a banshee as his repulsive form melted into the void. The horrifying Naraka realm beckoned.

The thick fog dissipated revealing a grey grassy field. Everything Kane spied was devoid of colour – just grey in all its hues. Grey fog, grey grass, even his limbs were a pallid grey. The chilled finger of dread traced along his spine. The hair on the back of his neck prickled. He had arrived in the dark world the Tibetan had prophesied, trapped for countless incarnations.

———— ❊ ————

My strength was gone, but I rushed to Keisha. Her rheumy eyes had filled and were on the brink. Her steely resolve had been tempered. I cut the ties at her feet and then her wrists. Her hands fell to entwine around me. Her bare and bloodied chest warmed against mine, revitalising my stamina. I felt the rapid beat of her heart. We soaked into each other, an embrace of our need to hold and to share the experience.

"Why did I ever doubt you?" she sobbed.

"I didn't know you did."

"Back at the Atlas Mountains. I should have told you what I had in mind.

She had held herself high after she had disposed of Anwar at the Basilica, but I had also noticed how her confident poise had been jaded. Right now, I felt her vulnerability, her exposure, but I also felt her need.

Keisha's sincerity washed over me as she buried her face against my cheek. "Come on, we're not safe yet. Let's get off this ship."

A voice from behind tamed our distress. It was Mitch. "The ship's secure, but it's wired with explosive. You're right; we need to get off the ship. Like now. We'll use the Blackhawk."

Mitch read my thoughts. "Don't worry Aiden; I know how to pilot the thing."

74

FINAL CONFESSION

THE VATICAN, ITALY

Antonio Cardinal Valla hesitated, but finally took the call. Only two men had access to this line. One was Veles Kane, Majestic's Intelligence Director of Global Studies and the other was a man he despised even more – the teflon-coated Giovanni Cardinal Agostino, head of the *Servizio Informazioni del Vaticano*, the enigmatic and secretive S.I.V. – the Vatican Intelligence Agency.

The line was installed purely for Kane's personal access to Valla, but Agostino had gained knowledge of its existence and he had the temerity to demand the same right of access. Valla had grudgingly acquiesced.

Kane was currently out of action, chasing the insane ramblings of the dead Tibetan, so Valla reasoned it must be Agostino. He gritted his teeth.

"Cardinal, I have some unfortunate news."

Typical arrogance, thought Valla. No greeting, just bad news. "That's your trademark Agostino."

"Yes, Your Eminence, but it's important that I see you straight away." Agostino's tone was absent of its usual contempt. There was an unmistakable urgency.

"Just tell me what you want so I can get on with my work."

"No. I need to see you now. Be at my villa within the hour."

The phone link disengaged. *Damn Agostino, every time he says jump, he expects me to jump.*

Valla reluctantly ordered his car. He felt fortunate that he had not actually had a personal meeting for over twelve months; the last time they spoke he was flying over the Atlantic. Meetings with Agostino always ended in the same antagonistic fracas that always left Valla cold. *The man's an evasive belligerent, a scheming chameleon.* Unfortunately, he wielded power and was not afraid to use it. His Jesuit attachments and membership of Opus Dei was contrary to everything that Valla held dear. It was the damn Jesuits for Christ sake who were probing the heavens with their damn telescopes, putting science above faith. They were a vile stain on the Church.

Agostino maintained a list of dubious associates outside the Holy Church that was deeply disturbing to the Cardinal. Dealing with Kane was one thing, that was personal, but Agostino's reach extended well beyond his own sphere of influence.

Forty minutes later, his car snaked the curved driveway. It was bordered by tall needle pines and lined with flowering lavender. Agostino's private quarters were set in a large walled enclave at Collis Quirinalis, one of the hills of ancient Rome. A circular fountain featuring a bronzed statue of Neptune sprayed a cool welcome on the large manicured lawn in front of the sumptuous villa. The portico was embellished by two large urns of perfumed annuals standing guard at the front entrance.

The Cardinal was greeted by the thirty-something housekeeper, an angelic vision of the female form. Housekeeper maybe, but she obviously performed other, more intimate duties. Her straight raven hair had a lustrous shine and hung in front of her shoulders in long groomed tresses, framing her perfect cleavage. It had the effect of drawing the Cardinal's eye to her feminine assets.

No-one from ecclesiastical circles had ever entered Agostino's private world. Now he knew why. The corner of his mouth visibly rose as he deposited this knowledge into his memory as future political capital. To be summoned here so urgently had weighty significance.

Valla followed her into the study. French style doors opened onto a terracotta terrace at one side of the villa. It overlooked a flat, billiard table lawn. Canopies of scented citrus protected an understorey of white lobelia which painted an artistic, horticultural backdrop. Agostino was sitting at a wrought-iron setting, glancing at the daily paper, Il Corriere della Sera. He struggled to rise from the chair in greeting and decided to remain seated.

Valla was shocked by the man's appearance. Agostino had lost a ton of weight since they had last met. He was etiolated and gaunt. Dressed in black pyjamas, his bony fingers clamped the lapels of his silk dressing gown. The garment hung like an oversized, empty sack from his once broad shoulders with his pectoral cross dangling like loose ballast from his deeply veined neck. He was clearly very ill, a once vital adversary now demolished with nowhere to hide. The Lord would soon deal with him.

"Thank you for coming Your Eminence."

Valla made no concession. "You better have a good reason. This is most inconvenient."

Normally Agostino would have shutdown such a jibe. But he responded in a manner befitting the position held by Cardinal Valla. "I understand, but time is of the essence. I can't guarantee the security of your private rooms, but I can guarantee we will not be heard here. I've asked you here to receive the Secretum Omega."

Valla knew of its existence and his chest palpitated with anxiety. He was not the Holy Father. Agostino had always been cunning.

His skill had been cast in the Banco Ambrosiano affair, and then the sudden and convenient death of Pope John Paul I. It had been moulded and refined ever since in the forge of political subterfuge and deal-making. Valla was deeply concerned. *Is the Pontiff in danger? Or is it me?* "Why me and why now?"

Agostino raised his ghostly hand and nodded in understanding. "Why you is because of your past. Why now is because I'm dying of cancer as you can see. I only have a week or two at most."

"I presumed the worst. May the Lord bless you."

Agostino controlled his condescension. "I can do without the platitude, and forget any ideas of grandeur. You can just listen and absorb. Got it?"

Valla acquiesced to the dying man, "You have the floor."

Agostino began a story that had been hidden from the world for decades. "My role at S.I.V. has had one overriding purpose. To suppress the Vatican's role in the 1954 meeting at Edwards Airforce Base. President Eisenhower asked us to provide spiritual counsel at that meeting so we provided the Bishop of Los Angeles, Richard McNamara. It was a meeting that brought him face to face with an alien delegation."

Valla had heard this type of gibberish from Veles Kane and remained unconvinced. "You mean demons. The president met with demons." He searched the man's sunken features. There was no equivocation.

"The meeting was with beings from another world and was captured on twenty minutes of film recorded by the U.S. military. Not demonic spiritual beings as you continually rant, but real physical entities like you and me. Flesh and blood. Each delegate was sworn to secrecy about what they had seen and heard. The bishop must have regretted taking his oath because it specifically included keeping the details secret from the Holy Father. He must have been spiritually challenged because three days later, he was received by Pope Pius

XII at the Vatican. Needless to say the Holy Father was incredulous. Pius meditated deeply about the implications of what he'd been told and decided to create the S.I.V. Our role was to acquire our own independent intelligence, separate from the crumbs that the U.S. military chose to feed us. Of course, our initial preoccupation was to reconcile the affair with our Lord and the Holy Scriptures.

"Events took a major turn. S.I.V. members made direct contact with an alien, Nordic type race who advised us that the Americans needed to be careful with the extraterrestrials they had encountered in the Californian desert. Contact even occurred here in Rome, within the gardens of the Vatican. Pius XII was there and met with their delegation.

"Imagine if that news had been leaked to the public. As you know, I've been involved with S.I.V. since the late eighties and I took over control in 1998. Needless to say, the Secretum Omega is the most highly secret compilation of material outside the U.S. military. The Holy Church has been fortunate. We span the globe and we've been very active in our research. I know you find it hard the bear, but the Jesuit study of the heavens with our radio telescope in Alaska has been vital to our research. You've been a fool in opposing it."

Agostino handed Valla a thick dossier bearing the official SIV wax seal. "This is a summary of our findings since 1954 and how they affect Church doctrine. It also contains the personal notes of Bishop McNamara describing the meeting and what was discussed. Pius also made copious notes of his thoughts at that time. They too are included. This is to be opened upon my death in the presence of the Curia. I want you to personally read the summary to them. The Church needs change Cardinal. Religion needs to change. It won't come from the Holy Father, so it needs to come from you."

To rise above the Holy Father weighed heavily. It was conspiratorial and would not sit well with the Curia. It would be professional suicide and would undermine the certainty of church doctrine. "What if I refuse or choose to destroy this dossier?"

"The dossier has already been violated. Its message will get out anyway, so you have no choice but to act."

"How could it have been violated? Only you had access to it."

"True, but somehow your infamous keeper has gathered the information. We believe he hacked into my personal computer files. It was a very technical operation, so we think he had outside help." Agostino reached deep into his dressing gown pocket. "I received a confidential delivery last week containing this memory stick. It contains everything in that dossier and much more, including a personal message for us both. Now that I have little time left, I have to say that I agree with him. He said, *It's time for the Church to open up and shape a new future*. He's given us an ultimatum Your Eminence. So, I've decided to give you an advantage. You can read everything on this memory stick before you open the file in front of the Curia. Only you can decide. Comte said, *There is no higher religion than Truth.* He's right."

Valla took the memory stick feeling the burden of its delivery.

"Thank you for coming Cardinal Valla. This is now your legacy. I hope you choose well – for your mother's sake. I need to rest now. Please find you're way out."

Agostino raised his wasted arm and waved a final dismissal.

Valla contemplated Agostino's bizarre confession about non-human entities, assessing the devastating global consequences. The Holy Bible certainly spoke of such beings throughout the scriptures. But the Church had already declared on such matters. Why raise all this inflammatory nonsense now, in a world already filled with confusion? The people needed to be led with a firm hand or else there would be anarchy. Valla also struggled with Agostino's expectations. Even in death he would be teflon-coated. He wouldn't be around to face the inevitable onslaught. As his car drove away from the villa and its luxurious grounds, Comte's words to Agostino resonated. *'There is no higher religion than Truth.'* Damn him.

The words of the Tibetan also rebounded. *'Your mother observes your suffering. She dwells within the light and cannot speak to you through your opaque shroud of deceit. Your attachments hold you back. Only you can find release. The eternity you seek is hidden until you rise in consciousness.'*

75

TRUTH

NEAR LUGANO, SWITZERLAND

Mitch had been a godsend. He located the first aid kit as I covered Keisha's torso with the captain's jacket that hung next to the navigation console. We hurried to the helipad. The pilot was lying on the deck next to the chopper, a large knife piercing his chest.

Mitch jutted his square jaw toward the carnage. "Collateral damage, I'm afraid. I had to liquidate them one by one. He was the last."

Mitch stepped over the body and climbed into the pilot's seat. We clambered into the rear seats and began to patch each other up. The chopper was in the air and banking away from the ship within seconds. I fastened a bandage along the cut down Keisha's torso and then she skilfully staunched the flow of blood from my own wounds.

Less than a minute into our flight, we watched the Ulysses Enterprise go down after it belched an explosive fireball. It lilted and sank before we had disappeared over the horizon.

The short hop back to Ercan Airport near Nicosia was over in twenty minutes. Mitch said he would deal with the authorities about the ship's explosion and the unscheduled arrival of the Blackhawk. He would keep our names out of it.

Mitch landed next to our original aircraft that flew us into Cyprus, a Challenger 604. We surreptitiously transferred, its pilot getting immediate clearance to depart. At a cruising speed of 880 kilometres per hour, we touched down three hours later.

We spoke little as we nursed our wounds and allowed fatigue to take hold. For much of the flight Keisha rested her head against my good shoulder, snuggling into my neck as she slept off her ordeal. I enjoyed the closeness. I knew what she meant to me. I had been close to losing her and was determined she would never face danger again, Elysius operative or not.

Philip and Mac were at Lugano-Agno airport to meet us and fifteen minutes later we were driving into the botanic surrounds of Philip's luxury estate in Croglio Lugano. Nobody would have realised that the estate housed a world class laboratory built two levels below the splendid villa, the home of a key Elysius nerve centre, communicating with a number of cells and lodges around the world. It was where the miniscule tracking device had been removed from my temple and our DNA tests on the mysterious bones were performed.

The villa appeared as a palatial double storey home spread over three wings, the central living area, the bedroom wing and an entertainment wing built over a six car garage. The grounds were spread over 25 completely private acres with views through a lush wooded valley.

I felt oddly at home. Our ordeal had culminated in a new bond between Keisha and I, and this had long been her family home. Philip had arranged for a doctor to examine our wounds. I was fortunate. The bullet had passed through my shoulder, leaving a clean wound. My side had suffered a shallow lesion. Antibiotics would kill any infection that might threaten.

Keisha too, was lucky. She had been more jaded than injured. The cut down her torso was shallow and clean. Any deeper and she would have bled much more profusely, healing with an ugly scar. She was relieved to have been so lucky.

Mac had also arrived at the estate with a heavy heart. His Parisian tryst had ended prematurely. He was anxious to return to the solitude of his home in Zurich, but as promised, he had waited for our return. Mac still seethed from his Marrakech experience. He gave a thumbnail version of his plans. "I stayed to make sure you two were OK, but I'll be leaving when I'm packed. I need a decent drive back home to think about my life."

"I'm glad you stayed, but drive safe and cut down on the Glenfiddich when you get back."

"OK, I'll drink Talisker instead," he teased.

"Seriously Mac, you need to stay focused. We've got enough to make a one-hour program, but I have to put out six episodes and I'll need your help." Keisha swung a dejected look at me. "We'll need your help too," I revised.

Mac did his best to console my concern. "I just need a few days Aiden. Call me when you're ready. You know me; I just need some time. She wasn't a bad sort, and besides I was looking forward to Paris."

Know him I did. After a high-speed drive through the mountains, two or three days and nights of blaring music, several joints and a few bottles of single malt, he would revive. He always did.

The seeds of Keisha's unconventional theory began to germinate. Mitch's DNA was pure sorcery. The results would send the scientific establishment into uproar. His karyotype displayed the same chromosomal pattern as the skeleton recovered in the Basilica of the Eastern Star – 44 chromosomes in 22 pairs. Unusually, the 22nd and 23rd chromosomes were fused. Mitch didn't appear to have any visible defect, yet he too, was an enigma. He was human, but not as I understood the word. We had met him, conversed with him, and been rescued by him. He was human in all aspects. The shortage of chromosomes put him into the realm of something that could not be categorised.

Keisha was more circumspect as she fleshed out her ideas. She was convinced we were delving into the chromosomal DNA of an extraterrestrial entity. She expanded her hypothesis by suggesting humans were a hybridised version between the primate and Mitch. Bizarre, but there was no simple explanation.

The question for Keisha was more academic. Her study of ancient Sumerian texts and her scholarship under the expertise of the renowned translator, Eli Rosen, convinced her she was correct. Genetic manipulation of hominoids, using extraterrestrial biological material created the modern human.

"Remember what Mitch said Aiden. *I'm one of their offspring just like you, but there's a subtle difference. I'm a direct offspring. You, however, like all modern humans were created in their image.'* He's already told us his genealogy. That's why he gave us his DNA. He wanted us to find the Truth."

I could deny it no longer. "And you say the ancient Sumerian texts confirm all this?"

Keisha was euphoric, her conclusion answering one of her 'big' questions. "Mitch is living proof of those ancient texts. We need to get him here."

Keisha decided to honour our achievements. "I've organised a treat. I've arranged a table at Santabbondio Restorante for tonight. It's up in the hills above Lugano. The food is superb and so are the views."

Dinner was a long awaited pleasure, giving us the opportunity to have more intimate conversation. I could tell she was very happy.

Not just because we were growing closer, but because I finally believed.

Keisha enjoyed the jumbo shrimp with three varieties of asparagus while I savoured the roast pigeon and pine nuts. The dishes were a harmony of delicate tastes, which we enjoyed with a crisp 1999 Pinot Grigio from Tenimento dell Örspar. We deliberately kept conversation away from our recent work, talking mainly about our immediate surrounds, the fond memories of our lives and the more intimate secrets of our enjoyable pasts. In truth, we were exploring each other.

Keisha wore a short black halter neck dress. She looked and smelled classy. It hugged her taut, lithe body and accentuated her delightful contours and vulnerable bare shoulders. I decided to shamelessly push the boundaries. I sensed she was being seduced by my visual absorption of her curves as plumes of blushing pleasure willingly vanquished her.

We were sharing a dessert of chocolate mousse with fresh loquats when I took my chance. I decided to finally solve the riddle of Keisha Petersen. "Remember that briefing you gave Mac and I when you met me at the villa."

"I'm not sure I do," she coquettishly teased. "Oh, wait, now I remember."

"I had been hoping for a more personal briefing."

Keisha interpreted the innuendo. "Comprehensive no doubt?"

"Very," I demanded.

"Aren't you still injured? You might not cope with the exercise. What if you do yourself an injury? I couldn't bear the responsibility."

I smirked, "You'll need to treat me gently then." I struggled not to laugh.

Keisha playfully giggled, "Come on then, let's go."

Mitch arrived the following morning. His overview of our questions started to provide some detail. A fantastic picture began to emerge.

He confirmed Keisha's hypothesis. He was indeed human with only 22 pairs of chromosomes. In fact, he stated he was human plus some additional strands of DNA. His genealogy belonged to a time long before the genetic cross-breeding of modern man. He was a direct descendant of the original 'gods', the Elohim who had come to Earth some 450,000 years ago. His forefathers were a human-like extraterrestrial race who had colonised the Earth in the search for minerals. Long before their arrival, they had established a way-station on Mars, prior to the collapse of its atmosphere. In the process of colonisation, the workers, known as the Annunaki in the ancient Sumerian texts, ultimately rebelled against the 'gods' and sought the creation of a hominid to act as labour slaves.

Enki, the being responsible for management of the Earth colony, decided to act, creating a 'man' using progressive genetic engineering techniques. Female Homo Erectus genes were combined with Enki's male genes, the resulting ovum being implanted into the womb of Ninki, Enki's wife. The melding of these genes created the first Homo Sapiens. *Us.*

Mitch claimed that the Annunaki continually bred with the females of this new species and corrupted their DNA. Ultimately, these beings were destroyed in the 'flood of the Bible' and a new man was created from the Elohim's own genes via direct cloning. This man, the Cro-Magnon was made in the 'image and likeness' of the Elohim.

Mitch told us that we were all innately inter-dimensional in nature, and that access to unseen dimensions had been sought after by the gifted for millennia. Various methods had been used over the ages in an effort to raise one's consciousness into these extra-dimensional realms. He mentioned the ingestion of the biblical manna that was used for this purpose. Over the millennia man lost his connection with the gods. Intervention occasionally occurred, the stories of various cultures confirming the presence of gods who walked among men.

In recent millennia, Jesus was one such individual who rose to understand the arcane knowledge of the past. After his physical death, he rose in his resurrection body as living proof that life indeed was eternal. But his teaching was distorted by those who craved control over the soul of each individual. The Church rose in power and paternalism ruled. Truth was replaced by dogma, preached by beings such as the wrathful Jehovah. Together with many other Nephilim, he inspired the orthodox, control based religions of today. The Knights Templar had uncovered the truth and were exterminated for their heretical knowledge. Yet the Founding Fathers of the United States had never forsaken the Templars, secretly following in their footsteps. They were committed to building a world for the benefit of everyone, rather than the religious and monarchical rulers of the world.

Mitch revealed there were periodic incarnations of enlightened beings on Earth and on other planets. These beings taught the few how to escape from the dust worlds. They taught the secret of enlightenment, the highest goal sought by the Egyptian Sons of Horus and later fellowships. It was a practise deeply cherished by the Elohim.

Mitch explained how the great thinkers of the past had understood the truth of man's eternity. He gave the example of the Cathars who were cut down and destroyed by the ignorant. They were individuals who understood the realms of existence beyond the physical, but were persecuted by the very Church that claimed to know better.

Mitch had provided the essence to my upcoming series. He promised to act as a special advisor during production and work on our project in any capacity that we desired. I was grateful for the offer and eagerly accepted.

But my gratitude also extended to Keisha's prodigious abilities. She assisted me throughout with her powerful, unconventional intellect, and last night she had sweetened the buds of my thirst. The tongue of her orgiastic fire had devoured me. She was discreet and undemanding and I wanted her in my life. I also wanted her in my next series. She was photogenic and had a presence that would translate easily to the screen. Keisha would emerge like fresh dew on the meadow.

I would ask her when the time was right. I didn't want to appear too eager. I could wait.

76

FINAL VISION

NEAR LUGANO, SWITZERLAND

The sense of nothingness gave way to a sense of space, the total absence of light transformed into a clear circle of visibility just forty metres around me. The small being was motionless, only a silhouette of its form visible. He was no longer the sickly child I had known for so long. He was restored to health. Without speaking, he told me my goals had been met.

The being asked me to close my eyes. As I shut them, a torrent of images cascaded before me. I ascended rapidly, moving close to a distant mountain. I saw the massive face carved upon it. As the angle of my ascent changed it became clearer. The face was similar to the Sphinx at Giza.

The usual sequence of cause and effect collapsed into the eternal now and I came to know. This was the planet Mars and a great civilization had once inhabited the planet. This civilisation had been seeded from another planet long venerated by the secret fraternities. I marvelled at the revelation. But a dreadful insight soon plundered my vision.

Those who had inhabited Mars detected it too late. They knew their time was at an end. An enormous comet passed too close and the resulting gravitational and electrostatic disturbance caused the atmosphere to rupture and dissipate into space. The majestic civilisation was devastated. They sought a new home – planet Earth. This event was the foundation of many myths and legends from our distant ancestors, about fiery clouds, flying serpents and beings that came to teach civilisation. However, the most precious knowledge was held within the mantle of the most arcane brotherhoods.

Mercifully, the beautiful and familiar blue planet drifted into my view. I saw the craft, 'stones of cloud by day and fire by night', vehicles bringing the first ones to Earth. Massive Seraphic Transports carrying the chosen to their new home before the devastation. Their planet was lost, its atmosphere destroyed. It was time to rebuild. But the respite was short-lived. A massive tectonic disturbance and catastrophic deluge plunged the Earth into chaos. Land rose, fell and was inundated by flood as the fledgling civilisation was annihilated.

The Hierophants who had inspired the earliest civilisations decided that their wisdom needed preservation. Pyramids were constructed on specific points around the globe with the largest in Egypt and Shensi in China. Mathematical proportions and astronomical calculations were coded into the massive stone monuments with architectural precision, to inform those who would come after them.

The child's silhouette solidified into form. I recognised him as Mitch. I had no doubt; he had reached for my hand when I needed to be shown. I was ready and the Master had indeed appeared. His previous sickly form was due to my ignorance, my prejudices. But my ordeals and experiences had made me more conscious. I could recognise him clearly now. He was the being in my dreams all along, waiting for me just beyond the veil of common life that blinds us.

77

ULTIMATUM

THE VATICAN, ITALY

Cardinal Valla began his day before the sun had risen. He cancelled all his activities and left orders not to be disturbed. Agostino was right. He had a brief window in which to weigh up the contents of the dossier and decide its fate.

He knew Comte would deliver on his promise. Even if Kane had tracked him down and disposed of him, Comte was shrewd. There would copies of this material everywhere.

Valla settled back in his leather chair and surveyed his Louis XIII desk. He had always admired the workmanship of its ebony and tortoise shell veneers. The art of creating beautiful handcrafted furniture was dying. The flat pack world of modern design just wasn't up to standard.

He filled his glass with a draught of the fresh spring water from his Waterford crystal jug which permanently clung to the corner of his desk. He swallowed a dose of his medication. It was not enough. The Cardinal reached into the bottom draw and pulled out a silver flask containing his Courvoisier cognac. He gulped down half of it, putting the flask back into the drawer. He was about to open Secretum Omega, the greatest secret of the Holy Church. His hands trembled slightly in anticipation. The memory stick in his USB port revealed one folder and two extra files. The folder was titled '*Evidence*', the others were named '*Agostino*' and to his surprise, '*Valla*'. It was his file that drew his immediate attention. He clicked the mouse.

Cardinal Valla,

If you are reading this, then Cardinal Agostino has done what I expected. He has little time left. After my years of research, I've now decided to expose Church deceit and in particular, your enmity towards the Truth.

I challenge you to re-read the Bible for what it actually says. I draw you to the very beginning of man. To see who Adam really is. It is a marvel of Truth, if understood with intellect and reason.

Take Genesis Chapter 1:26-28:

'God said, *Let us make man in **our image, male and female**.*' This is confirmed in Genesis 5:1-2: '*Male and female created he them, and **called their name Adam**.*'

The bold italics are mine Cardinal. As stated, the first man was male and female. They were the first hominids who bred and multiplied – these were the first Adam, created on the sixth day. Their name was Adam.

But what about the second Adam mentioned in Genesis 2:2-3, 5-7: It says that '***there was not a man to till the ground***'.

'*And the Lord God formed man of the dust of the ground, and breathed into his nostrils the breath of life; and man became a living soul.*'

'God' had already made the first Adam – male and female hominids. He rested and blessed all that He had made. But now, after the seventh day, the 'Lord God' saw there was no man to work. Don't you think this strange and contradictory?

But alas, for you and your petty sermons, there is no contra-diction. Lord God made a NEW man for the purpose of work, a being with heightened ability and skill, far exceeding that of the previous primitive hominid races. This new being became a living soul – a man with eternal life.

You spot the dilemma Cardinal, don't you? We have God who made the original hominids, the first Adam, and now the Lord God who made a new man, a new Adam, who possessed a soul – two separate entities, God and Lord God, two separate Adams.

This second Adam was genetically synthesised using the orig-inal hominid stock and the living soul of God, but the resultant hybrid offspring were unable to reproduce. They were sterile.

Further genetic manipulation was required. This is described as the making of Eve, the ability for sterile homo-sapiens to repro-duce. The operation is described in Genesis 2:18 and 21:

'And the Lord God said, it is not good that the man should be alone; And the Lord God caused a deep sleep to fall upon Adam and he slept: and he took one of his ribs, and closed up the flesh instead thereof.'

In the process, man lost the immortality of the gods. This is made clear in Genesis 3:21-24:

*'Unto Adam also and to his wife did the Lord God make coats of skins, and clothed them. And the Lord God said, Behold the man is become as one of us, to know good and evil:....**So he drove out the man**; and placed him at the east of the garden of Eden. Cherubims, and a flaming sword which turned every way, **to keep the way of the tree of life.'***

They were cast into a mortal skin, a body that genetically dis-integrated, one that lived then died. The tree of life was denied. Life eternal was lost.

It has been my life's work to bring back the tree of life to this world, as so many persecuted groups have tried to do throughout the ages.

I make one final plea to your mute senses. As you well know, Lord God breathed into man making him a living soul. Our flesh, our coats of skin, our bodies naturally die, but our soul lives on, it is eternal. Jesus taught this message. The Christ within us lives.

It's time the Church taught His story of resurrection more truthfully. The reason Jesus was not recognised when He appeared after the crucifixion was because He was not in physical form. The body was dead, but the living soul was alive. Christ was alive. St. Mark 16:12 says – *'and He appeared in another form.'* His companions only 'saw' Him when their consciousness was raised.

He first appeared to Mary Magdalene who 'saw' Him immediately, and yet 'they believed her not'. As the representative of the Divine Feminine, it is hardly surprising she had a raised consciousness. How the Church has castigated her for being so highly evolved. Damn the Church!

So ends the lesson, Cardinal.

You have always known the scriptures. You know them well. The world is screaming for change and you have the power to begin the transition. It's time to raise the consciousness of all humanity. Fairy tales are important for children, but the world has grown up.

It is time for full disclosure. The Templars, the Cathars and all the others who understood the Truth of the scriptures were hunted down and tortured in the name of your Lord. Was this the Lord of Light? Who did the Church serve then and who does it serve now?

The files on this memory stick will be revealed to the world's press six months from now. Together with other physical DNA evidence, they will be issued over a period of twelve months bringing to the world the truth of the gods and the truth of man's genesis.

It will be backed with proof. Ignore the proof at your peril. You have an opportunity to act in the best interests of humankind and your precious Church.

How ironic that the files that make up Secretum Omega were compiled by your very own! The time is NOW – don't waste it.

You already know that the Hosts of Gods – the Lord God and His companions were extraterrestrial beings who came and genetically manipulated the course of Earth's evolution. Yet you have always reconciled this knowledge by calling them either 'angels' or 'demons'. And so they are, like all of mankind, they serve either the forces of light or of darkness. We engage with one force or the other. And I'll ask you again. Who do you serve Cardinal?

I sign off thanking you for the opportunity you gave me in the Archive and for the compassion you never showed me. It gave me strength.

Your obedient keeper,
Comte.

The words of the valediction jammed into him. Fury bled into his hot veins. *Obedient. How dare he?*

Heat rose through the back of his neck, up into his face. Valla again opened his bottom drawer. He swigged another long draught, snuggled back into his thick leather chair and allowed his blood to cool. He then re-read the letter, slowly absorbing the message, allowing it to inform a decision he could live with. He reluctantly agreed with Agostino. He was right. Disclosure was unavoidable.

It pained him to admit that Comte was also right. He had reconciled his knowledge by dismissing the ancient gods as angels or demons.

As he grew into adulthood, he had always been concerned about who his mother had served during her trances. It had bothered him that she had served the forces of darkness who appeared in the form of the Third Reich.

But more than that, Comte had asked him who he served. That question cut deep, it rattled him. Suddenly, he felt like a shabby rent-boy who had plied his trade with no conscience. As a prostitute serves pimp and client, he had served the inner echelon of Majestic and of course, the Holy Church. Although he was fifteen years older than Agostino, Valla had always maintained a verve and intensity which was the equal of the younger man, but now, he felt defeated. Vitality drained out of him, becoming shrivelled like dried carrion at a drought-depleted waterhole. Just as Agostino would soon face judgement, he too, knew his day would come. Little did he expect it would come now and his judge would be Comte.

He pondered a precarious future. How could this be done to save him and maintain Church relevance? If the Church acted from the front foot, then he should be able to manage the fallout from a 'Christian' point of view. There was an added advantage. He could finally excommunicate himself from the Holy See of espionage, the nefarious world of Majestic. Handled with care, he recognised that disclosure could actually strengthen the Church's position. The populous at large would seek reassurance that God was the guiding hand in all of His creations – the Universal Hand that formed the Church would deliver strength by giving the ignorant masses the reassurance they would seek in uncertain times. Surely disclosure of contact with an alien race would cause the flock to seek ecclesiastical solace like never before.

As much as he hated to admit it, Agostino was a genius. He had chosen well and made a wise decision. Valla now saw the merit of what could be achieved, if conducted with the skill of a virtuoso. Agostino had known that only he could do it.

Valla had always thought the Second Vatican Council of 1978 had gone too far. Now he believed it hadn't gone far enough.

78

HIGHJUMP

BBC TELEVISION CENTRE
LONDON W12, ENGLAND

The studio personnel attached the miniature microphone to Ernst Volker's lapel. His interview was about to expose classified information, some of it hidden since the 13th century. I knew that his actions today could very well be his death sentence. It was a brave decision.

During our pre-interview discussions, Ernst had been straightforward about his involvement with Majestic and his subsequent recruitment by Elysius. He explained how Majestic had been swift to implement a complete restructure after the death of the sadistic psychopath, Veles Kane.

Both Ernst and Majestic believed that Kane had died on the Ulysses Enterprise as a result of an onboard explosion. The ship sank in fifteen hundred metres of water and the bodies were not recovered. Neither Keisha nor I divulged our involvement. That information died with Kane.

Ernst had been a valuable mole, but Philip felt that with the Majestic cleanout he could very well be vulnerable. Keisha had been brilliant in her negotiations. Ernst accepted her offer to appear in my television series which was designed to be an exposé on the origins of man, the ascent of human civilization and the deliberate cover-up of man's extraterrestrial genesis by both the Church and during the past seventy years, by governments and their clandestine agencies. It was the intimate details of the cover-up that he could expose.

Whilst concerned about his safety, he had seized the opportunity. His resignation from Majestic had been immediate. He knew he was on dangerous ground, but reasoned he was fortunate. His parents were dead; he had no siblings and he had never married. Elysius offered a new identity for him, so he took his chance. Today, he was not Ernst Volker. That man was no more. A million Euros deposited in a Swiss Bank and a new passport gave him a ticket to anonymity and freedom. Philip had made sure of it. Elysius always looked after their assets.

Ernst was a huge bonus. He provided several contacts that were able to provide further fragments of information. Some of them even agreed to feature in the series. But Ernst was the linchpin.

He was happy to answer any question during the interview as long as his face was pixellated and his voice digitalised. I had no problem agreeing to his request. It would add to the intrigue of his revelations.

The BBC wanted the series premiered within the next two months. We had been given a tight production schedule of six months and life had been frantic. This particular interview would be shown on the second episode.

Just prior to the interview, he told me that Majestic's worst fears were unravelling. Their close relationship with the Vatican had been compromised. Their man within was playing hardball. Antonio Cardinal Valla was refusing to honour a long-standing partnership that was forged soon after the war. The mortar holding Majestic and the Vatican together was crumbling.

With thirty seconds to go, activity was feverish. Studio lights blared. The cameras focused. The signal was given. The countdown was over.

I began the interview with Ernst by asking him about his curriculum vitae. It was impressive and set the scene for what was to come. He dropped bombshells, one after the other. He explained how the Pentagon picked him up after completing a PhD in ancient history, followed by his Masters in Middle Eastern history at Stanford. His eidetic memory was considered vital when he assisted the U.S. government during the unofficial negotiations in 1993 between Israel and the PLO. It was during this time that he had the opportunity to examine an ancient block of stone locked in a vault seventy seven feet below the Pentagon.

The stone block had been kept under wraps for almost forty years. Ernst was asked to study its secret inscriptions to see if it might provide some ancient insight into Middle Eastern history. Progressive translation over a number of years by the Pentagon and Majestic revealed a startling picture. The stone had been considered prophetic by the German Esoteric Bureau when it was smuggled out of Berlin through Soviet lines in the final days of Nazi capitulation. Engraved at least 4,000 years ago, it gave an account of the Elohim who came to Earth to teach mankind. It prophesied their return when mankind was at the brink of self-annihilation.

The timing of the Hiroshima and Nagasaki atomic explosions and the infamous mass sighting of UFOs over the Capitol building in 1947 were considered key markers of the prophecy, triggering the first modern day interventions by the off-worlders. World War II had left humanity bereft. Millions had died because of false religions, false ideologies and the conquest for finite resources. The Elohim knew only a spiritual evolution could prevent the destruction.

Ernst described the mood of the Allies after the War. Distrust of the Soviets was endemic and the U.S. was intent on establishing their own centres of power and influence. Nazi Germany had made unparalleled progress in developing a variety of new technologies such as rocketry, hypersonics, anti-gravity propulsion and hyper-dimensional energy systems. It was also found that the Nazis had used telepathic contact with extraterrestrial biological entities to enhance their technical knowledge. This was confirmed by the father of rocketry, Professor Hermann Oberth, when he stated that the Reich had been assisted in the advancement of certain scientific fields. When asked by whom, he had replied, *'the people of other worlds'.*

I asked Ernst what evidence existed for the assertion of psychic contact. He disclosed that Maria Oršić, another medium known only as Sigrun and Carla Valla, the mother of Antonio Giacomo Valla, one of the Catholic Church's most powerful Cardinals, had partici-pated in the telepathic communications. He confirmed that Oršić and Sigrun had disappeared, but that Carla had been murdered by the German Esoteric Bureau for her communication with the Allies. He produced two letters written to the Pentagon in 1960 by the young priest Antonio Valla. In his letter, he requested an explana-tion of his mother's trances and her involvement with the German Esoteric Bureau. The Pentagon ignored the letter, but he persisted and it wasn't until the 1980s that he received an explanation.

The second letter from Valla that Ernst produced was a complete denial of the findings. It was dated 15th February 1987. Valla was emphatic in his response. He wrote, *'I do not accept your assertion that my mother telepathically interacted with what you call, Extraterrestrial Biological Entities. I always believed she was talking to the Angels. From what you have advised they could only have been demons. God have mercy on her soul. May she avoid purgatory and damnation by the grace of God.'*

Ernst described the mood during the aftermath of the War. It was a time of heightened activity from the U.S. military. Intelligence had suggested that during German Antarctica research conducted in 1939, a discovery of a massive geo-thermal area, surrounded by brown hills studded with vegetation, had been made. The expedition took 11,000 photographs over an area of some 600,000 square kilometres, revealing ice-free, freshwater lakes dotted across the massive area. It was immediately claimed as German territory and named Neuschwabenland.

Intelligence had also uncovered a dangerous plan. Rumours had circulated that a selection of elite military and scientific personnel had fled Germany toward the end of the War and had established a community at the Antarctic base. It was presumed that the Nazi inner circle had built an underground military complex at Neuschwabenland. Evidence that certain elements of the Kreigsmarine, the German Navy were active in southern waters, operating either out of South America or the Antarctic was unequivocal. It was thought that the most secret Nazi technologies had been moved to this location. It was here that they continued their development of advanced aircraft based on extraterrestrial technology.

In response, the Americans launched Operation Highjump in August 1946, officially titled The United States Navy Antarctic Developments Program. It was organised by Rear Admiral Richard E. Byrd, the celebrated Antarctic explorer who had enjoyed a stellar career within the U.S. Navy.

Thirteen ships including the command ship, the icebreaker 'Northwind', the aircraft carrier 'USS Philippine Sea', the submarine 'Sennet' and the destroyer 'Henderson', together with 4,700 men and a multitude of aircraft were employed. The official objective of the mission was to determine the feasibility of establishing their own research base, and to consolidate and extend U.S. sovereignty over the largest possible area of the continent. But even before the expedition had ended, this objective was denied.

That denial was paramount in hiding the real objectives and the ultimate failure of the operation. Operation Highjump was in fact an invasion force which was made up of three naval battle groups. However, the operation encountered heavy resistance from flying discs, with unacceptable casualties and the destruction of one of their fleet. The operation was quickly called off.

An article in the Chilean newspaper 'El Mercurio' quoted Richard Byrd from an interview with Lee van Atta. The Admiral declared that the U.S. should immediately initiate defence measures against *'hostile regions'*. He stated it was *'a bitter reality that in any new war against the U.S. it would be attacked by flying objects which could fly from pole to pole at incredible speeds'.* Byrd later repeated these views in a news conference held for the International News Service.

Back in 1996, Volker interviewed a handful of still living personnel who had served during the operation. They confirmed there had been a number of aircraft destroyed. The Naval commanders of the time had unanimously declared that they had no understanding of what was really happening.

The formation of the United Nations also had undisclosed motives. One involved the removal and storage of discoveries of highly advanced human and non-human artefacts of antiquity from anywhere around the globe. Nations such as Iraq, Egypt, Tibet, Afghanistan and areas of Central America became highly prized geo-strategic assets. The Cold War masked much of the competing interests of Britain and the U.S. against Germany and France and also against the communist interests of China and the U.S.S.R.

Ernst described how Majestic had giving him the opportunity to access some of the world's most valuable documents. He had read the translations of the Dead Sea Scrolls and ancient Mesopotamian cuneiform tablets. He had also spoken to specialist translators to accurately decipher the writings.

The explanation of his views about those translations provided a timely segue into an episode that would feature Dr Keisha Petersen.

He mentioned the 6,500 year old Atrahasis tablet that details the ET manipulation of cross breeding. This tablet was much older than the block of stone stored beneath the Pentagon. The oldest cuneiform tablets, he affirmed, held the first written record about the extraterrestrial beings that came to Earth tens of thousands of years ago.

His final disclosure was dynamite designed to shake the foundations of the establishment. Backed by correspondence between the parties, he revealed how Majestic and the Vatican had worked hand in glove with key governments to suppress, discredit and ridicule any disclosure outside the accepted parameters. Shamefully, the Church had been complicit in this clandestine behaviour, cementing their own power base by the need to 'save the souls' of sinners.

When the program was due for screening, Ernst's disclosures would be interspersed with photographs, film and other archival material, including recordings and interviews with people of the era.

Old German SS film footage would be shown of the cuboid block of diorite centred in a bronze-age ring of stone slabs within the bombed-out building in Berlin. Volker had even been able to photograph the stone block in 1993 for further study. The pictographs and runes engraved into it appeared similar to the photographs that Aiden would show of his discovery in the Baalbek crypt.

German photographs taken in 1937 would show Neuschwabenland and the more temperate climate of that area. Modern film footage would also show the blue and green lakes of the area. Film of the 1947 mass sighting of craft over the Capitol building would also be put to air.

There was even a recording of Carla Valla during one of her trances that had collected dust in an East German archive until the fall of the Berlin Wall. Sixty six years after her death, her voice would be heard once again. The recording would be replayed and analysed during this episode.

Motion pictures of German flying saucers filmed during testing; together with U.S. footage taken at Area 51 of similar craft would be shown. The images had never been publicly available. Some had been supplied at great risk by Volker himself, but a great deal of the most secret material had been provided by a disfigured, renegade keeper of an obscure Vatican archive. Somehow he had obtained a collection of data that would fill several series.

The stage was set.

EPILOGUE

EDINBURGH, SCOTLAND

Mitch grabbed the remote and switched on the television. He tuned into BBC1. Five minutes from now, on prime time, Dr Aiden Keyes would introduce 'The Genesis Deception – The Genetic Manipulation of Humanity and its Modern Day Consequences." It had been advertised heavily for the past month.

It was now seven months since he had met Aiden and Keisha. He had noticed the chemistry between them during their ordeal on the Ulysses Enterprise. They were well suited. He knew the effort to put the program to air had been enormous. Thousands of man hours and thousands of travel miles had been expended. The achievement in such a short time frame was unprecedented.

Three months ago, the *Segretaria di Stato del Vaticano*, Cardinal Antonio Giacomo Valla, historically announced the formation of the Third Vatican Council to be held at St Peter's Basilica in the Vatican. The opening session was scheduled for six months after his announcement. The expectation of the Council was to integrate the biblical experience of faith with modern science. In a complete break from past convention, twelve commissions would be formed made up of Church Bishops from across the planet, and most remarkably, members of the scientific community who would represent a broad range of views from anthropology to astrophysics.

The scriptures were to be re-examined in light of modern discoveries and the reinterpretation of ancient texts. Even experts in ancient languages had been approached. Keisha was speechless when she received an invitation to give her input to the Council.

She had refused.

Mitch stood with his back to the fireplace, its hearth crackling with redundant pieces of old whisky barrels. Golden light spilled into the room, the air infused with the earthy scent of oak and peat. Mitch was elated. The program may never have gone to air without his sample of living DNA.

The door bell rang as Mitch poured a glass of wine. His special guest had finally arrived.

"You got here just in time. Here, give me your coat. Let me get you a glass of wine."

His guest hobbled to the kitchen. "I've brought a 1995 Clos du Mesnil and after that you can open some grappa?"

"Your right Comte, we'll celebrate with the best. Your taste in champagne is impeccable. There were only a thousand cases of these wasn't there?"

"Something like that. But hey, I just got in from Monaco so only the best will do, especially tonight."

Mitch smiled as he peeled the gold foil from the wired cork. "You look great after that dive of yours. You're very lucky."

"Luck had nothing to do with it. It was all a matter of ocean swell, accuracy and timing."

"Maybe, but the other guy drowned."

"That was the idea."

"What about the boy, Angelo?"

Comte's eyes brightened. "I've meditated a lot lately. Angelo's a priceless blessing. He's on the upward ascent and he'll be just fine. We'll meet again."

Mitch nodded and poured the light golden effervescence into tall crystal flutes. "So what do you think of Cardinal Valla's announcement? Quite a cunning move."

"I suppose, but wait until he's outed on the show. He's going to freak when he hears his mother's voice after all these years. Then he'll be catatonic when I send my new surprise."

"What've you got lined up this time?"

"When he hears about the bones from Morocco and then he hears about your DNA, I thought I'd send him a sample of mine."

Mitch grinned, "Forty-four chromosomes. That'll be enough to finish him."

"Brothers of the same mind Mitch." Both men laughed as the words 'The Genesis Deception' morphed onto the screen.

LONDON, UNITED KINGDOM.

Newspapers around the world were filled with front page captions. Headlines from Buenos Aires to Manila, from Reykjavik to Auckland screamed in bold print.

'VATICAN UNDER SIEGE'

'U.S. DENIES COVERUP'

'BIBLE NEEDS REVISION'

'CLAIM THAT MAN IS CROSSBREED WITH ETs'

'WE ARE NOT ALONE!'

We had several newspapers scattered across the breakfast table.

Last night, Keisha and I celebrated at the renowned L'Atelier de Joël Robuchon near Covent Garden. Delicious meal, delicious woman. Keisha had made sure of it.

She held up the front page of the *Daily Telegraph*. "There you go handsome. Check out the headline."

I cringed.

'KEYES PROVES THEM ALL WRONG'
'Church and State Conspire in Big Lie'

"The show's not about me."

"True, but it's the culmination of your life's work."

"Early days, let's see what happens over the next five episodes."

Keisha leaned forward, her silk dressing gown gaping open from the loose tie at her waist. A glimpse of her luscious curves was revealed. "I'd say the BBC will want a sequel. They won't be able to resist."

"I won't resist a sequel to last night."

Her beguiling eyes laughed as she held out her hand. "Come on, neither will I."

ABOUT THE AUTHORS

CRAIG STEVENS

Craig currently works on large infrastructure projects and has previously worked as an economic advisor, statistician, financial modeller and forecaster for the Australian government. Previously, Craig worked in corporate banking. Craig remains fascinated by ancient religious history, science, theology and esoteric subjects. He enjoys chess, cinema, music and fine scotch whisky.

WAYNE SHEPARD

Wayne has worked in the financial services industry for 40 years, currently employed as a Finance Broker. His interest and outlook in world affairs has been enhanced by his travel experiences. He has held an interest in mystical Christianity for the past 35 years. Wayne has two adult children and enjoys reading, gardening and a glass of red wine.

www.ingramcontent.com/pod-product-compliance
Lightning Source LLC
Chambersburg PA
CBHW051940020726
47501CB00001B/215